OUTSIDE INTERFERENCE

OUTSIDE INTERFERENCE

LONG JENN SILVA SERIES: BOOK 1

Jasmine:
Merry Christmas!,
Always fight for
what you believe in!

Scott

SCOTT QUINN

To my mother, my sister, my wife,
and my daughters...

You all are tenacious fighters,
each in your own special way.

0: AUTHOR'S NOTES ABOUT TIME

TIME plays an important role in this book/series.

The author utilizes flashbacks.

Various "alien" species travel through space, occasionally steering their space crafts through wormholes (folds in the time/space continuum).

The "PRESENT DAY" action in this book begins on:
JANUARY 1, 202_ (an unspecified year in the mid- to late-2020s).

Throughout the book, JANUARY 1, 202_ will be written as:
"YEAR 0 + 1 DAY/JANUARY 1st."

JULY 19th from the same year would be written as:
"YEAR 0 + 200 DAYS/JULY 19th."

JULY 19th from the next year would be written as:
"YEAR 1 + 200 DAYS/JULY 19th."

JULY 19th from twenty years earlier would be written as:
"YEAR -20 + 200 DAYS/JULY 19th."

1: KNOCKOUT

YEAR 0 + 1 DAY (JANUARY 1st)

"Welcome to The End Zone: Famous for Our Buns."

It was no secret that the restaurant followed a business model which centered around catering to sex-starved college guys. They made a small fortune off those who liked to gawk at scantily clad young women... all while downing pitchers of beer and watching sports on massive television screens. And management brazenly encouraged the customers to believe that each order included an implied invitation to study every square inch of the curvy coeds who served them their food.

A glance at her name tag would reveal the name of the breathtaking blond who uttered the establishment's shameless slogan at least twenty times a shift. "Tavia."

The glances seldom stopped at her name tag, though.

As she marched a group of frat boys to their table, Tavia could feel their eyes traveling downward along her frame. The gazes would not stop until they landed below her waist.

Like all female employees at The End Zone, she wore a company-issued bikini bottom that left half of each butt cheek hanging out for the world to see. Making matters worse, the marketing department stamped the letters "E.Z." across the seat. Though the letters were said to be an abbreviation for "End Zone," the result was that the restaurant's waitstaff became informally dubbed "The E.Z. Girls."

The uniform was equally scandalous above the waist. A tiny white T-shirt clung to Tavia's body and crept up to expose her midriff. Her employers provided a top that was at least two sizes too small. That was no accident. Royal blue letters spread across her chest and spelled out the name of the restaurant. Just beneath were the words that made up the burger joint's famous advertising mantra.

Her job made her feel like she was a couple of pieces of fabric away from being a stripper. She despised that fact. At least most of the time she did. She had to admit that the tips were damn good. Too substantial to pass up. She wouldn't bring home nearly as much cash waiting tables at any other place in the podunk college town where she went to school.

Under normal circumstances, The End Zone would be almost empty throughout Central Illinois University's Winter Break. The entire community cleared out when classes were not in session. Virtually all the students and much of the faculty returned home to celebrate the holiday season in Chicago or Peoria or Springfield or St. Louis. It didn't matter that the burgers were the tastiest in town. Barely enough people stuck around King City (population 20,000 and falling) to justify keeping the doors open over the holidays.

This was no ordinary night, though. The CIU Eagles were playing in college football's Tumbleweed Bowl. Tonight's contest marked the first time in school history that the hometown Eagles would take the field in a postseason contest. A win over the ninth-ranked Arizona State Sun Devils would give Central Illinois an outside chance of finishing in the Top Ten in the National Polls.

A tremendous amount of hoopla surrounded the big game. The place buzzed with excitement. Customers packed the restaurant. Locals filled many of the tables. Others were occupied by students who had journeyed back to watch the game on campus. That was a much more affordable option than road tripping all the way to Albuquerque to attend the Tumbleweed Bowl in person. And it made for a great excuse to come back to town early for all the New Year's Eve drinking and debauchery a college kid could handle.

On this night, the All-World Wrestling Association would broadcast their "New Year's Nightmare" Pay-Per-View extravaganza at the same time as the football game. Several pro wrestling fans added to the size of the crowd. Some of those enthusiasts were beer-chugging radicals who looked like they were one dirty look away from starting their own barroom brawl. Others were young families who were passing down their love of pre-scripted bloodbaths to their kids.

Every one of The End Zone's twenty-four televisions would display either the big game or the wrestling matches.

Tavia darted through the restaurant. She weaved between the wall-to-wall customers. Though the place was terribly understaffed, she placed beers, burgers, and buffalo wings in front of drinkers and diners with tremendous speed and precision.

She slid two bottles of light beer and one blue plastic cup of ice water in the middle of a table. The water drinker was a guy from a class she took during the previous semester. "Oh... hi there!" she

said, singling him out, even though she wondered if he would
remember her.

Her classmate lifted his cup. "I'm the designated driver
tonight." His explanation almost sounded like an apology.

Perhaps feeling somewhat self-conscious about the awkward
exchange, Tavia's classmate let his gaze drop to his black and
orange Central Illinois jersey. He looked up long enough to flash
the thumbs up signal. "Go Eagles!"

"He didn't recognize me," she muttered to herself as she
walked away from the table. Suddenly, Tavia found herself
unimpressed with this young man's decision to be responsible.
Customers paid four dollars a bottle for domestic beers. The water
was free. She wouldn't be able to afford to save up enough for her
Spring Break trip to Cancun if everyone ordered water instead of
Budweisers. That didn't mean she regretted flirting with him,
though. It might help reel in the big tip that she was counting on.
Plus, he was just about the cutest guy in the whole restaurant... even
if their brief conversation had been more than a little strange.

She squeezed between two other E.Z. Girls who stood near the
entrance to the kitchen. "How soon until those burgers come off the
grill?" Tavia asked the line cook. "Table Eight has been waiting for
quite a while now."

The burger-flipper made it no secret that the stress of the
evening was taking its toll. "We're doing the best we can!"

Turning to her fellow servers, Tavia reported, "Oh my God!
There's this hot guy from my Kinesiology class at one of my
tables."

"What is Kinesiology?" a redhead named Sierra inquired.

"Really? You're asking about the class and not the guy?"
Raven jumped in, frustrated because she knew that opportunities to
gossip would be limited on such a busy night.

"Sports and Society. It was a blowoff class where the professor was stuck in a time warp from when our parents were kids. He went on and on about how businessmen make million dollar deals on the golf course, and how teenage girls who take yoga classes are much more likely to become lesbians. The class sucked, but it was an 'easy A' that filled a prerequisite for my major."

"Ladies, your conversation is creating a fire hazard here!" Assistant Manager Todd complained as he turned the corner. He was a CIU dropout, and a good ten years older than any of the young women who worked at The End Zone. As Todd slid past, he allowed his hand to linger after it "inadvertently" came into contact with Tavia's backside.

Once the slimeball traveled through the door, Tavia informed the other two, "That perv totally just palmed my ass... *again*! It was no accident."

"Is it ever?" Raven asked. "Once, maybe twice, and I'd understand. But his grubby paws land somewhere they shouldn't almost every shift. I swear, if I was that man's wife..."

The restaurant overflowed with hungry, thirsty customers to a point well beyond capacity. There weren't enough servers on the floor. And Todd hadn't resolved to make *"Stop being a creepy pervert"* one of his goals for improvement in the new year. This terrible trifecta caused Tavia's heart to pound. "I swear to God, I need a cigarette!"

Though none of the three young women were regular smokers, each bummed a cigarette from one of the line cooks. After taking one or two puffs while enduring the frigid winter weather, Sierra and Raven had enough. They were ready to leave Tavia outside to seethe on her own.

"I'll be back inside in a sec," she told them.

☠ ☠ ☠

Brady Emerson. Marshall O'Neill. Greg Puckett. Perhaps it was a coincidence. Or maybe their first grade teacher thought she was being clever when she stuck Greg, Marshall, and Brady together at the same learning table. Either way, the boys quickly became best friends and the group known as "The Brady Bunch" was born.

Flip the calendar ahead sixteen years, and the inseparable trio soon would begin their final semester of college. For the first time in memory, they would go off in different directions. Greg's forecasted future included venturing south to Atlanta to work for his brother's promising start-up. Marshall's immediate plans involved law school. He was eyeing a cross-country move to Los Angeles so he could attend Pepperdine University.

Greg slapped their designated driver on the back. "Brady, I wish you weren't so absolutely oblivious. You could be swimming in an ocean of hotness."

"That doesn't sound comfortable."

"I mean hot, desirable women. You could be swimming in an ocean of hot women... and cold beer."

Marshall agreed. He offered a subtle nod and deadpanned, "Maybe not an ocean, *per se*. But at least a large tank full of hot women."

His friends were ganging up on him on this issue. Again. How frustrating! Sure, he boasted perfectly conditioned, wavy brown hair. Yes, his habit of spending two-and-a-half hours in the gym five days a week had worked. He was ripped. And good genetics and excellent dental hygiene practices resulted in a flawless smile that made him look like he had just stepped out of a toothpaste commercial. But that didn't mean every female 18 to 38 wanted to hook up with him. Did it?

"What...? The waitress?" Brady played dumb. Truth be told, he *had* detected a flirtatious tone in her voice. He didn't want them to know that, though. Acknowledging that attraction also would require that he own up to botching the exchange.

Placing his hand on his chest as if clutching imaginary pearls, Marshall mocked his friend, "You mean that smokin' hot blond who took our order and brought us our drinks? The knockout who looked like she was part fairytale princess, part swimsuit model... with most likely just a tad bit of crazy thrown in for good measure? That person?"

Greg shook his head and launched into an oft-given routine. He chided Brady about needing to step up his relationship game. "If you won't do it for yourself, please do it for me. If I'm forced to live vicariously through my much more desirable friend, I need that friend to get some action from time to time. I need *you* to get lucky so you can give *me* all the juicy details. That's how vicarious living works. Understand?"

Brady wasn't listening. Instead, he took a sip of water and stared off into space. A television was mounted onto the wall a few inches above Marshall's head. It was perfectly positioned in Brady's line of sight. As a CIU senior and a lifelong fan of the hometown Eagles, he came to The End Zone to watch the game. But kickoff wasn't for another twenty minutes. For the moment, his focus was on the knockout being interviewed on the TV.

Even with the sound muted, it was clear the wrestler utilized a pirate gimmick. Her wardrobe did not include a peg leg, a parrot on her shoulder, or an eye patch. Even so, her crimson and black costume made her character immediately identifiable. A red bandanna with several skulls 'n crossbones dotted across the fabric partially covered black hair styled in a pixie cut with tight curls on top. Gold, hooped earrings completed the look. But those would be removed before the match began.

Noticing that the primary target of his one-man comedy roast had zoned out, Greg snapped his fingers in Brady's face. "Earth to Brady. Earth to Brady Emerson... do you copy?"

"Sorry," was his absentminded response.

His pals lit up once they discovered where he was looking. "It's starting to add up now!" Greg declared. "Brady's too good for horny college girls. He's lookin' for a little more danger. He's lookin' for a woman who can kick his ass when he gets out of line!"

Marshall took the cue and continued the relentless ribbing of their friend. "Nah, it can't be that simple. I'm sure our lovely waitress... Tavia, is it? I'm sure she could kick Brady's ass if he got outta line. There must be something extra special about the luchadora."

Greg gave Marshall a curious look. He had used an unfamiliar term. *"Luchadora?"*

"Yeah... Weren't we all in Mrs. Carpenter's Spanish II class together?"

Greg still wasn't following his pal's line of thinking. "Yes, I was in *Señora Carpenter's* class. But that was six or seven years ago when we were still in high school. So please enlighten me... what's a friggin' *luchadora*?"

"Well, if you recall, we did a unit on popular Mexican sports. *'Lucha Libre'* is the preferred style of wrestling. The term literally means 'free fight.' And a *'luchadora'* is a female wrestler."

Greg nodded, then deadpanned, "I'm sure that'll come in handy when you go to law school."

Brady contributed nothing to the conversation. He continued to stare at the screen, wondering why he was experiencing such a powerful feeling of déjà vu.

Though it was a virtual certainty that he'd return to discussing Brady's love life (or lack thereof) later in the evening, Greg let off the gas for the moment. He surveyed his surroundings, then asked his friends, "Speaking of our lovely waitress... Where is she? It feels like we ordered our burgers forever ago. I'm getting hungry and the game's getting ready to start."

☠☠☠

Tavia took another puff from her bummed cigarette. She didn't like the aftertaste that came with smoking. It did nothing to quench her anger or calm her nerves. She looked down at the cigarette and wondered why she thought going outside and subjecting herself to frigid conditions would be a good idea.

She was about to stomp it out on the ground when a nearby vehicle caught her attention. The driver of a minivan jerked the wheel, whipping the van to a stop in front of her. The high-beams momentarily blinded Tavia. She lifted her forearm up in front of her face to shield her eyes from the bright lights.

With the lights still aimed directly at the waitress, the van's door swung opened and then slammed shut. A woman advanced towards her. She wore a look of panic or confusion as she called out, "Excuse me... Can you help me?"

Tavia said nothing. She was freezing. Her priority was getting back inside. She had no interest in giving some random single mom directions on how to get to the interstate.

"I'm looking for someone who works here..." the van's driver said as she rapidly approached.

Before Tavia could respond, the minivan driver moved directly in front of her. The woman looked vaguely familiar. She questioned whether she had seen her with...?

"TAVIA!!!" The woman shouted her name, indicating that she'd located the employee she was looking for. A second later, the wild-eyed woman blasted her target in the eyes with pepper spray! She barely got out a scream before the maniac from the minivan grabbed her by the hair on the back of her head. She drove Tavia's skull into the brick wall behind her.

"Todd is *my* man! He may be your boss, but he's *my* husband! He's the father of *my* kids!" she shouted. To add emphasis to her point, she kicked the waitress in her stomach every time she yelled the word "my."

Blood oozed out of Tavia's mouth. Barely conscious, she managed to focus just long enough to look this madwoman in her eyes and mumble, "I never touched your husband."

Panic struck Todd's wife. She whipped her head around in all directions to see if anyone had witnessed her attack. No one was around. Next, she made a second, more deliberate, scan of her surroundings. Confident there were no cameras in the vicinity, Todd's angry wife grabbed her victim by her feet and dragged her towards the side of her minivan.

☠ ☠ ☠

In professional wrestling lingo, a "ref bump" is the term for when a referee gets knocked out in the middle of a match. The trope gets used often because it opens the door for outside interference (or other types of cheating) to go unnoticed. When that happens, the loser invariably claims that a tarnished outcome resulted. If done right, it adds fuel to the rivalry. Fans demand to see a rematch.

Though she gave up at least a hundred pounds to the reigning champion, Jenn Silva had Savannah Lyons on her heels. The electricity in the crowd grew with every drop kick and every forearm smash. Lyons was out of gas and sucking wind. Though she was athletic, the large woman needed to roll out of the ring to buy some time and catch her breath. The pirate refused to let up. She hit her with a suicide dive, leaping over the top rope and blindsiding her unsuspecting opponent on the outside of the ring.

Once they returned to the squared circle, Lyons was staggering. The noise of the crowd rattled the roof. It looked like Jenn was about to take the AWWA Women's Championship. It was time to put away her opposition with a finishing maneuver. Unfortunately, the wily Lyons ducked out of the way of a running clothesline. The champ eluded Jenn. Her momentum forced her into a collision with the referee. The impact knocked the official "unconscious."

"What is he made of? Papier mâché?" the enraged announcer bellowed into his microphone.

Looking to take advantage of the ref bump, Lyons left the ring and retrieved a steel chair. While Jenn checked on the official, the champ returned. *SMACK!* The chair slammed across the fan favorite's back!

This brought another wrestler—Cocoa Freeman—charging down to ringside. Fans of the AWWA knew that Cocoa and Lyons had run through a series of red-hot matches over the course of the last year. They understood that Cocoa intended to stop Lyons from cheating before the dastardly champ could add Jenn to the list of wrestlers she'd injured.

Cocoa landed several blows, but Lyons wore the championship belt for a reason. She knew how to fight, and she didn't hesitate to fight dirty. The title-holder brought an abrupt halt to Cocoa's attacks by jabbing her thumb into her eye. This momentary pause was the opening that she needed. Lyons lifted Cocoa up and powerslammed her into the canvas three times in a row. She then turned and retrieved the steel chair that she had used to flatten Jenn.

The pirate recognized that her opponent's attention was fixated on punishing Cocoa. She perched herself on the top turnbuckle. When Lyons lifted the chair over her head to strike Cocoa, Jenn leapt. She drove her feet onto the top of the steel chair, forcing the foreign object downward and causing a thunderous impact against the champ's skull. The crowd erupted once again. The mighty Lyons dropped to the mat like a falling oak.

Jenn fell atop her opponent. The referee "conveniently" awoke at just the right time. He made a tremendous spectacle about moving five feet to his right to get into position to begin his three-count. *It was all part of the show.*

The rabid crowd screamed along. "One!!! Two!!! Three!!!"

Jenn lifted her arms up to the sky. She celebrated her win while surrounded by a trio of knocked out co-stars. Savannah Lyons (now the former champion) had been toppled. Cocoa Freeman took on a tremendous amount of punishment to keep Jenn from being the victim of a wrestling injustice. And it took all the remaining strength the exhausted referee could muster to bang his hand into the mat three times!

The finish may have been a little ridiculous, but Jenn's ear-to-ear smile was genuine. Years and years of hard work had paid off. She was the Women's Champion in one of the biggest wrestling promotions in the world!

☠☠☠

Tavia's face was bruised and bloodied as she laid on the side of a rural road. Her End Zone T-shirt had been ripped away, leaving her with only a soaked, mud-covered bra on top.

Snow began to accumulate in the few hours since she had been grabbed and taken from the sports bar's parking lot. It was cold, and the temperature was dropping. She needed to get help. The icy weather made the situation even more urgent. She had been beaten badly. Standing was out of the question. Her eyes fluttered as she tried to focus. Tavia didn't even think she could cry for help.

She was having difficulty keeping her eyes from rolling back in her head when she was hit with a blinding light. "Is that a car?" the young woman wondered aloud, her voice quivering.

She tapped into all her strength to open her eyes and raise one arm straight up in the air. It was at this point that she discovered that the bright light was not coming from a vehicle on the road...

It was coming from a mysterious craft hovering above her.

☠ ☠ ☠

EIGHT MONTHS LATER
YEAR 0 + 221 DAYS (AUGUST 9th)

Much to the dismay of the handful of passengers aboard, the commuter train did not move for several minutes. It idled in an underground station, all while Cocoa Freeman and Jenn Silva desperately needed to get to the venue for that night's pay-per-view event.

Once the train started moving, Cocoa glanced down at her cell phone to see if she had received any text messages in the last two minutes. Nothing.

"No signal?" Cocoa groaned as they emerged from an underground tunnel. Even though she knew that cell phone coverage is spotty at best in such a circumstance, she simply lacked the patience to deal with the laws of nature on this particular occasion. "I don't have time for this nonsense right now!"

The train pulled into the stop at Laclede's Landing. It was the final opportunity for passengers to get off on the Missouri side of the Mississippi River. Majestic views of the world-famous Gateway Arch could be seen through spectacular brick openings at this station.

Like the two stops before it, Laclede's Landing featured yet another unexpectedly vacant platform. Not a soul was there. There were no security guards. No baseball fans. No one heading to the popular bars and restaurants along the riverfront. No exhausted families finishing their afternoons on the Arch grounds. Not even a single homeless person was anywhere around.

A pudgy policeman stepped off, leaving only three riders aboard.

As the train rattled along the bridge over the Mississippi River, Brady Emerson moved from a seat farther back to one positioned immediately behind the two professional wrestlers. "Something doesn't feel right," he said.

Cocoa had more important things on her mind. "That may be, but our stop's right up here. As soon as those doors open, we're gonna get off and haul our happy tails into the ballroom of the casino. We've got too much stuff to do to worry about anything else right now." Then she added, "I can't wait to get off this God-forsaken bucket of bolts."

When the train pulled up to the platform, she exited the train with Jenn and the college boy close behind her. But there was no sprint to the nearby casino. And this time they didn't notice that they were standing at another vacant Metrolink platform that normally would have been packed with wall-to-wall passengers. Instead, the trio stood on the elevated mass of concrete and metal with their eyes fixated back across the river.

What they saw was horrific.

A 737 was gliding through the sky. It was close enough and low enough that the trio should have been able to hear the roar of the engine. Instead, it was silent. The airplane coasted through the air. Its movement was dictated by nothing but the downward tug of gravity and a side-to-side push from the wind.

The plane began to lean towards one side. The angle became more and more extreme until the portside wing snapped off. The descent of the plane became so rapid that the back third of the aircraft broke away and plummeted into the water.

What was left of the diving 737 slammed into the gridlocked Poplar Street Bridge. Dozens of cars and trucks dropped into the river below. With massive chunks of concrete and jagged metal toppling downward amid a wall of flames, it had all the signs of a tragedy with a death toll in the hundreds… if not thousands!

Under normal circumstances, the sounds of the crash should have included the public hysteria that would be expected to follow. But there were no screams. There were no sirens. From their vantagepoint, Jenn, Cocoa, and Brady should have been able to observe utter chaos. They should have seen people fighting for their lives, heroes rushing to save them, all while others desperately tried to get as far away from the danger as possible. Instead, there was no movement on what remained of the bridge (which now was ablaze with dozens of scattered fires). Stillness surrounded the riverfront. The city was eerily silent.

Brady looked up towards the sky. As if he was addressing the heavens, he asked, "What on earth is happening?"

2: FOREIGN OBJECT

"*You mindless dopes who call yourselves wrestling fans are all the same. You cheer that wannabe pirate who calls herself the champion. She only won the match because she smashed me over the head with a foreign object. The truth is Long Jenn Silva's a lousy cheater who couldn't beat me in a fair fight!*"

-SAVANNAH LYONS promo taped after losing the AWWA Women's Championship to Long Jenn Silva.

TWENTY YEARS EARLIER
YEAR -20 + 250 DAYS (SEPTEMBER 7th)

Cornell Bledsoe knew as much about making bourbon as any man in the Commonwealth of Kentucky. Other than the four years he spent serving in the U.S. Air Force, his entire adult life was spent holding one job or another at the Shotgun Bourbon Distillery near Bardstown. He retired after forty-five years at the SBD. But he still maintained a love for the one true American liquor.

"Remind me to call the boys tomorrow, Millie," he said as he greeted his loving wife on the back porch. "That five-year barrel is about ready."

Cornell accumulated a tremendous amount of knowledge over four decades at the distillery. He used that to produce his own single barrel batch of bourbon each year. That made 200 liters... actually, that number was closer to 175 after the "angel's share" disappeared into thin air. As much as he loved a glass with dinner and another just before going to bed, the old man needed a lot of help if he was going to get rid of almost 175 bottles of the stuff each year!

"I'm sure C.J. and Randy will be happy to take a case or two off your hands," she said as she pulled her soulmate towards her for a second smooch. "It would be nice if they brought the kids and stayed for dinner. It's a shame they always end up scurrying back to Louisville as soon as they load up their trucks."

"Speakin' of dinner, what's that I smell?"

"S'mores," Millie replied with a devious smile.

Millie's mouth-watering concoctions weren't the chocolate-marshmallow-graham cracker variety. Hers were a special dessert she called "Bardstown S'mores." She crafted the delicacy by drizzling a generous helping of bourbon caramel over fried apples.

The apples and a half scoop of vanilla ice cream were sandwiched between toasted grahams. The finishing touch was to cover all that deliciousness with a bit more of the gooey caramel. "I figure we're entitled to a bowl of our favorite dessert *before* dinner."

"And that, my love, is reason number four hundred sixty..." Cornell's compliment went unfinished. He allowed his words to fade as his gaze drifted above his wonderful wife. "I may have sampled a little more from that barrel than I realized."

It wasn't too much alcohol that had him distracted. It was the shiny silver aircraft. *Like one of those bobsleds from the Winter Olympics.* Whatever it was, it seemed to hover just a stone's throw away from the Bledsoe's back porch. "Honey, why don't you go inside and get those s'mores ready for us? Okay?"

She didn't have time to respond. In the next moment, the couple became enveloped in a blinding light. They never saw the burst of gas that knocked them unconscious... or the two blue men that collected their paralyzed bodies to be transported to their ship 180,000 miles above the Earth.

☠ ☠ ☠

FIVE MONTHS LATER
YEAR -19 + 32 DAYS (FEBRUARY 1st)

Two tall figures walked down a long corridor.

They were dressed in skin-tight flight suits. Each suit was lined with a gray, synthetic fabric that had been engineered to maximize its elasticity and breathability. An additional layer of material traveled from the neck down to just beneath the chest. This area shimmered with a near metallic sheen (amber, hunter green, navy blue, deep purple, or scarlet, depending on the wearer's primary specialty). Additional material of the appropriate color also covered the flight suit's forearms, crotch, and around the knees. It provided reinforcement for those areas one would be likely to sweat profusely or experience excessive wear and tear. At the bottom, the outfits tucked into black and silver boots with magnetic soles designed for zero gravity situations.

A sequence of dots, dashes, squiggles, and hooks were etched onto a patch that ran across the left side of the chest. When translated, the writings informed others of key information about the specific being that wore the suit.

The words "V-II 4/CARTOGRAPHER" were scrawled across the plum-colored strip worn by the taller of the two blue-skinned beings. His primary role was to program and map out complex realms of virtual reality. VR served an integral role when the scientists aboard the *Vilnagrom-II's* studied the psychology and physiology of abducted specimens.

Like the rest of the crew, the Cartographer was humanoid. Standing at approximately 6'7", he towered several inches above most of his kind. His cranium appeared noticeably more bulbous than an Earthly human's, but that perception certainly was impacted by the fact that there was no hair on his head or any other part of his body. Few wrinkles of blue-gray skin covered his forehead. Those likely would develop with advanced age.

The iris of this being's eyes glowed red. It rested in an orangish sclera, causing the orbs to look like burning suns.

A dark purple patch revealed that the other figure was designated "V-I 3/EXPLORER." He was one of the only survivors remaining from the crew of the *Vilnagrom-I*. That ship departed their home planet twenty years before the *V-II*. Based on the collection of wrinkles that were beginning to cluster near the top of his forehead, it was obvious that the Explorer was at least two decades older than his counterpart.

"I am eager to see the data the *Vilnagrom-I* collected over the time you have been orbiting O.E.," the young Cartographer proclaimed upon meeting the highest-ranking figure left from the mission's maiden voyage.

"O.E." (or "Original Earth") was how those from their home planet referred to the world that the Explorer had been observing. The *V-I* crew had orbited the planet for the last twenty years. During that time, they became so accustomed to the ways of the third planet from the sun that the term "O.E." sounded somewhat ridiculous.

"While we are waiting, I would like to ask you a series of questions. For example, I am curious about the synthetic food," the Explorer asked. "Have they managed to improve that in the last twenty years?"

"I am sorry to report that the food remains tasteless." Despite utilizing the wooden style of delivery so common among his people, the newcomer possessed a sense of humor. He joked, "Now we have options: tasteless and grainy, tasteless and gummy, or the traditional stale and tasteless. Though the reason remains a mystery, I have found that whichever variety is selected, it is most satisfying when consumed at a lukewarm temperature."

Reports flashed across a monitor that was imbedded in the wall. The Cartographer had been waiting for this interruption. He leaned in to quickly eyeball the information. It was his intention to conduct a much more detailed analysis later.

The Explorer shifted as he waited to hear a summary of the data. "I pray the unexpected attrition of our crew did not set back our progress too much."

Pray? That was a word that neither the Cartographer nor any of his fellow *V-II* crew members would have been accustomed to. It was a term that was seldom used and a concept that was infrequently explored on their home world.

The newcomer opted to address the broader question that had been posed. "I suspect the low number of crew members had less of a negative impact on the accumulation of usable data than did the fact that you were forced to work with such antiquated equipment. No doubt *that* would have impeded you, even if you had been operating with a full crew."

A series of tones announced the presence of other crew members. A moment later, two more from the *V-II* team arrived. Each was pushing a metal slab that hovered approximately three and a half feet above the floor. They were delivering a pair of live, but unconscious, humans.

"These are the only specimens you had in your life suspension tanks?" asked the Cartographer. He did very little to cover his disapproving tone.

"As you know, our crew was severely depleted. Abduction of test subjects is dangerous work. Additionally, such ventures are very taxing on our resources... particularly the crew members required for sedation and extraction."

The newcomer turned and examined the pair of senior citizens that lay on the floating slabs. "They appear so weak and frail? Are all the inhabitants of O.E. like this?"

"Negative. The average life span from their region is approximately 76 years. Both subjects were at least that old—if not older— at the time they were extracted."

"Hardly ideal," the Cartographer continued to criticize the methods of the *V-I crew*. "It does little good to study the habits of those on the fringe. Examination of the infirm and elderly will do little to educate our people on how we are to survive and thrive when living on the surface of the Earth."

The *V-I's* Senior Explorer began to allow his frustration to be apparent. "Again... With our depleted crew, it was no longer safe to abduct physically strong specimens. We did the best we could with a crew reduced from ten to three."

The younger officer raised his left hand in the air. He wiggled his long, blue fingers for a moment. This gesture customarily was given as an apology on their home planet. He then changed the subject.

He looked down at the elderly couple once again. They had been stripped of their clothes. The only coverings on their bodies were tight-fitting black undergarments. "What is this across the chest of the female?"

"Most adult women on Earth cover their breasts for support. They also do so out of modesty."

"Oh? How quaint." Next, he turned to the other two blue beings in the room. "Please proceed with hooking them up in the tanks. I am eager to show our friends from the *V-I* the advances that have been made in life suspension and virtual reality since they departed Na-Werss."

In theory, the process was simple. Pilots would fly a series of reconnaissance missions down to Earth. Making pass after pass over a certain area, they would travel close to the planet's surface, amassing images and meteorological data to be used by the Cartographer to map out the virtual reality realms housed within the ship's life suspension tanks.

Later, a Pilot and Explorer (or, for more complicated missions, a Pilot, Explorer, and an additional crew member acting as a Scout) would return to the Earth's surface. When it was safe to do so, the team would accomplish their abduction by sedating and extracting the subject or subjects. After each specimen underwent a preliminary medical inspection, they would be placed in the tanks for detailed study.

Unlike the much more basic programming utilized on *Vilnagrom-I*, the *V-II's* advanced system would allow the scientists aboard to observe the specimens as they lived in the virtual reality settings with amazingly significant attention to detail. On most occasions, those being studied would not remember or comprehend that they had been removed from Earth.

☠☠☠

FIFTEEN YEARS LATER
YEAR -5 + 149 DAYS (MAY 25th)

They called her Hazel. As one of the pilots aboard the *V-II*, she frequently shot down to Earth on reconnaissance missions. It was exhilarating to tear through the sky on a winged missile. The vessel looked like a silver bullet... or at least it would if the naked eye could catch up with the flash before it disappeared.

The advanced flying machine rocketed across hundreds of miles of sky in a matter of seconds, all while the onboard computers were recording images of the ground below. A slight manipulation of the controls redirected the path of the manned craft without drastically slowing its velocity. Frequent passes allowed the computers to layer extremely detailed maps—topographical, infrared, and meteorological. Those would be used by the Cartographer in his construction of the virtual realms that would be occupied by those Earthly beings who were being studied.

Traveling at such great speeds, Hazel could not afford for her mind to wander for too long. An inferno on the horizon grabbed her attention, though.

"I am observing a massive fire southeast of Akron, Ohio," she said, speaking in her native language to supplement the data her vessel was recording. "The fire was not present on my previous pass, but now…"

BAM!

The ship clipped a helicopter which had been life-flighting a patient to a nearby hospital. The chopper went down in a fiery crash, but not before ripping a gash through the outer walls of the foreign aircraft.

Hazel checked her flight panel, then shouted an expletive she had added to her vocabulary during her years of monitoring the people of Earth. Her shuttle was in no condition to travel into space. There would be no return to the *Vilnagrom-II*, a spacecraft she had called home for the last fifteen years. Making matters worse, she was too far from any of the vastly remote areas that had been predetermined as emergency landing sites.

"Dammit!" she screamed, realizing that she needed to act in the best interests of the mission, as well as her friends and colleagues aboard the *V-II*. She was going down. And since it appeared she would be going down in an area where she and her ship would be discovered, she knew what she had to do.

By pounding a sequence of buttons on her flight panel, Hazel prepared to drop the highly-explosive engine in a sparsely-populated area south of the historic battlefield of Gettysburg. Next, she angled the flight stick to take her into a nosedive. The impact would result in a violent explosion and would leave nothing for the inhabitants of Earth to study. The impact would obliterate the ship and its pilot.

But then instinct took over. Survival became her loan objective. Speaking for a final time into her flight log, Hazel said,

"Setting a course to crash into the Atlantic. Touchdown point thirty miles southeast of Ocean City, Maryland."

☠ ☠ ☠

Hazel never made it to the ocean. The silver bullet ripped apart in midair. What was left of the ship crashed on the 12th fairway of a golf course.

☠ ☠ ☠

FOUR HOURS LATER

Though Yaron Harazi had not yet reached his thirtieth birthday, he was one of the world's foremost experts on extraterrestrial communications and intelligence. He was an instructor at Johns Hopkins and worked for the Department of Defense as a consultant on issues related to unidentified aerial phenomena. ("Unidentified Aerial Phenomena" was the official term for what everyday people might refer to as unidentified flying objects or UFOs.)

The Yemeni-born doctor had been waiting by the door of his apartment building. Once he had slung his green canvas backpack over his shoulder, he jogged to the car. He wore khaki cargo shorts and a black T-shirt that featured a silkscreened logo of the classic video game known as Galaga. The casual attire created a stark contrast to the black suit worn by his counterpart.

Preston Ivy had worked for the U.S. Government for the better part of two decades. In that time, he learned to embrace the clichés of being a government agent. Doing so worked to his advantage on this occasion. The glare of the early morning sun was going to be

no match for his dark sunglasses and the tinted windows of his
SUV.

"Have you seen these images?" an excited Harazi asked before
he'd fully fallen into his seat.

"I have."

Ivy may have been every bit as excited as the doctor. They
likely were less than a one-hour drive away from the locale of the
most significant alien contact the U.S. Military had seen in more
than sixty years. But, thanks to years of Navy training, the
intelligence officer was far better at concealing his exuberance…
The dark sunglasses helped.

He eyed his partner's attire. "I know it's the weekend. But
those clothes! I think we can spare a couple of minutes if you want
to go back inside and put on a more appropriate outfit."

Harazi shook his head. Then he thumped the side of his
overstuffed backpack. "Drive. I've got a change of clothes in here.
I'll change on the way to our destination." After a brief pause, he
asked, "Where exactly are we going?"

"Westminster, Maryland," Ivy responded as he pulled away
from the curb.

"Never heard of it. Sounds fancy."

"It's not. Just a quiet little town near the Pennsylvania border.
At least it *was* quiet until a spaceship crashed at oh-four hundred
and added a crater to the toughest par five in Carroll County."

☠☠☠

Thirty miles down the road, Harazi had managed to wiggle into a
pair of tan slacks and a button-down dress shirt. He could feel Ivy's
disapproving glare bouncing off the mirror. "The shirt's made to be
untucked," he explained.

The military man shook his head and chuckled. What the ET expert chose to wear never particularly bothered him. And it certainly wasn't going to upset Ivy on this potentially historic day.

"There were people I worked with that thought I was nuts to transfer to the task force," he said of his reassignment within the intelligence community. "From counter-terrorism to Unidentified Aerial Phenomena? Some of my friends thought I was going through a midlife crisis. Others guessed I pissed off the Director." He laughed to himself, then added, "I even heard one rumor that I was in the doghouse because I'd slept with the Vice President's daughter."

"You slept with the Vice President's daughter?"

"I wish."

"Why *did* you join the task force?" Harazi asked.

"You ever hear the phrase 'needle in a haystack?'"

Harazi scoffed. "Of course. That's a very common saying. I was born in Yemen, but my parents and I moved to America when I was five."

Feeling no need to apologize, Ivy continued. "Well, I was in Somalia… not far from where you were born, I suppose. The night sky there is something I'll never forget. You look up into space and you can see millions and millions of stars. Here, the lights of the big city are never far away, so you can't see nearly as many. Over in East Africa, you get an entirely different perspective."

"What does that have to do with a 'needle in a haystack?'"

Ivy activated his turn signal. They were approaching the golf course and the site of the suspected alien vessel. "Most folks assume that people who spot UFOs are either crazy or on drugs or some lonely grandpa that's so desperate for attention that he'll gladly confuse a smudge on his glasses for a flying saucer. But I looked up into the blackness of the space above Somalia and I'm confident that I saw an alien space craft. One hundred percent. No doubt about it. It was much too fast and much too quiet to be manmade. I saw it with my own two eyes. I looked up into the sky and that's where I spotted an object that shouldn't be there. It was an object I had no business finding, short of a miracle. It was the universe's way of showing me that I was in the middle of a big haystack, and that I needed to be looking for that needle. A few weeks later I heard about D.O.D. forming this task force, and I jumped at the chance to sign up."

Harazi nodded his head. "Interesting."

Bright yellow tape surrounded the perimeter of the scene. Ivy pulled the SUV up as close to the action as he possibly could. As he climbed out of the vehicle, he told his young partner, "Today's the day I'm finally able to make my declaration. Today's the day I can tell myself that I'm not crazy. This may be the needle. If it is, I'll know that my decision to chase after UAPs was the most important decision I ever made in my life."

☠☠☠

An old man who identified himself as "Ellis" worked as the Head Greenskeeper for the golf course. No one bothered to ask if that was his first name or his last.

Ellis was the first one on the scene at the time of the crash. He quickly moved towards Ivy and Harazi. The greenskeeper was eager to share every detail of his discovery with the big shots from the U.S. Government.

"Bar none, it's the beatenest thing I ever saw," the old timer reported through a thick Appalachian drawl. "The blast was so dern loud! 'Bout scared the mess outta me! And it left a hole deep enough to bury a couple eighteen wheelers. Plumb near a dozen trees uprooted... most of 'em mighty oaks that were planted long before the course opened in the late-1960s."

Harazi feared he was about to be sucked into some phony baloney UFO tale that this guy may have been telling for decades. The government scientist had no intention of letting that slow his investigation today. "Is there anything left of the apparatus that caused the blast?"

"You mean the spacecraft?" Ellis asked, doing his best to cut through any official mumbo jumbo used by the Feds and designed to deny any knowledge of the existence of extraterrestrial beings or alien technology. "It's down at the bottom of the hole, right where you'd expect it. Looks like a bobsled. Shiny and metallic, though. Not fiberglass like the ones they use in the Winter Olympics."

Gesturing towards a golf cart, Harazi asked, "Please! Can you take us there?"

"I can..." Ellis said with a mysterious pause. "But I think what you really came to see ain't in the hole in the ground. Hung up in the branches of a tree over yonder, next to the Number Fourteen Tee Box... She ain't conscious, but I don't think she's dead."

3: KAYFABE

"When you live life as a pirate, there are a few lessons that you need to learn if you want to survive... You learn to never trust anyone. You learn to expect attacks from all sides. And you learn to keep your cool no matter what troubles arise on the high seas... I'm Long Jenn Silva. I'm a survivor!"

-LONG JENN SILVA promo taped prior to challenging Savannah Lyons for the AWWA Women's Championship as part of the "New Year's Nightmare" Pay-Per-View event.

THREE YEARS AGO
YEAR -3 + 36 DAYS (FEBRUARY 5th)

She was given the name "Jennysis Quevedo" at birth. But she abandoned that moniker when she was sixteen. That's when she moved from Florida to Puerto Rico to train under wrestling legend Manny Vargas. Fans of the masked young woman knew her as "Lady Pirata." Her portrayal of a leather-clad, post-apocalyptic pirate made her wildly popular.

After a couple years cutting her teeth and learning to run the ropes in Puerto Rico, larger paychecks and opportunities to gain notoriety lured her to Mexico. Though she had become a big star south of the border, Jenn hoped that she soon would enjoy success throughout the world as one of the biggest stars in the sports entertainment industry. That meant returning home and trying to make it in the U.S.

"I appreciate your commitment to kayfabe. But how do I put this...? The pirate gimmick may be a little dated."

Kayfabe. It was the long-honored tradition of protecting the secrets of the business of professional wrestling. Kayfabe was the process of presenting staged events as if they were genuine. Do not expose the secrets. *Never* let on that the show isn't one hundred percent real. That went for the performances in (and out) of the ring.

It also meant that the personas created and portrayed by those performers were to be taken seriously. Babyfaces and heels (good guys and bad guys, respectively) were never to eat or drink together after the match. To be seen doing so carried the potential of undoing all the hard work, spilled blood, and broken bones sacrificed to create the illusion that the combatants wanted to beat the holy hell out of each other!

Jenn had been told to expect the very words that were being spoken from across the massive desk. It was an appointment with Griffin Conrad, the head honcho of the International Wrestling Organization. The IWO was the biggest wrestling promotion in the world. Conrad had a reputation for scooping up existing talent, completely reworking their gimmicks, then claiming that all the success that followed was attributable to his magic touch... and his magic touch alone.

True to the Lucha Libre tradition, "Lady Pirata" refused to take her mask off in public. She insisted on keeping her face covered, even when meeting with the corporate big shot. She sat in the office of a man who could catapult her into superstardom or completely crush her career with the snap of his fingers. Was it courageous or foolhardy for her to balk at the suggestions being "offered" across the table? That was up for debate.

"I view pirates as 'classic' more than 'dated,'" the young grappler boldly responded. Her words were tinged with a hint of an accent that she picked up during her time in Mexico. "They loved it in Puerto Rico. And they've been eating it up in Mexico for almost five years now."

A brief smile appeared on the executive's face. Then that smile instantly disappeared. "We're not in Mexico now, are we?" He glanced down at his watch. "Let me cut to the chase. I've seen clips of you in the ring. Impressive. We think you have the look and the athletic ability to be considered a talent we can work with. However, this company is not interested in 'Lady Pirata.' If you'd like to lose the mask, I've got a couple of ideas for you. You choose which one you like. Then you can fight some dark matches with our developmental talent, and we'll see what works."

Though skeptical, she did not want to let this potentially life-changing opportunity pass her by. She leaned in. "I'm listening."

"Idea Number One. You'd be Margarita. A sexy Mexican señorita who loves tequila and long walks on the beach. But she's got a fiery temper. Or if you don't like that one…"

"I don't mean to cut you off, but I'm not really from Mexico."

Conrad ignored her interruption and continued his sales pitch. He did ad lib one minor change, however. "… If you don't like the sexy señorita, you could be Angelina. She's a sexy, yet street savvy girl and former *Puerto Rican* gang member… With a fiery temper."

Jenn waited to hear if there were any other proposals. Once it was clear that no other possible gimmicks were going to be suggested, she asked, "Can I have some time to think about it?"

The boss looked at his watch again, then nodded his head in the affirmative. "It's almost 10:30. I'm scheduled to be on a flight to Los Angeles at noon. It's about a five-hour flight. I could call you after I land… Or if you're thinking of hanging around Orlando for a few days, we'll comp you tickets for Friday's live show. You can give me your answer then if you prefer."

"I like that idea… Attending a live event sounds like a good time. Besides, I haven't been back to Florida for two or three years. I was hoping to spend a couple days visiting family and maybe even Mickey and Minnie while I'm in the area." (She already had her tickets to Disney World. But given Conrad's disdain for buccaneers, she resisted the urge to tell him she had made it a priority to book a FastPass reservation for the Pirates of the Caribbean ride.)

He pressed a button on his phone. It was a direct line to his secretary. "Sheila, make a call to the arena and tell them to hold two V.I.P. tickets for Friday's show…" Conrad lifted his finger off the intercom button and glanced across the desk. "We can't exactly leave the tickets for 'Lady Pirata,' can we? What name do you want us to use?"

Without hesitation, she came up with an appropriate alias on the fly. "Silva. Long Jenn Silva."

He smiled again. This one remained on his face a little longer than the last one. "Your commitment to kayfabe. I love it!" He pressed the intercom button once again and instructed his secretary, "Leave two V.I.P. tickets for Jenn Silva."

He got in the last word by leaving "Long" out of her name.

☠ ☠ ☠

ONE DAY LATER
YEAR -3 + 37 DAYS (FEBRUARY 6th)

Jenn hadn't been entirely forthcoming during her meeting with Griffin Conrad. Yes, she planned to be in Orlando for a few days. And, yes, she had a full day at the Magic Kingdom on her vacation itinerary. But her plans also included a marathon session with a local tattoo artist.

Lorenzo Momesso came highly recommended. Legendary Lucha Libre wrestler Hijo del Sanguinario swore by him... and with good reason. The Aztec-themed backpiece Momesso had done for Sanguinario was the most spectacular inkwork Jenn had ever seen.

Now Griffin Conrad wanted her to ditch the pirate persona. That unexpected turn put her in a bit of a quandary.

"Screw it," Jenn said aloud as she walked through the doors of the tattoo parlor. Conrad might have succeeded if he had simply tried to talk her into removing her mask. But she had been a pirate for the last seven years of her life! That had become her identity. In her mind, it wasn't negotiable. She would not compromise on that issue.

She marched right up to a counter in the front of the spacious room. "Hi! I'm Lady Pirata! I'm here to see Lorenzo. He's going to do my sleeve."

A heavily tatted woman acted as if it strained her to look down at the appointment book directly in front of her. "Oh yeah. 'Pirate Girl, the Latinx Superhero!' Gotcha right here," she said, making no effort to hide her disingenuous tone. "Lorenzo will be right with you."

The shop's owner strolled towards the front desk. He was much more pleasant than his receptionist. "Let me finish my java and I'm all yours."

After slurping down a gulp of overpriced coffee, the owner/artist added, "Cool mask, by the way. Lucha Libre all the way!" Then he escorted her towards the back of the shop.

Jenn took his comment about her mask as a sign that she was doing the right thing.

"I can't wait to show you my sketches! This is going to be quite the work of art!" he declared, excited by the opportunity to ink it onto her fleshy canvas.

If she liked the design, the sleeve would stretch from her shoulder down to her wrist. On her shoulder and bicep, a pirate galleon sailed under ominous clouds and over rough seas. The vessel flew the Jolly Roger. As the eye traveled down her arm, one would see a collection of skulls, a compass, and the helm of a ship. These images would rest with a tattered treasure map filling empty space and serving as a background. To cap it off, Lorenzo would tattoo a chest filled to overflowing with gold and gems on the luchadora's forearm, just above her wrist.

"We obviously can't do the entire sleeve in one sitting. But we can make a substantial dent in the process," he explained. "We can do the outline today. We will do the shading and add any color or finishing touches the next time you're in Orlando... I just want to make sure you're absolutely sure about this."

Jenn took a deep breath. She offered one final glance at her arm. It was tan and bare. There was no going back if she said "yes." Signing with the IWO? This tat was going to blow that idea out of the water. Literally and figuratively.

"Do it. I'm not just some fiery Latina. I'm Lady Pirata. I'm Long Jenn Silva. I'm a pirate, and I'm a survivor. No one's going to change who I am... especially not some pompous blowhard like Griffin Conrad."

☠☠☠

TWO DAYS LATER
YEAR -3 + 39 DAYS (FEBRUARY 8th)

Conrad spotted the beginnings of the luchadora's tattooed sleeve the moment he stepped into the V.I.P. box.

Jenn could have covered up the inkwork that had been permanently embedded into the skin on her left arm. But she displayed the fresh etchings as a badge of honor. She was proud of the character she had created, and the tattoo that celebrated it.

Conrad brushed past several glad-handers who were present. He marched straight up to Jenn. "Well, Miss Silva, I see I have my answer." If it disappointed him, he didn't allow any inflection in his voice to reveal that deeply buried secret. "I hope you enjoy the show tonight. And then your flight back to Mexico. I wish you luck scraping by with your mask and your pirate gimmick. Good night."

He pivoted and exited.

Jenn wondered if she'd see the wrestling big shot ever again... And she wasn't sure if she cared.

☠ ☠ ☠

PRESENT DAY
YEAR 0 + 1 DAY (JANUARY 1st)

Privacy was a rare thing in an independent promotion. On the road, they often wrestled in high school gymnasiums, county fairgrounds, and casinos. Many "locker rooms" had no lockers, much less separate changing areas for the male and female combatants. When they were fortunate enough to have separate facilities and functioning showers, many of the old schoolers felt their seniority entitled them to go wherever the hell they wanted. Sometimes that meant that the modern-day barbarians were parading their naked junk in front of the handful of women in the promotion. Those same scumbags weren't beyond more than a bit of "look-see" of their own on their way through.

Jenn developed a simple response to this problem. She adopted a habit of lingering in the backstage areas routinely open to members of the media, important guests, and others who were offered a glimpse behind the scenes. The pirate signed autographs and posed for selfies with anyone who wanted one. She gave interviews to the podcasters and local newspaper reporters who were covering the event. Invariably, she'd be one of the last wrestlers left in the building. And that's when she would hit the showers.

While seated on a bench in front of the lockers, the new champ went for the buckles to remove her black leather boots. She had purchased her authentic-looking footwear from an online company that sold upscale Halloween costumes. She chose to wrestle in men's boots. All the ones made for women came with ridiculous heels, and she valued function over fashion when she stepped between the ropes.

The next item Jenn peeled away was a hinged knee brace that she wore on her left leg. She began wearing it years ago to support the narrative of a kayfabe injury. She didn't need the brace for medical reasons, but it succeeded in making her look like she was a pirate who'd taken a few licks along the way.

Her tights were custom made. The right pant leg was black with red and silver markings. It was long and tucked into her boot. The left pant leg, however, was chopped off and frayed along the upper thigh. Complemented by her leg brace, she imagined that fans would buy into the story that she was a marauder who was lucky not to be walking on a peg leg!

The missing pant leg also allowed her to wear a thigh-high fishnet stocking on the leg. Cocoa Freeman suggested this sexy little addition when Jenn first began wrestling with the AWWA.

Above the waist, Jenn wore black fingerless gloves and matching elbow pads. She quickly discarded each of those items, leaving only a crimson halter top. It featured a lattice detail that gave the appearance of two strips of material being held together by twine. The glimpse of cleavage that could be viewed behind the strings that held her top together made this the piece of the wardrobe that amped the level of sexiness up to eleven.

Jenn took a moment to assess her wardrobe. Admittedly, it could be uncomfortable performing in such a complicated outfit. But none of that mattered at all right now! A smile spread across her face as she looked down at the pirate garb.

She glanced at the work of art etched onto her left arm, and said to herself, "I'm so glad I told Griffin Conrad to stick it. I'm Long Jenn Silva... And now this pirate is a World Champion!"

Jenn's little one-woman celebration came to an abrupt stop. She heard a noise coming from the shower area. She wrapped a towel around her, then tiptoed around the corner.

"Hello?"

There she was. Savannah Lyons sat balled up on the shower room floor. She was still wearing her wrestling Spandex. Her arms rested on raised knees. She buried her face in her arms and attempted to hide the fact that she was sobbing by sitting under a steady stream of running water.

The recently dethroned champion turned her head in the opposite direction, wiped away her tears, then slowly struggled to get to her feet and dry herself with a towel.

Jenn wanted to console the woman she had defeated in the ring. "Hitting you pretty hard, huh?"

"What? Losin' the strap?" Savannah was indignant. "That's part of the business. No! You earned your push. You deserved to be put over. That's not botherin' me in the least."

"Then why are you crying?"

Savannah stomped away from the showers and back towards the lockers. She turned back around and bellowed at the new champ. "If you must know, I'm pretty worked up about Cocoa."

"I didn't think you two got along," Jenn said. As soon as the words left her mouth, she realized that there was no actual animosity between the two wrestlers. Savannah came across as a genuinely unpleasant person. Maintaining the appearance of a legitimate rivalry was easy to sell. Even backstage. Even to someone (like Jenn) who had a reputation of keeping a commitment to kayfabe. "Wait... What about Cocoa?"

"Haven't you heard? They rushed her to the hospital right after our match. She couldn't move. She said the pain in her back was excruciating."

Jenn felt lousy. The new champ had been so busy basking in her victory she hadn't noticed that her closest friend in the promotion wasn't around to celebrate with her.

Savannah had her own concerns to worry about. She didn't
want to develop a reputation as someone who routinely injured her
fellow wrestlers in the ring. "Listen, I *did not* botch those
powerbombs. She landed just as we planned it out. I didn't do
anything out of the ordinary. Nothing that should've hurt her... You
know that's right, don't you?"

Jenn had been a little preoccupied at the moment in question.
She was busy steadying herself for her own high-risk maneuver.
Seeing no harm in being diplomatic, she agreed, "Everything
looked 'by the book' to me."

☠☠☠

After she took a quick shower, Jenn slid into a pair of black
leggings and a Lucha Libre T-shirt she had picked up during her
days wrestling in Mexico.

Dragging her rolling suitcase behind her, Jenn climbed into an
Uber.

"What an honor! I'm driving the new champ! Long Jenn
Silva!" the heavyset driver declared as soon as Jenn sat in the back
seat. "Congrats!"

"Thanks," Jenn smiled. "Did you see the match?"

"Sure did. Me and a bunch of the guys got together and
watched the pay-per-view at a friend's house... Man oh man! Did I
let out a scream when you nailed Savannah Lyons with that move
from the top rope!"

Jenn smiled back. She didn't offer much of a response, though.
She was too preoccupied with her concerns about Cocoa being
rushed to the hospital.

The driver continued to offer his post-match analysis. "When
the ref got knocked out, I thought to myself, 'Here we go again.

Savannah Lyons is going to cheat and steal a win like she always does.' Man, I was so glad when that didn't happen. She's such a... b-word, if you know what I mean."

Jenn thought about her locker room conversation with Savannah. "Ah, she's not that bad."

The driver held his hands up in submission. "I get it. The sport is fake and you're probably all good friends behind the scenes."

Those were words that made the new champ grimace. She hated hearing others declare that wrestling was fake. Try telling that to Cocoa Freeman. For almost two decades, she had sacrificed her body to entertain others. It had reached the point that she was lying in a hospital bed in unbearable pain.

Jenn's nostrils flared. She had slipped and momentarily broken the kayfabe façade. That façade was a part of the business that a heel like Savannah took seriously.

"No..." Jenn tried to correct her earlier blunder. "I was just being polite. But you're right. I can't stand her. Savannah Lyons is nothing but scum. She's an absolute dirtbag."

4: THE BOOKER

"It bothers you that I've never had a door slammed in my face? You say that every opportunity was handed to me on a silver platter? Let's stop right there... Yes, my father is a legend in the business. But I don't know anything about doors being open or doors being shut. When I come callin', I don't knock. I kick the damn door down and march right in!"

-COCOA FREEMAN promo taped three years ago, when she was one of the most popular female wrestlers in the country.

EIGHT MONTHS LATER
YEAR 0 + 221 DAYS (AUGUST 9th)

She stood at a height a few inches above most women in the business of professional wrestling. Even so, Cocoa preferred to wear heels instead of flats. When she was around her fellow grapplers—male and female—she liked to present herself as confident and in control. Her sleek gray pants suit showed off her slender frame and long legs. Her appearance made it easy for one to recognize why she once was one of the most downloaded women in all of professional wrestling. Confident she looked the part, Cocoa carried herself in a manner that left onlookers wondering if she was a runway model or if she owned the company that manufactured the clothes she wore.

As she sat behind the wheel of a 14-passenger van, she listened to the radio sputter out noise. She despised classic rock almost as much as she loathed the traffic jam she found herself in. Cocoa didn't particularly care if her passengers were enjoying the music or not. Her choice to leave the sound turned down low was deliberate. It enabled her to eavesdrop on the conversations that were happening behind her, while continuing to listen for the commercial for tonight's event to hit the airwaves.

A voice called out from the back seat. "You'll be able to save some time if you take this exit."

Cocoa was skeptical. "That's not what the app says."

"Trust me. I grew up here."

"*You* grew up in St. Louis?" she said, completely blown away by this revelation. "I thought you were from France."

"Nope, born and raised in the U.S. of A..." The surprising declaration came from the young man who called himself Henri Arceneaux (usually pronounced with an exaggerated, stereotypical

French accent). He suddenly abandoned the cadence and inflection that he employed when portraying his character. "I grew up in a suburb called Creve Coeur. That's French for 'Broken Heart,' but it's really right here in The Lou. Practically under the shadow of the Arch, the Gateway to the West, Home of Toasted Ravioli and Ooey Gooey Butter Cake... Now turn left here. Another left at the end of the next block, and you're there."

Henri was right. Deviating from the directions that the cell phone application provided saved them at least twenty minutes.

Once they pulled into the children's hospital, a handful of behemoths spilled out of the van. A giant dressed in a tattered Kris Kringle costume was the first to emerge. "Santa Saws" looked more like a chainsaw-wielding psychopath than a jolly old elf. His red suit had seen better days. He had torn away the sleeves, exposing a mosaic of biker tattoos painted over massive muscles. No one would dare pull the bushy black beard on his face. It wasn't the flimsy shopping mall St. Nick variety. He'd been working on that monstrosity of facial hair for months, if not years. A kid foolish enough to tug on his whiskers wouldn't get the desired result. He might earn the spanking of a lifetime, but the beard wouldn't budge.

A monolith equally large in stature was the next to exit. His inkwork was more tribal in nature. It was blanketed across his shirtless torso to reveal his Samoan heritage and his storyline status as a warrior.

Manu "The Samoan Warrior" moved his head from side to side, studying his surroundings. He wondered aloud, "Are they going to let me into the hospital without a shirt on?" His tone would have sounded shockingly normal to anyone who overheard him while passing by.

Saws glanced towards the entryway. He then shrugged and gave his counterpart a grunt. He was not sure of the answer. The

Samoan then reached back into the van and grabbed a black T-shirt that featured a cartoony caricature of himself. The marketing gurus graffitied his name underneath. "When in doubt, wear the merch," Manu declared with a smile running across his massive face.

Two more beefy wrestlers followed Saws and Manu out of the vehicle. Then came a leggy Hawaiian princess in skin-tight jeans and fringe-covered cowgirl boots. Above the waist, Ailani Diamond wore a purple bikini top that was completely bedazzled with rhinestones... and it took *a lot* of rhinestones to cover her top!

Henri and two video camera-toting men exited through the sliding side door, leaving only Jenn and Cocoa.

"Go on in... we'll be right behind you," Cocoa called to the characters that had already vacated.

After exhaling the deep breath she had just sucked in, Cocoa turned in her seat and began a conversation that she'd been dreading. "I don't think this will really come as much of a surprise. We're going to have you drop the title to Ailani tonight."

The pirate momentarily bit down on her bottom lip. She wanted to keep herself from saying anything that she might later regret. "I can't say I'm surprised. It's just that..."

"Hold that thought," the executive interrupted while turning up the volume on the radio.

The radio announcer's enthusiasm was over the top. He sought to capture the listener's attention with his aggressive emphasis of almost every third word in the ad copy. "One night only...! *Tonight...!* The All-World Wrestling Association and the Camelot Casino present... the Third Annual *Black & Blue Bonanza*! Eight matches! In action tonight... Fireball Freeman, Braxton Gore, Henri Arceneaux, The Great Kayzo, and Manu 'The Samoan Warrior'... Plus, a twelve-man battle royal, Caribbean beauty *Long Jenn Silva* defends her Women's Championship against *Ailani*

Diamond... and in the *Main Event*... Hardcore Champ *Santa Saws* defends his title in a *'No Holds Barred' match...!'"

Satisfied with the ad, Cocoa nodded her head in approval. Her father, wrestling legend Fireball Freeman, was a pioneer of sorts. It would be fair to call him one of the most successful black wrestlers in history. This was an especially remarkable accomplishment given that his heyday came in an era in which most African-Americans struggled to get the time of day in many of the regional promotions. Now, even in his sixties, Fireball still strapped on the boots from time to time to generate buzz for the AWWA. He was the principal owner and the face of the promotion. His daughter was recently elevated into the role of the promotion's top booker. Who won, who lost, who got the push and who didn't? That all went through Cocoa.

Once the commercial concluded, she signaled that Jenn was free to speak again. The tone of her voice, however, signaled that the outcome had already been decided and was not up for debate. "You were saying?"

There was little to gain in complaining about the inevitable result of the upcoming match. Jenn had seen the poster. They brought a stack of them to autograph and give to the kids. Ailani's picture sat smack dab in the middle... positioned in the center of a bunch of other more talented and far more experienced wrestlers. Ailani Diamond had the movie star good looks and the enormous boobs. As long as she showed an ounce of promise, she was going to get the push. Tonight it was Jenn's job to help Little Miss Double D's get over.

Instead of starting an argument in the parking lot of the children's hospital, Jenn shrugged it off. "At least they called me a Caribbean beauty."

Cocoa reached back and gave Jenn a couple of taps on her knee. "Good girl. Now grab those posters and come on. I've gotta get into this hospital before one of those fools does something stupid. That's all we need. Freaking all these kids out... And I need you to come with me. Hospitals give me the creeps, you know?"

☠☠☠

SIX MONTHS EARLIER
YEAR 0 + 1 DAY (JANUARY 1st)

It was almost midnight. Because of the late hour, Jenn was met with resistance when she stepped off the elevator and into the dimly lit hallway.

"Ma'am...!" the crotchety nurse declared as she sprang up from her seat. Moving with surprising speed, the old woman darted into Jenn's path to prevent her from advancing closer to Cocoa's hospital room. "Visiting hours are from 8:00 a.m. to 8:00 p.m. Only immediate family can be here at this hour. I'm going to have to ask you to leave."

The luchadora took a step back and tried to assess the situation. *Was this woman always so rude? Or did her aggression have something to do with Jenn's almond skin tone?* Deciding that neither of these possibilities was acceptable, Jenn snapped, "Excuse me, but you don't even know who I'm here to see!"

A gentleman emerged from one of the rooms further down the hallway. Fireball Freeman called out, "Jenn! We're down here!" He shifted his focus to the gatekeeper/nighttime nurse. "She's Cocoa's sister."

The nurse made no effort to hide her skepticism. Fireball rolled with it, though, adding a believable detail to his fib. "Same father, different mother."

Jenn shimmied past the nurse. Playfully giving her boss a kiss on the cheek, she placed her hand on Fireball's shoulder and said, "Thanks, Papa." Then she softly tapped on the door to Cocoa's room. In a voice just above a whisper, she called to her dear friend, "Knock knock."

"Get in here, Champ!" Cocoa called from her bed. Other than eyes made drowsy by the late hour and the effects of her pain killers, she looked fantastic.

Fireball popped his head into the room. "I know I just risked the wrath of Nurse Ratched to get Jenn in here, but Cocoa really should be getting some rest soon. I'm gonna go check out the snack machine so you can talk in private for a minute or two. But when I come back, it's gonna be time to say *sayonara* for the night."

The ladies agreed. As he was making his exit, Cocoa called to him, "Pops? Can you get me some peanut butter cups?"

After some congratulations and chit chat about winning her first championship, Jenn told Cocoa about how Savannah Lyons had been sobbing in the shower.

"I'm touched that she was concerned about me," said Cocoa. "But, no matter what she said, I suspect she may have been a little worked up over dropping the title. Mark my words, when the booker tells you you're gonna lose it, part of you can't help but feel like you might never win another championship ever again. It feels like a sign that the end of your career may be just around the corner. Trust me, I'm speaking from experience."

"Damn, girl, that's depressing." Fireball's voice gave Jenn a start. The old man had a way of slipping into a room unnoticed.

"Well, the doc *did* say that my wrestling career was over," Cocoa reminded him.

This revelation shocked Jenn. "What?"

"I've had back issues for years. Takin' so many bumps for so many years… It's done a number on my spine. Tonight's was a real doozy. I couldn't move. The doctors here ran some tests, talked to my specialist back in Memphis, and everyone agreed. Time to hang up the boots."

"What about a second opinion?"

Cocoa shook her head. "I heard the first opinion loud and clear. If I wanna keep wrestling, that means major surgery. I'd be out a minimum of six months. And did I mention I might not ever walk again? If that's even a remote possibility, it ain't worth the risk. I'd say surgery is for the birds."

Tears ran down Jenn's face. She was flabbergasted by the news. "I can't believe how well you're taking this."

"It's the drugs," Cocoa joked.

Fireball placed a comforting hand on Jenn's shoulder. "Besides, we knew this day was comin'. Cocoa's cool with never steppin' in the ring again. And to be honest, I'm happy about it."

Jenn was shocked by what she was hearing. "What?"

"Oh, don't get me wrong. I hate seein' my baby girl in pain," he said in an effort to restate his sentiment. "But I've still got plans for her. Bigger and better things, in fact… Every time I've asked for Cocoa's input on who to sign or who should win the belt, her instincts have proven to be spot on. I've been lookin' forward to the day that my daughter would transition to becoming the full-time top booker of the AWWA. Looks like that day is here."

☠☠☠

PRESENT DAY
YEAR 0 + 221 DAYS (AUGUST 9th)

Jenn and Cocoa walked towards the front door of the children's hospital. The soon-to-be former champ kept glancing towards the woman who was both her boss and friend. She kept hoping that Cocoa would offer a promise. *Something like "we are going to have you win the title back when you have your rematch" would be nice.* If not that, at the very least she'd like to receive some words of encouragement. *Hearing "don't worry, we've still got big plans for you" would help soften the blow.* Instead, she was showered with awkward silence.

Jenn paused. "Do you mind if I make a call first? I'll be in right behind you."

Cocoa weighed the situation and agreed. She'd blindsided her friend with the news. She should have told her weeks ago about the plan to put the championship on Ailani. But Cocoa avoided filling her in because she was continuing to try to craft an angle that allowed Jenn to hold the title for a while longer.

Once Jenn was alone, she pulled out her phone and attempted a video call to her husband. The call went straight to voicemail. *He was most likely working out. Lazz spent a lot of time at the gym.*

She left a message and went inside.

☠☠☠

The moment she stepped off the elevator, Jenn was approached by a nurse and a hospital administrator. The administrator greeted her with a smile. "Miss Silva… Or is it Captain Silva? Thank you so much for being here today. We've set up a station over here for you to take a few pictures with some members of our staff and a few of our patients."

Jenn suppressed a laugh as the administrator went on about how wonderful it was for the AWWA Women's Champ to take some time out of her busy schedule to visit their facility. This welcome was quite different than the one she received the last time she set foot in a hospital. It was just a few months earlier that the night shift nurse almost tackled the luchadora while trying to prevent her from entering Cocoa's room.

The administrator escorted Jenn to an area where she was asked to pose for a picture with Ailani and a trio of doctors. While waiting for the Hawaiian princess to stop flirting with one of the younger MDs long enough to snap a few photos, the pirate got distracted. There was a commotion coming from down the hall. She stepped away from the photo opp to investigate.

Turning the corner, she spotted Cocoa standing between Santa Saws and a concerned father.

"I'm sure you mean well and that deep down you're a nice guy," the father said as the giant in the tattered red suit towered over him. "But you've got to understand... my son just turned seven. We let him watch wrestling from time to time. And he gets very confused by your tough Santa character."

"'Character?' Are you suggesting there's something about me that's not real?"

Kayfabe. Saws apparently didn't understand that sometimes it was appropriate to abandon (or at least deviate) from the tough guy act. Especially when you were visiting kids in a children's hospital.

The chaos that had erupted in his doorway left the seven-year-old boy in tears. As soon as he spotted Jenn, however, the crying stopped. "Lady Pirata!" he cried out. His enthusiasm resembled that shown by other kids when they received a new bike as a birthday present.

Jenn smiled at the fact that he had addressed her by the name she used when wrestling in Mexico. "Step aside, Saws. The kid is a *bona fide* fan." The women's champ slipped past the mountain of a man, smiling and winking as she did so. "My fans can't be left waiting any longer." She tugged on the father's arm, pulling him into the room before shutting the door behind them.

Finally able to give her young supporter her undivided attention, Jenn looked towards the bed. "Did I hear someone say 'Lady Pirata?'"

The kid suddenly got shy. Instead of answering the question, he slammed a pair of wrestling action figures against one another.

"This is Michael. He has a rare blood disorder. He's in and out of the hospital quite frequently," the boy's father explained. Knowing that he had brought down the room with his introduction, he turned the topic back to wrestling. "Michael is a big fan of the sport. We've been trying to use that to teach him Spanish. His mom and I have been letting him watch videos of Mexican wrestling on the internet. Isn't that right, big guy?"

Michael put his toys down long enough to look up at his visitor.

Jenn took a step towards the boy's bed. She spoke to him in Spanish. *"¿Estas aprendiendo mirando la Lucha Libre?"* (Which means "You're learning by watching wrestling?")

Michael stared at her.

His dad stepped in and offered an explanation. "He's just learning. He isn't quite fluent yet."

"Ah! *Un poquito.*" (Which means "a little.") "Maybe I can teach *Miguel* a few words before I leave."

☠☠☠

Cocoa peeked her head into Michael's room. "It's almost time for us to load up the van and head back to the casino for tonight's matches," she reported.

"Oh my!" Jenn declared. "We spent almost two hours together, Miguel!"

"I wondered where you disappeared to. A few other kiddos were asking about you, but I was too busy putting out the fires created by Manu and Saws to hunt you down."

"Please tell me they didn't actually start any fires," Jenn said, all the time grinning as she looked into the eyes of her new, young friend.

"No. No actual fires… But we do need to go."

Jenn said her good-byes to Michael and his father, then stepped out to talk to Cocoa. "I feel awful about not visiting any of the other kids. Do you think maybe you could take everyone else back in the van, and I'll catch an Uber in a little bit? A half hour is all I need."

Cocoa took a moment to study the reigning champ's mannerisms and expressions. On one hand, Jenn was a good friend, had always been a team player, and helped out today by getting Saws to leave poor, frightened Michael alone. On the other hand, she had just been given the news that she was going to lose the title at that night's pay-per-view. It would be disastrous if the pirate jumped ship and didn't show up for the performance.

"How 'bout I stay with you," Cocoa suggested. "Henri apparently knows the streets of St. Louis like the back of his hand. He can take everyone else back in the van. You and I can head back a little bit later."

5: BABYFACE

"Let me tell you one thing, you miserable Soviet... When you threw that apple pie in my face, you weren't just attacking me. You were attacking this great country that I love with all my heart. I won't stand for that! I'm going to beat you in the center of the ring, then send you high-tailin' it all the way back to Moscow... U-S-A! U-S-A! U-S-A!"

-CORPORAL CHAMBERS promo recorded during his feud with Boris Sputnikov at the heart of the Cold War in the mid-1980s.

ONE WEEK EARLIER
YEAR 0 + 214 DAYS (AUGUST 2nd)

"You shaved your goatee!"

Brady ran his hand across his cleanly shaven face and nodded. "Yeah... It was starting to get a little hot and itchy in the summer heat."

"And who are you wearing today?"

It was a question Brady got asked frequently. The recent college grad estimated he owned somewhere between thirty and forty sports jerseys commemorating his favorite teams and players. Jerseys or shirzees—which were much less expensive replica T-shirts designed to resemble a player's uniform—were just about all he ever wore.

Baseball, basketball, football, hockey, and even a little professional wrestling, as of late. It didn't matter. If it aired on ESPN, Brady was watching. He could name almost every starting lineup in all of professional sports. Passion for the games we play was his way of filling the void created from losing both parents shortly after his eighteenth birthday.

Brady's fun-loving father dropped dead of a massive heart attack at a co-worker's wedding reception. It struck while he was dancing to the "Beer Barrel Polka."

His strict mother quickly realized she didn't have another friend in the world. She overdosed on her husband's muscle relaxers a few days after his funeral.

Brady looked down at the outfit he had pulled out of his closet for the day. He had chosen a red and black Chicago Bulls jersey over a plain white T-shirt. "Number 23. Michael Jordan."

"Oh of course. The baseball player from that Bugs Bunny movie... *Space Jam*."

Brady peered in at Pastor Winston. *Was he serious? Or was he joking? It was hard to tell with the straight-as-a-string minister of King City's largest non-denominational congregation.* "He was a pretty good basketball player, too."

The Pastor agreed. "You've gotta be... if you're going to beat those cartoon aliens in a game of hoops."

"He was *pulling my leg,"* Brady finally concluded.

Pastor Winston turned to the woman behind the counter and placed his order. "I'd like to order two chocolate covered long johns... and whatever my friend is having."

Brady wasn't expecting free donuts. "Thanks!"

"Don't mention it," the pastor replied before reminding him of their appointment later in the day. "And we're still on for three o'clock?"

"I'll see you then."

☠ ☠ ☠

Brady still lived in his childhood home. It was just two blocks from the Daisy Donut Shoppe and about six blocks from the Main Campus of Central Illinois University. He would have no problem downing a dozen donut holes on his walk to the campus bookstore.

The next item on the day's to-do list was an attempt to sell back as many used textbooks as possible. The recent graduate felt he had wasted most of his senior year taking a schedule full of general studies classes. To him, they were "pointless" courses that the university required for graduation. It never occurred to him that it may have been short-sighted and insensitive (if not unintentionally xenophobic) to grumble about the classes. At the moment, however, he found himself unable to think of a single practical use for the books he had been forced to purchase to study Art History, Latin American Culture, and World Religion.

The bookstore employee made two piles. The much larger stack was filled with books that the store would not buy back.

"Why not?" Brady asked even though he had endured this process in each of the last four summers.

"Most of these texts have new editions coming out. A couple of them were used for classes that will no longer be offered due to university budget cuts," she begrudgingly explained (probably for the fiftieth time to the fiftieth different broke student this week).

Brady stood in silence. Complaining might make him feel better, but he knew that doing so would serve no purpose.

"Ready for the good news?" The bookstore employee pointed to the smaller stack.

That pile was made up of three texts from a World Religion class. Although the course had been just about the only one Brady found at all interesting in the second semester of his senior year, he was eager to see how much money he could recoup. After all, he'd shelled out nearly three hundred dollars to purchase the books. He could think of plenty of ways he could put the recovered cash to good use.

"I can give you thirty for these."

"Thirty dollars each? Ninety bucks isn't bad."

"Sorry. I would if it were up to me," the worker apologized. "But thirty dollars is all I can do. Thirty dollars total."

Brady looked down at both stacks. He did his best to suppress his anger as he stuffed the three World Religion texts into his backpack. "No. I think I'll keep these. You can throw the other ones in the garbage."

Then he left. He had other errands to run. He hoped those would be more fruitful than the trip to the bookstore.

☠ ☠ ☠

The next stop was to swing by the little league fields. He needed to
pick up his weekly paycheck and get the schedule for the games he
would be umpiring for the final two weeks of the season.

"Oh good. Brady, I'm glad you're here."

Brady peaked his head into the concession stand. League
Director Toby Pendleton was stocking the fridge with bottles of
water, Gatorade and soda.

"You needed me for something?" he asked, mindful that the
realtor was scheduled to stop by over the lunch hour with a
prospective buyer. Brady had gotten an early start on the day, but
he still wanted to get back to the house and do a little spot cleaning
before the lady from Century 21 arrived.

After putting the last bottle into the refrigerator, Pendleton
stood and looked at the reliable umpire. "Did you hear about J.R.
Whitten?"

"Who?"

"Head coach of the KC Automotive team in the 11 & 12 Boys
Division? The guy that always rolls up his sleeves to show off his
huge biceps."

Brady shook his head from side to side. "No. What about
him?"

"Feds popped him. Apparently, he wasn't just importing car
parts, but all sorts of synthetic drugs from China. News report says
he's probably gonna get at least twenty years in prison."

"Wow. I didn't see that coming. Was he using the drugs or
selling them?"

"Definitely selling," Pendleton reported. "I suspect he was
dipping into his supply from time to time. He hadn't been himself
lately... One of his players complained about how much time the

coach had made him sit the bench. J.R. told the kid 'You know there's no I in TEAM. And if it were up to me, there'd be no U on my TEAM'… Kind of a lousy thing to say to an eleven-year-old, if you ask me."

Brady agreed. He still wasn't sure how this concerned him, though.

The League Director got around to the reason he stopped him. "I was hoping you could take over coaching the KC Automotive team for the rest of the season."

Brady glanced at the paycheck in his hand. Other than a bit of cash he received from renting his third bedroom, umpiring was his only source of income. Even though his parents' old house was paid for, he had to bring in enough to cover food, taxes, utilities, and incidentals. He had applied for a few jobs, but so far there wasn't much available in a rinky dink town that was saturated with the cheap labor of college students.

"We really need you to step up and do this," Pendleton explained. (The news had broken only a few hours earlier. Brady was confident no one else had been asked to fill the coaching vacancy. But his boss was looking to solve this problem quickly and efficiently.) "*The kids* need you to step up and do this. Come on, Brady. You're not going to let down the kids, are you?"

☠ ☠ ☠

By the time he had walked to the donut shop, the campus bookstore, and the little league complex, made a stop at the bank to deposit his check, then returned home, Brady had worked up quite a sweat. Turning the corner and seeing the For Sale sign in front of his parents' home brought a little smile to his face. "I can't wait to feel that air conditioning!"

The feeling of joy vanished, however, when he spotted a towering pile of dishes in the kitchen. That mess hadn't been there when he walked out the door earlier in the morning. "What the…?" he muttered, stopping before allowing himself to finish the thought out loud.

He tossed his keys on the counter and spotted a handwritten note. It was from Valērijs, his happy-go-lucky Latvian roommate who was about to begin his sixth year of college with no end in sight.

The note read: *"Brady, I know I still owe the July rent, but an old friend came into town. We are going on a road trip to Colorado and Wyoming. Be back in two weeks. I will give you the rent for July and August then. Val!"* (Whether he intended to was uncertain, but the Latvian included a pizza sauce impression of his thumbprint directly beneath his signature.)

He knew he should have seen it coming. Val hadn't bothered to chip in for groceries for the last few weeks. "Why pay your rent? Why pay for your share of the groceries if you can save up that money for a nonstop party in the Rocky Mountains?" Brady moaned while resisting the urge to fling a dirty bowl across the kitchen.

☠ ☠ ☠

Pastor Winston gestured to the chair across from him. "Come on in and sit down."

He dropped into the seat for his weekly half-hour with his mentor and spiritual advisor. Pastor Winston carefully watched over all the members of his flock. He made every effort he could to be there for Brady after his parents passed.

Over the course of their session, Brady told Pastor Winston about his frustrations at the bookstore, being pressured into giving up a paying umpire gig so he could "volunteer" to coach a team of eleven-year-olds, and how his ridiculous roommate prioritized his ability to party far above paying Brady the money he owed him.

"Brady, pastors don't always say things like this, but you're too nice. You shouldn't allow people to take advantage of your kindness all the time."

He shook his head. "You bought my donuts today. That was nice."

The pastor elaborated. "I did that because I wanted to. I didn't do it because I felt guilted into doing it. I didn't do it because someone made me feel obligated."

"The kids needed me. The kids needed a coach." Brady realized what it sounded like as he was making excuses for the people who walked all over him. But he continued anyway, "My roommate needed the money for his trip. He'll catch up on the rent when he gets back. I don't have that many bills. And with Val out of town, the grocery bill won't be nearly as big. The house is paid for. I just need to bring in enough money to cover the taxes and utilities."

"And clothes. You need cash to take young women out on dates. You need money to tuck away for a rainy day." Pastor Winston looked at the clock and shifted in his seat. "I've got another appointment coming in at any time. But here's what I want you to do… Let me reword that… Here's what I want you to pray about. Pray about lowering the price on your mom and dad's house. Sell it. Put a big chunk of cash in savings. Then get an apartment with a short-term lease. If you find a job or a girl that takes you out of King City, go for it. Don't fight so hard if you detect God's trying to nudge you out of the nest."

Despite the leather cushions clinging to his sweaty skin, Brady quickly shot out of his seat. "I guess you've got it all figured out then."

"I'd never be so bold as to presume to know God's plan," Winston responded in what Brady took to be classic pastor-speak. "But I pray you won't hesitate when He sends an opportunity your way."

"Hesitate?"

"Hesitate because you've got a ball team to coach. Or because you feel sorry for your roommate. Or because you feel guilty about accepting something less than a top dollar offer on your childhood home."

Brady had heard enough. He threw two dollars onto the desk. "That's for the donuts!" He headed towards the door.

Pastor Winston stood to offer one parting piece of advice. "Brady, please don't clutch to the anchor. Seek adventure. Even when you feel most alone, God will be with you. And with His help, you can change the world... Maybe even save it."

☠☠☠

ONE WEEK LATER
YEAR 0 + 221 DAYS (AUGUST 9th)

The inseparable trio known as the "Brady Bunch" was about to split up and head off into different directions. If all went according to plan, Greg would relocate to Atlanta to take a new job, while Marshall journeyed to Los Angeles for law school. Both were scheduled to pack up and leave their cozy little Southern Illinois hometown of King City by the end of the month. None of that would happen before the gang got together for one final, memorable weekend living it up in St. Louis.

The itinerary included drinking and golfing by day, followed by drinking (again), watching baseball, and trying their luck at the blackjack tables at Camelot Casino. They might even consider heading to one of the many strip clubs on the East Side if Greg and Marshall managed to convince the conservative-minded Brady that getting a lapdance wasn't an unpardonable sin.

Signs, posters, and the marquee over the hotel's front entrance announced the All-World Wrestling Association's Pay-Per-View event that was being filmed at the Camelot Casino that night. Brady kept his head on a swivel as his trio checked in at the front desk.

"Did you know there was wrestling here tonight?" he asked Marshall while Greg took on the duty of getting the keys to their suite.

"Not until I saw the sign. But don't go getting any crazy ideas. You can't be in two places at once, and we've got some pretty expensive baseball tickets in our pockets."

"Oh, I wasn't wanting to go to the matches..." he responded while continuing to scan the vicinity for any recognizable figures who might be wandering through the lobby. Unfortunately, the perpetually nice guy wasn't a very convincing liar. It was no secret that the rabid sports fan had developed a bit of a crush on the AWWA Women's Champion. Ever since he first spotted her on a television screen seven months earlier, Brady had dedicated quite a bit of time to daydreaming about Long Jenn Silva.

"Tell you what, loverboy... I'll chase her down and get her autograph for you, if I happen to see her before you do," Marshall joked. "If I thought you'd act on it, I might even try to get a key to her room for you. But we both know that would be pointless. You'd just end up embarrassing yourself because you wouldn't know what to do with a woman."

☠☠☠

Brady never managed to spot any wrestlers at the casino.

After he and his lifelong pals showered and dressed, they hopped on the westbound Metrolink train towards the ballpark. Once they were there, they headed over to the collection of bronze statues that had been erected to celebrate the finest baseball players in the storied history of the hometown team.

Greg handed his phone to a passer-by and asked him to take a few pictures of "the Brady Bunch" next to a statue of Stan "The Man" Musial. Though they tried to act nonchalant about the whole thing, all three young men took the photo op very seriously. After all, they knew that the picture likely would resurface on social media. It might even be displayed at future weddings or high school reunions.

As they prepared to take another photo, Greg eyed Brady's black and yellow Pirates throwback jersey. "How many baseball jerseys do you own?"

"Baseball? Probably fifteen or sixteen… That's not including the game-worn Jack Flaherty jersey. I'll only wear that to a game when the Cardinals make it to the World Series."

"Fifteen or sixteen…?" Greg said as part of the group's constant friendly ribbing of one another. "But you wore *that* to tonight's ballgame?"

It was a valid point. First place was on the line, and Brady was wearing the colors of the opposition. Willie Stargell had been his dad's childhood favorite. And since this would have been his dad's fifty-eighth birthday, Brady felt that it was a fitting tribute to wear the replica 1979 Stargell jersey and matching hat.

Instead of reminding his fellow Brady Bunchers of his father's all-too-early demise, he chose to shrug it off and offer an excuse.

"Sorry. Dylan Carlson's in the wash... I did pack an Ozzie Smith for tomorrow's game, though."

Ozzie was a St. Louis legend, and another favorite of Brady's father back in the 1980s. "Can't blame a guy for wanting to turn back the clock," Brady said, smiling to himself about the double meaning of his words.

That smile quickly left his face, however, when he discovered that his ticket was not in his wallet. "Ah, crap! I must've left my ticket back at the hotel room."

Quick to turn Brady's words against him for another friendly gibe, Marshall said, "I bet right now you're wishin' you could turn back the clock to about thirty minutes ago. Then maybe you wouldn't have forgotten your ticket."

"Crap!" he blurted out once again.

That was about as vulgar as Brady would get. Back when he was eleven, he made the mistake of reciting a movie quote that included a four-letter word. His strict mother washed his mouth out with soap. That taught him an important lesson. Ever since, curse words rarely crossed his lips.

(He did say "shit" when she died, though.)

Greg offered to contribute ten bucks. "Find a scalper," he suggested. "Buy the cheapest seat you can find. Who cares if it's in the nosebleeds? You won't actually be sitting up there. You'll just use that ticket to get in the stadium."

Brady thought about the fact that tonight's game was going to be a sellout. Even the cheapest single ticket would carry a hefty price tag. Besides, leaving the ticket back at the hotel was his own stupid mistake. "Go on in, you guys," he responded. "I'll get on the train, run to the hotel, and I'll be back before they throw out the first pitch."

6: STANDING ROOM ONLY

*"You feel that chill in the air? Santa Saws is
flying down from The North Pole to bring all
your hopes and dreams crashing down. Your
journey ends tonight... You may not believe in
the fat man in the red suit, but soon you'll know
that Santa Saws is the real deal!"*

*-SANTA SAWS promo recorded in
advance of his match against Braxton Gore at
the AWWA's Third Annual Black & Blue
Bonanza pay-per-view event.*

PRESENT DAY
YEAR 0 + 221 DAYS (AUGUST 9th)

Bumper to bumper traffic towards the bridges meant that an Uber to the casino was going to take an exorbitant amount of time. "You'll get there a lot faster if you take the MetroLink," suggested a hospital staffer.

As Jenn and Cocoa were approaching the nearest commuter train stop, a blast of heavy metal music interrupted them. The noise came from Jenn's phone.

"Is that your husband's entrance music?"

"Yep." Jenn's radiant smile revealed how much she continued to be smitten with the man. She had known him for two years. They recently celebrated their first anniversary. "Scares me half to death when he calls in the middle of the night."

"You better take that. Please don't be too long. I'm giving you five minutes," Cocoa said before stepping in the direction of the automated machine to purchase two one-way tickets.

Jenn swiped her finger across her phone, gladly accepting her husband's request to videochat. Once she answered, she saw that he had propped the phone up and stepped back so his bride could see a full body view of him. He was lifting weights.

"Hi, sweetheart! I see you're pumping iron."

Laszlo Barba first appeared on the national stage as a member of Team USA's weightlifting squad. After accomplishing his dream of competing in the Olympics, he made the jump to the world of professional wrestling. Griffin Conrad snatched him up and gave him a gimmick of a Gold Medalist from Romania. Lazz did not mind, though, because the change included a rocket push to the top of the International Wrestling Organization's championship picture.

"Gotta stay in tip-top form in case I ever decide to step in the ring again," Lazz said, referencing his recent decision to take some time away from sports entertainment. "You're geared up awfully early."

"Yeah," she replied, glancing down at the attire she was wearing while standing at a crowded commuter train stop. Jenn snickered to herself after realizing how odd it must be to see her riding public transportation in her wrestling garb. "Cocoa took a few of us to sign autographs at the children's hospital before tonight's pay-per-view. Some good publicity. You know the drill."

"You should remind Cocoa that you're the champ, and that the publicity trips should be reserved for mid-carders."

Jenn nodded her head and hoped that her boss didn't somehow overhear that part of the conversation. "Eh, we're already done. I'm standing outside the hospital right now... I'm hoping it wasn't just good publicity for the company, but some good karma for me."

Lazz instantly recognized the concern in his wife's voice. "Is there something I should know?"

"Eh." Jenn tried to wipe her mind clean of any concerns she was experiencing. "You know how I told you it felt like Cocoa might be avoiding me? Well, spoiler alert... This afternoon she told me I'll be dropping the title in tonight's match."

"That sucks."

"Yeah. I wish she hadn't waited until the last minute to break the news. Makes me feel like I'm no longer in their long-term plans."

Though her concerns sounded plausible, her husband did his best to reassure her. Then he changed the subject and told her a funny story so she would stop dwelling on work worries, particularly those that were out of her control.

They had been talking for more than the allotted five minutes when Cocoa waved to get Jenn's attention. She pantomimed pointing at an imaginary watch, a motion intended to tell the luchadora that it was time to wrap up the call.

"I better go before Cocoa pitches a fit."

"Well, from everything you told me, it doesn't sound like she's avoiding you," Lazz said, attempting to encourage his wife. "Based on how you handled the situation in the hospital, it sounds like she needs you now more than ever."

"Thanks."

"Before you go, I want you to remember two things... I love you. You can call me any time. You're a survivor. And right now you're the champ even though there are some people in the business who thought you'd never make it."

Jenn wiped a tear away from her cheek. The man she loved had spoken the exact words she needed to hear. "Lazz, that was at least three or four things. Not two." She chuckled, then she blew a kiss into the phone before signing off. "I love you too. I'll call you tonight after the match. Win or lose."

☠☠☠

A pudgy cop glanced at their tickets. He looked none too thrilled to be assigned to the Public Transportation Unit. There were many riveting law enforcement jobs out there. Verifying that each boarding passenger possessed a validated MetroLink ticket was not one. He did, however, study Jenn for quite some time as she walked by. "Definitely the most interesting getup I've seen all day," he said.

She and Cocoa stood among a curious collection of characters on the platform. A handful of medical professionals were waiting for the next eastbound train. They were overworked doctors and nurses coming off long shifts at the children's hospital. Given their conversation, however, it became obvious these heroes weren't headed home for a well-deserved rest. Rather, their plans included downing a few frosty brewskies while taking in tonight's ballgame.

Considering the hospital's affiliation with a local Catholic university, the presence of a nun on the platform shouldn't have been too shocking. Still, it was somewhat unexpected to see the Sister wearing a baseball glove. Even more startling were the dark sunglasses and the thick layer of face paint. Every bit of the youthful woman's exposed skin was either powder blue or red in support of the local baseball franchise.

"You are going to want to take this train."

This bit of unsolicited advice surprised both Jenn and Cocoa... mostly because it came from the baseball-crazy nun. Before either could offer a response, the Red Line Train came screeching to a stop at the Grand Avenue Station.

A quick glance towards the train revealed that every car was jammed completely full of riders. Virtually everyone aboard was wearing some combination of red and white (and a smattering of blue) in the form of caps, jerseys or T-shirts. The passengers knew that a couple of claustrophobic MetroLink rides beat paying for grossly overpriced parking. Plus, it allowed them to avoid the horrific traffic jams that came with selecting the lots near the stadium.

"Trust me," the enthusiastic nun said leading into her explanation, "There is a big game tonight. Every train that rolls through this stop for the next hour and a half will be just as full as this one. Hop on."

Jenn and Cocoa gave one another a momentary glance. When neither detected an objection from the other, they stepped through the doors and into a wall of red and white.

The seats were filled with riders who had boarded several stops up the line. The two women followed the nun's lead. They reached up, clutched the metal bar overhead, and hung on once the train started moving.

"I am Sister Monroe," the nun said, introducing herself before any further casual conversation. "Redbirds versus the Pirates. First place is on the line tonight..." She was interrupted before she could complete her pregame analysis.

An overzealous and obviously intoxicated fan leaned towards the trio and blurted out his disapproval of tonight's opponent. "PIRATES SUCK!!!" A mixture of spittle and light beer sprayed out of his mouth.

There was little doubt that the jeer was intended for Jenn. After all, she did appear to be the only person on the train who was dressed in genuine swashbuckler attire.

The champ rubbed a bit of spray off her face. More importantly, she resisted the urge to kick the fool in the groin. Instead, she turned to Cocoa and half-jokingly remarked, "Maybe I should rethink my decision not to wear an eyepatch as part of my wardrobe."

Meanwhile, Sister Monroe lasered a nasty glare directly at the drunk aggressor. He immediately slunk backwards, slithering away from Jenn and towards the center of the train.

The Sister appeared eager to defend the city's reputation as having the "best baseball fans in America." Turning back towards Jenn and Cocoa, she offered, "Cosplaying in the ballpark of the opposing team is a bold move, but I suspect you will find that most folks here in St. Louis will treat you well enough."

Experienced grapplers were masters of the art of giving their counterparts nonverbal signals. Part of their trade involved in-ring winks and nods that were imperceptible to the untrained eye. An ever-slight, half shake of her head was all Cocoa needed to convey a message to Jenn. There was no need to burst this delightful woman's bubble by telling her that they wouldn't be joining her at the ballgame.

"I've been to St. Louis a number of times," Cocoa began her truthful but purposely evasive reply. "I've always loved it here. Great people. Great food."

The train made its next scheduled stop at the Civic Center Station. A few prospective passengers were waiting to board. But as soon as the doors opened, Sister Monroe set them straight. In an interesting departure from the "hop on" sentiment she had expressed just a couple minutes prior, she informed this batch of eastbounders, "This train is full. Wait for the next one."

☠☠☠

Cocoa nearly lost her balance when the Metrolink slowed to a stop. She hadn't noticed the automated voice come through to announce: "Stadium Station. Please use all doors and exit to your left." If she had, maybe she wouldn't have had to lean on Jenn for support.

"Here we are!" Sister Monroe happily declared while pounding her fist into the palm of her glove. She looked like a shortstop getting into defensive position before a pitch.

"Oh, we're not getting off here," Jenn confessed.

"I know," Monroe said. With a nod and a smile she added, "Travel safely."

With that, like scores of other passengers who were exiting the commuter train at the Stadium Station, the memorable nun was gone.

Jenn and Cocoa settled into two of the many recently vacated seats within the train. While the champ found them ridiculously uncomfortable, the booker was relieved to be off her feet. The rocking and swaying they endured while standing was particularly stressful on the muscles in Cocoa's lower back.

The automated voice made another announcement. "Doors are coming to a close."

Shortly before the train's doors shut, a single baseball fan slipped onto the train.

"Are you lost?" Jenn asked jokingly as she eyed the attire Brady was wearing. "This is the ballpark stop. If you're going to the game, you need to be getting out here."

"I left my ticket back at the hotel." His explanation was accompanied with a subtle reddening of his face. Being spoken to by such an exotic knockout was flattering. Admitting that he'd done something stupid like forgetting his tickets was embarrassing.

Jenn's jesting continued. Acknowledging the shirzee he was wearing, she said, "Hasn't anyone ever told you the Pirates suck? At least that's what I've heard."

The fact that his exotic antagonist was *dressed* as a pirate was lost on him. So was the fact that the heckling was coming from a woman who had become a bit of an obsession of his over the last few months. Maybe he didn't recognize Jenn because she was sitting down. Or it may have been because he wouldn't expect to see her riding a commuter train. Or perhaps it was because he was 23 years old and still somewhat oblivious to the ways women flirt. Whatever the reason, instead of continuing the conversation, Brady maneuvered his way back to a seat a few rows behind Jenn and Cocoa.

"Aren't you married?" Cocoa smirked as she elbowed her friend.

The train pulled away from the Stadium Station platform and soon moved into a tunnel that would take them beneath the busy streets of Downtown St. Louis.

The next stop was at Eighth & Pine. This station was cold and dark, cave-like. And it was empty. The train stopped for what seemed to be several minutes with no one getting on or off.

While the eastbound train remained motionless, a westbound train made a brief appearance at the station. Not a single person was aboard.

Brady turned to the police officer who had been standing near the back of the car. "Shouldn't that train be loaded with people going to the game?"

Officer Grayson shrugged. The question pulled him out of a bit of a trance... something that came frequently since he'd been assigned to the monotonous duties of the Public Transportation Unit. "I never know why they do anything," he complained.

Grayson tried to radio the driver of the train to find out what was holding things up. All he got was feedback as soon as he hit the button on the radio.

☠☠☠

It was three hours until opening bell. Jenn could see that Cocoa was agitated, desperate to get to the venue to oversee the countless tasks that needed to be completed before the live broadcast began. But the champ was running out of time to voice her objections about dropping the title at tonight's show.

"I get it that you want to put the belt on Ailani eventually, but don't you think a little buildup would lead to an even bigger payoff in a month or…"

Cocoa glared at Jenn. Her recent transition from a wrestler into a high-level executive within her father's growing promotion meant that she was being put in awkward positions more and more often. Jenn was her friend. But business was business. And she was practically begging for a result that Cocoa was unwilling and unable to deliver. Since she was pressed for time and still had tons to do in the next couple of hours, she flashed an expression intended to make it clear that she was not willing to discuss a last minute audible.

"…two?"

Frustrated by the idling train, Cocoa voiced her disgust. "You can't tell me driving back to the casino would've taken longer than this!"

Jenn wasn't sure if Cocoa was expecting a response or not, but she was determined to give her one. "It would if we were stuck in a traffic jam. Then we wouldn't be moving at all."

Cocoa glanced down at her cell phone for yet another look at the time or to see if she had received any text messages in the last two minutes. Nothing.

"No signal? I don't have time for this nonsense right now!"

The luchadora looked down. Focusing her attention on her boots seemed more productive than to continue to plead her case to Cocoa… *and it was sure a hell of a lot more enjoyable than to listen to her complain about things that were out of her control!*

Once the cop had exited, the doors shut behind him and the train rattled along the bridge over the Mississippi. Brady took the opportunity to move from a seat farther back to one immediately behind Jenn and Cocoa. "Something doesn't feel right," he said to them.

Cocoa had more important things on her mind. "That may be, but our stop's right up here. We're gonna get off the train and haul our happy tails into the ballroom of the casino. We've got too much stuff to do to worry about anything else right now."

For the fourth straight station, there was no announcement of the upcoming arrival over the train's intercom. The only sound the three passengers heard was the high-pitched squealing of the commuter train as it came to a stop.

Cocoa stood up and took a couple of wobbly steps towards the exit. "I wanna step off this God-forsaken train as soon as these doors open."

As they moved onto the vacant platform, the trio stood with their eyes fixated back across the river they'd just crossed.

"That plane's flying awfully low," Jenn observed.

A 737 floated like a leaf that had fallen from a tree. With the city skyline in the background, the silence that accompanied the airliner pulled the three viewers back into a state of consciousness necessary to appreciate what they were witnessing.

The plane was close enough and low enough that they should have been able to hear the roar of the engine. They saw it gliding downward, but there was nothing anyone could do. Tragedy appeared inevitable.

None of them could look away.

Soon, the plane began to lean towards one side. The angle became more and more extreme. The portside wing snapped off. The descent of the plane became rapid. The back third of the aircraft broke away and plummeted towards the muddy yet mighty Mississippi.

The silence was only broken when the nosediving 737 slammed into the gridlocked Poplar Street Bridge. Dozens of cars and trucks dropped into the river below.

Each member of the trio stood motionless, allowing the magnitude of what they had just witnessed to soak in.

Under normal circumstances, the crash should have been blanketed with a cacophony of hysteria. From their vantagepoint atop the East Riverfront platform, they should have been able to observe many signs of chaos: People fighting for their lives. Heroes rushing to save them. Others desperately trying to get as far away from danger as possible. Instead, there was no movement on what remained of the bridge, now was ablaze with dozens of scattered fires. Stillness surrounded the riverfront. No activity was coming from the city or the nearby ballpark, either.

"Something ain't right. Why don't I hear any sirens?" Cocoa asked. "Where are the screams? Why is it so damn quiet? The only thing I can hear is my own heart pounding in my chest!"

Jenn was mystified. "Unreal..." It was the only word that came to mind. She stared at the wreckage and kept repeating that single word. "Unreal."

7: WORKING AN ANGLE

*"Perfect hair, perfect smile, perfect body. I'm a
beauty to behold... You can look, but you can't
touch. Because I'm a whole lot more than a
pretty face. I'm the best women's wrestler in the
world. I've got the championship belt to prove it.
No one can touch me. I'm simply the best."*

*-AILANI DIAMOND promo recorded in
advance of her AWWA Women's Championship
title defense against Kelly Ka-Pow.*

PRESENT DAY
YEAR 0 + 221 DAYS (AUGUST 9th)

Jenn whipped her phone out of her back pocket and tried to call Lazz. "No signal!"

Brady had the same idea. He said a silent prayer as he tried to reach Greg and Marshall. "No signal!"

When Cocoa saw that her phone wasn't working, she raced down the stairs of the East Riverfront MetroLink Station. She sprinted across the parking lot towards the Camelot Casino. Her accumulation of injuries had prevented her from moving with such speed for a long, long time. But she had to get to her father, and her chronic aches and pains were not going to slow her down.

Upon reaching the front entrance of the hotel, Cocoa stopped long enough to survey her surroundings. She wasn't greeted by a friendly doorman, and there were no valet workers around to park arriving automobiles. When she walked through that same area just a few hours earlier, it had been overrun with people hustling and bustling in all directions.

Likewise, there was no one at the front desk, the concierge station, or anywhere else in the spacious hotel lobby. Not yet ready to surrender to the notion that everyone had disappeared, Cocoa decided to try her luck by moving her search to the floor of the casino.

"Hello! Is anyone here?" she shouted.

There was no response.

The only sounds she heard came from the digital slot machines. Their pre-programmed pinging and dinging were designed to attract gamblers, beckoning for them to slide their debit cards inside for a chance to win big. These computerized games were much more confusing than the classics they had replaced. But since they were themed around blockbuster movies or popular TV game shows, the flashy slots were the most profitable, and addictive, machines in the casino.

"Dee-dee-ding... Dee-dee-ding... Jackpots every hour!"

☠☠☠

"Nothing," Brady reported as he made a final attempt to start his car. "I had almost a full tank when I pulled in here earlier today. Now it's like my tank is bone dry."

"I wish I knew more about cars. Maybe it's the battery or alternator or something?" Jenn suggested.

"Could be. I don't think so, though." Brady grabbed a handful of change out of the cupholder. "Who knows when a pocketful of coins might come in handy? They certainly won't do me any good sitting in this broken-down vehicle." After stuffing the silver into his pocket, he shut the door behind him. Then he suggested, "There are a bunch of cars in this parking lot. Maybe I can get one started while you find your friend."

Brady and Jenn walked across the asphalt parking lot, each looking around an observing how normal their surroundings seemed to be. "The sun, the wind, the temperature. It all feels the same..."

Jenn interrupted him. "But it also feels completely different!"

"I know!" Brady agreed. "That was what I was about to say. No car alarms going off. No horns honking. I don't even hear any birds. It feels the same, but it seems so strange."

Jenn stopped in her tracks. She held out her hand and offered to shake. "By the way, my name is Jenn."

Brady smiled. His face momentarily flushed red. "I know. I figured out who you were when we were still on the train."

"Are you a wrestling fan?"

What the heck? Why be bashful? "I'm not so much a fan of the sport, but it's fair to say I am a fan of one particular wrestler."

"Oh? Who's that?"

He shrugged. Somewhat sheepishly, he admitted, "Long Jenn Silva. My buddies and I were watching the night you won the championship. I was hooked. There was just something about you." He chuckled. "I've watched quite a few of your old matches online."

"It's always nice to meet a fan."

☠ ☠ ☠

Cocoa's search for survivors took her into the backstage area. Unfortunately, each time she called out, she was met with no answer.

She located the door to her father's private dressing room. Out of habit, she knocked before walking in. "Hello? Pops?"

Silence.

Cocoa turned around and punched the door. Then she dropped to the floor and covered her face, all while tears streamed down. Everyone was gone. *Everyone.* Including her father. But, for some reason, she had been left behind.

She wiped the tears away and investigated the room. There was no sign of a struggle. No reason to believe that he had suffered. He simply vanished.

Fireball left his phone and watch behind. They had been placed neatly on a table. "He was probably changing for tonight's show," she guessed while clutching his treasured timepiece.

☠☠☠

After saying some private "good-byes," Cocoa joined Jenn near the slot machines. Brady approached from the other direction.

"I grabbed a bunch of keys from the valet parking," he reported. "I tried seven or eight cars before I gave up. Not a one of them started. I couldn't even get a radio to work."

Jenn stated the obvious. "That is so strange."

"So now what do we do?" Cocoa asked.

Brady shushed her.

"Excuse me?"

Ignoring her angry tone, he asked, "Do you hear that?"

Before waiting for an answer, he bolted towards a set of swinging aluminum doors that led to the kitchen. The women followed.

Once in the kitchen, Brady stood perfectly still and listened. After a few seconds, he heard something. *A thump. A thud. A knock?* He ran in the direction of the muffled sound, coming to a stop at the walk-in freezer.

"What is it?" Jenn asked.

Brady opened the freezer door.

It was a young woman in a royal blue party dress! She collapsed, slowly and stiffly. With her light blond hair, she looked like a snow-capped tree chopped on Christmas Eve. She dropped straight into Brady's arms.

He began to lower her onto the ground. Once he took a look at the cold, hard floor, he thought better of it.

"No..." She struggled to spit her words out. The co-ed's skin was frigid. Her lips were as blue as the dress she wore.

"She's been in there a long time!" Jenn worried aloud.

Tavia looked into Brady's eyes. "Hold... close... freezing."

With a bit of panic in his voice, Brady yelled, "Somebody get her a blanket!"

Cocoa shook her head. She had seen *a lot* today. She'd seen a plane crash and a city vanish. As far as she could tell, the girl who ended up stuck in the freezer for a few minutes got off fairly easy. "We're right here, kid. No need to yell. We'll find blondie a jacket or something, but for now why don't you hold her close and warm her up with a little body heat."

He seemed unsure.

Tavia agreed. Nodding her head, she mashed her chest into his. She pressed her icy cold cheek against him.

"She's shivering. I can feel her teeth chattering!" Brady declared, hopeful that a blanket would be coming soon.

"Your body temperature should be around ninety-eight point six degrees. That's a good start," Cocoa said as she exited the kitchen area.

Eager to be a hero, he rapidly ran his hands up and down Tavia's back. He hoped the friction would warm her. "I'm Brady. Can you tell me your name?"

☠☠☠

Thirty minutes and two cups of coffee later, Tavia was ready to shed the cocoon of tablecloths that had been stripped off banquet tables and wrapped around her.

"Sorry about the coffee," Jenn apologized. "It kinda tasted like dirty water to me. And I couldn't figure out how the coffee maker worked, so I know it wasn't as warm as you would've liked."

Tavia shook her head. "Don't be silly. I'm used to bland tasting food. That was anything but bland. In fact, I'd say it was the best I've had in months... While it wasn't the hottest cup of coffee I've ever had, it warmed me up. That's all I really cared about." She turned to look at Brady. "I'm glad you showed up when you did. I'm not sure how much longer I could have lasted in that freezer."

A set of aluminum doors separated the kitchen from the dining area. Those doors swung open. Cocoa walked through carrying a platter with freshly grilled T-bones piled one on top of the other. "I hope neither of you are vegetarians because Chef Cocoa has prepared steak... and more steak. They're a little tough. I may have overcooked them, but protein's protein."

"I'm starved!" Brady announced, clearly approving of the lone dinner option.

Tavia sat up in her seat when she saw Cocoa. "Did you say your name is Cocoa? You must be Cocoa Freeman?"

She was surprised to be recognized. The bubbly young woman didn't seem to land in the AWWA's target demographic. "I am. Are you a wrestling fan?"

"I wouldn't say that," she responded. "But I did meet your dad earlier today... Based on what you guys told me about everyone disappearing at once, I figure I'm just about the last person to see him alive."

Cocoa simultaneously let a smile creep across her face while she fought back a tear. She turned her head to the side, sucked in a deep breath to suppress the urge to weep, then turned back to look at the group. "That's a story I'd love to hear."

"Serve me up one of those steaks and I'll tell it."

Jenn interrupted. "First things first... we need beer. Beer and my personal favorite, tequila. I have a feeling we're going to tell quite a few stories around this table tonight. Don't start until I get back from the bar."

☠☠☠

THREE HOURS EARLIER
YEAR 0 + 200 DAYS (AUGUST 9th)

Casino workers were setting up a buffet of catered food in the backstage area. Many of those wrestlers who hadn't accompanied Cocoa to the children's hospital would be filling plates from the buffet. It would be their final meal before the night's matches began.

Before it was mealtime, however, Fireball Freeman utilized the room. He was there to prep the five beauties who were going to be participating in a pageant scheduled to be part of the pay-per-view extravaganza.

"I wanna thank you lovely ladies for being here this evening." He walked up and down the line of young women, glancing down at a clipboard and saying each prospective contestant's name after he gave her a quick visual inspection. The wrestling legend spent an extra amount of time looking at the copper-haired contestant dressed in a tight, emerald green tube top. "A-O-I-F-E? Young lady, do you pronounce your name 'Ay-fuh' or 'Oy-fuh?'"

"Eee-fa."

"Why thank you, *Eee-fa*," he said as he gazed at her for a moment longer.

Next, he took a step back and addressed the entire group. "Tonight we're gonna work an 'angry beauty pageant contestant' angle as part of the show."

Tavia interrupted. "What do you mean by 'angle?'"

Fireball lowered his head and looked at her over the top of his glasses. "Please... If you can just hold your questions to the end, I'm sure it'll all be clear as mud." He took another step back and returned to giving his instructions. "As I was saying... At various

points in the evening, you five ladies will be on stage with two of
our girls: Devon and Cindy May."

To the surprise of several of those in the audition, Fireball
informed them in no uncertain terms, "Cindy's gonna win the
crown. Devon's gonna get all pissed off, smash Cindy's crown into
a million pieces, and then drag her into the ring for a match right
there in their high heels and evening gowns." He waved his hand
through the air because he knew he was providing too many
specifics. "But those details aren't important right now."

Aoife did not like the sound of participating in a contest with a
predetermined outcome. She stormed off, complaining she could
make more cash tending bar than "finishing third in a phony beauty
pageant."

Fireball tilted his head to one side. He made no effort to hide
the fact that he was admiring how her plump backside filled her
blue jeans. "Sorry to see you go, Aoife."

Once the Irish lass had made her exit, Fireball attempted a little
damage control. "It's true the outcome of our little contest has
already been determined. But you should know that there will be
thousands of people watching this event live on the internet. All
over the country. All over the world. This could be your big break
into acting or modeling or even wrestling if that's what you're
interested in… Normally my daughter Cocoa would be the one to
run through the particulars, but she's still at the children's hospital."

The brunette standing next to Tavia expressed concern.

"She's not a patient! She's a grown-ass woman. She just took a
vanload of talent there to sign autographs, take pictures, that kinda
stuff…"

He continued, speaking over a couple more murmurs. "Cocoa
will be here soon. She'll have releases for you to sign. She'll be the
one to pay you at the end of the night. That's all you need to know

for now. Go on and get changed into your dresses so we can take some promotional photos. Those'll go up on the big screen and the internet page during tonight's event. The photographer should be here in..." He stopped long enough to stare at his watch, squinting to read the time. "...ten minutes or so."

☠☠☠

THREE HOURS LATER
YEAR 0 + 221 DAYS (AUGUST 9th)

Tavia concluded her telling of the story by explaining, "After I changed into my dress, I made a wrong turn and ended up in the kitchen. I held the freezer door open for one of the caterers who was carrying a big metal dish full of carved turkey and roast beef. Somebody pushed me into the freezer. I guess the door locks when it shuts. As a result, I almost froze to death... I suppose I'd be frozen stiff by now if you guys hadn't found me."

Cocoa motioned for Jenn to splash another ounce of tequila into her shot glass. She held it up in the air, then slightly tilted it towards Tavia. "I'm glad we found you. You, my friend, are a gifted storyteller. Every little detail of that story sounded just like my pops. 'Clear as mud!' 'Grown-ass woman!' God, I miss him so much already!"

Tavia clinked her beer bottle against the shot glass.

Brady returned to the dining room with two bottles of water, one for him and one for Tavia. As he delivered the bottle, he sat in the chair next to the blond beauty. He said, "I figured out why you look so familiar."

"Oh?"

"You went to CIU. You were a waitress at The End Zone, weren't you? You went missing... A detective even came to my house and interviewed me about it," he told her.

"They did?"

"Yeah... I wasn't a suspect or anything," he wanted to make that point very clear. "It's just that you were our waitress the night you disappeared. The night of the Tumbleweed Bowl."

She looked away. After a long drink, she unleashed an ear-to-ear grin and asked, "I never heard... Who won the game?"

"Arizona State killed us."

She laughed and put her hand on his knee. Her hand remained there for a long time. "I didn't really go missing, ya know?"

This response confused Brady. "There was a vigil on campus. My whole church prayed for you."

"Thanks for that." She finally removed her hand from his knee. She took another drink. This one was more of a seductive sip. Her lips danced across the rim of the bottle as she kept her eyes locked on his. "Truth is, there was this guy that was a little obsessed with me. More than a little, actually. He was married. His wife caught wind of his undying love for me. Next thing you know, she lost her friggin' mind. She tracked me down and attacked me in the parking lot... That night, right outside the restaurant."

"Are you serious?"

"She sprayed me with pepper spray, banged my head against a brick wall. She kicked me in the stomach and in the ribs until I was black and blue. She did quite a number on me... All this happened while you were inside, probably enjoying your burger and an order of curly fries."

"That's terrible."

"You're tellin' me."

By this point, the others had been drawn in by Tavia's story. "So why did they think you disappeared?" Jenn asked.

"Oh, I did disappear. I just didn't go missing... You see, I didn't know if that maniac wanted to kill me or what the hell she intended to do. So I tapped into all of my strength and let out a scream. She took off in her minivan. Afraid she was gonna get caught, I guess. I crawled over to my car, got in, and drove as far as I could... not very far given the condition I was in."

"Why didn't you call the police?" Brady asked.

Tavia shot him a look as if he had just asked her the stupidest question in the world. "I was scared. I had just gotten beaten to a pulp and I was confused. She beat me so bad I was hallucinating."

"Sounds like a really bad concussion," Jenn said, speaking from experience.

Cocoa agreed. "Definitely. You got your bell rung."

"I hid out at my friend Liz's place for the night. She filled up my car with gas and loaned me two hundred bucks. The next morning, I got on the road and drove six hours. I moved in with my cousin in Ohio, got a job and took some classes at the community college..." She paused to measure her audience's interest in her story. Seeing that they were leaning on every word, she added a specific detail to the narrative. "Clark State Community College. Their sports teams are called the Eagles, just like CIU."

"Did they ever catch the woman that attacked you?" Jenn asked.

"Nope." Tavia bit down on her bottom lip and looked away. Once she appeared to compose herself, she looked back and finished her story. "But a few weeks ago, my family hired a private investigator. He asked around and determined that she loaded up her minivan and left town for good... When I heard that, I decided to come back home and start living my life again."

The four sat eerily still.

Brady broke the silence by declaring, "Sounds like our prayers were answered!"

Cocoa was a bit more cynical. "Why are you so damn joyful? From where I'm sittin', it looks like we may be the last four fools left on Earth."

"Wait!" Jenn jumped out of her chair, knocking over the bottle of tequila as she did so. "We're not the last four! What about the cop? The cop on the train... He's out there somewhere!"

8: JOBBER TO THE STARS

"People are calling Grizzly Jack the underdog. They say I've got no chance. But I've got news for you, folks. Ol' Grizzly Jack's fought some of the biggest stars in the business... I'm going to shock the world and win the IWO Championship tonight!"

-GRIZZLY JACK GRISSOM promo given minutes before his match against IWO Champion Ace Cutler. Grissom lost to Cutler in a bout that was over in under two minutes.

THREE HOURS EARLIER
YEAR 0 + 221 DAYS (AUGUST 9th)

The train pulled into the stop at Laclede's Landing. It was the last opportunity for eastbound passengers to exit the MetroLink on the Missouri side of the Mississippi River.

As an officer in the Public Transportation Unit, Corporal Arnold Grayson dealt with plenty of headaches. Those ranged from fare evasion to loud music to riders taking open containers of alcohol on the train. He was deputized and authorized to work on either side of the river. Even so, he typically exited at Laclede's Landing, letting one of the East St. Louis cops handle any problems that happened on the Illinois side.

No one could be found on the platform at The Landing. There was not a soul to be seen, eastbound or westbound. It made no sense. Grayson had set foot on this very slab of concrete at least a hundred times in the past month. Whether it was at six in the morning or eleven at night, he always saw at least three or four people at the Laclede's Landing Station.

Where were the vacationing families? This was the station nearest the City's most recognizable landmark: the Gateway Arch. Though painfully humid, it was a picture-perfect day by St. Louis standards. There were no clouds in the sky on this beautiful summer weekend. Available activities included going up in the Arch, seeing the museum that highlighted Lewis & Clark and the country's westward expansion, taking a cruise on an old steamboat, riding in a horsedrawn carriage along the riverfront, or simply picnicking on the Arch grounds. Thousands of visitors would have been expected to be in the area on a day like this one. So where were they?

Where were the baseball fans? First place in the division was on the line. The rivalry between St. Louis and Pittsburgh had grown into one of the bigger feuds in the sport. Each team had postseason aspirations, with their division rivals being one another's primary obstacle. Tonight's game wasn't scheduled to start for at least an hour. Experience told the policeman that there should have been dozens of baseball fans waiting to hop on the train for a ride to the stadium.

Where was Otis, the legless man who sat near the stairwell seven days a week? This guy called out "Spare any change?" to every person who rode the train. He routinely stayed in his cherished location from sunrise to well past sundown. There was no reason to think that he wouldn't be occupying his familiar spot.

Another attempt to use his police radio was met with more high-pitched feedback. "What the hell is going on?"

Grayson exited the station to evaluate the situation from the street. He hoped and prayed that he could get a cell phone signal once he was down there. Much to his dismay, he quickly discovered that nothing could be seen or heard from that location either.

The silence was interrupted by the momentarily deafening sound of the commercial airliner crashing into and completely destroying the Poplar Street Bridge! "What was that?" he cried out. Now he was thoroughly confused.

The bridge was about a mile away. Though he wasn't in outstanding shape, the corporal was in no danger of getting booted from the police force... At least not based on being physically unable to perform his duties, that is. Grayson knew he could cover that distance in about ten minutes.

He chose a route along the western edge of the Arch grounds. He made a quick detour, however, when he noticed a pileup of cars and trucks on the adjoining interstate highway.

Grayson hopped a fence and scanned the stretch of visible pavement for any automobiles that may be barreling towards the wrecked vehicles (or him, for that matter). Nothing. Only silence. There were no sounds. No screams, sirens, or even the rumbling of car engines. "What's going on?" he blurted out again, not at all concerned that he kept repeating himself.

The first disabled vehicle he reached was an oversized pickup truck. The gas guzzler rested against the guardrail. There was no sign of a violent impact. No driver or passengers were anywhere in or around the vehicle. "The engine isn't even running," he said aloud. "It's as if this thing just ran out of fuel and coasted until it hit something."

Again and again he observed the same situation with every car or truck stopped in the roadway. The conditions were identical. No drivers, no passengers, no violent impacts. He could think of no logical explanation for why the engines were not running and would not start.

"What a friggin' nightmare!" he groaned, still somewhat frightened that at any moment he would be hit with an onslaught of interstate travelers caught completely unaware by the vacated automobiles that were blocking the road.

Those interstate travelers never appeared. Not a one. It was a crossroads where Interstate-70 merged with I-55, I-44 and I-64. Thousands drove that section of road each hour. Even with those who would have used the Poplar Street Bridge being unable to get through, there should have been hundreds of cars whipping by... "Cars *with* people in them," Grayson reminded himself, half-jokingly, half-terrified.

Curiosity led the cop to walk towards what remained of the plane crash. He no longer felt any urgency. Why run? "I'm betting there won't be anyone there either," he told himself. "I'm betting that plane didn't have a single passenger in it by the time it took out the bridge."

Was he beginning to piece things together? Even if his hunches were correct, Grayson couldn't help but be unnerved when walking by the baseball stadium. Less than one hour earlier, he had seen hundreds of people spilling out of the train at the Stadium Station. The game was expected to be a sellout. The sounds of the bustling ballyard should have been heard from several blocks away.

Instead, the whisper of the wind was all he heard.

He had to see for himself. He altered his intended course by a couple of blocks so he could swing by the ballpark and confirm his fears. "Not a soul in sight... Arnie Grayson, you're in Hell."

Investigate the plane crash? "Why even bother?" Instead, he wandered into the stadium. Just inside the gate, the cop paused and helped himself to a complementary bobblehead. The collectible was to be handed out to the first 25,000 fans with a paid admission. Grayson quickly tore into the box and pulled out the figurine commemorating one of the best outfielders in the long and storied history of the team. A little tap on the doll's cheek was all that was needed for its plastic head to shake violently from side to side. The entire time it did so, it looked back at the Public Transportation Officer with a menacing smile.

Returning the creepy figurine to the pile, Grayson moved towards a nearby concession stand. He retrieved a hot dog that rested under a heat lamp. Unfortunately, the first bite had no taste whatsoever. "I must be in shock," he hypothesized. But after smothering the frankfurter in ketchup and mustard, his next bite tasted like wet cardboard, instead of just cardboard.

"What the heck, I'll have a beer... What are they gonna do, fire me from being a cop in Hell?" he said aloud. He decided that verbalizing his thoughts might help keep him sane. At least for a little while.

The beer was flat. "Tastes like dirty water. Or worse."

The nachos were off, too. "Warm snot on a Styrofoam cracker!"

The peanuts were horrible. "Oh! Now that's just sad... Can't even enjoy peanuts at a baseball stadium."

☠☠☠

After a "private tour" of the clubhouse, Grayson decided that he probably needed to head back to his apartment. He held on to a glimmer of hope that his cat hadn't disappeared. He knew it was probably wishful thinking. As far as he could tell, every other living creature in the entire State of Missouri had vanished.

He made a couple of weak attempts to start two or three of the nicer cars in the nearest parking lot. He couldn't find any keys and didn't know how to hotwire a car. Carrying the duffle bag full of "souvenirs" he'd lifted from the clubhouse would make the four-mile walk to his apartment a little more annoying. But what did he care? This was Hell.

"Annoying is par for the course. Get used to it, Grayson," he said to himself. Then another thought occurred to him. "'Par for the course?' I'll be able to play eighteen holes at Spring Valley Country Club whenever I want! Maybe there are a few perks to living in Hell, after all."

A surge of energy gave the policeman a renewed purpose and a bit more bounce to his step. Thoughts of additional benefits that came with being the last man on Earth caused him to daydream about taking a detour and stopping by the Anheuser Busch Brewery. "Stocking up for the apocalypse doesn't sound like a bad idea," he thought before vetoing that notion as quickly as it came to him.

"No thank you," he muttered to himself as he considered the route necessary to make such an epic beer run. He'd be forced to trudge past the offices of Blake, Jennings & Ross. Those were the bastards who sued the police force on behalf of a 21-year-old punk who fell off a roof.

"Blame the cop," Grayson complained at the time, "instead of the fact that the dumbass had one too many shots of cheap whiskey."

The personal injury lawyers claimed that the first officer on the scene (Grayson) delayed in requesting an ambulance. They went on to allege that the delay contributed to the severity of the kid's brain injury and the blindness that resulted.

"I think I'll save myself the headache. I can pick up all the beer I want at the convenience store down the street from my apartment," he said through his tightly-clenched jaw.

☠ ☠ ☠

NINE MONTHS EARLIER
YEAR -1 + 305 DAYS (NOVEMBER 1st)

"Officer Grayson, I'd like to direct your attention..."

"*Captain* Grayson." It felt good to correct the sleazebag who'd dragged him in for a deposition on his day off.

Like most cops he knew, Grayson didn't particularly enjoy testifying in court proceedings. He had encountered more than his share of overpriced lawyers trying to justify huge retainers. One of their favorite ways to do so was to twist the words of a policeman, trying to make him look like a fool. At least in the courtroom Grayson could rely on the assistant prosecutor to make an objection. Plus, most of the judges did their best to take care of law enforcement. They would put a stop to it if the defense attorneys were harassing the witnesses too aggressively.

Depositions were altogether different. Much worse. There was no judge in the room. When a question crossed the line, the police department's attorney might look up from his cell phone long enough to make an objection. In the next breath the poor witness would be told to answer the question anyway. *What good did that do?*

Xavier Ross cleared his throat and rolled his eyes. He then made a quick glance to his right to measure whether Grayson's obstinance came as a result of instructions from the police department's attorney.

"*Captain* Grayson, I'd like to direct your attention to Page Two of your report... What time did you receive the call from dispatch?"

He looked down at a report that he had written a few months earlier. "Approximately 0130. That's 1:30 a.m."

"Just a minute ago, you said you weren't called until almost 2:00. Now you say 1:30. Which was it?"

Grayson shook his head from side to side. He fought the urge to tell everyone in the room what he really thought of the ambulance chaser. He had a feeling that the three hours he was scheduled to be deposed were going to be three of the most tedious hours of his life.

Already frustrated, Grayson gave in to the temptation to spar with the opposition. With a smug look running across his face, he responded, "Maybe where I come from, 1:30 *is* almost 2:00. Maybe I don't see a difference."

The personal injury attorney matched the policeman with a self-approving look of his own. "Well..." Xavier Ross said as he straightened his papers and considered whether it was worth the effort to strike. "My client comes from a world where there is ample medical evidence available. That evidence shows that every minute wasted was a minute that increased the likelihood that the injuries he sustained would stay with him for a lifetime. I understand that the difference between whether the call came in at 1:30 or 1:50 isn't that big of a deal to you. But I also understand that if my client had gotten to the Emergency Room twenty minutes earlier, his prognosis might not include a lifetime of living with total blindness. His condition might not require years of physical therapy just so he can complete simple tasks like walking in a straight line or lifting a spoon to his mouth!"

The rest of the time in the deposition was equally as brutal. The lawsuit was settled a few days later. And *Captain* Grayson was fortunate that the worst he received was a demotion to corporal and a reassignment to the Public Transportation Unit.

☠☠☠

PRESENT DAY
YEAR 0 + 221 DAYS (AUGUST 9th)

He trudged through the streets of St. Louis. With each step, Grayson became more and more convinced that skipping the extra detour was the right decision. Lugging a duffle bag full of purloined sports equipment proved to be more trouble that it was worth. He dropped third base onto the sidewalk about a mile and a half away from his apartment. "Not sure why I pulled that out of the ground in the first place. What was I gonna do with it?" he wondered aloud. Before he made it home, some catcher's equipment, two game-used bats and a batting helmet were jettisoned. The only items left in his bag were a couple of hats and jerseys.

Grayson called for his cat as soon as he walked through the door of his apartment. "Bacon Breath?" He had held out hopes that he'd be greeted with the friendly meows of his tabby. He let out a disappointed sigh, followed by a low whistle just in case his pet had been napping. "Bacon Breath?"

Nothing.

The cop's next move was to set his sidearm down on the kitchen counter and pick up the television remote. It was an exchange the lifelong bachelor had made thousands of times through the years. He traded off his gun for the remote as fluidly as Mister Rogers swapped his dress shoes for sneakers.

He was a little hesitant to hit the "Power" button on the remote. There had been nothing but feedback on his police radio. He had no luck getting a cell phone signal. If the TV didn't work, he just might shoot the damn thing.

"Thank God!" he declared, momentarily abandoning the theory that he was in Hell. The television turned on! Frantically, he flipped through the channels, desperately hoping to learn that he had survived some sort of regional disaster and that the rest of the world was A-OK.

"Nothing!" every channel on his TV featured the same image: the White-Yellow-Aqua-Green-Pink-Red-Blue test pattern. "Jeez!"

He dropped the remote. The AA batteries that had been nestled inside jumped out as soon as the channel-changer hit the faux hardwood floor. The batteries rolled off in opposite directions, never to be found again.

Grayson waved his hand in frustration but made no effort to retrieve the remote or its batteries. Instead, he moved towards the laptop computer that rested on his kitchen table. No matter how many times he pressed Control-Alt-Delete or pounded the on/off button, the screen remained an obnoxious shade of blue. "Give me a friggin' break!"

He grabbed a can of beer and a piece of leftover pizza from the fridge. "At least the beer's cold," he said to himself as he sank into his smelly old recliner. Staring at the television screen, he wondered aloud, "When was the last time I saw the test pattern?" he quizzed himself at full volume. "Maybe I'm not in Hell. Maybe I've traveled back in time to the 1980s."

He cracked open the beer, tilted his head back, and took a mighty gulp. Like the beer at the ballpark, this one was flat and tasteless. "Nope. It's definitely Hell."

☠☠☠

Exhausted from his trek across Downtown St. Louis, Grayson swapped his police uniform for a pair of sweatpants and a white, cotton T-shirt. He dragged himself back to his recliner and quickly fell into a deep slumber.

After sleeping for several hours, the police officer awakened to see that same test pattern staring back at him. This caused him to seethe. Everyone he cared about and everyone he knew was gone! Even his damn cat who missed the litter box half the time had vanished! No TV! No computer! The food sucked! Even the beer sucked!

He thought about a classic *Twilight Zone* episode... The one where Burgess Meredith was an avid reader who took every available opportunity to dive headfirst into the pages of a book. Doing so often angered his abusive boss or his hateful wife. Then nuclear war came, sparing the bookworm and leaving him by a public library with a lifetime worth of written treasures to devour. Unfortunately, he broke his glasses. His vision was so bad that he couldn't see the hand in front of his face. That meant he couldn't take advantage of his unique opportunity. Even though he had all the time in the world, he wouldn't be able to spend it pouring over the beloved works of Charles Dickens, H.G. Wells, or Robert Lewis Stevenson. Instead, he would be destined to spend his remaining days in turmoil.

Grayson vowed that he wasn't going to suffer the same fate as poor old Burgess Meredith. If the rest of the world had checked out, Grayson saw no reason to stick around and endure months—maybe years—of torturous solitude. That would be no way to live. Such conditions inevitably would cause him to lose his mind.

He stood and walked slowly towards the kitchen. It was only a few steps. It was a distance he could have managed in a couple of seconds. But his heart pounded and each step took a tremendous amount of energy. If he was going to blow his head off, his body had no intention of making it easy on him.

Grayson took a deep breath as he examined his Glock 19. One shot to the temple would do the trick. He had no doubt about that.

He set the gun back down and headed for the door.

Peaking his head out of his apartment, he looked down the hallway and made a desperate call for his pet. "Bacon Breath? Here kitty!"

Grayson examined the hallway, knocking on the other two doors on his floor. He certainly wasn't surprised that no one from the Bosnian family in Apartment 8-C was home. Though he never said a word to any of them—and wasn't entirely sure they spoke a word of English—Grayson would have rejoiced if even one of his neighbors had come to the door.

Next, he tried Apartment 7-C. The elderly lady who lived inside seldom ventured out of her apartment. He knew it was a bad sign when she didn't answer her door.

"Bacon Breath?" he called one last time.

Then he returned to his apartment, picked up the gun once again, and settled into his recliner.

Corporal Arnold Grayson lifted his Glock 19 to his head and squeezed his eyes shut. His entire face reddened and his hand trembled. He whispered a silent prayer asking God to forgive him, and briefly fantasized about being reunited with his mother and father in heaven.

His finger twitched. He was about to pull the trigger when he heard a noise in the hallway. *Was that a knock? A thump? A thud?*

Wiping tears away from his face, the policeman called out. "Hello?"

No response. Did he imagine the sound?

Grayson walked towards the door. He traveled every bit as slowly as he did when he traversed the room earlier to retrieve his firearm. "Hello? Who's there?"

He opened the door but saw no one. He craned his head to look down the hallway. And there it was...

A stuffed animal. A little purple kitty like he might have won at the county fair when he was a kid. Attached to the toy was a note with three simple words: "DON'T DO IT."

9: LUCHAS DE APUESTAS

> *"Fans of Lucha Libre! From the deadly waters of the Caribbean... this is Lady Pirata! She will cut your throat if you get between her and her one desire... GOLD! If you have a championship belt, let this serve as your one and only warning. Lady Pirata is coming for you!"*

> *-LADY PIRATA promo, spoken by her maestro MANUEL VARGAS, as she glares through the eyes of her crimson mask.*

NINE YEARS EARLIER
YEAR -9 + 101 DAYS (APRIL 11th)

Jenn—then just sixteen years old—dove for the ball. Fully extended, she snatched it out of the sky. Landing on the hard ground knocked the wind out of her, but she had succeeded in keeping her struggling soccer team from falling even further behind.

The arrogant private school girls on the opposing team didn't care that they were already up by six goals. It didn't matter to them that only a couple of minutes remained on the scoreboard clock. The contest may have been out of reach, but the strikers in green and gold desperately wanted to get one more ball past the tenacious goalkeeper. Jenn was just about the only one with any talent on her team... and the opposition wanted to punish her for having the audacity to put up a fight.

With the netminder having the ball sufficiently secured, the offensive players should have backed off. Instead, two forwards charged on and blasted the ball *(and the goalkeeper)* with a series of severe kicks. They threw in a few taunts as they did so. "Give up, loser!" one yelled while driving her spiked shoe into Jenn's ribs.

An official's whistle eventually stopped the attack. Jenn rose to her feet, waving off a pair of concerned teammates who went to check on her. "Not even a yellow card?" she complained, shouting at the coward in the striped shirt.

The referee had no intention of doing anything about the opposition's blatant attempts to hurt her. That meant the goalkeeper was going to need to take matters into her own hands. She spiked the soccer ball into the ground and chased down the offender who had kicked her in the ribs. Before there was any opportunity to react, Jenn raced towards the offending player and leapt at her. She blindsided the bully with a spinning clothesline that she improvised while in mid-air. Now sitting atop her opponent, Jenn rubbed the girl's face in the mud.

Her team had no chance of mounting a glorious comeback. But achieving a little bit of revenge felt damn good. "Give up! I wanna hear you say it! Give up!"

☠ ☠ ☠

Jenn sat alone at the end of an aluminum bench. The game was over. Her time playing high school soccer most likely was, too. She had been suspended for the season and kicked off the team. Though she suspected she was packing up her gear for the last time, she didn't regret the fact that she had sought a little vengeance.

An imposing man approached. He wore the colors of the opposing team.

Perhaps a little part of her wished that she could turn back the clock and rethink her actions. When Jenn managed a second look in his direction, she recognized that this was no ordinary soccer dad. He was the meanest looking, most musclebound monster she'd ever seen. Now this guy was headed directly towards her!

She was uncertain if she should run or scream. She also was unsure if anyone in the vicinity would care if something bad happened to her. She wondered if her ostracization extended to a collective indifference. Her now *former* teammates might not lift a finger to help her if an angry high school soccer fanatic decided to give the vigilante goalkeeper exactly what she had coming.

Then he smiled.

"Rough day out there," the man said as he plopped down next to her on the bench.

Jenn sat in silence.

He nodded. It was his way of acknowledging the confusion she understandably was experiencing at that moment. "You had a difficult day. But I believe everything happens for a reason. Don't you?"

She shrugged. *Where was this conversation going?*

"You know who I am?"

She shook her head "no."

He held his hand out, welcoming a handshake as he greeted her. "Manuel Vargas. Manny. At one time or another, I've claimed ownership to every professional wrestling championship in Puerto Rico. I've also competed in Mexico, the United Kingdom, and Japan. Now, I'm in what they call 'the twilight of my career.' I split my time between wrestling gigs back home in Puerto Rico and training aspiring grapplers here in Florida."

The legend's forehead was covered in scars from years of slicing himself open with a razor. He sacrificed his appearance in this manner because fans of Puerto Rican wrestling were known to crave matches that featured fire, weapons, and blood. Especially blood.

After his brief introduction, Manuel informed her, "That girl you clobbered was my niece."

The last thing Jenn wanted to do was say that she was sorry. His niece was a spoiled brat. She deserved every bit of the punishment Jenn had dished out. But there was no denying that this man was extremely intimidating. She might just give him a bare bones apology to avoid any retribution. "Listen, I..."

Manuel held up one finger and shook his head from side to side. The gestures were intended to cut her off from saying anything. That included an apology. "Have you ever wrestled before? The move you used on my niece is called a 'sling blade.' I've seen guys who have been in the business for years who weren't able to execute that very move with such precision. I was impressed. And I'm not easily impressed... Listen. I'm looking to transition into coaching, training, and managing on a full-time basis. You've got a lot of heart, that much is obvious. And from what I can see, it looks like you've been gifted with plenty of natural ability. I'd love to coach you... if you're interested."

☠☠☠

TWO YEARS LATER
YEAR -7 + 69 DAYS (MARCH 10th)

"Hola. Mi nombre es Lady Pirata de Puerto Rico. Estoy emocionada de estar en Mexico. Quiero ser una estrella en la Lucha Libre." Translated into English, the masked wrestler's awkward promo sounded like this: "Hello. My name is Lady Pirata from Puerto Rico. I am excited to be in Mexico. I want to be a star in Lucha Libre."

Once the cameras stopped rolling, she turned to Manny and asked, "How was that?"

"Ehh... not bad," he told her, making his best effort to be supportive. "But that's okay. Pre-match promos aren't really that big of a deal in Mexico. We'll keep working on it."

Jenn was only eighteen at the time. She was still adjusting to being away from her mother and her home in Orlando. She was a fan-favorite when she wrestled alongside Vargas in Puerto Rico. In Mexico, she would be booked as a *rudo* (aka a "bad guy"). Eager to improve, she pressed her *maestro* on how she could be a better heel.

"You aren't there yet," he told her while being mindful that he needed to keep things light with his apprentice. "People will watch that and think, 'Cute girl. I wonder if she would like to earn some extra money on the side by babysitting my kids next weekend.'

Instead, you want to strike fear in your opponents. A good heel will be hated so much that, deep down inside, the fans actually like them because they do such a fantastic job playing the villain."

Part of her wanted to cry. Jenn was relatively new to the sport and had a long, long way to go. Her goal was to be headlining in the main events (which were known as *"Luchas Estrellas"* in Mexico).

The masked luchadora pounced towards her *maestro* and playfully put him in a headlock. She only kept him in the hold for a moment, before letting him go and jokingly sticking her middle finger in his face. "Still want me babysitting your kids? Or are you scared of me now?"

"Neither one, actually," he laughed. "But at least now I know Lady Pirata is supposed to be a *rudo*."

☠☠☠

Manny set up quite a bout for Jenn's Mexican debut. He would join his student in a mixed tag team match against a pair of Lucha Libre superstars.

Relámpaga (whose name sounded like the Spanish word for "Lightning") wore a bright green mask with a golden lightning bolt piercing the middle. She chose her name because her high-flying style electrified the fans of Mexican wrestling. Vargas knew that Relámpaga would be a good counterpart, and perhaps future rival, for his protégé.

Hijo del Sanguinario (whose name meant "Son of the Bloodthirsty" or "Son of the Torturer") had been one of the biggest figures in the sport for many years. Over the past decade, he and Vargas fought in a series of epic matches in Mexico and Puerto Rico. Though they were bitter enemies inside the ring, Manny considered Sanguinario one of his true friends.

"Don't let his scary mask or the bloody skeleton costume he wears give you the wrong impression," Manuel told Jenn. "Sanguinario is a pro. He will jump around and do some amazing moves, but if you're in the ring with him, he will make sure that you get a chance to show off what you can do. People like that stay in the business for a long, long time. Everyone loves working with them. Remember that. It's not just about looking great. The best wrestlers make their opponents look good, too."

☠☠☠

SIX DAYS LATER
YEAR -7 + 75 DAYS (MARCH 16th)

Manny arranged for Jenn to participate in several interviews to promote the upcoming contest. He wanted Lucha Libre fans to be getting excited about the match, and more importantly, about his promising young pupil who had come over from Puerto Rico to take on the best Mexico had to offer.

The teenaged wrestler's interviews were every bit as wooden as her awkward attempts to cut a promo. "Don't worry about it," the coach encouraged his protégé. "The promos and the interviews will come with time. If you put on a great show and excite the crowd, the fans won't remember or won't care what you sounded like before the match. They're simply going to go home knowing that they got a glimpse into the future... a look at the young woman who is going to be a top luchadora for years to come!"

Once the opening bell sounded, Relámpaga began with a flurry of dazzling moves that sent "Lady Pirata" to the floor to regroup. As she huddled with Manny, Jenn looked up just in time to see Sanguinario bounding over the top rope with a "suicide dive." He soared through the air, having his fall broken as he crashed into his helpless opponents. The crowd exploded as they voiced their approval. The opening blows of the match had been dished out by the Lucha Libre favorites.

Later in the match, Jenn found herself squaring off against Sanguinario. The bloodthirsty demon pounded her with an open-handed slap that made a thunderous noise.

"That's going to leave a handprint across my chest for days!"

The newcomer returned fire, nailing her opponent with a slap that boomed every bit as hard and loud as the one she had just received. The crowd collectively let out "oohs" and "aahs" as Sanguinario staggered backwards. Then they didn't exactly know how to react when Jenn unleashed at dropkick that sent the veteran wrestler sprawling backwards over the top rope!

Relámpaga ran in. As if she was sneaking under a limbo stick, Jenn dodged the wild swing of her opponent. Then, in the first of a fluid series of movements, Jenn swept her leg towards Relámpaga's, taking her out at the ankles. With the woman now in a seated position in the center of the ring, Jenn took a running start, bounced against the ring ropes to gain momentum, and leapt towards her opponent. She drove her knees into the shoulders of Relámpaga. This sent her back into the mat, with Jenn perfectly positioned and seated atop her chest. It was a flawlessly executed running meteora.

The referee slid into position. 1-2-3! Lady Pirata amazed the crowd. It was shocking to see the newcomer from Puerto Rico score the pinfall against a couple of Mexico's favorites.

Manny looked across the ring and smiled. Jenn had come a long way in a short amount of time. From where he stood, it looked like she could surge all the way to becoming one of the top women in the sport... and not just in Mexico. She could be one of the best in the entire wrestling universe.

☠ ☠ ☠

FIVE YEARS LATER (TWO YEARS AGO)
YEAR -2 + 110 DAYS (APRIL 20th)

Despite being rejected by Griffin Conrad and the IWO, Jenn (still competing as "Lady Pirata") continued to have her eyes on making the jump to wrestling in one of the big American promotions. That took her to an upstart women's wrestling organization based out of Texas, New Mexico, and Arizona.

"Luchadora USA" was a company that granted quite a bit of freedom to the women on its roster. In fact, Jenn was planning on taking advantage of her newfound liberty to follow in the footsteps of her *maestro*. Like Manny had years earlier, she made plans to travel to Japan for a month so she could wrestle a series of matches with one of their women's wrestling outfits.

Her longtime rival, Relámpaga, made the jump to Luchadora USA at roughly the same time. The two of them had been booked in a long-running three-way rivalry with the champion. Having accumulated nearly thirty years of experience, Tigresa Roja had achieved legendary status in Lucha Libre. She was the only Luchadora USA champion in the three and a half years that the promotion had been in existence. The conventional wisdom was that she soon would be passing the torch to either Lady Pirata or Relámpaga.

A sellout crowd was expected at the upcoming Cinco de Mayo show in El Paso. "The timing is not right," Tigresa Roja told her much younger colleagues. She had a bad habit of assuming the role of booker to her own matches. Even worse, she possessed the power to get away with doing so. "We need to continue to build the story... to increase the anticipation. We do that by having our own *lucha de apueste. Máscara versus Máscara.* " Her phone buzzed before the trio could finish their conversation. Looking down, then back up to Jenn and Relámpaga, she apologized. "I'll be back."

Relámpaga raised both of her middle fingers into the air as soon as the champion exited the room. "She may relinquish the belt eventually. But she'll never let one of us take her mask."

Jenn bit her lip as she considered what it was that the cagy veteran was trying to pull. Literally translated, *luchas de apuestes* meant "betting matches." The contests typically included wagers in which the loser would forfeit her mask or allow her hair to be shaved off. They were among the most popular bouts in Lucha Libre.

Relámpaga continued, "So maybe it's up to us to decide."

"What do you mean?" Jenn asked.

"You're so damn pretty. You've got a new American boyfriend and a foot out the door."

"Foot out the door? What are you saying?"

Relámpaga didn't tiptoe around the issue. "I'm saying I should take your mask in El Paso. You'll be headlining in Japan or starring in one of America's big promotions by this time next year. I'm Mexican. I'm Lucha Libre for life. The mask is sacred to a Mexican wrestler. Give me the win in the Triple Threat match. We will tell Tigresa together... and insist she drop the title to me at the next big event."

Jenn didn't like the sound of that. "What do I get out of it?"

Relámpaga's plan was well thought out. It was almost as if it was rehearsed. "You and I can wrestle a whole bunch of matches after the old lady's out of the way. You'll take the title from me. A few months later, I'll win it back. The fans will love it."

☠☠☠

TWO WEEKS LATER
YEAR -2 + 125 DAYS (MAY 5th)

The El Paso crowd was a boisterous bunch. They knew their
wrestling. They greeted Relámpaga with an explosion of cheers,
clapping, yelling, and whistling. The bright lights that came with
appearing in the Lucha Estrella (Main Event) caused her golden
lightning bolts to flash. The fanatics in the seats recognized that she
was the future of Luchadora USA, and they cheered her
appropriately.

Lady Pirata was the next to make her way to the ring. She had
never been a dirty wrestler. But in playing the role of a *rudo*, she
often bent the rules by pulling her opponent's tights or using the
ropes for leverage when attempting a pin. And, when the referee
wasn't looking, she would occasionally pull her foe's hair or hit
them with a foreign object. If there was an advantage to be had, the
beautiful buccaneer took it. She was good at what she did.
Accordingly, she was met with a chorus of boos.

Tigresa Roja entered the ring with the pomp and circumstance
of a fan favorite and longtime champion. As her name implied, she
wore a red and black tiger-striped bodysuit and a matching mask.
Much of the audience sang along with her well-known, custom
theme music, while some of her biggest supporters waved red or
black flags or blew into plastic horns. She was a legend in the
business. And she was greeted as such.

Once the bell sounded, Tigresa Roja looked a lot less like a
legend. She took the first available opportunity to roll under the
ropes, then out of and away from the squared circle. She would last
longer that night—and throughout the remainder of her career— if
she could spend most of her time parading around the ring. Letting

the others do the bulk of the work was much safer than taking bumps on the inside. This meant that Jenn and Relámpaga needed to provide most of the action.

The twosome had squared off against each other on numerous occasions throughout Jenn's time in Mexico. Because of their familiarity with one another, they were able to fly around the arena with one exciting spot after another. "If I'm going out, I'm going out with a bang," Jenn whispered to her friendly rival during one headlock.

She pulled out every flashy move in her arsenal. She nailed Relámpaga with a sequence that included a hip toss, a knee lift, and a drop kick in rapid succession. Turning her attention to her other opponent, Jenn surprised Tigresa Roja as she loitered outside the ring. She garnered her own roar from the crowd by high jumping over the top rope, executing a perfect front flip in midair, and splashing down on top of the champion.

The audience roared with approval. "Some of the loudest cheers I've ever received." Jenn smiled as she whispered to Tigresa Roja while pulling her into the ring.

For the next several minutes, Jenn continued to dazzle with spot after electrifying spot. When both of her opponents began to suck wind, the champion signaled for the three of them to begin their scripted finish.

Jenn was perched atop a ladder that had been stored under the ring. She motioned for those seated in the audience to rise to their feet. Then she prepared to dive off the top of the ladder and onto the belly of the prone champ. Relámpaga scrambled to her feet. She managed to push the ladder out from under Jenn a split second before she would have made her jump.

Lady Pirata came crashing down. The crowd gasped. The landing looked awkward... and extremely painful. Jenn was fine,

though, and stuck to the script as Relámpaga and Tigresa Roja
latched onto one another at the wrist. They hit the dazed
swashbuckler with a double-clothesline. Then they both dropped
down to cover her. 1-2-3!

The *Máscara versus Máscara* match was over. Relámpaga and
Tigresa Roja had joined forces to best Lady Pirata.

☠☠☠

When a luchadora is forced to shed her mask in public, oftentimes
that moment is a very emotional one. In the past, many Mexican
wrestlers have felt humiliation after losing a *lucha de apueste*.
Tears are not unexpected when the losing combatant is paraded in
front of the crowd for a post-match interview.

Lady Pirata's unmasking was quite different than the norm.

"We are here with Lady Pirata," Luchadora USA's promoter
and English language color commentator said as he led her into the
center of the ring. "You fought an excellent match tonight.
Unfortunately, you came up on the losing end at the last moment.
Do you have any comments about tonight's match?"

"I have a motto. Always fight to win. Tonight, Tigresa Roja
chose the coward's way. She was fighting not to lose. Yes, she and
Relámpaga joined forces so they could keep their masks. But
tonight they lost a lot of dignity. I'm standing tall right now. I'm
proud of my performance."

The crowd erupted. Jenn lost the match, but she had won the
approval of the fans.

Jenn had performed as a *rudo* for the last five years.
Knowledgeable Lucha Libre fans respected her even if they didn't
exactly pull for her. The roar of the El Paso crowd signaled that
everything was about to change.

"Well said," the promoter remarked. He briefly scanned the faces in the crowd, as he was buying time after being caught off guard by Jenn's unscripted analysis. "And now, please remove your mask and tell us your name."

The primary color of the mask was crimson. The eyeholes were outlined in a tan material that looked like well-weathered leather. A white skull 'n crossbones was embossed across the forehead. She peeled the disguise over her curly, black hair. Then she winked and handed the mask to the official. With that, Lady Pirata was no more.

Instead of tears streaming down her face, Jenn met the camera with a confident smile. It was almost flirtatious. The crowd clearly supported the former villain as she transformed into a fan favorite right before their eyes. Her change in status was based on the audience's respect for her tremendous performance in the ring, as well as their appreciation for how she conducted herself after the final bell.

Picking up on their response, the promoter blurted out, "Very beautiful. *Muy bonita!*" After another surge of cheers, he asked again, "Lucha Libre fans everywhere want to know… What is your name? And what are you going to do next?"

In the blink of an eye, her expression changed from confident and flirtatious to deadly serious. Thinking back to the alias she had given Griffin Conrad a few months earlier, she looked into the camera and said, "My name is Long... Jenn... Silva. You ask what I'm going to do next? I'm a pirate. There are only *two* things a pirate ever desires: gold and revenge. Next time I fight Relámpaga, I will get my revenge. And the next time I face Tigresa Roja, I will take the gold from around her waist."

The audience erupted with a deafening noise.

Still standing at ringside, Tigresa Roja and Relámpaga looked at one another. Neither took the loss in the big match. Neither had to relinquish their mask. "Is it just me or did we somehow walk into a trap?" Tigresa Roja asked her counterpart. "We got exactly what we wanted, but Long Jenn Silva is the only one anybody's going to be talking about tomorrow."

Once the roar of the crowd died down to a low rumble, the pirate spoke a final threat. "I'm Long Jenn Silva, and I'm coming for you."

10: BLACK AND BLUE

"Harley Harris says my career's going downhill? Look at this body. Look at these muscles. I will crush anyone that gets in my way... like an avalanche rushing down the side of a mountain. You don't want to get in my way! This Saturday night, at the Columbia County Fairgrounds, Harley Harris is going to find out you don't step in the path of an avalanche!

-LASZLO BARBA promo before his final match.

PRESENT DAY
YEAR 0 + 222 DAYS (AUGUST 10th)

The Vanishing. They kicked around a few names, but that's the one Jenn and her fellow survivors settled on when discussing the mass disappearance of everyone else in the St. Louis area. Collectively, they refused to believe that the tragedy spread across the entire country or—God forbid—the whole world. But they grew more and more concerned the longer they went without being able to reach faraway loved ones. They wondered why they hadn't seen any military vehicles riding to the rescue. With every hour that passed, they worried more and more that it might not be simply a regional event.

Though they had an entire hotel at their disposal, no one felt comfortable sleeping behind closed doors. They also feared spending too much time on an upper floor might leave them vulnerable. Vulnerable to something. No one knew exactly what.

"I wanna be as close to the exit as possible," Cocoa remarked. "Just in case."

Ultimately, they decided to change into more comfortable clothing and spread out in one of the casino's ballrooms for the night. The four of them slept on mattresses that Brady and Jenn dragged out of some second floor suites. "Then we'll go looking for other survivors first thing in the morning."

Jenn never managed to get any meaningful sleep. She tossed and turned, prioritizing her frequent attempts to reach her husband over rest. She tried calling Lazz every hour on the hour. Her phone never got a signal. She couldn't call. Couldn't text. Couldn't e-mail.

She finally drifted off around six in the morning. She was awakened a little before seven. Tavia's shrill scream got everyone's attention.

"Wonderful! Absolutely wonderful!" Her voiced echoed throughout the large convention space. "I'm stuck here with the last man on Earth… and he's a friggin' creeper!"

Jenn sprang up from her mattress and rushed towards the commotion. "What's going on?"

Tavia was up and she was agitated. She was dressed in the royal blue party dress that she had been wearing when the others found her trapped in the walk-in freezer. The blond college student weaved a number of vulgarities among words like "sicko," "pervert," "deviant," and "menace."

It didn't take long for Cocoa and Brady to join them. With all four together, Jenn asked again, "Tavia! What's got you so freaked out?"

The beauty in the blue dress stopped pacing. She glared at Brady. Pointing, she screeched, "I'm freaking out because of HIM!"

The lone male in the group, Brady was perplexed as to why Tavia's anger was directed towards him. "What are you talking about?"

"When I went to sleep, I was wearing a pair of running shorts and a T-shirt. When I woke up, I'm wearing this dress again! I know I didn't change into it!"

"So why are you mad at *ME*?"

"Those shorts and T-shirt didn't magically disappear! This dress didn't magically jump off the hanger and back onto my body! Somebody undressed me and then put me in this. And I think it was you!"

The accusation caught Brady off guard. If it hadn't, it may not have taken him so long to notice that he too was back in the clothes he was wearing prior to going to bed. Gone were the basketball shorts and the Central Illinois University tank top he had pulled from his suitcase just before midnight. He was inexplicably back in his Pirates throwback jersey and cap.

"I'm sorry..." he began.

"So you admit it!"

"No...! No..." He struggled to find the words to convey his simultaneous feelings of empathy for his new friend, and the frustration he felt from being wrongfully accused. "I'm sorry that something like that happened, but please know that it wasn't because of anything I did... Look! The same thing happened to me. I wasn't wearing these clothes when I went to sleep. But I am now. I don't know how and I don't know why. I don't have an explanation. But I can confidently say it wasn't me!"

It sounded ridiculous.

"Liar!" Tavia screamed.

"Honey, wait!" Cocoa shouted as she stood there in the same gray pants suit that she wore on the previous day. Then she gestured towards Jenn (once again dressed in her Long Jenn Silva wrestling attire). "The same thing happened to all of us."

The co-ed's arms flailed as she threw a brief, silent quasi-tantrum. "That doesn't make any sense."

"*Nothing* makes sense right now!" Jenn interjected. "Do I need to remind you of what happened yesterday?"

Tavia challenged her. "I still don't know. Someone locked me in a freezer. So why don't you tell me...? What *did* happen yesterday?"

☠☠☠

Once the commotion subsided, the group devised a plan. It included crossing the Eads Bridge and going into the city. As scary and unpleasant as it sounded, they knew that they needed to assess the damage and search for other survivors. That included the police officer who had exited the train at the Laclede's Landing Station.

But first... breakfast.

"Do you mind looking for a cooler and maybe packing some food for our adventure?" Brady asked as he and Jenn stepped into the kitchen. "I'll take care of making breakfast. I'm hoping that things will cool down once everyone gets some scrambled eggs and toast in their bellies."

"You honestly think that's all it's going to take?" Jenn's skepticism was obvious from her tone. "I'm not sure if you noticed, but Cocoa's father and brother and just about every friend she ever had just disappeared last night. Poof! Gone into thin air. I think it's going to take more than a tasty breakfast to change her mood."

"True." Brady got quiet and broke a few eggs. After a lengthy silence he said, "Hey, Champ... Thanks."

The pirate wasn't exactly sure why he was thanking her.

"My parents died a few years earlier. I rarely speak to my older brother. He works as a political aide in D.C. We call each other on our birthdays and Christmas. That's it. Now it appears my two best friends in the whole world just vanished with the rest of the city..." He paused to wipe away a single tear. "I guess I deal with grief a little differently than most people..." He stepped towards Jenn and wrapped his arms around her neck. Pulling himself in for a hug, he finally finished his thought. "And by 'different' I mean 'possibly annoying.' So thanks for saying something. Seriously."

Jenn stiffened. She wanted to comfort her new friend. But she didn't want to send any wrong signals to Brady. *Who knew where a hug might lead? Especially when everyone's emotions were all over the place.*

"Just to be clear, I stayed up most of last night trying to call my husband. As far as I know, he's back at our condo in Florida freaking out because he can't get ahold of me."

"I get that," Brady pulled away. He was having to apologize a lot over the last hour. "I wasn't trying to hook up or anything like that. Sorry if I made you feel uncomfortable."

"You didn't," Jenn tried to reassure him. "That's my way of nipping it in the bud. And as far as we know, this vanishing—whatever it was—only happened here. If that's the case, your brother in Washington and my husband in Orlando are worried sick about us. We need to be making plans to get out of St. Louis and start working our way towards our loved ones. Or at least to somewhere where we can get a phone signal."

☠☠☠

THREE YEARS EARLIER
YEAR -3 + 39 DAY (FEBRUARY 8th)

Venom spewed from the mouth of Griffin Conrad. "Well, Miss Silva, I see I have my answer... I hope you enjoy the show tonight. And then your flight back to Mexico. Good luck scraping by with your mask and your pirate gimmick. Good night."

He pivoted and exited.

"It looks like you probably won't be joining the ranks of the IWO anytime soon." These unexpected words came from over Jenn's left shoulder. It wasn't the sentiment that was surprising. She simply didn't think anyone else was involved in the conversation.

"Too bad too... I was looking forward to running into you backstage and around the gym."

Who was this lug? Was he for real? Hitting on Jenn moments after she'd been told that she may never make it onto the biggest stage in professional wrestling? The guy had a lot of gall.

She turned around and bumped into an enormous hunk of humanity.

"I'm Lazz. Laszlo Barba," he said, holding his hand out as he introduced himself.

"The way you say that reminds me of 'Bond. James Bond.' I guess that might explain why you were spying on my private conversation."

Lazz stood motionless. He was dumbfounded.

The olive-skinned wrestler was massive. He stood at just under 6'4" and tipped the scales at exactly 275 pounds. That was pure muscle. Prior to joining the International Wrestling Organization, Lazz set several American records in Olympic Style Weightlifting. On this particular occasion, however, he was on crutches. "Broken foot," he explained. "That's why I'm shaking hands and signing autographs in the V.I.P. box instead of crushin' someone's head between the turnbuckles."

"Well, Lazz... Do you make a habit of flirting with girls moments after they've had their *dreams* crushed?"

"Never," he answered truthfully. "I'm usually a big wimp when it comes to approaching gorgeous women. I take weeks, maybe months, to work up the courage. I usually figure out some reason why I shouldn't stick my neck out on the line... next thing you know, the opportunity passes me by. But since it sounds like it won't be easy for me to casually bump into you after tonight, I decided to take a leap of faith and introduce myself."

Maybe this guy wasn't a total sleazeball. Still, Jenn worried this might be a line he used on all the ladies. "You said I was gorgeous? How can you tell? Dude, I'm wearing a mask."

"Your voice is mesmerizing. I love your accent. That got me to take notice. Then your eyes pulled me in. That crimson mask can't hide those." Why lie? Lazz was laying it all on the line. "And that tattoo. Griffin Conrad may have gotten all bent outta shape about it, but it tells me 'there's something unique about this girl. She's someone you're going to want to take the time to get to know.' So here I am. Hoping Conrad and his lack of vision doesn't get in the way of true love... And even more importantly, that you don't think I'm some sort of clown or some sort of jerk. Because it would be even worse knowing that it was my fault. It would be torture to know that *I* was the one that screwed up my shot with you."

Jenn paused and weighed her options. Everything happens for a reason, right? "Griffin Conrad may be powerful, but he's not enough of a big shot to get in the way of true love. Besides, I don't think you're a clown *or* a jerk. Maybe you and I could go get a drink or something? After tonight's matches?"

☠ ☠ ☠

TWO YEARS LATER (ONE YEAR AGO)
YEAR -1 + 163 DAYS (JUNE 12th)

Jenn was at their condominium in Orlando. Lazz was in Minneapolis. Wrestling in competing promotions meant that the lovebirds found themselves in different cities more often than not. Thankfully, video calls and text messages helped them bridge time zones and hundreds of miles. Still, it was going to make scheduling a "proper" honeymoon difficult. *They tied the knot in May, but only had a couple days together before work took them in opposite directions.*

On this night, Lazz was scheduled to appear on "IWO Thursday Night," the country's highest rated weekly wrestling program.

Jenn zoomed the camera in on her wedding ring while waiting for him to answer.

"Well, hello there!" he said upon accepting the call.

Jenn zoomed out, revealing that she was wearing the black bikini that she bought on the day they were married.

Lazz "corrected" himself. "Well, hello there, *Beautiful!*"

The camera finally focused on her face, revealing that Jenn was wearing the crimson mask she once wore as "Lady Pirata." It was the mask she was wearing when the two of them first met... and also the time they first made love.

"Damn! You haven't said a word on this call, and I'm already trying to figure out a way to blow off tonight's show so I can hop the first plane down to Orlando!"

"As nice as that sounds, you can't do that. We've got bills to pay and fancy vacations to save up for... You'll just have to wink into the camera. That way I'll know you're thinking about me during tonight's match."

Her husband sighed and momentarily looked away from the phone. "Not sure there will be time to do that."

Jenn instantly recognized the frustration in her man's voice. "What's up?"

"I'm free fallin'. Not in a Tom Petty good way. Two months ago I'm main eventing the biggest pay-per-view of the year," he held his thumb and index finger less than an inch apart, "this close to winning the title. Now I've slid down to the mid-card, being booked to take embarrassing losses to newcomers. I thought last week's double-DQ against a has-been like Coyote Jack was bad enough, but..." His voice trailed off. He didn't want to tell his bride

the details of the humiliating loss that had been booked to go down
in a couple of hours.

Jenn did her best to cheer him up. It helped a little when she
reminded him that she loved him no matter the outcome of his
matches or where he was positioned on the card. Promising a night
of fantastic sex the next time they were together helped more.
"Now go out there and do your best. Your biggest fan will be down
here in Orlando pulling for you. And I'll be wearing this smokin'
hot outfit while I'm watching."

☠☠☠

That night, the heavy metal chords that served as Lazz's entrance
music played early in the show. Dressed in jeans and a white tank
top instead of his typical in-ring gear, the kayfabe Romanian
Olympian grabbed the microphone and spoke through his fake
accent. "Look aht dees moss-ahls! I iss-oo opahn challenge to in-ee-
one een da IWO... I vill crush you!"

His boasting got cut short. Specifically, it was interrupted by
upbeat mariachi music. Someone was there to answer his challenge.

The enthusiastic television announcer caught the at-home
viewers up to speed. "That's Margarita Relámpaga... She's one of
the biggest female stars from Lucha Libre wrestling. And now she's
looking to make a name for herself in the IWO!"

Jenn's stare came dangerously close to burning a hole in the
television screen. Her biggest rival in Mexico was making her debut
in the IWO? What happened to being Lucha Libre for life?

Relámpaga still wore her trademark green with gold lightning
bolts, but her mask was gone. This was quite a change from the
proud luchadora Jenn once knew. She always maintained that a
wrestler's mask was sacred, and that the mainstream American

promotions were far inferior to those that honored the well-establish traditions of Lucha Libre. Now Relámpaga had signed with the IWO! And she was stepping into the ring with Lazz?

What the hell?

The challenger snatched the microphone out of Lazz's meaty hands. "I am Margarita Relámpaga. And I am here to announce to the world and to the IWO that no one is safe with me around! No one… I accept your challenge."

She spiked the microphone at Lazz's feet, then slapped him across the face. A split-second later, she drilled the bewildered brute with a standing drop kick. A referee appeared from out of nowhere. The official waived his arms and signaled for the bell to ring. The match was on. Right then, right there.

Lazz made it to his feet just in time to be hit with a second drop kick. He got up a little less quickly this time but was met with the same fate. A third dropkick. This one kept him down.

With the sellout crowd cheering the exciting newcomer, Relámpaga sprang up the turnbuckle pads and leapt from the top rope. She executed a picture-perfect frog splash, landing across the much larger man's chest. The ref slid across the ring and counted Lazz out: 1-2-3!

The bell rang again. Lazz had been slaughtered in under thirty seconds.

In wrestling, a "burial" is the opposite of a push. It is a deliberate lowering of the status, credibility, or popularity of a once popular star. They often are accomplished by subjecting the wrestler to embarrassing defeats and losses to lesser opponents. The burial of Laszlo Barba had become obvious. And, based on the luchadora they used to humiliate him, it looked like this punishment was because Griffin Conrad didn't approve of his choice of a wife.

☠ ☠ ☠

NINE MONTHS LATER (THREE MONTHS AGO)
YEAR 0 + 91 DAYS (APRIL 1st)

Jenn was set to wrestle in Phoenix when she got word of her
husband's injury. She rushed to the airport with the objective of
getting to the local medical facility in Columbia County, Georgia,
as quickly as humanly possible. Unfortunately, "humanly possible"
meant fifteen hours. Her trip included a flight from Phoenix to
Chicago, a lengthy layover in the Windy City, a second flight from
Chicago to Charleston, a ridiculous wait in the line for a rental car,
and a two-hour drive to the community in northeast Georgia.

Lazz's doctor looked up from his chart. "Ah, Ms. Barba, thank
you for coming."

Jenn chose not to correct the doctor. She had opted against
taking her husband's name when they were married. A detail like
that seemed trivial at the moment. "Jenn," she said, indicating that
he could address her by her first name. "Doctor, how is my
husband?"

"He's heavily sedated." The physician stepped aside to give her
an unobstructed view of her sleeping husband. Lazz had a large
bandage along his hairline. "He came in with quite a gash on the
top of his head. Should heal up just fine, as long as he doesn't mind
a wicked scar."

The cut on his head was not his only injury. "We were far more
concerned with the trauma to the neck and spinal cord. I don't know
much at all about pro wrestling. But from what I've been able to
gather, it sounds as if his opponent really screwed things up.
Dropped him..." The doctor paused long enough to correct himself.
"...actually, *slammed* the top of your husband's head directly onto
the concrete. No padding whatsoever."

Jenn held her hand up, covering her mouth in a failed attempt to hide her worry. "Damn small-time promotion."

She stood over her husband for hours. During that time, Jenn came to the conclusion that her anger wasn't directed towards the wrestling wannabe who screwed up and slammed Lazz's head into the concrete. She also wasn't angry with the outfit that had put on the show at the Columbia County Fairgrounds.

No, her anger was with Griffin Conrad and the IWO. If Mr. Bigshot himself hadn't blackballed Lazz simply because he didn't like his choice of a wife, then he wouldn't have been forced to fight an inexperienced hack for a bush league promotion. "That scumbag," she said with her jaw clenched.

"Huh?"

Lazz was waking up! He sounded extremely groggy, but he was waking up!

"Jenn...? Is that you?" The weightlifter-turned-wrestler squinted as his eyes adjusted to the light. "I guess Harley Harris botched his big move pretty bad."

The pirate sniffled and wiped away a few tears.

"Oh... hey..." he continued. "I had the craziest dream about you. Crazy, but super vivid. You ever had one of those? It was so real..."

"Oh yeah? What was I doing, *querido*?" (*"Querido"* was a Spanish term that was similar to calling a loved one "dear.")

"'*Querido?*' It's been a long time since you called me that..." After a pause, Lazz resumed telling his bride about his dream. "You weren't doing anything all that extraordinary. Just looking at your phone. Maybe reading a magazine. But it was so real. And there were aliens. Green... No, *blue*. Blue men watching you. They weren't doing anything else. Just watching you while you were playing on your phone... Weird, huh?"

11: SWERVE

*"The lights have gone out here in the arena...
Okay, now they're back on. But where is The
Great Kayzo? One minute he's knocked out in
the middle of the ring. The lights flickered off
and on, and now he's gone! The champ is irate!
He doesn't know what to think... quite frankly,
folks, neither do I."*

*-ROOSEVELT HILL'S on-air
commentary from when The Great Kayzo
"teleported" in the middle of his match against
AWWA Champion Braxton Gore.*

TWO DAYS AGO
YEAR 0 + 220 DAYS (AUGUST 8th)

After studying the people of the "home planet" for one year, the crew members of each *Vilnagrom* ship followed a custom of choosing a new "Earth name." They felt it helped them identify with the specimens they were observing. Most often, the blue-skinned beings selected monikers that served as a tribute to historical figures or cultural icons they admired. Sometimes a crewmember opted to take the name of a giant in Earth's equivalent of his or her field.

The *V-II's* Cartographer selected "Polo." It was a fitting choice, a nod to the famous Venetian explorer, Marco Polo. The Cartographer's primary responsibility was to utilize maps and thousands of other types of data to create a vast observatory. Those abducted by his people were placed within the virtual reality world that he crafted. That is where he and the scientists aboard the ship could study the psychological and physiological effects that various stimuli had on humans.

The primary purpose of Project Vilnagrom was to conduct this massive experiment. Those they abducted were not placed in life suspension tanks and plugged into a world of virtual reality because the interstellar travelers were sadistic monsters. (They were not.) They were gathering information that would be highly valuable when making their peaceful transition from living in space to attempting to settle on Earth.

Ideally, the VR settings closely resembled the lives from which those being studied had been removed. Often external stimuli would be used. Doing something like inserting a pack of lions into an otherwise quiet neighborhood allowed the team of scientists to observe and record how each specimen responded. The physiology of the citizens of Earth was not much different than their own. It was believed that emulating the survival methods and social interactions of the planet's original inhabitants would be imperative to thriving on this "new" planet.

A tremendous amount of planning went into each instance of extracting a human from his or her home on Earth and transplanting the specimen into the tanks for observation. On the horizon was the most ambitious abduction mission in the (nearly) forty years that their people had been orbiting the planet. Every available Pilot, Explorer, and Scout met with the Cartographer in the *V-II's* theater. Their sole purpose was to discuss the final details of the mission.

On most occasions, one or two people were grabbed while they were in remote areas or otherwise vulnerable. Polo would then be tasked with hurriedly throwing together a virtual reality setting in just a couple of days. He always believed that operating in that manner did not maximize the effectiveness of their observations. "I simply cannot create a fully believable façade in that short amount of time!" he argued, insisting that they needed to do things differently.

"This process works most effectively if we can successfully trick those being observed into believing that they have remained in their native environment. Every minute detail I am able to include increases the believability of the illusion. The experimentation is compromised when the subjects begin to suspect that they have been abducted," Polo reminded his colleagues.

Not everyone shared Polo's enthusiasm as they assembled to discuss the most complex group of abductions in the history of Project Vilnagrom.

"We are talking about taking five specific humans from a busy metropolitan area on the same day..." one skeptic complained. "Are we confident we can do this?"

"Subject Patton should not be difficult," Polo responded. "It is a matter of grabbing a person out of an unguarded, and otherwise empty, hospital room."

After some additional chatter, the Cartographer reiterated why it was so important to handle the extractions in this new, aggressive manner. "This will drastically increase the effectiveness of our studies. That is, after all, the point of the abductions," he reminded them, doing little to mask his confidence. "With these specific individuals, I... *we* have had more than seven months to prepare. That seven months was not wasted. It was used to collect as much information about these specimens and their surroundings as we possibly could. Our scouts and explorers have done a phenomenal job assisting me in collecting that data. And I dare say that *I* have done a phenomenal job sewing that into our observation arena... If Subject Freeman walks into a restaurant in VR, she will see an exact replica of the same menu that she would have if she walked into that restaurant in Downtown St. Louis. If Subject Grayson looks in his dresser, he will see his socks balled up and his underwear folded the way he always keeps them."

The skeptic remained unconvinced. "Even if you had seven *years*, you could not possibly cover every square inch of a city that size. What happens when Freeman walks into a place that has not been so thoroughly mapped?"

"We keep her from going in such places."

"How?"

"Set the building ablaze. Have it collapse. Our subjects are going to find themselves in a scenario in which the world as they know it has changed in the blink of an eye," Polo insisted. "They will seek to avoid additional danger, not go running towards it. Once we unite our new subjects with our existing one, I am

confident we will be able to steer them away from unmapped areas
within the virtual realm."

☠ ☠ ☠

PRESENT DAY
YEAR 0 + 222 DAYS (AUGUST 10th)

The four bullet shuttles zoomed into the *V-II's* landing bay several
hours ahead of schedule. "Something must have gone wrong," Polo
worried as he left his sleeping quarters and rushed to greet his
returning comrades.

Movement from one section of the ship to another required
passage through one or more air locks. It could be a lengthy
process. By the time Polo arrived to greet the returning ships, the
docking area was nearly empty. "Where did everyone go?" he
asked.

The Scout known as "Monroe" was the only one in his
proximity when he asked his question. She was gathering her nun's
habit and various other props that were used to pull off the
abductions in the highly populated area. "Delivering the five human
subjects to the medical team for analysis?" Her tone indicated that
the answer should have been obvious to the Cartographer. "The rest
were moving towards the theater to celebrate a successful mission."

"Success?"

"An overwhelming success," Monroe beamed. She ran her
hands through her strawberry blond hair, which had been surgically
implanted into her scalp. "As expected, Subject Patton was alone in
a hospital room. That extraction was easy. Speaking of hospitals…"

"I adore it when you talk like an Earthly human. I lack the
ability to do so," Polo interrupted.

"Speaking of hospitals…" she continued, while beginning to wipe red paint away from her face and unwrinkled forehead, "Subject Grayson followed his routine and boarded the eastbound train as expected. What we did not foresee was the fact that Subjects Freeman and Silva were going to board the train at the same station!"

"What?"

"The plan was to grab them after the wrestling matches later that night. But they were among a group that visited patients at the children's hospital earlier in the day."

"Incredible."

"For a moment, I thought Grayson was going to follow us aboard— me, Subject Freeman, and Subject Silva. He took a great interest in Silva's wrestling attire. But then he stuck to his routine, and boarded two trains later… At 6:00 p.m. Central Daylight Savings Time, exactly as we had anticipated."

Polo could not believe the good fortune enjoyed by the extraction team.

Monroe continued. "Freeman and Silva were sedated and seized at the planned extraction point…" She stooped over to look into the front seat of her shuttle. "According to the log, they were taken at 5:55 p.m. Two trains later, Grayson was taken when his train arrived at 6:15 p.m."

"And Subject Emerson?"

"We needed to separate Subject Emerson from his friends. As we anticipated, he chose to return to his hotel alone once he realized he did not have his ticket for the baseball game. The timing was perfect. He boarded the train in between the one ridden by Grayson, and the one that Freeman and Silva were aboard. Emerson was sedated and seized at the same extraction point at 6:05 p.m."

"Outstanding! I suspect I will encounter little difficulty in weaving their virtual reality settings to make all four believe they were passengers on the same train. It should be the easiest introduction into VR of any of the specimens in the history of Project Vilnagrom."

☠☠☠

THE FOLLOWING MORNING
YEAR 0 + 222 DAYS (AUGUST 10th)

Grayson stirred as soon as the day's first light beamed through his window. He was not at all surprised to discover that he had fallen asleep in his recliner. He was, however, quite perplexed to see that he was back in his police uniform.

"What the hell?"

The corporal scanned his surroundings. Had someone—or *something*— entered his apartment in the night? He didn't detect any indicators that would lead him to believe that that was the case.

He let out a tiny chuckle when he spotted the stuffed animal in his kitchen. He had left both the purple kitty and his Glock 19 on the counter. Grayson scolded himself for leaving his firearm out in open view. "That's a good way to get yourself shot with your own gun."

After holstering his sidearm, he examined the notecard that had been left with the mysterious toy. "DON'T DO IT" was etched in black ink.

He flipped the notecard over and studied it. Once he determined that there were no additional clues to extract from the note, he pulled a pen out of his desk and wrote on the other side. "Who wrote this?"

Next, he stepped into the hallway. He placed the stuffed animal and his note down in roughly the same spot that he had discovered them the night before.

Grayson then began his systematic search of all three buildings clustered together in the apartment complex. Each of the three stone structures stood four stories tall, with ten units in each building.

Starting in Building C, Grayson went from the single Apartment on the fourth floor and worked his way down. He began with a polite knock. "This is Arnie Grayson. Is anyone in there?" When no one answered, he utilized his police training to kick down the door.

Repeating this process 29 times should have been murder on his 46-year-old knees. But he felt no pain. He was, however, pissed off that he never found the person who left him the note. He didn't locate any other survivors, for that matter. But at least his old body wasn't breaking down on him.

Grayson paused on his way back to his own building. He called out. He hoped that some other survivor would hear his shouts and come running. "Hello! Is anyone there? Hello!"

He shouted until he was hoarse. Then he headed back to Apartment 9-C for some water. "Maybe I should eat a couple Pop Tarts and then take a nap."

Once up the final flight of stairs, Grayson glared at the purple cat. Was he going crazy? Was someone playing a twisted, metaphysical joke? Whatever the hell was going on, the cop decided that taking a running start and kicking the stuffed animal would help.

With a form similar to a placekicker on a professional football team, Grayson blasted the toy up into the air and across the hallway. In doing so, however, he lost his footing and landed on his tailbone. While still seated on the floor in front of the door to his apartment, he laughed at himself and proclaimed, "It sure felt damn good to kick that friggin' cat!"

After rising to his feet and dusting himself off, Grayson walked through the door marked 9-C.

"What the Holy Hell?"

Grayson had stepped through the door to his apartment, but that doorway no longer led to his 790 square foot unit. Instead, he found himself standing in the lobby of the Camelot Casino.

☠ ☠ ☠

Jenn, Cocoa, Brady, and Tavia finished breakfast. The luchadora excused herself to make another attempt to call her husband.

Cocoa cleared the dirty plates. "I know it's silly," she told Brady and Tavia. "We're leaving this casino in a few minutes and most likely won't ever come back here. I could leave our dishes on the table, but I just can't. Maybe it's because this is where my pops and my brother were at the time of The Vanishing... Anyhow, I'm going to go throw these in the sink."

She hadn't been gone long when Tavia and Brady heard a sound coming from the lobby.

"Did you hear that?" Tavia asked.

"It sounded like a man's voice," Brady replied.

"Let's go check it out."

Brady's instincts told him to wait for Jenn and Cocoa. But with his attractive counterpart showing no fear, he accompanied her.

Tavia led the way, marching confidently towards the archway that led into the lobby. Without warning, she grabbed Brady by the arm and jerked him away from the exit. Pulling him into a corner, she whispered, "Did you get a look at him? It's a police officer."

"I didn't see him... But it's probably the guy who was on the train with me and Jenn and Cocoa."

"Well, cops make me nervous," Tavia confessed.

"Why?"

"As far as the authorities know, I'm still a missing person. We can't tell this guy my real name."

Brady shot the co-ed a puzzled look. "You didn't do anything wrong. You're not wanted... Right?"

"No. I'm not a fugitive or anything like that. Like I said, the police freak me out..." Her eyes raced along the walls of the ballroom until she focused on artwork that resembled the face cards from a standard deck. "We're going to tell this guy my name is 'Tavia Queen.' Do *not* tell him my real name under any circumstances. Got it?"

Brady was still confused. "Heck, as far as we know, we're the only five people left on Earth. Even if you were wanted for murder, I don't think he's going to care."

Tavia glared at Brady. "Do I look like a murderer to you?"

Grayson's voice was getting closer. "Hello?"

Tavia did her best to explain her concern. "In my experience, guys with badges aren't trusting people. First chance this cop gets, curiosity is going to get the best of him. He's going to run our names. I don't just have a couple of unpaid parking tickets. I was on a missing persons list. When he finds that out, he's gonna have a million and one questions. Can you please just respect me on this? My name is 'Tavia Queen.'"

"Yeah, sure... Absolutely."

While Tavia and Brady were ducked into the corner, Cocoa returned from the kitchen. "Don't you hear that? A man's voice?"

Brady stayed silent. He was unsure how Tavia would want him to respond.

Cocoa rolled her eyes, then broke into a slow jog as she headed towards the archway. Though she was moving towards the lobby, she momentarily turned her attention back to them and asked, "Were you guys too busy playin' kissy-face to hear that man calling out?"

☠☠☠

This whole situation was extremely bizarre. Grayson knew to proceed with caution. With each step he took, he glanced around to all sides. He was constantly checking his periphery.

Seeing Cocoa running towards him was unexpected. She was closing the gap between them at a rate that made the longtime member of law enforcement rather uncomfortable. Seeing no other alternative, Grayson raised his weapon and went to pull the trigger.

The panicked policeman screamed one final warning. "Not another step! Freeze!"

Cocoa complied. She stopped dead in her tracks.

Then she began laughing hysterically. Though his posture suggested otherwise, the police officer was not aiming a firearm at her. He was trying to shoot her with a toy. He was trying to shoot her with a stuffed purple kitten.

12: DISTANT TERRITORIES

"FIREBALL FREEMAN! You look into the sky above and think of it as a galaxy far, far away! I look TO THE STARS and I see the place I call HOME! When you and I meet in the ring, I'm going to send you INTO THE ABYSS! Then you will desire the unknown... a far better option than the turmoil you'll face where I AM SENDING YOU!"

-THE GALACTIC WARRIOR's scream-laden promo filmed for "Wrestling's Greatest Matches: Volume VII," a collection released exclusively on VHS in 1988.

PRESENT DAY
YEAR 0 + 222 DAYS (AUGUST 10th)

Following their initial introductions, Grayson spent the next couple of hours telling the others everything about the craziness he observed after being separated from them. "There wasn't another living creature on that side of the river. Nothing but empty cars on the interstate. No people on the Arch Grounds. No one in or around the ballpark... You guys are calling it The Vanishing? I'd say that's a perfect name for it. The rest of the world vanished while we were sitting on a train stopped in an underground tunnel."

"The rest of the *world*?" Jenn didn't like the sound of that.

The group traded theories until the policeman's stomach started to growl. "I haven't had breakfast. And decent food could be hard to come by before long. We should load up while we've got the opportunity." He suggested that they grab lunch at a nearby fast food deli. "I'm not much of a cook, but how hard can it be to slap some cold cuts and a few veggies on some bread? I say we head there now."

Once they made their way to the sandwich shop, Brady piled sliced meat high atop a loaf of day-old bread. Turkey, ham, roast beef, salami, and bologna. He smothered the meat with a generous heap of mayonnaise, along with cucumbers and tomatoes.

Jenn joked, "Jinkies, Shaggy... Did you leave Scooby-Doo back at the haunted casino?"

"Grayson said to load up, so I'm loading up. Besides, I'm a growing boy," he said with a grin.

The young man crammed the massive sandwich into his mouth. Then he made a face. Fighting the urge to gag, he couldn't hide the fact that it took him forever to choke that first bite down.

"Too much mayo?"

"Too much everything. This sandwich has no taste whatsoever. I'd rather eat the bark off a tree."

Grayson used his teeth to tear off another bite of his concoction of ham, mustard, pickles, and extra onions. "Yeah, I personally prefer Subway or Jimmy John's to this place. But it was close by. And since we haven't been able to get any cars to start, it looks like we're gonna be hoofin' it wherever we go. That being the case, my vote is we save ourselves the two-mile walk and eat here."

"Speaking of walking, where do we go now?" Jenn asked the group. "I mean, does anyone see any point in sticking around here any longer than we have to?"

"It might be nice to search the city a little more thoroughly to see if there are any other survivors," Brady suggested.

"Are you looking for anyone in particular?" Tavia asked. "Family? Maybe a girlfriend?"

Brady shook his head from side to side. His parents died a few years earlier. His older brother took a job in D.C. after grad school. Greg and Marshall were nowhere to be found. It appeared the other two members of "The Brady Bunch" had disappeared with the rest of the city. That left nothing (and no one) to tie the recent college grad to St. Louis or his nearby hometown of King City.

Tavia turned to Grayson. "How about you?"

He looked at the stuffed animal that he'd been carrying. "Nah. I've been a loner for most of my adult life. Never married. I've got no family. And now even my cat's gone... My real cat." He looked again at the purple kitty. Had he imagined the knock on the door? Had it been some self-preservation mechanism that he subconsciously triggered when he had considered taking his own life? He searched the area quite thoroughly and found no sign of anyone who might have left the toy and the note. "I say we get the hell away from St. Louis as soon as we can."

Tavia tilted her head at an angle and asked, "Did you seriously just suggest we should get out of town because your cat's gone?"

"No..." The cop fought to hide his embarrassment. "Yes, my cat's gone. But I think we need to get out of town because we don't know how widespread this is. Is this event you call *'The Vanishing'* limited to the St. Louis area or is it all over? We've gotta try going somewhere if we are going to have any chance of finding out."

Jenn was quick to jump in to agree with Grayson's sentiment. "Definitely. So *where* do we go?"

Grayson shrugged. "Beats me. Have any of you had any dreams about an old, black lady named Mother Abigail?"

No one picked up on his reference to Stephen King's classic book—*The Stand*. Instead, the rest of the group collectively glared at him.

It didn't take long for the silence to become awkward. Rising to his feet, Grayson stood and made a suggestion. "I don't particularly care where we go, but I don't intend on wasting any more time in here talking about it." He walked towards the door. Before exiting, he jammed the stuffed animal into a trashcan. "Who's with me?"

☠☠☠

"This is exactly why I hated group projects in college," Brady remarked after they had been standing outside the sandwich shop for more than ten minutes. "Can't come to a decision. Nobody knows anybody all that well, so nobody wants to make a suggestion for fear of ticking off someone they just met. I say we stop talking about it and take it to a vote."

Jenn decided it was time to interrupt. She continued to hold out hope that Lazz was still alive and well. She desperately wanted to head towards Florida. She didn't want the group choosing their next move based on an uninformed vote, indifference, or a coin toss. She couldn't chance a decision to go in the opposite direction based on the outcome of a game of Rock-Paper-Scissors. "I personally would like to head towards Orlando."

"Florida? I don't know how well you know your U.S. geography, but that's hundreds of miles away!" Grayson did little to hide his concerns about subjecting his body to such a lengthy journey. "How do you expect to accomplish that with no planes, trains or automobiles?"

"We walk? Ride bicycles?" Jenn said, her reply sounding as much like a series of questions than suggestions. In the next breath, she felt the need to make it clear that she was born and raised in the United States, and that her knowledge of the nation's geography was quite thorough. "And for your information, I grew up in Florida. I've wrestled from Seattle to Boston, from L.A. to Miami, and just about every stop in between. I think I've got a pretty strong grasp on the fifty states. Thank you, very much!"

"Enough!" Cocoa wanted to keep them from bickering. The conversation needed to remain focused on their next move.

Tavia didn't like the idea of journeying all the way to Florida, either. "That's a thousand miles from here. My family used to take me and my brother to Disney every year. I like to ride Space Mountain as much as the next girl. It's the oldest ride in the park, but it still has the longest line... Even so, I don't see how we can travel that far even if we were on bicycles."

"What about Memphis?" If the pirate could convince the group to go there, they'd be significantly closer to her hometown... and her husband. "That's where Cocoa lives. And it's not nearly as far as Orlando."

Cocoa chimed in. "It's about three hundred miles... give or take. But please don't think about going there on my behalf. My dad, my brother, and pretty much anyone else that was important in my life disappeared from the Camelot Casino last night."

"Three hundred miles..." Jenn did the calculations. "Walking at a reasonable pace, we go at least three miles an hour, probably closer to four. If we walk ten hours a day, that's thirty miles... even with breaks every hour or so. We could be in Memphis in ten days."

Grayson spoke up, presumably speaking for the rest of the group. "But why? I mean, what's so special about Memphis?" They all seemed unconvinced.

"Because there's no point in staying here. There's nothing here. Things could be totally different three hundred miles away. Between here and there, we might find other people. We might get a cell phone signal or find a mode of transportation that actually works. If we don't find anybody, at least we've got a place that we can stay for a while to regroup and rest up until we decide where to go from there."

"What the heck? You talked me into it. Sounds like an adventure." Tavia made a show of lifting her hand into the air. "Anyone else wanna go to Memphis with me and Long Jenn Silva?"

Brady raised his hand.

Though the look on his face revealed that he remained unconvinced, Grayson went with the majority.

Cocoa was the last to agree to the plan. "I'll go with the group, but only as long as my back can take it. Thirty miles a day sounds pretty extreme. If I say we've gotta stop, we stop. Is everyone cool with that?"

☠☠☠

ON THE PLANET NA-WERSS
TWO THOUSAND YEARS INTO THE FUTURE

Several centuries had passed since a few desperate space pioneers established a small colony on Na-Werss. Over time, their descendants replaced the ways of the old world with their own language and culture.

They began as a handful of astronauts searching for refuge. Their numbers surged and the single colony became many. They grew into a people who occupied most of the northern hemisphere of the second planet from the star/sun they called "Simeon 9."

Microevolution led to changes in physical appearance. Some were subtle. Others were obvious. They grew considerably taller than their ancestors. Hair no longer appeared atop their heads or on their bodies. Their noses grew wider and flattened to the point to where there was almost no bridge at all.

Most notably, though, exposure to high levels of silver caused fair, tan, and brown skin tones to change gradually into various shades of blue. Pigmentation varied little. Whether the skin was cornflower, cerulean, robin's egg, or turquoise, it all looked blue through the weak, red eyes of the people of Na-Werss.

Silver. High levels of silver in the atmosphere and water choked the life out of the Nawerssians. It was a slow death for those that occupied the planet's northern hemisphere. But they would not be able to endure living in a world with such conditions forever.

Nawerssian technology had advanced exponentially through the decades. They operated computers and machines that featured a sophistication that would have been unimaginable to their ancestors.

☠☠☠

The engine pulled water molecules out of the atmosphere, separated the hydrogen from the oxygen, then propelled the craft by the nuclear fission of the hydrogen. Not weighed down by large amounts of fuel or massive tanks needed to hold it, this silver streak in the sky had the potential to save the Nawerssians from being poisoned out of existence.

The Pilot zipped across hundreds of miles of sky in a matter of seconds. With a slight manipulation of the controls, he was able to penetrate the lower atmosphere and climb towards space. A moment later, he directed the machine to dive between two silver-topped mountain peaks.

"That was the most amazing ride of my life!" he declared once he returned to solid ground. "Does this aircraft have anything to do with what we will discuss at the briefing scheduled for later today? If my suspicion is right and it does, I need no further details. Sign me up for the mission!"

☠☠☠

Ten blue-skinned figures—six males, four females—sat in a military hangar. They wore skin-tight flight suits.

The Pilot was still riding the high from his exhilarating flight from earlier in the day. "Our boots have thick metal soles. I presume these are for when we must resort to electromagnetism for our artificial gravity." He wore the designation "V-I 7/PILOT" embossed on one side of his uniform. Like all pilots and navigators, his gray flight suit was accented with amber over the shoulders and across his chest.

"These flight suits are waterproof." He hypothesized this was necessary to maximize the collection, filtration, and re-use of every available droplet of water. Turning to the male seated next to him, he added, "That means we are in for a long mission into deep space. Am I correct?"

The Pilot voice his speculation toward one designated "V-I 3/EXPLORER."

The Explorer nodded. Privy to a few more details than most of the others gathered in the hangar, he leaned in to whisper a couple of key pieces of information to his longtime friend and partner. Before he could do so, however, the entire group was interrupted by a loud tone. This obnoxious noise alerted all ten blue beings to rise and stand at attention.

An image appeared on a large black monitor. Depicted on the screen was Magistrate Mua-Quana Eesafoa, the highest-ranking political figure in the region. "Greetings and congratulations!" he began. Unlike those of the youthful soldiers in the hangar, the Magistrate's forehead was covered in wrinkles upon wrinkles of baggy skin. "You have been selected to participate in a monumental mission that will alter and forever improve the course of history for the people of Na-Werss."

Na-Werss. The name the blue-skinned beings gave their planet evolved over time. Much like how many long-term residents of New Orleans were said to pronounce the name of their city "N'awlins," the planet originally dubbed "New Earth" gradually found its name modified to "Na-Werss" by a people that were once known to hiss their "S" sounds if they were not careful.

A period that would have equaled two thousand years on Earth had passed since the Nawerssians first colonized their world. Hundreds of years earlier, the leaders of the original Earth ("O.E.") determined that a doomsday scenario appeared imminent. The space agencies of the United States, the United Kingdom, Russia, Japan, China, India, Israel, and possibly others launched manned missions deep into the galaxy. Each team left the solar system and traversed the galaxy. The goal was to discover habitable planets in other solar systems. The purpose was to settle and build permanent colonies. They hoped that human life would be preserved and the culture and customs of Earth would continue on at least one of those new worlds. Preservation of humanity depended on at least one of the missions succeeding.

The Magistrate continued his announcement. "You have been selected for Project Vilnagrom."

(Loosely translated, *"Vilnagrom"* meant "return home" in the language spoken by the Nawerssians.)

Several scientists and military officials gathered in the front of the hangar to explain the project far more thoroughly. Four reconnaissance teams would be sent to Earth—O.E. These missions were scheduled to take place over sixty Earth years.

"The mission requires a precise launch date," said V-I 1/GENERAL in a voice that was much more weathered than a typical Nawerssian.

The General was a popular figure in the northern hemisphere. Specifically, he was a war hero with a collection of well-earned momentos. This included one large seam that came when shrapnel embedded in his face. The scar traveled from the top of his head to the midpoint in his cheek. It was a miracle he kept the eye. It was doubtful that he could see out of it, but the General was a hero... and a fantastic liar when the occasion called for it.

He explained, "Our opportunity is limited. The wormhole will only be in range for a brief period of time. It will not return to within a close proximity of Na-Werss for another twenty Earth years."

The Pilot raised his hand. "What is on O.E.?" he asked. "I was under the impression the entire world was completely obliterated more than a thousand years ago."

"True. Our best intelligence reveals that all life was destroyed, but the planet remains intact." The General's reply included a bit of excitement coloring his tone. An adventure emerged on the horizon, and it was clear he was eagerly anticipating the launch. "Regardless of its current condition, we have charted a course that will allow us to observe O.E. before and during its catastrophic event."

A buzz of confusion spread within the hangar. Attempting to return to the script, the General jumped back in. "There is a simple answer to the questions many of you are asking. The wormhole will not only allow us to cover an incredible distance in a short amount of time..."

The Pilot figured it out as the General was in the process of answering the question. "It will allow us to go back in time to a point before the destruction of Original Earth."

"Correct!" the General said, his gravelly voice permeating through the growing number of questions arising from the collection of officers in the hangar.

The Pilot knew the science. Such a journey was theoretically possible. He jumped up to explain it. "When you look into the night's sky, we see light that the stars emitted many, many light years ago. If the star we know as Dosta-Gloys was extinguished today, we would continue to observe the light that came from that star for three hundred more years from our vantage point here on Na-Werss. If we were looking from Original Earth, we would continue to see that light for eight hundred more years after that... The wormhole allows us to travel to the exact point in space and time that the light first went out. In theory, we could travel fast enough to reach Dosta-Gloys before it was extinguished. Likewise, a trip through the right wormhole could put us near Original Earth at a time prior to its doomsday."

"Correct!" he said again, bubbling with enthusiasm.

The Pilot turned and looked towards the General and the Magistrate who was still participating via the monitor. "I have one question... How do we get back? Under the theory, we can travel fast enough to reach a point in the past. But, as I understand it, a wormhole is a one-way portal. We cannot outrun light that has yet to be emitted. Traveling into the future simply is not possible. If we go, we can never come back. Am I right?"

"You are correct."

Quiet filled the hangar.

The Magistrate broke the silence. "Your primary role will include observing O.E. at a point in its history in which the planet was thriving. You will study their weather, geology, and agriculture. You will study the people of O.E., including their physiological and psychological capabilities and, of course, their culture. When the time comes, we will be neutral observers as their catastrophic event occurs. After that, we should be prepared to take the information we have gathered and use it to aid our people in their move onto the surface of O.E."

Upon hearing this, more than one person asked, "They are our ancestors. Why would we not help them?"

The Magistrate was quick with his answer. "Our objective is in the name of the mission. *Vilnagrom*. Return home. We want to prepare O.E. so that the people of Na-Werss can return home."

Though the Magistrate had more to say, he paused to allow the assembled heroes to ask their questions. Once satisfied that most of their concerns had been addressed, he continued. "By traveling into the past, you will be taking historic first steps of our people. Steps into the past which, in reality, will be steps into the future of our people. Yours will be the beginning of our long-promised return home. You will leave as Nawerssians. You will arrive at O.E. as the first New and Future Earth Dwellers... Heroes unlike any others in our long and glorious history."

The Explorer sat motionless. None of this was a surprise to him. He had been in countless preliminary meetings with the General, the top scientists of the region, and the Magistrate himself. In fact, he played a significant role in selecting the members of the crew for the *Vilnagrom-I* voyage.

The Pilot looked at his closest friend. He shook his head from side to side. Unable to mask the hurt and betrayal he felt, he said, "This is a suicide mission. We will never see our families again. You knew... All this time, you knew, and you signed us up... And you did not tell me."

VILNAGROM MISSION ROLES:

1. MILITARY OFFICER- Commanding officer during military conflicts... Assesses the risk prior to launch of any Earth Recon or Abduction Missions.

2. SKIPPER- Pilots ship through intergalactic space and wormholes... Maintains the structural integrity of the ship, repairing damage inside and outside... Mans bridge/control center while ship is docked.

3. EXPLORER- Organizes and plans all Earth Recon or Abduction Missions... Participates in Earth Recon or Abduction Missions... Assists Cartographer in constructing maps and blueprints for virtual reality.

4. CARTOGRAPHER- Aids Explorer in Earth Recon and Abductions... Principal engineer in charge of constructing maps and blueprints for virtual reality.

5. NAVIGATOR- Assists Skipper piloting through intergalactic space... Assists on bridge/control center while ship is docked... Directs shuttles in and out of landing bay.

6. PILOT- Transports Explorers and Scouts in Earth Recon and Abductions... Assists the Skipper in maintaining structural integrity of the ship... Assists on bridge/control center while ship is docked.

7. PILOT- Transports Explorers and Scouts in Earth Recon and Abductions... Assists the Skipper in maintaining structural integrity of the ship... Assists on bridge/control center while ship is docked.

8. PHYSICAL SCIENCES OFFICER- Science Officer with special emphasis on study of the geologic makeup and meteorologic patterns of the Earth, its atmosphere, and its bodies of water... Assists Doctor with medical procedures.

9. BIOLOGICAL SCIENCES OFFICER- Science Officer with special emphasis on study of the agricultural, biological, and zoological trends found on the Earth, its atmosphere, and its bodies of water... Assists Doctor with medical procedures.

10. DOCTOR- Primary physician for crew... Conducts medical experiments on Abducted Specimens... Assists Science Officers with experimentation.

13: RITE OF PASSAGE

"They say you know you've made it in this business once you've fought in Madison Square Garden. Tonight I have my first match in wrestling's most sacred venue. I guarantee you it won't be the last."

-BRICK VANDERWAL promo prior to his first match in Madison Square Garden.

FORTY YEARS AGO (ABOARD THE VILNAGROM-I) YEAR -40 + 201 DAYS (JULY 20th)

The *Vilnagrom-I* looked like a large jellyfish. A massive jellyfish, actually, approximately 63 meters (206 feet) from top to bottom and 40 meters (131 feet) wide.

Almost half of the height represented the "bell" portion of the ship. To a human's touch, that section would more closely resemble rubber or silicon than the cold, hard, metallic feel one might expect when coming into contact with the outer surface of a spacecraft. That was by design. The bell became the nose of the ship when traveling through deep space, and the design allowed it to absorb impact and repel foreign objects much like the function of a cowplow on an old locomotive.

When the *V-I* was at rest, either docked or in orbit, the bell was designed to appear as the "bottom" of the craft. The mechanisms for the collection, filtration, cleaning, and storage of water were located deep inside that important part of the craft. Also stored in this area were the incubators, as well as rows and rows of tanks needed to breed, warm, and grow the algae-like organisms which served as the primary source of food and protein for those beings living in space.

Extending out from the widest section of the bell were at least twenty long, narrow corridors that resembled arms or tentacles. These extensions were filled with the living quarters of the ship's occupants, as well as libraries and laboratories for their work. When the ship was in motion through deep space, the arms were electromagnetically drawn and held together so they would not snap off while traveling at velocities that approached the speed of light. Those connections also could be used to pull any two of those arms together. This feature was particularly useful when a crew member wanted to move from one section of the ship to another.

While the *Vilnagrom-I* was traveling through deep space, the bridge served as the center of the spacecraft's nervous system. It housed a bank of computers at stations that monitored the communications, navigation, flight, and integrity of the ship.

The Communications Grid would keep track of those within the ship, and later would be a lifeline for those flying observation, collection, or abduction excursions down to the surface of the Earth.

The Navigation Grid would be manned by a specialist on the first leg of the voyage. Precise readings from the maps and star charts were imperative if the *V-I* was going to enter the wormhole during the appropriate window.

There were several military pilots who shared the duties at the Flight Grid. It was not exhilarating to those who had flown wartime missions. If the ship crashed into an asteroid or flew into a comet, fault likely would lie with the Navigator. Until they could fly the bullet shuttles down to Earth, the only time true piloting skills would come into play would be if they encountered an unfriendly ship from another solar system. That was an occurrence that would be extremely unlikely to happen.

The Integrity Grid was operated by the ship's Skipper. It was his job to ensure that the *V-I* remained structurally sound. If there was significant damage to the outside of the ship, the entire vessel could be ripped apart moments after entering the wormhole. Additionally, the water collection and filtration, air scrubbing and circulation, and artificial gravity systems were monitored at that area of the bridge.

Gunner stations were positioned on the port and starboard sides. From there, a crew member could fire stunning blasts, laser cannons, or-in extreme situations—nuclear warheads.

"The ship looks magnificent," the General commented as he rested in the Captain's Chair.

"Yes, it does," agreed the Explorer. Then he added, "And that is a good thing, since each of us will live the duration of our lives in space."

☠☠☠

Tey-rixia Eesafoa was the niece of the Magistrate and the spouse of the *V-I*'s Skipper. Regardless of her connections, she was chosen to be part of the mission based on her own merit. There was little argument that she was among the top biological scientists in the northern hemisphere of Na-Werss.

"This is Tey-rixia. Requesting link to Corridor 3."

A series of tones rang out from the control panel. Buzzing and humming sounds echoed through the hallway. Then came another tone. "This is the Control Center. Electromagnetic Connection of the Corridors has been completed. Please enter the safety code when you are ready to activate the air lock."

Once she made the transfer to the appropriate section of the massive spacecraft, Tey-rixia advanced down the corridor and entered the bathing facility. She moved towards a panel on the far wall. Lost in thought, she walked right past the pool of murky, orange liquid without noticing that the Pilot and the Explorer were standing in the waist-deep cleaning solution.

"Science Officer Tey-rixia," the Explorer called out, hoping to announce his presence without startling her.

The woman whipped her head around. Her unblemished face could not hide her surprise. "I did not expect anyone else to be in here at this hour," she apologized. "I can come back if the two of you prefer to be alone."

No one knew if the voyage through the wormhole would take two hours, two years, or somewhere in between. Before entering the passage, most of the crew would be placed in hibernation for the inter-dimensional journey. Those who spent the passage in hibernation would be contained in the life suspension tanks. While in the tanks, the aging process would slow significantly, but each would remain alert and conscious of the virtual reality setting around them. For most, it would be like a vacation to the paradise of their choosing.

Unfortunately, at least two crew members had to remain on the bridge to navigate in and out of the wormhole. The Pilot had been chosen to join the Skipper for that essential segment of the trip to Original Earth. That meant that he and the Explorer were about to be separated for an undetermined period of time.

The Explorer had hoped for a few moments of privacy with his partner before going into the life-suspension tanks, but the high-ranking officer knew better than to ask Tey-rixia to leave. Though they had only been in space for the equivalent of a few months on O.E., requests for secrecy or privacy already had become a way of arousing suspicions among the crew.

"Nonsense," he replied. "Join us." The pool was large enough for several Nawerssians to bathe at the same time. The substance used to clean them was designed to pull any grime down to the bottom and directly into a drain. Because of this, they believed sharing "bath water" was in no way unsanitary. And since the people of his world possessed few qualms about the naked form, the suggestion to join them was neither unexpected nor inappropriate.

Tey-rixia smiled. "Very good."

The Biologist moved to the far end of the compartment. She tapped a code into a panel. A flat slab emerged from the wall. This was where she would place her clothing. It would disappear into the same wall. While she bathed, the slab would return with her flight suit and undergarment scrubbed clean and ready for another seven days of wear.

She first removed her boots, then lifted two fingers to the neck of the flight suit. Those two fingers glided smoothly towards her waist, "unzipping" the garment as her touched traveled downward. She peeled her outfit over her hips, tugging at it until she pulled it over her ankles. Once she removed a black undergarment that resembled boyshorts, she moved towards the pool.

Being naked in front of two males caused her no concern. She was not ashamed, nor was she "strutting her stuff" like a woman from O.E. might do in an effort to seduce one or both of them. Naked was the way they were created. To a Nawerssian, it was as simple as that.

"This feels wonderful!" Tey-rixia exclaimed as she stepped into the pool. The temperature throughout most of the *V-I* was set at approximately 86 degrees Fahrenheit (30 degrees Celsius). Being required to constantly wear the water-resistant flight suits made the extreme heat even more intolerable. Stepping into the cool pool for a twelve-minute bath was one of the highlights of each seven-day period.

With the "water" only coming up to her midsection, Tey-rixia dropped to her knees and slowly lowered her body downward until even the top of her hairless head was submerged. She rose to a standing position and concentrated on the sensation of how the gritty solution crept down her body. As it did so, the orange goo extracted any dirt, grime, dead skin cells, etc. from the surface.

After a bit of the Nawerssian equivalent of small talk, the Explorer informed the Skipper's spouse, "I was about to continue my final internal inspections before we enter the wormhole. My next stop is in Corridor 12…" He paused when he heard his laundry slab slide out of the wall. This not only signaled that his clothes were clean, but that the allotted time for his bath was done. Acknowledging the end of his respite, he remarked, "I suppose the next time you and I likely will interact is in VR during our time in the life suspension tanks."

Positioning himself under a showerhead just outside the pool, he was hit by a brief avalanche of water. This final spray removed any remaining bits of the orange solution that may have adhered to his body. Then came a rapid blast of air to dry him.

"That was what I was hoping to discuss…" Tey-rixia said as she turned towards the Pilot. "I know you were assigned to remain in the Control Center with my spouse during the passage through the wormhole."

"Yes?"

"I want to take your spot."

The Pilot protested. "As much as I would enjoy a virtual vacation with my own partner, I cannot. I have received specialized training…"

"You and I both know the Skipper handles navigation into and out of the wormhole," she protested. "Your role is to be there to make sure that someone can pull the rest of the crew out of hibernation if anything unexpected happens to him."

"My assignment is a little more complicated than that."

"I *need* to take your spot. *My baby* needs me to take your spot. He cannot…"

The Pilot made no effort to hide his shock. The women of the crew had been instructed to take every precaution to avoid conception prior to passing through the wormhole. There were too many uncertainties regarding how traveling through a fold in space and time could affect an unborn child. "You are pregnant? ...Now?"

Tey-rixia felt her throat tightening. She responded in a voice just above a whisper. "Yes."

☠☠☠

FOUR MONTHS LATER
YEAR -40 + 285 DAYS (OCTOBER 12th)

Sweat streamed from the pores atop Tey-rixia's head.

"Drink some water," her spouse reminded her.

"You fly the ship!" she snapped back. "I will decide when I need to drink!"

She was right. As much as the well-being of the laboring mother concerned him, the Skipper's attention had to keep returning to the flight deck. The fate of the entire crew and the mission required that his primary focus remain on the control panel.

Alarms flashed continuously.

Many mysteries and countless dangers accompanied any passage through a fold in time and space.

From the Communications Grid, utter chaos rang through the speakers. Thousands of years' worth of radio broadcasts burst through at once. Some of the frequencies carried communications from decades ago, while others carried messages that would not be spoken for centuries.

Integrity alerts buzzed one atop another. This part of the journey was wreaking havoc on every section of the *V-I*. Somewhat panicked, the Skipper voiced his frustrations. "We are coming to the end of the wormhole! Light. Gravity. Space. Time. There are no laws of physics here!"

"Relax." The word was spoken between desperate breaths. They were gasps taken to avoid being strangled by a room suddenly robbed of oxygen. Tey-rixia attempted to soothe the Skipper and herself at the same time. It was not working.

The Skipper ignored the flashing lights and warning tones. He dove across the control room to give an oxygen mask to the mother of his unborn son. Unable to hide his worry, he mouthed the words "How soon?"

Tey-rixia's honey-colored eyes glowed a fiery red as they rolled back in her head. After another gasp, she regained consciousness. Reaching out and clutching her partner by the wrist, she told him, "Soon... Very soon."

A deafening tone sounded along the flight deck. The Skipper recognized the alert, but had only enough time to shout, "Hold on!"

The *V-1* shook violently and abruptly. Artificial gravity was lost, sending the bodies of both Nawerssians soaring into the air until they crashed against the ceiling. Then they dropped just as suddenly.

With a steady stream of blood flowing from a massive tear in the skin atop his head, the Skipper scrambled to put gravity boots onto the feet of his otherwise naked spouse. "To keep you from flying around the room if that happens again," he said before pulling himself back towards the control panel.

"Hang on, my love!" the Skipper yelled. The vibrations of the spacecraft continued without ceasing. "We are right on the edge. Hang on, my love!"

A low, steady rumble followed and seemed to linger for several minutes. It caused the Skipper's bones to rattle. Several of his teeth spilled onto the floor. He gagged as his mouth filled with a bitter pool of blood.

They were surrounded by brief, but total, darkness that was interrupted only by a couple of popping fuses across the flight board. Then came an eardrum-rupturing explosion that momentarily knocked the Skipper unconscious. He scurried to his feet, observing a bright light through the portside window. A second later, the blinding rays came from all directions and the ship was pelleted with small rocks and chunks of ice. "We... are... through!"

The *V-I* shot out of the wormhole like it had been blasted from a cannon. It zoomed through the vacuum of space at a velocity that approached the speed of light. With an orange, gassy giant behind him and an asteroid belt fast approaching, the Skipper didn't have much time to look to his passengers.

"Did you hear that, my love? We made it through."

She didn't reply.

The Skipper attempted to use the arm of his flight suit to wipe away the blood that gushed from his head. The he glanced back and saw his spouse lying lifelessly in a crimson pool. There was so much blood. It made the tiny trickles flowing from the Skipper's head and out of his mouth look trivial. Even so, Tey-rixia looked peaceful.

It was as if she died with a smile on her face.

The newborn baby boy was still attached to his mother by the umbilical cord. He too was peaceful... and perfectly healthy.

The baby cooed as he gazed at his father with honey hued orbs. The soft, sweet sound was a drastic contrast to the symphony of terror and chaos the Skipper observed as he guided the ship through the wormhole mere moments earlier.

Mentally and physically exhausted, he kissed his son on his head and told him, "We made it through."

☠☠☠

A YEAR AND A HALF LATER
YEAR -38 + 120 DAYS (APRIL 30th)

Nine Nawerssians—ten if the infant held by the Skipper was included in the count—gathered in the theater of Corridor 2. The Explorer stepped to the front. With the approval of the General, he began the festivities by addressing the crew:

"We have spent a tremendous amount of time in this room over the last few weeks and months. On the screen behind me, we have watched films and television broadcasts intercepted from Earth. We have heard their music and listened to their radio programs. We have done so for the equivalent of 365 days on Earth. One year. And so tonight we gather to celebrate... to remember... and to ceremoniously take the next step in our transition from citizens of Na-Werss to residents of the planet of our ancestors. Na-Werss is light years away. The lives we knew when it was home...? They do not begin for another two thousand years." He pointed towards a digital map of Earth that always appeared on the wall of the room. "Our home is no longer Na-Werss. It is not the *Vilnagrom-I*. It is the Earth that we orbit. The Earth that we have studied for the last year, and will continue to do so until the *Vilnagrom-II* arrives many years from now... Tonight, we choose our new names. Our Earth names."

Most of the crew members cheered in traditional Nawerssian fashion. They made a fist, pumping their right arms into the air. As they did so, each would rapidly vibrate his or her tongue against the roof of their mouth. The result was a clicking sound that resembled a jackhammer.

The Explorer and the Pilot, however, clapped their hands together. Spotting this, the General smiled and gave the duo a thumbs up sign. "Already adapting to the ways of Earth. I love it!"

After a little more fanfare, the General hobbled forward. His war-worn voice filled the room as he spoke. "The Naming Ceremony... We have been observing the media and culture of our Earthly ancestors. We have made numerous discoveries while studying their history. And now, each of us is tasked with selecting an Earthly name. As your General, I will go first... Any guesses?"

"Blackbeard!" one crew member called out.

"Hook!" offered another.

"Captain Kidd!"

The Explorer jokingly added a suggestion of his own. "Scurvy Dog, the swashbuckling land lover!"

"Now that is a mouthful!" he laughed.

The names made sense. The General had a gravelly voice. His vocal cords were badly damaged from years of shouting instructions to Nawerssian soldiers. The condition was made much worse when he was nearly killed in an explosion. While serving in wars back on Na-Werss, he developed a reputation for using unconventional tactics with outstanding levels of success. And since they had been watching hours and hours of films and television from Earth, it was no secret that he quickly became enamored with pirate-themed stories.

The General imitated a buccaneer. "Argh! Good suggestions from the lot a' ye! But I gots no hair on me face, so Blackbeard won't work, now will it? And I gots two good hands and a full complement of fingers, so I can't exactly go wit' Hook... As fer Captain Kidd? That's outta the question. I not be willin' ta take a demotion in rank..."

"So what is it?" the playful audience wanted to know.

Still talking with a tinge of his forced pirate accent, he announced, "As much as I have an affinity for the demons of the high seas, I picked a name based on me sympathy for the devil hisself... and my inability to obtain satisfaction. Therefore, please call me 'JAGGER' from here on out."

Jagger's declaration was met with cheers. One of the crew members passed around containers of Meezuh, a fermented tea that was served during celebrations on Na-Werss.

The Skipper was the next to announce his chosen name. His presentation was much more somber. His spouse, Tey-rixia, began the *Vilnagrom-I* mission as one of its Science Officers. She became the mission's first fatality after encountering difficulties during the birth of their son. The Skipper's vitality disappeared following her death. Though he was one of the three highest ranking officers on the *V-I*, he frequently commented that his primary purpose had been served after the passage through the wormhole was complete.

"I am going to take on the name Magellan," he said, acknowledging the obvious comparisons between his voyage through space and the Portuguese hero's historic circumnavigation of the Earth.

"Magellan" then raised his young son up for all to see. "And since he is the first-born child of the mission, I hope you will indulge me... I would like to call him 'Adam.'"

No one quarreled with either of those names.

Following Magellan, several other crew members selected their monikers. Inspiration came from various sources. The Pilot chose "Avis" because it was the Latin word for "bird." The *V-I's* Geologist would be known as "Mantle." He selected that name as a dual homage to New York Yankees baseball legend Mickey Mantle and the layer of rock just below the crust of the Earth. And the ship's Doctor looked to popular culture when she selected "McCoy" as a tribute to the blue-shirted character from *Star Trek*.

The Explorer was the final Nawerssian to announce his new name. As he stepped forward, he was prepared to call himself "Tenzing" in honor of the Sherpa that accompanied Sir Edmund Hillary on his historic climb to the top of Mount Everest.

Jagger stopped him. "Not so fast, matey!" Mission plans dictated that the hierarchy of authority was to be shared between the General, the Skipper, and the Explorer. Since the moment Skipper Magellan lost his wife, he contributed very little to Project Vilnagrom. With Magellan serving as little more than a feckless tiebreaker, the General and Explorer had been butting heads more and more frequently over the last several weeks.

"Yer about to pick some modest name. 'Tis written all over that ugly mug a' yers…" *(The others in the theater looked around. Was Jagger drunk on Meezuh? Many were uncertain if he was joking or about to make a power play.)* "What this crew needs is for you to pick a name that makes a bold statement. I'd humbly request that ya consider my suggestion… Ya looks like an 'Armstrong' ta me. And since ye 'll be the first of yer people to set foot on Planet Earth, I think it would be a damn fine name for you to choose."

The Explorer stood in shock. Up to that very point, it had not been decided who would be the first to place their boots on the ground. There was speculation that the General's ego would result in him assigning the task to himself.

"Armstrong…? I like the sound of that." The Explorer raised his container of Meezuh. "And I like the sound of being the first blue man on Earth even better."

VILNAGROM-I

CREW MEMBERS (AFTER ONE YEAR ORBITING EARTH)

ROLE	CODENAME
V-I 1/GENERAL	JAGGER
V-I 2/SKIPPER	MAGELLAN
V-I 3/EXPLORER	ARMSTRONG
V-I 4/CARTOGRAPHER	CROCKETT
V-I 5/NAVIGATOR	*VALENTINA*
V-I 6/PILOT	*LINDY*
V-I 7/PILOT	AVIS
V-I 8/PHYSICAL SCIENCE	MANTLE
V-I 9/BIOLOGICAL SCIENCE	*TEY-RIXIA* (deceased)
V-I 10/DOCTOR	*McCOY*
V-I 11/UNASSIGNED	ADAM (son of Magellan & Tey-Rixia)

14: THE FEUD

"The Galactic Warrior may be the Flavor of the Week. But those don't stick around all too long. As for Fireball Freeman? I've got staying power. Long after the snot-nosed kiddies are done shoutin' your name, Fireball Freeman's gonna be there in the middle of the ring... knockin' out the next Flavor of the Week."

-FIREBALL FREEMAN promo filmed for "Wrestling's Greatest Matches: Volume VII."

NA-WERSS – APPROXIMATELY FORTY-TWO YEARS AGO
YEAR -42 + 77 DAYS (MARCH 18th)

The surgeon stepped in. She was young and talented. A rising star in the Nawerssian military. She soon would join Project *Vilnagrom* and adopt "McCoy" as the name she would be known by for the remainder of her life.

Under normal circumstances, she would tap a button on the wall, and then a medical chart would be displayed on the monitor. She didn't need it for this patient, though. Gar-Vizza Rey'otia was a hero. And it was the surgeon's job to make sure that the hero survived to tell his story and inspire his people to continue to fight the advances of the cyborg devils from the southern hemisphere.

Gar-Vizza and his troops were greatly outnumbered and caught in the middle of a Cyborg Storm. He was the only one on either side to walk away from the pivotal battle. And he didn't exactly walk away.

McCoy greeted her patient with a smile. "Good morning, Gar-Vizza..."

The patient attempted to reply. As soon as the man who would later call himself "Jagger" opened his mouth, he winced. The hero raised his blue hands to cover his throat.

"Please do not attempt to speak. You sustained significant damage to your vocal cords. I was pulling cyborg shrapnel out of your face and neck for a substantial portion of the time you spent in the operating room... Do not worry. Our doctors can clean up the scar tissue once your body has more fully recovered. Your voice will be restored to as good as before. Better, perhaps. For now, however, you need to figure out a way to communicate non-verbally."

Though it pained his body to do so, Gar-Vizza reached down to assess another of the many injuries he had sustained. He mouthed the words, "My leg?"

The surgeon shook her head from side to side. "We had no choice but to amputate from a point just above you right knee."

Nawerssian technology had advanced to a point that a prosthetic could be attached, fully connected to his nervous system in such a way that no one could tell that he was walking on an artificial limb. He knew the doctors could reconstruct him to a level of health and mobility equal (or superior) to his original condition. But he had no intention of permitting the doctor to perform any procedures that would take him closer to living like the cyborg bastards from the southern hemisphere. He refused to consider the possibility.

"The other alternative is a prosthetic like 'the ancients' would have used. You would rest what remains of your leg into an artificial limb that features no true range of movement... and there would be no way to synch it to the nerves in your leg," the doctor explained.

He mouthed the word "yes" as his response. He would much rather hobble around like one of the ancients than take on an appendage that made him resemble a cyborg devil.

The doctor argued against this decision. "You will not be very ambulatory. You will have to use your hip to swing the heavy prosthetic in front of you to propel yourself forward. The consequences of walking in such an unnatural manner will begin with a profound limp. After the passage of time, you can expect your daily life to include severe pain in your hip and lower back. Additionally, there will be constant friction between the artificial limb and the stub at the end of your leg. That, of course, will result in constant discomfort." She paused, hoping this list would cause him to reconsider his stance.

The war hero looked the doctor in the eye. Though he knew that doing so would be painful, he spoke his answer aloud in a voice that sounded like a growl. "I can handle the pain... *Better my body than my soul.*"

💀💀💀

EARTH - FOUR AND A HALF YEARS LATER
YEAR -38 + 313 DAYS (NOVEMBER 9th)

The Pilot occupied the front seat of the silver bullet shuttle. Like peas in a pod, five additional seats were placed behind him, one behind another, behind another, etc. The manned missile shot through the sky at a velocity so great that it was almost impossible for a human eye to see... especially when flown against the backdrop of an overcast sky or on a moonless night.

Seated in the second row, Armstrong reached forward and placed his hand on his partner's shoulder. He asked, "Are you ready to make history?"

The shuttle was blasted away from the *Vilnagrom-I's* launch tubes and dissected the vacuum of space. Entry into the Earth's outer atmosphere caused the vessel to glow red and shake violently. With the planet's gravity now adding an additional pull, the shuttle ripped through the night sky, leaving a subtle mist of vapor in its wake.

"Yeeeeeeeeeeeeeeaaaaaaaaaaaa!!!!" Avis had flown above the surface of the Earth previously, but the Nawerssian still experienced quite a sensation from traveling under these conditions.

Moderately concerned by the unexpected yell, Armstrong asked, "Is everything alright?"

"Never better!" Avis replied as he raised the nose of the shuttle to reduce the speed. Remembering his protocols, the Pilot reported back to the big ship. He spoke in English, but his words would sound like gibberish if any Earthly beings somehow stumbled onto their frequency. Decoded, his message was: "*Vilnagrom*, this is the Alpha Shuttle. We will be touching down in the Mojave Desert in approximately four minutes. Going dark until our return."

☠☠☠

ABOARD THE VILNAGROM-I – ONE DAY LATER
YEAR -38 + 314 DAYS (NOVEMBER 10th)

The Alpha Shuttle pulled into the landing bay. Though the Skipper (Magellan) and Navigator (Valentina) were needed in the Control Center, every other member of the *V-I* crew was there to greet the returning heroes.

Jagger greeted Armstrong with a mighty embrace. "Armstrong, m'boy!!! How did it feel to drop yer big blue feet on the Earth's surface?"

"Fantastic!"

As the other members of the crew approached, the Explorer reached back into the shuttle and pulled several cannisters out of the back seats. "I have gifts!"

The first container was small enough to fit in the palm of his hand. He handed it to the *V-I's* Cartographer, Crockett. "Since you are the mission's top biological scientist now that Tey-Rixia is gone... We brought you a spider and a portion of its sticky web."

Next came two cannisters that were much larger. "For our Geologist... Dirt and several rocks from the Mojave."

Armstrong went on to pass out creosote branches and a few other items for the ship's scientists to discover. "And maybe the best for last…!" he announced as he motioned for everyone to gather around. "Avis and I also made a quick detour to a filling station." Seeing a bit of confusion on some of the faces of his fell crew members, he explained, "It is where Earthly humans go to put fuel in their automobiles."

"Were you seen?" one concerned Newerssian asked.

"Negative. It was the middle of the night."

Avis jumped in to reassure the group. "We were in a very secluded area. The filling station was closed. Still, we took precautions and used our infrared scanners so we could be certain. No one was within twenty miles of this place."

"What about cameras?"

Avis assured them that they followed each of the mission's safety procedures. "We utilized an electromagnetic surge to disable the power grid for the surrounding area."

Armstrong was eager to show off the treasures he had collected. "If there are not any more questions… I helped myself to a case of beer, several bottles of orange soda, and three bags of potato chips. We have Original, Barbeque, and Sour Cream & Onion."

Several Nawerssians cheered. Each of them had watched dozens of hours' worth of television and movies from Earth. They had seen advertisements for beer, soda, and chips in the media they viewed, but had never tasted any food from the planet where their ancestors had once lived.

Slapping the Explorer on the back once again, Jagger directed McCoy to test the foods to make sure they were safe for consumption. "But don't cha take too much, ya hear? Armstrong 'n Avis were nice enough to go on the mission's first beer run. We wanna have plenty o' the good stuff so we can all enjoy more than one bite and a couple sips!"

☠☠☠

ABOARD THE VILNAGROM-I – THREE YEARS LATER
YEAR -35 + 162 DAYS (JUNE 11th)

Jagger paced around the launch tubes. He held a cylinder, approximately two feet in length. The General practice whipping the device out from a spot in which it was concealed inside the leg of his flight suit.

"What are you doing with that Stun Blaster?" Armstrong asked. The Explorer then took a few steps back when his counterpart twirled the weapon.

"Ah, 'tis nothin' to worry yer bald little head about. This blaster's not charged."

"Why is it not either in your quarters or in the armory?"

"Just wanted to feel what it be like ta hold a blaster. It's been a while. And since I'm itchin' ta make another trip down to Earth, I thought I'd work on me quick draw skills."

Armstrong did not like the sound of that. For one thing, they were on a tight time frame. The *Vilnagrom-I's* timeline dictated that they should be abducting their first humans for observation in the next few weeks.

Jagger waved off his concerns. "I may only have one good leg and—between you and me—only one good eye, but I be capable of gassin' and grabbin' a human every bit as much as ye. 'Tis simply a matter of pluckin' the right lamb from the flock. Takes more brains than physical ability."

"Are you thinking of pulling me from the first abduction? We should consult the Skipper if you are considering such..."

The General held his hand in the air and shook his head from side to side. "Don't cha worry. I ain't gonna steal yer glory. You'll be the man for the job when the time comes for the first abduction.

That bein' said, I *will* be doin' some of me own grabs down the road a bit."

His answer opened the door for Armstrong to raise his second concern. "The blaster? Mission protocols dictate that we are never to take them to the surface of O.E. The blasters contain technology that is far more advanced than any handheld weapons on the planet."

With a quick flick of his wrist, Jagger charged the blaster. He stared into Armstrong's eyes as the firearm hummed an implied threat. It was a supercharged weapon that held one or two shots, depending on the settings selected by its operator. One hit by a stun shot would find the target's body momentarily engulfed in an electronic field. Unless heavily armored, it would paralyze the victim for at least thirty minutes.

If set to stun, the blaster held two non-fatal shots. It took roughly half the energy to disable a foe than it did to issue a fatal shot. If the situation made it necessary, the blaster could be set to kill. It was up to the shooter to determine if he or she was better off with the opportunity to subdue two victims in rapid succession or to render a single target dead with one terrible blast.

Two disabling shots is the preferred setting, unless one absolutely must shoot to kill.

"Relax, Armstrong. I've got no plans to take this blaster to Earth… or ta use it to blow a hole in your blue backside, for that matter." He twisted the weapon once more and the humming stopped. "Besides, ye should know that I prefer knives over guns, blades ta lasers."

"Of course," he replied, trying to humor the General.

"The pirate in me likes the ol' fashioned kind o' steel."

☠☠☠

ABOARD THE VILNAGROM-I – TEN YEARS LATER
YEAR -25 + 17 DAYS (JANUARY 17th)

Magellan sat in the Captain's Chair on the Bridge. It was a seat he had occupied quite frequently since his spouse died in childbirth fifteen years earlier. Though the Skipper did his best to maintain the appearance, he was not doing much to control the ship.

For one thing, the *V-I* was not in motion. It was in a docked position, cloaked and floating around the Earth as the crew members studied the planet from an orbit almost 200,000 miles away.

More significantly, however, was the fact that Magellan had grown quite indecisive since Tey-Rixia's death. "I had to fly the ship. I had no choice," he once told McCoy in a counseling session. "I had to steer the *V-I* through the wormhole. I was keeping the ship from tearing apart. The entire time, I could hear the only woman I ever loved dying in agony."

Under official Project *Vilnagrom* protocols, the Skipper, the General, and the Explorer were to serve as the three Senior Officers aboard the spacecraft. If two disagreed, the third broke the tie. But Magellan's inability to act frustrated the crew on numerous occasions. As the philosophical differences between Jagger and Armstrong widened, the Skipper's breakdown was becoming more and more crippling to the crew.

"You cannot possibly think this is a good idea!" Like most of those from Na-Werss, Armstrong did not raise his voice often. When he did, it signaled that the topic was of great importance.

"Surprise, surprise! The ever-cautious Armstrong wants to take the safe approach!" Jagger mocked his rival. As time aboard the *V-I* passed, the General's ideas had become more and more extreme.

His plan to hijack a NASA space shuttle and abduct the entire crew of astronauts was met with significant resistance. Thus, it became the latest point of contention between the two officers. Given the potential consequences, things had reached a boiling point on this occasion.

"Do you realize what happens to this ship if we are discovered?" Armstrong continued. "The Americans, the Russians, the Chinese... Every nation on Earth would unite against one common enemy. Us! They would launch every nuclear warhead in their arsenals until we were totally obliterated. After that, they would watch the skies every night from now until the *V-II* showed up. Then they would destroy them too! What you are proposing would lead to total destruction of this mission... and possibly all of the people of Na-Werss when they come here years from now!"

Jagger fought back. He paced around the room, deliberately causing his metal leg to clank on the surface beneath him as a reminder of his past wartime heroics. "For a man who calls hisself an 'Explorer', ye don't have much of a sense of adventure. When I fought in the wars back home, I learned that ye don't succeed if ye not be willin' to take a risk from time to time. It's those unexpected risks that bring the biggest rewards."

"Maybe that is true in war. But we are *not* at war with O.E. We are simply observing them. On this ship we are scientists and archeologists far more than we are soldiers."

"Then why did the ol' Magistrate send a team of ten military men and women instead of professors and executives? Because Project *Vilnagrom* is a military endeavor, that's why!" Jagger whipped around and snarled at the third man in the room. "Ye've been awfully quiet, 'Gelly. Whose side are ye takin', Skipper?"

"Gentleman, you both make good points. Perhaps I should take some additional time to consider your arguments."

☠☠☠

ABOARD THE VILNAGROM-I – ONE DAY LATER
YEAR -25 + 18 DAYS (JANUARY 18th)

"Avis, ye may be buddy buddy with the Explorer, but I'm still the General on this ship. That means I outrank ye," Jagger glared at the Pilot. "Get in the shuttle. I'm not gonna ask ye again."

Already strapped in to a second shuttle and occupying the lead position in the launch tube, Navigator Valentina and Cartographer Crockett were ready to go. "The intercept point will be here soon. We need to launch immediately!" Valentina called out.

Avis glanced in the direction of approaching footsteps. Reinforcements had arrived. Armstrong and McCoy appeared. Adam, the oldest of the youths born on the ship after the *V-I* departed Na-Werss, followed in behind them.

Primed for a fight, Jagger looked past Avis and towards the one that he felt was causing dissention on the ship. "Are we gonna have us a good ol' fashion showdown, Armstrong, me lad?"

"There is no need... Jagger! Stop and consider what you want to do. Hijacking a NASA shuttle and abducting the crew? It is madness!"

McCoy yelled at her partner. "Crockett! Why are you doing this?"

He held up his hands in surrender. "I thought I was following orders." The Cartographer rose to a standing position and prepared to exit the shuttle.

"Don't ye go anywhere!" Jagger said, using a tone that made clear that it was a threat that was passing over his lips.

Valentina joined the argument. Turning to Armstrong, she said, "You may call it 'madness,' but there are those of us that believe there is no better way to study the technology of Earth than to observe the sharpest minds on the entire planet."

"It would jeopardize our mission! NASA is watching that shuttle every second it is out in space. Even with our ability to cloak the ship, their astronomers would discover us!" Avis protested.

Ignoring the Pilot, Valentina reminded Jagger, "We are going to miss the intercept point if we do not launch immediately!"

Keeping his cool, Jagger spoke into his personal communications link. "Control Center... Jagger here. Please issue the following alert: 'All crew members to the launch tubes immediately.' We've got some mutineers that need ta be dealt with."

Armstrong followed with request of his own. "Control, this is Armstrong. There is no mutiny. Manually override the launch tubes so..."

Jagger interjected, "Belay Armstrong's order! He's the coward leadin' the mutiny!"

☠☠☠

Lindy (aka *V-I* 6/PILOT) was positioned at the Communications Grid. "Skipper, General Jagger and Explorer Armstrong have given conflicting orders. What do you want me to do?"

The hollow figure in the Captain's Chair offered no response.

"Skipper? Magellan! What do you want me to do? Should I sound the alarm?"

Magellan sat motionless.

The woman at the Comm Grid took it upon herself to reply. "Armstrong... Jagger... Those are conflicting orders... Control is seeking further instruction."

Jagger voiced his anger over his comm link. "Bloody Hell!"

Lindy dropped her head. The situation was about to escalate to a point of no return. There was nothing she could do to stop it. She turned to Magellan once again and remarked, "A lack of action from the bridge can be every bit as dangerous as an incorrect response. What are your orders?"

Still, he said nothing.

☠☠☠

Young Adam had endured the indecisiveness of his father for years. It infuriated him. "Armstrong, tell my father that I will put a stop to this if he cannot!" Then the first Nawerssian born aboard the *Vilnagrom-I* rushed towards the General.

Jagger quickly assessed the situation. He abandoned the idea of hijacking the NASA shuttle. His focus shifted to survival. As he would later confess, his plan was to kill those that opposed him in at the launch tubes, steal a shuttle, and try to find some place on Earth where he could live out his days in seclusion.

The General pulled out a pair of daggers that were tucked away in his flight suit. He had intended to use those to aid in the abduction of the NASA crew. He ended up using them to strike down Adam.

Jagger took the dagger in his left hand and plunged it deep into Adam's side. An instant later, he jammed the second blade into the young man's eye.

In a moment of panic, Valentina mashed a sequence of buttons on her shuttle's dashboard. The first caused the rapid closure of its doors, bringing its overhead metal cover zooming above her and enclosing her inside.

Because Crockett had been standing in his seat, he was not fully inside the vehicle when the shuttle cover reached him. The razor-sharp metal guillotined into his stomach, nearly slicing the blue humanoid in half.

McCoy ran towards her maimed partner. She pulled him out of the shuttle, then held him close. Though she tried to reassure him, the physician knew that there would be nothing she could do to save him.

The second in the sequence of buttons that Valentina pressed into the dashboard of her shuttle resulted in the immediate launch of the rocket. There was no countdown. No warning. Just a fiery burst followed by a bang and the silver missile being propelled into space.

White hot flames shot out. They consumed McCoy and Crockett, killing them instantly.

Jagger extracted the bloody dagger from his first victim. He snarled and focused his attention on Armstrong. Jagger's attack ended, however, when Avis struck him down with a shot from a Stun Blaster.

With electricity pulsing through his body (enhanced due to an extra powerful surge along his metal leg), Jagger jolted and shook before he dropped. As he fell, his head smacked against a metal beam. Blood gushed onto the floor, mixing with that which had been spilled from Adam's fallen body.

The Pilot looked at the fallen General. "He will be alright." Then he apologized to Armstrong. "I am truly sorry."

This confused the Explorer. *How could Avis possibly blame himself for this tragedy?* "You could not have gone with them to hijack the space shuttle. The result would have been disastrous."

"No..." Avis shook his head. "I am apologizing because I should have set the blaster to 'Kill.'"

☠☠☠

ABOARD THE VILNAGROM-I – TWO HOURS LATER
YEAR -25 + 18 DAYS (JANUARY 18th)

"What? You're in charge now?" Jagger's words came out as a growl. A saturated bandage was plastered against the side of the deposed general's bulbous head. His good eye was swollen completely shut as a result of his fall. "If it weren't for these restraints, I'd still choke the life outta ya!"

Armstrong offered a cold stare into the cell that now housed Jagger and Valentina. "Drop the act, General. You are not a pirate."

"*Armstrong?* Looks like the joke's on me. I shoulda never given ye that name. Turns out ye be more cowboy than explorer. I shoulda called ye 'John Wayne.' How's that sound, *pardner?*"

The Explorer did his best to keep his cool. The death of the youthful Adam was enough to enrage him. The deaths of Crockett and McCoy were even more upsetting. Because of Jagger's impulsive act, their two tiny children—Greta and Monroe—had been orphaned. "You are in no position to be hurling insults."

"Are ye gonna execute us? Do ye have it deep down in yer innards ta do so?"

Armstrong turned his head, momentarily calculating the risks of marching Jagger down the corridor and blasting his body out the launch tube and condemning his rival to a near instantaneous death. *The mere thought of seeing Jagger hurtling into the blackness of space was momentarily intoxicating... and that option would help guarantee the survival of the Project Vilnagrom.*

"No. No one is getting executed today. Enough of our people have died already. They died because of the two of you." He looked directly at Jagger as he clarified his statement, "It was your ambition," then he turned to Valentina and looked directly at her, "and your inability to think for yourself. You were willing to follow a man mad with power without ever stopping to consider that his ridiculous plan could destroy the entire mission."

"Ye think you've got it all figured out, but ye can't even decide what yer gonna do with us."

"Once again you are wrong." Armstrong did not hesitate. "The two of you will be held until we, as a crew, determine the proper response to your actions."

"I did nothin' but defend myself and my ship against a mutiny. Aye, you were successful. But ye still be a mutineer."

Valentina took a less aggressive stance. After flying away, she returned to the *V-I* voluntarily. The Navigator hoped her peaceful surrender would merit some consideration. "I was only siding with the General because... because he was the General. Please do not send me out through the launch tubes."

Armstrong tilted his head at a slight downward angle and shut his eyes for a moment. Then he raised his head and looked directly at the prisoners. "As I said, no one will be executed today." After a long pause, he added, "I intend to recommend that we hold you in the brig until the *Vilnagrom-II* arrives. Then the duties belonging to this crew and this ship will be complete."

"That's another five years!" Jagger protested. "That's a long time!"

The Explorer kept his cool. Ignoring the interruption, he continued. "When the *V-II* arrives, those of us that remain able will join their crew. We will take what materials we need from this ship. And then we will set the *V-I* on a collision course with a nearby star. Those in the brig will die upon impact."

Valentina no longer felt the need to conceal her disdain for Armstrong. "If that is our fate, execute us now, you coward!"

Jagger held his hand out, signaling that his cellmate should cool down. "Don't give the mutineer the pleasure of seein' ye get angry." He pivoted and struggled to glare at his captor through his one good eye. "Yer makin' a big mistake, John Wayne. One day the tables 'ill be turned... Ye can bet I'm gonna get ye before I die!"

<u>*VILNAGROM-I*</u>

CREW MEMBERS (AFTER 15 YEARS ORBITING EARTH)

ROLE	CODENAME
V-I 1/GENERAL	JAGGER (in the brig)
V-I 2/SKIPPER	MAGELLAN
V-I 3/EXPLORER	ARMSTRONG
V-I 5/NAVIGATOR	*VALENTINA* (in the brig)
V-I 6/PILOT	*LINDY*
V-I 7/PILOT	AVIS
V-I 8/PHYSICAL SCIENCE	MANTLE
V-I 12/UNASSIGNED	MONTANA (child of Mantle & Lindy)
V-I 13/UNASSIGNED	GRETA (child of Crockett & McCoy)
V-I 14/UNASSIGNED	MONROE (child of Crockett & McCoy)

<u>DECEASED:</u>

V-I 4/CARTOGRAPHER	CROCKETT
V-I 9/BIOLOGICAL SCIENCE	*TEY-RIXIA*
V-I 10/DOCTOR	*McCOY*
V-I 11/UNASSIGNED	ADAM (child of Magellan & Tey-Rixia)

15: HEEL TURN

"Wooooo! Do I feel good! It was one of the greatest moments of my life when I nailed Sir Lancelot with my 'Sorry Charlie' Superkick... Lance, I should've dumped you as a tag team partner a long time ago. Expect more of the same tonight, brother. Another Superkick for you, and another win for Prince Charles. Woooooo!!!"

-PRINCE CHARLES (age fourteen)
promo prior to Backyard Mania 5.

PRESENT DAY
YEAR 0 + 227 DAYS (AUGUST 15th)

The march to Memphis continued. Fatigue was setting in on Grayson's fortysomething body.

"Pick up the pace, lawman," Cocoa chided him while playfully smacking him on his back. She was feeling great. The aches and pains that had been part of her day-to-day life had not manifested themselves since The Vanishing.

"I'm doing my best," Grayson panted. "It's just that I'm carrying at least seventy-five pounds and ten more years of wear and tear on my body than any of you."

Cocoa was quick to dispute his point. "I'll give you the weight. But try almost twenty years in the wrestling business. All the bumps and surgeries that came along with that career choice..." She shook her head. "I've got you licked on wear 'n tear."

"Maybe I've got a little less pep in my step because there's nothing waiting for me in Memphis. That's *your* hometown. Remember?"

Cocoa returned fire. "Did you have something special happenin' that made you wanna stay in St. Louis? Because I sure didn't hear you say anything about it at the time. You seemed every bit as eager to get outta town as the rest of us."

Tavia jumped in before the travel conversation got any more contentious. "I love Memphis," she told the group. "I was actually thinking of moving there after graduation."

"As a lifelong resident, I'd recommend you reconsider," said Cocoa.

"My brother took me down there a couple weeks before I started my freshman year of college." The happy memory caused her to glow. "We called it the Four Kings of Memphis tour. First,

we went to Graceland. That's where Elvis lived. He's the King of
Rock 'n Roll. That night we went to B.B. King's Blues Bar,
listened to amazing music and got super drunk..."

"Wait. How old were you?" Grayson asked.

"Eighteen. I turn nineteen in a week or two. Maybe three. With
all that's been happening, I've lost track of what day it is," she
replied. "But relax. I had a fake ID."

Cocoa motioned for Grayson to stop interrupting. "Back off,
old man! I'm willing to bet Memphis is out of your jurisdiction."

The entire group was interested in her story. With no realistic
prospects of vacations on the horizon, any future travel adventures
most likely would come vicariously through the stories of the
others. "That's two kings. Who are the other two?" Brady asked.

"Number three was Martin Luther King. Doctor King was
assassinated in Memphis..."

"Not my town's brightest moment," Cocoa interjected.

"Memphis has—or 'had,' I suppose I should say—an amazing
civil rights museum. Right there at the same place where he got
shot. I'm a privileged white girl from a rich suburb. I got a brand
new car the day I turned sixteen, and had my entire tuition paid for
me to go to some generic college in boring old Illinois... But going
to that museum really opened my eyes. It helped me understand
how important Martin Luther King was. And I think it is absolutely
amazing that they took a place where such a terrible thing
happened, and they made it into something that would have a
positive impact on so many people."

There was a long pause as the walkers let the wisdom of the
18-year-old waitress sink in.

Finally, Brady asked, "Who is the fourth king?"

Tavia's smile returned. "Wrestling legend Jerry 'The King'
Lawler. He had a restaurant right on Beale Street. Live music.

Amazing barbeque. Videos of old school wrestling playing on every TV. If I'm being honest, I'd say that going there was probably the highlight of the vacation. We got really drunk for the second night in a row. It was a great end to a great weekend."

☠☠☠

As they continued their trek towards Memphis, Grayson made conversation by comparing their current plight to that of the characters in a classic television program. "Any of you ever watch *The Twilight Zone*?"

Cocoa and Brady had. Jenn wasn't sure.

Tavia said she knew of the show, but added, "I never had any desire to watch a show that wasn't filmed in color."

Her comment led to a lengthy tangential debate over the quality of television classics like *Leave it to Beaver, The Lone Ranger*, and *I Love Lucy.*

"Anyway...!" Grayson elevated the volume of his voice so he could redirect the conversation back to his originally intended topic. "There's this classic episode of *The Twilight Zone* called 'Five Characters in Search of an Exit.' The story is about a military man, a clown, a ballerina, and a couple other people who are trapped in this big, tall cylinder. They don't know where they are or why they are there in the first place."

Jenn was curious where the boob tube-loving cop was going with this story.

Grayson continued. "The way I see it, the cast of that show seems a lot like us. Instead of the military man, we got me. A police officer. And instead of the clown, we've got a pirate. Long Jenn Silva..."

"You think I'm a clown?"

"Not at all," he quickly replied, instantly regretting wording his comparison as he did. "I can be the clown and you can be the military man if you prefer. That's not my point. What I'm trying to say is this... they were five characters in search of a way to get out of that tall cylinder. We are five characters: a cop, a pirate, an athlete with a made-for-TV smile, an executive who looks like a million bucks, and a drop dead gorgeous sorority girl..."

Now Tavia was the one taking offense. "What makes you think that I was in a sorority?"

Jenn didn't understand why Tavia was so upset. "At least he said you were gorgeous."

Grayson shrugged. But then he had to know if his quick assessment of the young college student had been correct. "Are you... in a sorority, that is?"

Tavia shook her head. "No. My parents weren't going to pay my tuition if I couldn't maintain at least a 'B' average. I had a roommate who rushed Zeta Tau Alpha, but it seemed like too much of a time commitment to me. I chose to focus on getting good grades and working as many hours as I could at The End Zone."

"Sorry. I guess you just have that 'sorority girl look.'"

"You shouldn't judge a book by its cover. There are lots of things about me that none of you know. I'm willing to bet some of those things would come as quite a surprise. I know you guys look at me and think I'm some spoiled, helpless blond. Sorry to burst your bubble, but I think you'll find me quite capable."

Grayson nodded his head in agreement. Then he got quiet. There was no need to continue analyzing the television classic if doing so was going to bring offense to the other members of the group.

☠☠☠

SEVEN YEARS EARLIER
YEAR -7 + 151 DAYS (MAY 31st)

"Careful, Tavia! You're gonna break dad's camera!" Charlie Patton (aka "Prince Charles") scolded his kid sister.

Tavia was younger than her brother by two and a half years. She idolized him. He was a wrestling fanatic. So that made her a wrestling fanatic, too. Together the Patton kids watched all the television programs, and saved allowance money to buy posters and magazines and T-shirts depicting their favorite grapplers. They even created their own backyard wrestling organization in their suburban neighborhood.

Charlie ignored the scoffs. He never hesitated to tell his elders that he wanted to be a megastar when he grew up. It had been his dream for as long as Tavia could remember. And until that day came when he stepped into the squared circle as a professional, he intended to bide his time putting on amateur shows in his back yard.

His best friend Lance (aka "Sir Lancelot") was the neighborhood kid with the second most natural talent. It was a no-brainer that they would make up the top tag team in the "Patton Wrestling Entertainment Universe."

"Things are getting a little stale in the PWE," Charlie told his pals as they mapped out the plan for Backyard Mania 4. "Things are getting a little predictable."

"You could add a women's match," blurted out twelve-year-old Tavia. Deep down inside she knew that most of these boys were annoyed by her participation. She didn't care that they weren't all that interested in the input of Charlie's pest of a little sister. How would she earn her spot on the card if she didn't assert herself? "I could fight my friend Liz."

"Women's match?" Lance said laughing. "Don't you have to stop sleeping with a teddy bear and playing with Barbies before you can call yourself a woman?"

The other boys laughed. Charlie gave his buddy a high five.

Tavia was undaunted. "Women's match. Divas match. Whatever you want to call it. Liz and I would be better than most of you. Most of you look like a bunch of chumps out there!"

It may have been true. Charlie was never going to admit it in front of his friends, though. He shut down the idea as quickly as it had sprouted. "No divas match! Period! Parker's mom is super religious! She would throw a fit if she found out there were girls wrestling here! She probably wouldn't even let him come over. Besides, I know exactly what it is that we need to spice things up... We need a heel turn."

"A what?" Parker asked between oversized bites of an oatmeal cream pie.

Tavia wanted to prove her value to the group. She still held out hopes that she could get assigned a task other than operating the camera. "A heel turn is when a good guy turns on his partner and suddenly becomes a bad guy. A 'heel' is a wrestling term for bad guy. Charlie wants to turn on Lance because they're the two best wrestlers in the neighborhood. Your matches would be more entertaining if Charlie and Lance actually wrestled *against* each other, instead of on the same team."

Charlie nodded his head in agreement. "The kid knows her stuff. Maybe she should be our announcer."

Announcer. That was a step in the right direction. She loved her big brother!

☠☠☠

ONE YEAR AGO
YEAR -1 + 181 DAYS (JUNE 30th)

When indie promotions like Fireball Freeman's All-World
Wrestling Association stopped in a town, they often invited aspiring
wrestlers to try out as Local Enhancement Talent. If they passed the
eyeball test, they'd get to show off their skills in an empty ring. One
or two might be selected to perform on that night's show.

"This should go without saying, but... if you get picked, you're
not gonna win. That should be clear as mud. If you get picked,
you're gonna get squashed. That's what jobbers do," Fireball
explained to a collection of hopefuls who were lined up in the ring.
"You'd let our star toss you around and get over at your expense.
It's a chance to get a foot in the door. It might be your first step at
being offered a contract to wrestle with the AWWA."

The six aspiring wrestlers included a pair of self-proclaimed
aerial specialists. They came dressed in matching Speedos. Neither
one tipped the scales past 150 pounds. Fireball looked down at his
clipboard and greeted the duo. "Mr. Winningham and... Mr.
Winningham? Brothers I take it?"

"Cousins."

He shook his head. They didn't pass the eyeball test that the
wrestling legend had warned them about. "Sorry, Winningham
cousins, but it's a 'no.' You just don't have enough meat on your
bones."

"We're high-flyers," the first Winningham protested. "We've
got drop kicks and moves off the ropes that you wouldn't believe."

"That may be," Fireball replied, somewhat irritated by the
backtalk. *It reeked of desperation.* "But if you come into the ring
looking like you'd struggle to carry a bag of groceries into the

house, no one's gonna believe you're a formidable opponent for
Hal Hitchcock or Santa Saws... It's a 'no.' Sorry, boys."

Next in line was an extremely tall man with a bushy beard. His
outfit consisted of a pair of dirty overalls. He wore no shirt
underneath, and no shoes on his feet. Fireball looked down at his
clipboard even though he was familiar with this prospective jobber.
"Welcome back, Mr. Brunansky. Goin' for the classic hillbilly look
this time around... Stick around, but get some boots on. I think the
'barefoot hillbilly' is a little over the top."

Fireball started to move down the line, but then doubled back.
"And you can't use the name 'Bruno.' Sounds like you're a
mobster, not a pig farmer. Think of somethin' a little more 'country
boy,' if you get my meaning."

The next two aspiring wrestlers were the only two women in
the bunch. Fireball quickly rejected the one dressed in a Harley
Quinn Halloween costume. "Been there. Done that. Next."

He came to Tavia! She wore a pair of leggings and matching
sports bra, both black covered with a pattern of skulls that were
emerging from white, red, and purple flowers. Fireball looked down
at his clipboard. He looked back up at Tavia, studying how
perfectly her athletic, yet curvy, body filled her outfit. Then he
looked back down at the clipboard again.

"Drove four hours to get here, huh?"

"Something like that. I slept much of the way while my brother
did the driving," the young, blond wrestling enthusiast admitted.

"Trained under Boris Sputnikov?"

"Both me and my brother," she replied, again reminding the
wrestling legend that she hadn't come to the tryout alone. "We
work out and run through drills at his gym in St. Louis three or four
nights a week."

"Boris was pretty much a cartoon character when he went to the IWO. But back when he wrestled up in Calgary and then down in New Orleans, that man was one of the meanest mofos you ever saw... I'm sorry, Tavia Patton. Please... *PLEASE*... come back in a few months. Our insurance absolutely, positively will not let us use wrestlers under the age of eighteen," he informed her. "You've trained under Boris and I love your look. I just can't use you tonight because of your age."

Despite the encouraging words, Tavia had to fight back the urge to cry. She had hoped that this would be the night she and Charlie launched into careers within the wrestling universe. She managed to keep from tearing up. Instead, she focused her attention on her brother. After all, he was the main reason they'd driven down to Memphis for this tryout. This was his night to shine. Her opportunity would have to wait for a few months.

Finally, the wrestling promoter looked towards Charlie. Gone was the "Prince Charles" moniker and the King Arthur-esque attire. Now he went by the name "Patton Charles" and dressed in his college singlet. The outfit was complimented by wrestling headgear and a Central Illinois University letterman's jacket. "Goin' for the collegiate star goes pro gimmick?" Fireball observed. "I can work with that. Why don't you and Hillbilly..."

"Cousin Bubba!" Brunansky announced his new persona by yelling across the gym.

Fireball winced. "I'm not sure about that name, but we'll see." Turning his attention back to Charlie, he said, "You two show me what you can do in the ring. If I like what I see, there may be a slot for you in tonight's show."

Tavia squealed with excitement and wrapped her arms around the neck of her brother. "This is awesome! You're going to do amazing! Your dream's coming true!"

☠☠☠

SIX HOURS LATER

Charlie (aka "Patton Charles") sat alone in the men's locker room. Attempting to distract himself while he waited on the legendary wrestler and booker to give him the verdict, Charlie put his gear in a bag. He took it out again, verified that he hadn't misplaced anything, then shoved the equipment inside once more. He repeated this exercise a handful of times before Tavia approached.

"Great match tonight, Brother."

Charlie tried to discourage the compliments. "Ah, it was a squash match. Pinned by The Great Kayzo in under three minutes."

"Yeah, but how many people even get the chance to wrestle someone like The Great Kayzo? Besides, you got off a couple of big moves. That gut wrench suplex got a big pop from the crowd. And even *I* thought you knocked Kayzo's teeth out when you hit him with that flying forearm!"

"It *was* pretty awesome, wasn't it!" her brother said, suddenly unable to hide his excitement. He followed this up with a nervous sigh. Fireball Freeman had asked Charlie to wait in the locker room while he discussed the issue of an AWWA call back with his team. "Now we wait to see if I did good enough to go on the road... one match at a time, training with the best and workin' my way up the card. That's the dream."

Tavia was unable to control her need for answers. *Was this the night that her brother was going to finally be rewarded for years of hard work in Boris Sputnikov's dark and smelly gym?* Feeling the need to quench her curiosity, the teenager wandered down the hallway trying to locate Fireball in time to make an argument on Charlie's behalf.

☠☠☠

"I liked the Patton kid," Fireball told Cocoa as the two sat in the women's locker room discussing whether they were going to hire Charlie or Cousin Bubba. Then again, hiring *both* hopefuls or *neither one* were other available options on the table.

Cocoa wasn't convinced that Patton Charles was all that impressive. "You mean the kid from Central Idaho State?"

"It was Central Illinois University."

That made little difference to Fireball's daughter. "Same difference. Not exactly a big-time college program, am I right?"

"Fine. We can tweak the gimmick. Make him from a bigger school. I'm sure we can look online and find him a letter jacket from Michigan or Syracuse or Oklahoma," Fireball mentioned these specific Division I schools as a reference to the members of the Varsity Club, a classic tag team from the 1980s. "The school can change. But I like the idea of a successful college star trying to make it in pro wrestling."

"He just seems like another scrawny white boy to me. I like Bruno—er, Cousin Bubba—better," Cocoa argued. "He's big. Actually, he's huge."

"Yeah, but that hillbilly gimmick. That was a tired act..."

Fireball got distracted as Jenn walked by. Soaking wet and wrapped in a towel, she was coming out of the shower. The wrestling legend paused to compliment her. "Nice match tonight, Silva. There's no denying that you've got great in-ring skills. The fans dig your look..." He hesitated for a moment, as if he was contemplating the appropriateness of his next remark. "I, myself, am a fan of *everything* you bring to the table. The total package, so to speak."

Cocoa was a little grossed out that her dad was being such a pervert. Sadly, that was the culture that permeated the industry, particularly years ago when wrestling was dominated by musclebound macho men who assumed that they were God's gift to all of womankind.

Cocoa snapped her fingers in her father's direction. "You were saying?"

Picking up right where he left off, Fireball's analysis continued. "The hillbilly gimmick doesn't do it for me. It didn't do it for me twenty, twenty-five years ago. It sure doesn't work now."

"But like you said..." Cocoa enjoyed playing booker. She secretly hoped she would hold that job in the future. It could keep her making money in the business for a long, long time. "We can tweak the gimmick. Remember when Bruno tried to pitch the mobster character with slicked back hair and a thick New York accent?"

"Yeah. That sucked too."

"Hear me out. What if we took his mobster character and dressed him up as a hillbilly?"

Cocoa's suggestion caught her father off guard. "Come again?"

"Have him lose the beard, lose the cowboy boots, lose the country boy accent. Instead, he's a New Yorker on the run from the mob. He puts on a pair of overalls as a disguise. Then he comes to the farm to lay low. He's still got that New York accent, the ridiculous amount of gold chains, and the fancy Italian shoes. But he tries to hide the fact that he's a New York gangster by dressing like a hillbilly... Now that's a great character that wrestling fans are going to love. Kinda like 'My Cousin Vinny' in the ring. I think Bruno could do it. We'll call him 'Bubba Brunocelli' and give him a legit push."

Fireball nodded his head as he chewed on Cocoa's suggestion. Then he looked over his shoulder. "Let's ask the new girl. You break the tie, Long Jenn Silva. Do you like Patton Charles the Collegiate Champ? Or do you prefer Bubba Brunocelli, the mobster who hides out on the farm?"

Jenn stood there for a moment. She hadn't exactly heard the entire conversation. She had been more concerned with whether or not she should just drop her towel and hurriedly change in front of Fireball or if she should wait him out. From the part of the conversation she managed to hear, she agreed with Cocoa. Bubba Brunocelli sounded like a persona that had a world of potential.

"No offense, Fireball, but I agree with your daughter."

The wrestling pioneer smiled. Pressing his hands down beside each knee, he pushed against the bench to help him rise to a standing position. "I'll go break the news to the boys. Bruno's going on the road with us..."

"If he'll shave the beard," Cocoa interjected.

Fireball nodded once again. "Yes. If he'll shave the beard... And I'll tell Charles that it's a 'no' for now."

Tavia bit down on her lip. Hard. She had been eavesdropping from just outside the locker room. She couldn't see them, but she heard everything that was being said. Unfortunately, the conversation had not gone the way she had hoped.

"Oh, hey... Tavia," Fireball said as he exited the women's locker room and almost trampled the teenager. "I hope you enjoyed tonight's show. Your brother did a fine job. I hope you'll both come back in a few months and try out after you've turned eighteen."

The only response she could muster was a quick "yeah." Her brother was going to be devastated. Fireball would have signed him. But Cocoa Freeman and Long Jenn Silva voted him down.

Cocoa Freeman and Long Jenn Silva.

☠☠☠

PRESENT DAY – ABOARD THE VILNAGROM-II
YEAR 0 + 284 DAYS (OCTOBER 10th)

Polo walked with a purpose as he advanced down Corridor 16. His recent trials implementing highly advanced external stimuli had been a success. The *V-II* Cartographer's request to move forward with even more aggressive testing was approved by his superiors. The manipulation of the newest batch of test subjects was about to get a lot more intense.

Of course, it was all being done in the name of science. The objective remained to prepare his people to return "home" once Earth's current residents were no longer in the way. ("It should yield some fantastic results on how our subjects react to rapid, unexpected changes to their surroundings," he had told the Senior Officers.)

The Nawerssian approached the massive tank. He gazed longingly at the five figures that floated in that murky, purple liquid. He appreciated them... much like a family might appreciate the delicious spread of food set on the table for Thanksgiving Dinner.

Polo stepped back and prepared to enter a complex sequence into the computer. Then fate intervened.

It was at this moment that a meteor struck the space craft. With the *Vilnagrom's* artificial gravity surviving the impact, the collision created a violent jolt the sent the blue-skinned Cartographer to the floor. He looked up and noticed a massive crack in the life suspension tank. The breach in the glass traveled from floor to ceiling.

Lights flashed. Alarms sounded.

"Alert! We have a potential..." Polo's warning was cut off as he was engulfed by a crushing wave of slimy liquid.

Many of the wires used to record the psychological and physiological effects of the VR experiments snapped. One by one, Grayson, Brady, Cocoa, Jenn, and Tavia road the wave of violet ooze out of the tank and onto the floor. They flopped like trout being dumped from a bucket onto the bottom of a fishing boat.

"What the hell?" someone blurted out.

Polo attempted to warn his fellow crew members about the breach. In doing so, he called attention to himself.

Grayson wobbled and slipped, eventually making it to his feet. He was covered in purple goo and smelled like piss. But his adrenaline was cutting through the sedation the Nawerssian doctors had administered. And there was no mistaking what stood before him.

"A friggin' alien!"

It took no time at all for the abducted police officer to close the gap between him and a trembling Polo. With Grayson's fists balled up, he pounded the "alien" with punch after punch to the head.

The first impact landed just above Polo's left eye. The next was a left cross that caught him on the side of the head. With his foe now on the ground, he continued to pound away with blow after blow. He would not relent. Grayson had no intention of stopping until he was completely confident that this unknown combatant would be unable to strike like a viper if given an opportunity.

Tavia was the second of the five to make it to her feet. "Grayson! Stop!" she screamed.

Ignoring her demand, the cop remained intent on beating this freak well past the point of submission. With a knee on Polo's chest, Grayson continued punching. Right, left. Right. Looking to deliver the knockout blow, he switched strategies and repeatedly

struck the spaceman with his dominant hand. Reaching back,
Grayson pounded him with right after right.

The barrage ended suddenly.

Grayson's red blood joined Polo's to discolor the puddles of
purple ooze that had collected on the floor. Tavia stood over him.
She had driven a large shard of glass deep into the back of the
police officer.

She yanked the shard of glass out of Grayson's back. She held
it like a sword as she inched her way into the corner of the room.

Jenn made it to one knee. She analyzed her surroundings. She
and her friends were knee deep in neon purple slime. That slime
was beginning to harden against her nearly naked body. Wires had
been attached to her. Some had snapped in two, but others
continued to dangle from her chest, back, or forehead. And since it
felt like she may have been drugged, she decided that it might be a
potentially fatal move to attempt to disarm the angry college girl...
especially now that her previous boast had rung true. With one bold
move, Tavia Patton had proven herelf quite capable.

Cocoa laid face down in the ooze. She had felt no pain in days.
Now spasms shot through her back like lightning, practically
paralyzing her. She cursed as she spat out a mouthful of the murky
liquid and struggled to push herself up into a seated position.

Brady rotated into a crouch. As he slowly rose to stand, he held
his hands out as a sign that he didn't want to be the next person
fileted by Tavia and her jagged weapon. Trying not to look directly
at her in her state of partial undress, Brady called out, "Tavia...
what's going on? Where in the world are we?"

"Not exactly *on the world*, actually," she responded, refusing to
abandon her defensive position.

Jenn jumped in. "What does that mean?"

At that moment, the lights stopped pulsating and the alarm was no longer blaring. The image of a bald and blue-faced figure wearing dark glasses appeared on the room's telecommunication monitor. Speaking with no obvious accent, this figure announced, "This is Navigator Baron. A large meteor has struck the vessel. Most systems are now secure... An integrity alert has been detected in your compartment. Cartographer Polo, please report."

Badly beaten and pinned beneath Grayson's lifeless body, Polo called out, "I cannot stand."

Baron turned and looked over his shoulder. Another blue figure stepped into view on the monitor. "This is General Hannibal. Tavia Patton, please assist Polo in getting to his feet... Subjects Silva, Emerson, and Freeman, do not make any efforts to stop her. We will gas the entire room if any threats emerge. Please do not take any measures which will require us to respond with such action."

The waitress-turned-killer leaned her weapon against the door, then rolled Grayson over and off Polo.

Jenn spoke for the group. "Tavia, what exactly is happening?"

Hannibal gave his next order once Tavia had helped the Nawerssian stand. "Tavia Patton, the door will open for you in a moment. Please assist the Cartographer down the corridor... Subjects Silva, Emerson, and Freeman, you are directed to stand by. Each of you will be escorted to a debriefing room so we can thoroughly explain your current circumstance. In the meantime, do not make any aggressive moves and do not try to impede Miss Patton from exiting the room."

This time with more urgency in her voice, Jenn asked the question again. "Tavia, what's going on?"

16: THE PLANT

"I feel sorry for you, Lance. I keep beating you. But since you can't figure out when enough is enough, I'll accept your challenge to fight next week at Hardcore Mania VI... And to give you a fighting chance, you can have any tag team partner you want. Heck, I'll even let you pick __MY__ tag team partner. Woooooo!!!"

-PATTON CHARLES (age eighteen) promo prior to Hardcore Mania VI.

PRESENT DAY – ABOARD THE VILNAGROM-II
YEAR 0 + 284 DAYS (OCTOBER 10th)

A thirty-second blast of water was all Jenn was given. It was sufficient to remove the purple goo that had pasted against her body and caked in her hair. As instructed, she slipped into a new set of the skin-tight black undergarments and wrapped herself in a shiny silver robe that was not nearly as comfy as it looked.

The door slid open. A tall blue figure walked in and introduced himself. "My name is Armstrong. I understand you have a myriad of questions. If you would please come with me, I will do my best to answer as many as I can in the time we have."

He escorted her down the corridor to a room that resembled an office. Armstrong sat in a chair on one side of a table and motioned for Jenn to sit across from him.

"Listen here, scumbag...!" the luchadora began, refusing to sit. She balled up her hands into fists. Grayson managed to beat the crap out of one of these things. She was ready to see if she could do the same to this blue freak.

Armstrong casually shook his head from side to side. "Please... Remember, they are always watching on the other end of that monitor. I acknowledge that you are a strong woman, Miss Silva. I acknowledge that you possess the physical strength to overpower me. If that happened, other members of my crew would gas you and plug you back into another virtual reality chamber without you ever getting the chance to learn any answers. Who does that benefit?" He paused. Seeing that she didn't have an answer at the ready, he continued. "Sit. If you listen to what I have to say, I believe you will discover that we share some common interests... even though our physical appearances admittedly are quite different."

To further entice her, Armstrong slid a can of ice cold root beer across the table.

"I'm guessing you're the 'good cop.' Is that it?"

Ignoring Jenn's attempt to bait him, Armstrong continued, "From my personal stash. I empty a soda machine every time I visit Earth. That has become a rather frequent occurrence lately. My most recent visit was August 9th."

Jenn was doing her best to keep her anger and her confusion at bay. She needed to maintain a level head. Upon hearing the date of Armstrong's last visit, it took her little time to connect the dots. "The day of The Vanishing."

"What seemed like a 'Vanishing' to you," Armstrong said as he watched the young woman study the can of root beer. "Please, drink it. It will taste better than anything you have consumed in the last few weeks. Trust me, the drink has not been poisoned."

She glared at him. If poison was the way she was going to die, so be it. It sounded preferable to being poked and probed on a flying saucer. And it sure beat being carted off to some alien planet to be fattened up and eventually eaten.

She pressed down on the top of the can to open it. Still somewhat uncertain, she pulled the soda to her mouth and began to sip it. Once she got a taste of the sweet beverage, she was convinced. Her slurping turned to guzzling. "This *is* good!"

Armstrong continued. "As I was saying... To you, the event seemed like a 'Vanishing' of everyone on Earth. In actuality, it was quite the opposite. The only people who disappeared on that day were you, Cocoa Freeman, Brady Emerson, and Arnold Grayson. Four passengers in an otherwise empty commuter train."

"And Tavia Patton?" Jenn interrupted, her words being as much a question as a statement.

"No. She came to our ship some time earlier."

☠☠☠

NINE MONTHS EARLIER
YEAR 0 + 1 DAY (JANUARY 1st)

Tavia's face was bruised and bloodied as she laid on the side of a rural road. Her End Zone T-shirt had been ripped away, leaving her with only a soaked, mud-covered bra on top.

Snow began to accumulate in the few hours since she had been grabbed and taken from the restaurant's parking lot. The temperature was dropping. She needed to get help. The icy weather made the situation even more urgent. She had been beaten badly. Standing was out of the question. Her eyes fluttered as she tried to focus. Tavia didn't even think she could cry for help.

She was having difficulty keeping her eyes from rolling back in her head when she was hit with a blinding light. "Is that a car?" the young woman wondered aloud, her voice quivering.

She tapped into all her strength to open her eyes and raise one arm straight up in the air. It was at this point that she discovered that the bright light wasn't coming from a vehicle on the road.

It was coming from a mysterious craft hovering above her in the night sky.

☠☠☠

They wore surgical masks. Sets of red and yellow eyes peered down. The young woman lay on the operating table. Polo assisted, as Medical Officer Dorothea and Science Officer Carver took the lead in the efforts to save their newest arrival.

Speaking with a degree of urgency in her tone, Dorothea assessed the situation. "The subject was nearly frozen to death by the time they located her. It is obvious that she was the victim of severe trauma unrelated to the abduction..." As the frustrated doctor struggled to keep the patient from dying on the operating table, she added, "We would have been better off taking an alternative subject. With the injuries this young adult female has sustained, we are forced to work with many unknown variables. I am not sure we are equipped to do so... We may need to call for help."

The doctors on the *Vilnagrom-II* continued to work to stabilize their patient. As they did so, the highest-ranking officers on the ship debated whether they should cease the recovery efforts and dispose of their newest arrival.

Because of the condition she was in prior to abduction, the Nawerssians underestimated how much anesthetic needed to be administered. The substances they had pumped into Tavia's system were wearing off more quickly than originally anticipated.

Dorothea barked out her instructions. When they were met with hesitation, she snapped. "We are in unknown territory here! Polo, we need to prepare for the worst!"

"What, may I ask, do you consider 'the worst' possible scenario?" the tall, thin Nawerssian asked.

(Those involved in the medical procedure previously had removed their communication links before stepping into the room. The devices could interfere with their instruments and confound their efforts to treat their patient. Because of this fact, Polo would be required to exit the operating room to make his call for help.)

The young woman on the table began to twitch. Her arm lashed upward. "Stop wasting time!" Dorothea yelled. "Go! Get help! We need help in here now!"

Each and every time before, studying Earthly humans followed a specific process and a certain order: Abduction. Sedation. Testing and experimentation. Euthanasia. Disposal.

It was a cruel practice, but one designed to ensure that the abducted could not somehow rise up and revolt. Even a couple of loose humans could—in theory—kill crew members, sabotage the ship, and completely wreck all that those associated with Project *Vilnagrom* had been working towards. The scientists were unsure if their small crew was adequately prepared for what they feared was about to happen.

Tavia woke up on the operating table.

She let out a primordial scream. Energized by a blast of adrenaline, the frantic young college student twisted and thrashed and coiled her body as she attempted to get away from the hideous eyes that stared down from above.

Startled by the sudden movement (and the scream), Carver dropped her instruments and took a couple of steps back. Polo, who never made it out to get the assistance Dorothea had requested, pivoted and triggered an alarm on the wall behind him.

"What's going on?" Tavia shouted. "Where the hell am I?"

Quick to notice how her abductors recoiled when she yelled, Tavia lunged towards the closest figure (Dorothea).

Carver kept her cool, however. She held a silver robe and slowly closed the gap between Tavia and herself. "Relax, Miss Patton. My name is Carver. I am a friend. You can trust me. Please calm down. Give those of us on this vessel an opportunity to explain."

"Vessel? *Vessel!* Where the hell am I?"

"This is madness!" Polo said, protesting Carver's efforts to calm the abductee. "Do not talk to her. We should be putting her down!"

Dorothea supported Carver's approach. "Polo, leave! This is my operating room! I call the shots in here. And right now I want you out of here."

When Polo hesitated, Carver pointed towards the door and said, "Go."

Dorothea took the silver robe and tiptoed towards Tavia. "Miss Patton, someone attacked you and dumped your body in the snow. You were minutes away from dying of hypothermia when we found you. Do you remember any of that?"

Tavia grabbed the robe and hurriedly wrapped it around her. "I remember a bright light... And I remember being in the back of a van." At this point she lifted her hand to her mouth to cover her gasp.

Emboldened by Dorothea's success in speaking directly to Tavia, Carver stepped forward and added, "It appears that you were involved in a significant struggle... Tavia, if I asked the male members of our crew to remain outside of this room, will you promise to remain calm?"

Tavia nodded her head. It was a sudden shift from the violence she was ready to inflict just a few moments earlier. But that was before she began coming to the realization that these blue space creatures actually saved her, and that the real monster was her assistant manager's delirious, jealous wife back on Earth.

Carver tapped a couple of buttons on a side panel. Four seats from inside the wall instantly slid out. "Would you like to sit down?" she asked while settling into one herself.

Unsure if it was a demand or an offer designed to put her at ease, Tavia complied and sank onto the cold, hard metal that had emerged from out of nowhere.

"We obviously look very different than you..." Carver began.

"No kidding! So which is it...? Are you from Mars or Venus? Or a galaxy far, far away?"

The scientist held her hands up, a gesture intended to get Tavia to stop interrupting. "We were born on a planet that is many light years from Earth. More important than that distance, however, are the similarities between our DNA and your DNA... Our DNA is almost identical."

Though the Nawerssian paused, Tavia's only response was a shrug. She needed more information before she could process exactly what was happening.

Carver continued, "You see, in just a few years from now, the destruction of Earth as you know it is going to occur. It is our belief that all human life on the planet will cease to exist at that time."

That piece of information was enough to elicit an immediate response. "Wonderful! You're here to blow us up or start some sort of worldwide plague? And what do you mean by 'a few years?' Two or three? Or two or three hundred? Because if it's a hundred or more, I couldn't care less. Do what you want. Just have Scottie beam me back down to Earth. I'll be on my merry way. And I won't tell a soul about you, your spaceship, or the fact that the whole world is doomed. 'Don't ask, don't tell' works for me."

Carver held her hands up again. "It is nice to know you are willing to negotiate. Still, this will go much more smoothly if you stop interrupting... I will do my best to answer your questions."

☠ ☠ ☠

THREE YEARS EARLIER
YEAR -3 + 169 DAYS (JUNE 18th)

After the *Backyard Mania* series proved to be far more than a passing fad, Mr. Patton succumbed to the requests of his children.

He shelled out the cash necessary for Charlie and Tavia to get some real instruction by training with Boris Sputnikov. The rugged old Russian was a former grappler who became a local legend back when "Wrestling at the Chase" was one of the most popular television programs broadcast in St. Louis.

Mr. Patton coughed up more dough so his kids could buy some wood, ropes, canvas, and more than thirty used tires. He hired a handyman to construct a 16x16 wrestling ring in their back yard. Then, after a few more months of seeing growing crowds attending their weekly matches, he bankrolled the purchase of bleachers and lights so Charlie and his friends could perform nighttime shows.

"The 'Patton Wrestling Entertainment Universe' is getting more and more legit all the time!" Charlie declared as he showed off the new sound system that his father had installed on his eighteenth birthday. "Kids from school are paying five dollars a pop to buy Hardcore Mania DVDs. Our online videos are getting a ton of likes. And I'm getting contacted by people I don't even know who want to be part of our shows."

Charlie and Lance renewed their rivalry. However, they no longer called themselves "Prince Charles" and "Sir Lancelot." Charlie had begun dressing in amateur wrestling attire. Wearing a singlet, headgear, and a letterman's jacket, he fought under the name "Patton Charles." He played the role of a ring technician quite well.

Lance went the other direction. His latest gimmick showcased his acting chops. Playing off the growing popularity of the superhero genre, his character went by the name "Lance Smith: American Hero." He was an average Joe with no real special powers or abilities, except for a strong desire to save the day and take down the bad guys. He played that role no matter the cost. And in the PWE matches, it usually resulted in him being bashed with a steel chair, slammed onto a pile of thumbtacks, or something equally painful.

Even with several aspiring wrestlers joining their ranks—including a couple of other teens who trained under Sputnikov—Charlie and Lance remained the most talented grapplers in the PWE. With that in mind, the marquee match of *Hardcore Mania VI* would be a tag team contest in which the underdog—Lance—got to pick the partners for both himself and Charlie.

"It's gonna be great! We've got an awesome swerve and no one's gonna see it coming!" Charlie told his best bud as they were planning out their match. "Especially if I sell it right. When you reveal who you've picked as my partner, I'm going to go berserk and act like I'm absolutely furious."

☠☠☠

The PWE's ring announcer was a guy everyone called Scoop. His parents bought a tuxedo for him during his freshman year. The idea was that he'd wear the fancy duds to every Homecoming, Prom, and Sweetheart dance during his time in high school. They didn't account for him growing six inches taller or gaining 75 pounds. So now he had a tuxedo that was too small to wear to dances... but it fit well enough to wear as supporting talent for a backyard wrestling organization.

Scoop climbed into the ring to make the introductions for the main event. "This tag team match is scheduled for one fall..."

At just a few months shy of her sixteenth birthday, Tavia was blossoming into a beautiful woman. Since she was dabbling on the sidelines of a team that regularly practiced kayfabe, her ability to make herself appear significantly younger occasionally served her purposes.

Charlie's friend Parker glanced towards the bleachers. Right there in the front row was Tavia, sitting beside her friend Liz and two of the most desirable girls in the sophomore class. "What's with Tavia's getup?" Parker asked moments before Charlie was to run down the aisle. "I'm cool with your kid sister hanging around us, especially when she brings her smokin' hot friends with her. But I gotta ask... Why is her hair in pig tails? And why is she wearing a shirt with a pink unicorn on it?"

"That's an old pajama top," Charlie responded.

Parker looked at his pal. "Even worse. Why's she dressed that way? She looks like she's about ten or twelve years old."

"Trust me. She's dressed like that for a reason. I picked the outfit out myself," he assured his pal while simultaneously gesturing for him to shush so he could hear the ring announcer.

"Introducing first, from New York, New York... weighing in at 245 pounds... The American Hero, LANCE SMITH!" (In actuality, Lance was from the St. Louis suburb of Chesterfield, Missouri. And he only tipped the scales at about 160 pounds.) "He has selected as his tag team partner... From Tokyo, Japan, weighing in at an even 200 pounds... Hiroyuki Z." (Tony Aoki lived in Downtown St. Louis. He contacted Charlie after watching several of their videos on the Internet. He was a huge fan of *puroresu*, a style of wrestling that was prominent in Japan and featured a combination of martial arts moves and submission holds.)

Heavy metal music blasted through the Patton's new sound system. "And their opponents... First, from Hollywood, California... weighing in at 205 pounds... PATTON CHARLES!"

Charlie high fived several fans and neighbors on his way to the ring. He rolled under the ring's bottom rope and glared at Lance and Hiroyuki. "And now..." Scoop paused for dramatic effect,

"Lance, who have you selected as a tag team partner for Patton Charles?"

Lance shielded his eyes as he pretended to survey the audience. Then he turned, smiled at the camera, and spoke into the microphone. "The girl in the front row... I pick you."

Tavia's friend Liz pointed to herself and mouthed the words, "Who? Me?"

Lance shook his head. "Not you. The little girl next to you."

Charlie stomped his feet and flailed his arms. "That's not fair! This is an outrage!"

Tavia looked shocked. "Me?"

Charlie grabbed the microphone out of his opponent's hand. "You can't do that! That's not fair!"

Lance shook his head and flashed a devious smile. "Last week, at *Hardcore Mania V*, you said that I could pick whoever I wanted to be my partner. And you also said I could pick whoever I wanted to be *your* partner. That's what you said. I know because I paid five bucks of my hard-earned money to buy the DVD. I watched it again just to be sure I heard you say what I thought you said... And I definitely heard you right. Patton Charles, I'm selecting this cute little girl as your partner. Deal with it, stupid!"

Eventually Charlie decided he'd milked his faux temper tantrum for all it was worth, and the match began. Patton Charles got in a few big moves early, but refused to tag Tavia into the ring. This strategy appeared to backfire as the match went on. Hiroyuki and Lance double-teamed him, nailing him with a bevy of kicks, clotheslines, and elbow drops. Charlie narrowly avoided losing the match on several occasions. Each time Charlie kicked out, the referee's hand was dangerously close to hitting the mat for a third time.

With Charlie being pounded nearly to the point of exhaustion, he managed to scramble to his corner and reach Tavia's outstretched hand. She paused long enough to peel her unicorn pajama top over her head. This revealed the sports bra she wore underneath. It matched the spandex leggings she had been wearing. She was a wrestler. And she was dressed for the part.

"She looks a lot more mature without the unicorn," Parker observed while watching from his ringside seat. "I better not let my mom see the DVD of this match!"

Tavia sprang into the ring and leveled Lance with a dropkick. Hiroyuki came in to aid his partner, but he met the same fate. She delivered another fantastic dropkick that caught him on the right shoulder. (To the naked eye, it would have looked as if she hit him square in the jaw.)

Charlie pulled himself into a standing position. Tavia climbed atop her brother and stood with her feet on his shoulders. After pointing towards the sky, she jumped off Charlie's shoulders. She soared through the air until she landed with her outstretched elbow hitting Lance across the chest.

The referee dropped into position and performed an exaggerated three-count. Tavia was victorious in her wrestling debut!

Charlie snatched the microphone away from Scoop. He looked into the camera, and boasted, "Poor, poor Lance. Beaten again. I bet you're wondering, 'How *does* he do it?' Well, today you chose my sister. Yep, you chose *my sister* to be my tag team partner. Just like I knew you would. We set you up... In the future, you'd be wise to remember this one important lesson..." He leaned down and raised his voice to taunt his best friend/in-ring rival. "I'm always gonna be one step ahead of you!"

☠☠☠

PRESENT DAY – ABOARD THE VILNAGROM-II
YEAR 0 + 284 DAYS (OCTOBER 10th)

Having concluded his own shower and debriefing, Brady was wrapped in a silver robe and marched down Corridor 16. His escort was female. Unlike her fellow crew members, she wore a wig of strawberry blond hair with a braided ponytail flopping over her right shoulder. She also had opted to have her nasal passage surgically enhanced to give her nose a shape much like one belonging to an Earthly human. "It is a fashion choice," the Nawerssian revealed after noticing that her features had caught Brady's attention. "I travel to Earth from time to time... and I have not seen one bald, blue woman on the cover of any fashion magazine. Plus, it helps me blend in."

Brady did not respond. The day had been rather traumatic. He wasn't quite ready to chit chat with any of his alien abductors, no matter how pleasant they might appear in person.

They stopped in front of a doorway. "This is our stop," she was deliberate in her effort to incorporate a figure of speech often used on Earth. A second later, a buzzing sound interrupted the silence. The door vanished into the wall. Gesturing towards the opening, she said, "Please step inside."

Brady entered a room that was identical to the one he had left sometime earlier. A large tank filled with a murky purple liquid was built into the far wall. The Nawerssian entered a code into a panel. Four chairs emerged.

"Sit here," she told him. "The others will be joining you soon. Then we will bring you food. It may not taste like much, but you need to eat it. Your body will need protein for what lies ahead."

Brady looked at his counterpart and gave her a half smile. He was unsure about who he could trust. But he felt reasonably good about his escort. "Thank you."

She responded with a nod of her head. Prior to exiting the room, she turned back and remarked, "By the way, you and I met briefly once before... You were getting onto a train as I was stepping off." She held out her hand for him to shake.

Though they stood almost eye-to-eye, her fingers were considerably longer than Brady's. Her skin was unexpectedly soft. Touching her delicate skin was a sensation that made him glad he worked up the courage to shake.

"My name is Monroe," she told him. Aware that someone from the Control Center may be watching, she whispered another familiar phrase. "Hang in there."

☠☠☠

Brady was not left alone for long. A swishing sound filled the air. The metal that had been blocking the doorway once again disappeared into the wall. "Tavia?"

Unlike Brady, Tavia wasn't dressed in a short, silver robe. She wore a flight suit exactly like the ones worn by their captors. However, she chose to wear hers "unzipped" down to the waist. This allowed the top half of the garment to fall and dangle behind her, much like a flannel shirt might if she tied it around her midsection. On top, she wore a black sports bra with purple, red and white skulls. (It was the same one she wore more than a year ago to the wrestling tryouts in Memphis.) And instead of wearing the heavy, black and silver boots that made up part of the Nawerssian uniform, she was permitted to wear a pair of gym shoes that she previously wore while cross training.

"I'm pretty sure they asked you to sit down," she said as she entered the room. "Better listen, before they gas us both. Then again, they might just zap you with the electroshock wave."

"They can do that?"

With another swishing sound, the doorway closed behind her.

"Hell if I know..." she answered truthfully. "But I *do* know quite a few things. We don't have much time. Sit down and listen so you and I can get on the same page."

A lot had transpired since they were jolted out of virtual reality. Brady couldn't exactly calculate how many hours it had been since he was sprawled out on the floor in a massive puddle of purple slime, but he did know that everything was happening at a blistering pace.

Tavia killed Grayson. *Why? Because the police officer was beating the tar out of a blue alien?* Now she was dressed like them. *Sort of.* Brady was unsure of his next step. *Could she be trusted?*

"Should we wait for Jenn and Cocoa?" he finally asked.

Embracing her elevation in status, Tavia made no effort to hide the fact that she loved holding power over Brady. Her shoulders momentarily sagged and she exhaled in an exaggerated manner. "You seemed so much more intelligent when we were in that kinesiology class together back at CIU... I said 'you and I'. I'm not sure there's anything I can do for Miss Cocoa for Cuckoo Puffs or her little lapdog El Chico Pirate-o."

"Huh?"

"It's you and me and no one else... I've been hanging around these Great Gazoos for quite a bit longer than you. And while living in their virtual reality world has some perks, I'm ready to hop off this rocket and set foot on terra firma. You play your cards right and you can come with me. What do you say?"

The door zoomed open before Brady could ask any other questions.

Like Brady, Cocoa had been given a silver robe. She moved very slowly. Being violently ejected from the life suspension tank aggravated the former wrestler's chronic back injury.

Cocoa's Nawerssian escort instructed her to sit by Brady. Sit and wait. "Once Subject Silva returns, we will prepare you for reentry into the tank. You will be in a new virtual reality setting, and your back will feel much better."

A split second after the blue man exited, Cocoa bounced to her feet. Pressing through the pain, she lunged towards Tavia. She shouted, "I'm gonna kill you!"

Tavia easily side-stepped Cocoa's initial advance. She then returned fire, pounding her adversary with a closed fist to the side of her head. The impact sent Cocoa to the ground.

With her foe on one knee and struggling to stand, Tavia lifted her right leg and stomped on her back.

Brady stood by and watched. He was frozen with fear.

Seeing her opposition lying face down on the floor, the co-ed moved in to finish her off. In one fluid motion, she yanked the back of Cocoa's silver robe over her head, then jerked it around her throat.

"Tavia! Please! You're choking her!" Brady yelled.

After strangling Cocoa for a few more seconds, Tavia let up. She drove her gym shoe into the former wrestler's back once more. "Never threaten me again! If anyone does any killing here, it's going to be *ME*!" Tavia wanted the message to be delivered loud and clear. She leaned downward and screamed at her fallen nemesis. "You think you're somethin' special. You may be in charge back home… But we're not in your daddy's little indie wrestling promotion. This is *MY* turf, and *I* call the shots here!"

17: SQUASH MATCH

"*Like his mighty ancestors of days gone past,
The Warrior has come from PARTS UNKNOWN
to bring TOTAL DESTRUCTION to the
Wrestling Universe! The Warrior begins his
journey battling FIREBALL FREEMAN on
tonight's SATURDAY NIGHT SLAMFEST! The
Warrior takes no prisoners and The Warrior
leaves NO SURVIVORS!*"

*-GALACTIC WARRIOR #2 promo before
his match against Fireball Freeman on the
IWO's "Saturday Night Slamfest."*

Cocoa's lip was bloodied and she was gasping for air. Brady knelt to check on her. Once her breathing steadied, he tried to help her to her feet. She pushed him away, shouting, "Nobody touch me!" Though the pain in her back was agonizing, she eventually made it to her feet.

Once his offer of assistance was rejected, Brady shifted his focus to Tavia. He had no words. He simply glared at the young woman.

The corner of her lip curved upward. "Big things are about to happen. Some of us are playin' chess. Others are still playin' checkers. You need to choose the right team, Brady, before it's too late."

Brady continued to bite his tongue. He wondered what could have happened in Tavia's life to cause her to become such a cruel and calculating person.

The door to the compartment slid open. A massive Nawerssian stepped through the opening. General Hannibal was the *V-II's* top military officer. When they feared a particular abduction would require heavy lifting or held the potential for a physical confrontation, the General participated in the excursion.

Hannibal stood every bit as tall as Polo. That was where the physical similarities between the musclebound General and the rail-thin Cartographer ended. Even while covered by a full-body flight suit, it was apparent that his body was contoured in a manner that would rival anyone in the wrestling business. There wasn't even a hint of a wrinkle on his bulging forehead. And his eyes burned a haunting hue of orangish-yellow, almost like Dijon mustard. Taken together as a package, Hannibal was the Nawerssian who would inspire both the awe and fear of all those with whom he came into contact.

His voice boomed considerably lower than any other Nawerssian Brady or Cocoa had heard speak. "Tavia Patton. Come with me."

"Am I in trouble?" she asked. Despite this question, the tone of her voice and the look she gave Brady made it clear that she did not think there would be any negative ramifications for the beatdown she had dished out to Cocoa.

Hannibal and Tavia exited the compartment. Brady and Cocoa were alone. While Cocoa sat in one of the chairs, Brady stood against the opposite wall. Neither said a single word.

The awkward silence was broken when Jenn was escorted into the room. Upon spotting Cocoa, Jenn rushed towards her friend and asked, "What did I miss? What the hell happened?"

Cocoa said nothing. Instead, she looked away, unwilling to accept any assistance from the luchadora, and refusing to fill her in on the details of the attack.

Jenn whipped her head around and glared at Brady. "Are you going to tell me what's going on?"

"Tavia's either lost it or she's some sort of evil mastermind. I haven't figured out which one it is... But she almost beat Cocoa to death. Literally. She was strangling her, and she wouldn't let up. It was pretty scary."

Jenn looked to Cocoa for her version, but the booker still wasn't talking. She was deliberate in her efforts to turn her head even further away.

"This is crazy." Now taking seriously the suggestion that their captors were always watching and listening in on them, Jenn whispered a plan to Brady. "I don't care who it is. We attack the next thing that walks through that door. I don't care if it's Tavia or one of the blue skinned bastards. We give 'em all we got... Unless you have some other idea?"

He whispered back, "I don't know what to think. We're in uncharted territory here. But the way I see it, doing nothing isn't an option."

"Doing nothing is the only choice that makes any sense," Cocoa jumped in, speaking at full volume. "First of all, don't you know they can hear everything you say? There won't be any element of surprise. All that's gonna happen is you're gonna get beat half to death like I did... or maybe worse."

Jenn whispered her response. "You do what you think's right. Right now, Brady and I are weighing options. And that may include fighting these oversized Smurfs and trying to take control of their spaceship."

With that message delivered, Jenn turned to Brady and mouthed her words. There was no audible sound.

Cocoa took another run at trying to discourage them. She chose her words carefully in her effort to talk them out of their foolhardy plan. "What good's it gonna do? Do you have a little friendly robot that's gonna give you a blueprint to this ship? For that matter, do you know if we're on some massive mothership or something much smaller? Even if you make it out that door, you won't have the slightest clue where to go or what to do... You're gonna get yourselves (and maybe me) killed. I'd rather take my chances goin' back in the purple soup, where at least my back don't hurt."

☠☠☠

TWENTY-TWO YEARS AGO
YEAR -22 + 163 DAYS (JUNE 12th)

The Freemans were in the home stretch of their two-hour drive from Winona, Mississippi. Fireball had dropped off the kids—

Cocoa (age 14) and KaPhonso (age 9)— for a weekend visit with grandma and grandpa. Cocoa and her little brother spent most of the drive back to Memphis in a series of highly competitive back seat contests. First it was "I Spy," and then "The Alphabet Game."

Cocoa was scanning billboards and license plates for the letter "Y" when her mobile phone rang. She did not recognize the incoming number. "Hello?"

Her father frowned. He'd told her time and time again that he'd gotten her the phone for emergencies... and only emergencies. "Cocoa, who's callin' you?" (His tone implied that they'd be discussing the parameters of her cellphone usage once the call was completed.)

The sassy teen resisted the urge to roll her eyes. Instead, she shook her head and listened intently to the caller on the other end. Then she passed the phone over to her father. "It's for you."

"For me?"

Fireball had made the conscious decision to not own a mobile phone. He'd been told that it wouldn't be long until *everyone* carried one. But he intended to avoid that so-called "technological advance" for as long as humanly possible. ("Those things will turn folks into mindless robots," he predicted. "People will be dilly dallyin' with their handheld phones all the time instead of havin' honest to goodness conversations. Not for me. No thank you.")

He reluctantly grabbed the phone from his daughter. "Hello? Who's this?"

It was Griffin Conrad. Though he was head honcho of the wildly popular International Wrestling Organization, Fireball wasn't exactly impressed. "How did you get my daughter's number? ...No really, how did you get it?"

While Fireball was trying to get to the bottom of that mystery, KaPhonso pulled him into another parenting situation. "'S' on

Shooting Star Gentlemen's Club!" the nine-year-old proudly announced.

"Kayzo, don't be lookin' at that! Cocoa, cover that boy's eyes!"

"I should get double points for that one!" the boy declared.

Cocoa reached to cover his eyes. "Dad said don't look at that sign... And when did you find a 'Q,' cheater?"

Enough was enough. Conrad finally got down to business. "In all seriousness, I didn't have a good number for you. Thankfully your daughter gave this number when she signed up for the Rosey Hill Fan Club on the IWO webpage."

Most of what Conrad had just said was gobbledygook to the old grappler. Roosevelt Hill, however, was Fireball's former tag team partner. He'd moved on to bigger and brighter things in the IWO. It made sense to him that Cocoa would sign up to be a member of Rosey's fan club.

"I know you've said you're retired. And I know you don't want to sign a long-term deal with the IWO because it would take you away from your family. But hear me out..."

"I'm listening."

Conrad got into his pitch. "I want you to appear on next month's 'Saturday Night Slamfest' broadcast to put over one of my new wrestlers. One night only. It would be a national audience and a big payday."

In wrestling lingo, one "put over" another wrestler by losing to him. When an established wrestler fell to a newcomer, it helped that newcomer gain notoriety, credibility and/or popularity with the fans.

If Fireball was going to be showing up to lose a match in order to boost the popularity of Conrad Griffin's latest project, he wanted a few more details. "Tell me about the job. Who would I be facing?"

"His name is Galactic Warrior #2."

Fireball participated in a long and memorable feud with the original Galactic Warrior back in the late-1980s. They weren't his favorite bouts. The Galactic Warrior wasn't easy to work with. He had a terrible habit of "no-selling" his opponents' attacks (Fireball's included). Making matter's worse, years of rampant juicing left him in a perpetual state of 'roid rage. It made it impossible to discuss creative differences with the alien-themed wrestler.

The veteran fired off a sarcastic response, "That's a creative name."

"You won't believe it. This guy looks exactly like the original Galactic Warrior. It's not just a casual resemblance. He could be his clone," Conrad explained.

"Who on God's Green Earth would ever want to clone a moron like the Galactic Warrior!"

Ignoring Fireball's comment, Conrad continued. "We brought in G.W. to team with the new guy. But then the dumbass blew out his ACL playing in a charity basketball game. We wanted to stick with the Galactic Warrior #2 gimmick, so we put our heads together and decided to give you a call."

It was a tempting offer. The IWO had landed a contract that allowed them to air one live, one-hour, primetime broadcast each month on network television. The show got great ratings. Like Conrad said, it would be a big paycheck. Plus, it would put Fireball's name out there again. That may have been a bigger perk than the quick cash. It certainly couldn't hurt... especially if the veteran wrestler decided to go through with his idea to start up his own independent promotion.

"Lemme sleep on it for the night. I'll call you with my answer tomorrow morning."

☠☠☠

TWENTY-TWO YEARS AGO
YEAR -22 + 198 DAYS (JULY 17th)

"This is my first match in five years. Kayzo's seen tapes, but he's never seen me wrestle live. It might be my last time in the ring, or it might be the thing that kickstarts me to start my own promotion. Either way, we're going to do this up big-time!" he had told Cocoa after she questioned him about the high price of round-trip airfare for three.

The taxi approached the arena. "Here we are, kids," Fireball announced.

Nine-year-old KaPhonso seemed puzzled. "Is that a church?"

"What? No. That's where your dad's gonna fight tonight," he told his son.

"It looks like a big church to me."

Fireball shook his head. "No. I'm pretty sure this is the arena. It's where Hakeem and the Houston Rockets play. They have big concerts here. And tonight there will be a great big wrestling ring in the center of the arena."

"You ever fought here before, Pops?" Cocoa asked.

"Once or twice. I took part in a big battle royal here just a few days before Kayzo was born."

Cocoa laughed. "Oh yeah!" She laughed at her little brother. "Pops had a big ol' busted lip in the pictures of him holding you at the hospital!"

☠☠☠

EIGHT HOURS LATER

Because "Saturday Night Slamfest" aired on live TV, the network insisted on Griffin Conrad putting the marquee matchup at the top of the show. If the Main Event went longer than expected, they could tweak the matches of lesser importance. (Though this sometimes compromised the quality of the later bouts, this adjustment was preferable to having to cut paid commercial breaks.)

A production assistant approached Fireball and the Galactic Warrior #2. It was less than ten minutes before they were set to do battle. "The tag team championship match went longer than expected. We're going to cut your match down from eight minutes to four." Recognizing the frustration on the faces of both the returning veteran and his young opponent, the P.A. shrugged and offered a weak apology. "Sorry. It's out of my control."

Fireball turned to his in-ring foe. "That doesn't give me much time to get my licks in before I put you over..." The duo went on to agree on a modified plan for their match.

The P.A. returned seconds before Fireball's entrance music was set to begin. This time he had Griffin Conrad with him. "Sorry, gents," Conrad began. "The network is telling us they've only got two and a half minutes for your match."

Fireball protested, "What? We can't hardly get down to the ring in that amount of time."

Conrad patted him on the back. "Sure you can. Galactic Warrior #2 sprints down to the ring, just like the original used to." He leaned in and whispered into Fireball's ear, "I'm sorry. It couldn't be avoided. Live TV is a different animal. Talk to me after the show. I've already got a plan on how to make this right."

As if on cue, Fireball's music began blaring over the loudspeakers.

He was a pioneer in modern professional wrestling. He didn't want to pull any stunts that might tarnish his reputation in the business. Plus, he didn't want to do anything that might hurt the debuting rookie. *(This debacle wasn't his fault.)*

He wasn't happy. But Fireball Freeman donned his trademark white fedora, then jogged to the ring. He even found it in him to wink into the camera and flash a smile for the national audience.

Cocoa and Kayzo were seated in a pair of seats in Row 5. They—along with a smattering of fans who knew of his importance in the history of sports entertainment—shouted their support. Fireball gave the thumbs up signal to his kids.

In the next instant, speed metal music signaled the upcoming entrance of the Galactic Warrior #2. He raced into the ring. The crowd roared over the sound of pyrotechnics. Once the newcomer's boots hit the ring, he pounded his chest then flexed his unnaturally large muscles.

Then, without any further warning, "GW2" leveled Fireball with a flying football tackle.

The veteran scrambled to his feet, but immediately saw his opponent giving the signal to begin the final sequence. GW2 threw Freeman against the ropes, caught him on his return, and powerslammed him into the mat.

The match lasted less than sixty seconds from bell to bell.

Fireball picked himself up off the canvas. He heard shouts like "You shoulda stayed retired!" and "You're nothin' but a bum!" and "You suck, old man!" Those taunts normally would not have bothered him. But hearing them while seeing a stream of tears roll down KaPhonso's face made the entire experience hard to swallow.

☠ ☠ ☠

ONE DAY LATER
YEAR -22 + 199 DAYS (JULY 18th)

The return flight to Memphis would take less than two hours.

KaPhonso was content to sit in the window seat, alternating his attention between staring at the clouds and playing his handheld video game.

Cocoa leaned against her father. Resting her head against his shoulder, she remarked, "You haven't said much since last night's match. You okay?"

"Yeah." His voice trailed off in the middle of the word. This made his answer thoroughly unconvincing. "Just got a lot on my mind."

Cocoa thought she had a pretty good idea what her dad was thinking. She waited for him to tell her to study hard and go to college. She didn't think he wanted her anywhere close to the wrestling business that had, once again, broken his heart.

Fireball surprised his daughter with the next words that came out of his mouth. "Griffin Conrad offered me a two-year contract after last night's match... He apologized for how things went down, and how they had to change things to a squash match at the last minute. He even promised that they'd book me to win the rematch on the next 'Saturday Slamfest' show."

Cocoa lifted her head off her father's shoulder. She tilted her head and tried to look into his eyes to see if she could figure out what he intended to do.

She went from surprised to stunned when Fireball continued to verbalize his thoughts. "You should start comin' with me to the gym. I'd like to begin training you. I could teach you everything I know about the wrestling business, in and out of the ring... If you want to, that is."

"Really? After last night, I figured you were done with the business for good."

"Nah. Wrestling's in my blood. I could never be done with it forever... Griffin Conrad? Now, that piece of garbage is another story. He better hope I never see him again. But that would probably be wishful thinkin' on his part."

"Why's that, Pops?"

"Whatever that bull hockey was that got pulled last night..." He shook his head and spoke with a newfound confidence in his voice. "It reminded me that I gotta take care of me and mine before anyone else. It gave me the shove I've been needing. Now I'm definitely startin' my own promotion."

☠☠☠

PRESENT DAY – ABOARD THE VILNAGROM-II
YEAR 0 + 284 DAYS (OCTOBER 10th)

As expected, the Nawerssians didn't leave their specimens alone for long. A tone sounded. It was followed by instructions for Brady and Jenn to sit in the chairs next to Cocoa.

The door slid open. The imposing Hannibal entered, followed by the *V-II's* Doctor (Dorothea). "Cocoa Freeman, I am here to assess your injuries and overall condition. Would you prefer I examine you here or take you to a more private setting?"

"NOW!" Jenn sprang to her feet. Brady did the same a split second later.

Utilizing a maneuver that she occasionally used as "Long Jenn Silva," the luchadora leapt into the air. As her downward momentum brought her back to the floor, Jenn flattened Dorothea with a "Superman punch." Her closed fist crashed into the doctor's cranium, knocking her to the floor in a single blow.

Brady attempted to surprise the much larger Hannibal. He drove his foot between the legs of the Nawerssian. He hoped that a shot to the groin would be every bit as effective against the blue-skinned aliens as it would be when striking an Earthly human.

The impact sent the mighty General staggering backwards, and he dropped to one knee. Brady continued his attack. He cocked his right arm back before mashing his fist into his foe's skull. The punch landed squarely, and phased Hannibal for another moment. Unfortunately, Brady couldn't take advantage and follow it up immediately. He was too busy shaking off the pain that came from giving himself a boxer's fracture.

That hesitation was the only opening the physically superior Nawerssian needed. He rose to his feet and backhanded Brady across the face.

With Dorothea incapacitated, Jenn tried to assist her friend. She slipped in behind Hannibal, wrapping her arms under his armpits and over his shoulders. She hoped to keep him from moving his own arms, thus leaving him vulnerable to more offensive moves from Brady.

Recognizing his opening, Brady charged forward and drove his shoulder into the General's stomach.

The recent college grad's attack ended there. Cocoa grabbed Brady from behind, tugging at his long, curly hair. With a loud grunt, she jerked him around and slammed his head into the wall.

With it now a one-on-one battle against Jenn, Hannibal moved to finish the fight. He stood straight up, then surged backwards. He smashed the much smaller combatant between his massive body and the wall.

Seconds later, five more Nawerssians rushed into the compartment. Jenn and Brady were outnumbered. And now Cocoa had turned against them, too!

Jenn's mouth dropped open as she stared at her friend. "Help me understand."

"I don't have it in me to play rebel or pirate or whatever it is you guys thought you were doing." Tears rolled down her cheeks. Cocoa quoted her father as she explained her actions. "'I gotta take care of me and mine.' Right now, for me that means cooperating with these bastards. That means going in the tank, hopin' and prayin' that we can make a deal and they'll let us go home when they're done with us."

18: BACKSTAGE HEAT

"Sometimes championships are won and lost on the other side of the curtain. Backstage. If you treat your fellow wrestlers like garbage, you ain't long for this business. You could be the most talented athlete on the planet, but your days are numbered if you're going around actin' like a horse's ass."

-FIREBALL FREEMAN shoot interview on "Chatting with Champions" podcast.

PRESENT DAY-ABOARD THE VILNAGROM-II
YEAR 0 + 285 DAYS (OCTOBER 11th)

The door slid open. Though she wore only a short, silver robe, Dorothea invited Monroe to enter. "Carver is getting the children ready."

Cleo and Ptolemy were the only children on the *V-II*. Their mothers believed that continuing the Nawerssian bloodline was important. But neither woman had any interest in a monogamous relationship with a male member of the crew. They opted for artificial insemination, and to raise their children together.

One of Monroe's primary roles on the ship was to aid in the education of the children. On most days, their lessons began with time observing the specimens in the life suspension tanks followed by a discussion of the behaviors they observed.

"With all of the chaos that transpired in Corridor 16, what do you propose I do with the children today?" Monroe asked the Doctor.

"Most importantly, please keep them away from the theater. Much of the crew will be meeting there to discuss what we are to do with Subjects Silva, Emerson, and Freeman."

Carver approached. The Nawerssian children stood at each side. The Biologist's son, Ptolemy, was the older of the two. The Doctor's daughter, Cleo, was born a year later. But she had grown almost as tall as "Toly" in her six years of living in space.

"I suggest you take Toly and Cleo to view the subjects in Corridor 15," said Carver. "Observing Mr. and Mrs. Bledsoe will be a healthy change from watching Tavia's never-ending manipulations."

As Carver spoke, Cleo shifted from being positioned at her side to a spot where she could hold one of her instructor's hands. Ptolemy continued to clutch his mother's leg.

Monroe told them, "It is time for your lessons. Say good-bye to your mothers."

The boy refused to move.

"Toly, if you come with me, I will let you hold my purple kitty during your lessons."

"Can I keep it?" he asked.

"No. It was a special gift given to me when I was even smaller than you," Monroe answered. "You can play with it, but I want it back."

He nodded his head, then took Monroe's other hand.

☠☠☠

TWENTY-FIVE YEARS EARLIER – ABOARD THE VILNAGROM-I YEAR -25 + 18 DAYS (JANUARY 18th)

With Jagger and Valentina secure in the brig, Armstrong returned to the theater in Corridor 2. Avis was with Mantle (aka V-I 8/ GEOLOGIST) and Lindy (aka V-I 6/PILOT).

"Where is everyone else?" Armstrong asked.

Mantle was approaching a breakdown. "Dead. In the brig... Other than the children, this is it."

Avis was not so dramatic with his response. "Magellan needed some time alone. As you can imagine, our Skipper is nearing his breaking point. First his wife dies. Now his son... It is unthinkable."

"Adam was just one of the deaths this crew experienced today," Lindy said, pulling the group back into the discussion they were having prior to Armstrong's return. "Let us not forget that the deaths of Crockett and McCoy orphaned two young girls."

Monroe was only a few weeks old at the time of the Launch Bay Clash. Her older sister, Greta, was a month shy of her fifth birthday.

It did not take the surviving Nawerssians long to decide that Magellan was in no condition to care for two young children.

"That leaves the two of us," Lindy said, referencing her relationship with Mantle. Then she gestured towards Avis and Armstrong, "Or the two of you."

Armstrong asked, "Would it be appropriate to split up the girls? Or would it be best to keep them together?"

Being the only woman in the group, Lindy felt the need to speak on behalf of Greta and Monroe. "They have already been prematurely separated from their parents. It would be cruel to split them from one another."

The three males agreed.

Likewise, it didn't take long for them to arrive at a consensus on who should care for them. "We already have one child. We can handle the girls, too. We will be one big, happy family," Mantle declared.

Lindy looked towards her fellow pilot, Avis. "I suspect I will need you to fly a little more often. Not all the missions. I still want to travel to Earth from time to time."

☠☠☠

TEN MONTHS LATER – ABOARD THE VILNAGROM-I
YEAR -25 + 244 DAYS (SEPTEMBER 1st)

The *V-I* was well cloaked. Since the spacecraft drifted almost 200,000 miles away from the Earth, it was quite safe from accidental detection by astronauts or satellites that happened to be flying nearby. That might not be the case, however, if their communications were overheard. Radio transmissions to and from the *Vilnagrom-I* were discouraged. Even though their messages were encrypted, they did not want to risk having them intercepted by those on Earth. That could draw the attention of astronomers and militaries on the planet. If they were aware that they needed to be looking, it could direct them to where they needed to focus their efforts.

"Lindy left on her reconnaissance flight more than thirty hours ago!"

It took approximately eight hours to travel from the space craft to Earth, and another ten to make the return trip. The Pilot should have returned hours ago. Understandably, Mantle was concerned about the wellbeing of his partner.

"You have been through this before," Armstrong admonished the nervous Geologist. "You know that the mission requires limited radio communication any time a shuttle penetrates the atmosphere."

"We have heard nothing? And Lindy has not activated the distress beacon?"

Avis looked at the instruments in the Control Center. "The beacon has not been activated. Of course, Lindy would only utilize it if she was adrift or lost in space. If something happened while they were within the atmosphere of the Earth, the beacon would not be enabled."

"What are we supposed to do?"

Armstrong offered the only answer he could. "We wait and we monitor radio broadcasts from Earth."

The waiting continued for hours. Lindy never returned. She may have crashed. She could have been captured. There was no way of telling until they could pilot another shuttle down to the surface to investigate.

Armstrong did not support the idea of going on such a mission. "If we took a shuttle to her charted coordinates, whatever befell her could doom those in the second shuttle. If she was captured by the U.S. Military, for example, it is likely that they would continue to maintain a presence in that area. It is too dangerous. And we do not have any crew members we can spare. Even if we had volunteers, there is no one we can risk on an exploratory mission."

"I wonder if your position would be the same if Avis was the pilot who disappeared?"

Armstrong repeated his prior assessment. "We do not have any crew member we can risk on an exploratory mission... particularly one in which there would be such a high probability of negative consequences."

Mantle gritted his teeth together. His red eyes beamed with anger. He nodded his head and said, "Not a single *crew member*. Understood. Thank you for helping me consider the dangers and the 'negative consequences.'"

☠☠☠

SIXTEEN HOURS LATER – ABOARD THE VILNAGROM-I
YEAR -25 + 245 DAYS (SEPTEMBER 2nd)

Jagger and Valentina were scheduled to be in the brig until the *Vilnagrom-II* arrived in about four years. Armstrong took on the task of taking meals to the prisoners twice a day. Undoubtedly, the worst part about that was having to endure Jagger's verbal attacks, insults, and taunts.

"Ah! 'Tis Armstrong... Captain, Admiral, and King of the *Vilnagrom*. Top o' da mornin', Yer Highness!"

"I am in no mood."

Armstrong went silent.

For once, Jagger made no effort to fill that silence. Instead, he watched and studied the face of his adversary. Then he let out a monstrous belly laugh.

"WHERE IS VALENTINA?" Armstrong demanded.

She was not in the brig.

"Yer yella bellied geologist may not have been as big of a coward as we always thought," Jagger gloated. Following a dramatic pause, the former war hero revealed that he was holding a tiny piece of parchment.

"I almost forgot… Mantle left a note." Pulling the sheet close, he squinted one eye shut to allow the other to focus. Paraphrasing where he saw fit, Jagger read the note aloud, "'There be too much death on this ship. 'Tis no place to raise a child. I'm takin' Montana and Greta. We're goin' to look for me partner.'" He stopped reading and filled in the remaining details in his own words. "You see, ol' Mantle sprung Valentina. Needed a shuttle pilot… Gonna look for the missing missus. But I suppose if they don't find her, Miss Val will be able to keep him warm at night…" Jagger smirked as he watched his seething rival fill with rage. "Mantle 'n Val even helped themselves to me plan to find some remote island and live out their days on O.E… Away from all that death. Away from King Armstrong. I find it curious, though, how they took the oldest kids and left the wee little tot behind."

The Explorer wanted to murder him. Though vulgarities seemed unnatural to most Nawerssians, he allowed himself to dip into the vocabulary of those from Original Earth. "You bastard!"

Jagger held up his hands in surrender. "Now don't go killin' the messenger… That little girl, on the other hand? How are you and Avis and Magellan gonna raise a baby? I'd suggest ye save yerselves a lotta trouble and just put little Monroe out the launch tubes."

☠ ☠ ☠

PRESENT DAY-ABOARD THE VILNAGROM-II
YEAR 0 + 285 DAYS (OCTOBER 11th)

The V-II's Senior Officers congregated in the theater. Hannibal (aka V-II 1/GENERAL), Oya (aka V-II 2/SKIPPER), and Atlas (aka V-II 3/EXPLORER) would cast the deciding votes. Armstrong was included in the meeting based on his status as Explorer on the original *Vilnagrom* crew. Rounding out the participants were Dorothea and Polo. They were there to discuss whether there was any scientific value in continuing to observe the four Earthly humans in the virtual reality experiments.

As the various crew members vocalized their positions, it became clear that Hannibal and Oya preferred to wipe the slate clean and euthanize all of the subjects who had spilled out of the life suspension tanks.

"We have been safe and productive throughout our time here," Hannibal explained. "I will not jeopardize our legacy. Having problematic test subjects aboard when the *V-III* arrives could tarnish how we are viewed in history."

Armstrong disagreed. "I must remind you that Polo and the rest of you were extremely displeased with the fact that we only turned over two elderly subjects upon the arrival of the *V-II*... And that was with good reason. With a crew down to three, we did not have the resources to travel to Earth to abduct additional subjects."

"Precisely," Hannibal declared. "We have a full crew. That gives us the ability to be rid of the problematic subjects and replace them with a new, untainted group to be observed. If all goes according to schedule, the *V-III* will be here within a few months. We need to act quickly."

Polo spoke up. "There are experiments that can be conducted utilizing subjects that know they are being observed. Such experiments would allow me to try new techniques in manipulating the events in virtual reality. If my hypothesis is correct, observing them in such circumstances would be highly relevant to Nawerssian adaptation to living on O.E after the cataclysmic event occurs on the planet... The data collected would be highly valuable. More so than any experimentation we have been able to conduct up to this point."

Though the Cartographer's input impacted the tone of the conversation, it was clear that the majority of the decision-makers remained unconvinced.

Dorothea joined Polo in his request for a humane approach to dealing with the Earthly humans. "We gave our word to Tavia Patton. She bares no blame for the fact that the life suspension tank ruptured. Plus, I believe her quick response to the attack against Polo saved his life. I ask that our logs reflect that I object to discarding her in such a manner."

"I did not agree with the deal that you made with Tavia Patton. However, I believe a promise from a member of this crew should be honored," said Hannibal. "Atlas, please retrieve Tavia Patton."

☠☠☠

Atlas returned with Tavia. He refused to take any chances. He held a Nawerssian blaster inches away from her back as he marched her into the theater.

Being treated like the enemy did not set well with the fiery co-ed. She had been working with them for months! *She'd lived up to her end of the bargain one hundred percent of the way!*

Tavia shouted at the group as soon as she entered the room. "What's the meaning of this? Why are you treating me like some sort of criminal? You should consider me a hero, not a prisoner! I've done everything I was supposed to do. I even killed the guy that beat one of you to within an inch of his life! I don't know what you've been talking about in here, but the story better end like this: You fix my brother. Then you drop me and Charlie back on Earth... as promised. I know my cover story like the back of my hand. No one will ever know where we went, how his blindness was cured, or anything about you."

Hannibal held up his hand to signal that he was going to speak for the group. "Was that rehearsed?"

Tavia offered a half shrug and admitted, "A little bit... I'm a damn good actress. That's why everyone will believe it when they hear we joined a cult and a faith healing witchdoctor restored Charlie's vision. No one will ever suspect aliens played a role in any of our lives."

Hannibal quickly tired of Tavia's routine. "Dorothea, please provide an update regarding your progress in restoring the vision of Charlie Patton."

The Doctor stepped forward. "His vision has not yet been fully restored. Additional procedures will be required."

"How many?" Hannibal asked.

"At least three. There is a recovery period required between each surgery."

"How long?"

"Between thirty and forty-five days."

Tavia interrupted. "I don't want to spend one more night on this flying saucer! Even if his eyesight isn't perfect... It'll have to be enough. Just put us on the next flight out of here."

The General whispered in the Skipper's ear. "We have heard enough. We are declaring a State of Emergency. As for the three in Corridor 16, put them back into the life suspension tanks immediately. Polo, you will provide daily reports on your experiments with the subjects who are cognizant of the fact they are in virtual reality. If we do not see progress or do not like the results, Subjects Silva, Freeman, and Emerson will be euthanized."

"What about me and my brother?" Tavia asked. Her tone had shifted from demanding to fearful.

"As for Subject Tavia Patton, put her in the tank so she can say her good-byes to her brother. We will devise a plan to return her to Earth immediately. We will return Subject Charlie Patton once the additional procedures have been completed."

"Wait!" Tavia called out. After silencing the room, she took a moment to consider her next move. She had been the one who selected the recent abductees. She had hoped to ignite a relationship with Brady Emerson, but no spark ever developed. She wanted Arnold Grayson, Cocoa Freeman, and Long Jenn Silva to pay for their past sins. So far, only Grayson had been killed.

"I'm confident you'll return my brother once you've fixed him. I'd rather wait until then to see him," she said, concealing her actual motivation. "But as for Brady… I didn't leave things right with him. If it wouldn't mess up the experiment, I'd like to be put back in the tanks with Brady and Jenn and Cocoa long enough to bid them a proper farewell."

"You understand it is highly unlikely that Jenn Silva, Cocoa Freeman, and Brady Emerson will ever return to Earth?"

Tavia stood confidently before the powerful Nawerssian. "I was listening closely. And I understood every single word that you said, General. *'Highly unlikely.'* I understand."

☠☠☠

IN THE VIRTUAL REALITY TANKS—ABOARD THE VILNAGROM-II
YEAR 0 + 286 DAYS (OCTOBER 12th)

Jenn, Cocoa, and Brady awakened to find they had been sleeping on concrete. It took a few moments to adapt to the rapid reentry into the life suspension tanks. Once they were able to assess their surroundings, they discovered they'd been returned to a familiar setting.

"Do either of you recognize this place?" Jenn asked.

Brady nodded. "We're back in Downtown St. Louis. This is the train station across from the baseball stadium." There wasn't another living creature anywhere around. "It looks like they put us back in the spot where we first met..."

The luchadora finished the sentence for her friend. "Only this time they've bumped the clock forward to a point after the rest of the world vanished." She glared at Cocoa. If she hadn't interfered in their revolt, they might not have been returned to this cruel déjà vu setting. Almost snarling, she asked, "How does your back feel?"

Cocoa stood. She puffed out her chest and balled her fists. Throughout her wrestling career, she never faced "Long Jenn Silva" in a match. Maybe it was time for them to square off to determine who was the top dog.

Brady interrupted the showdown. "Guys, did you hear that?"

It was a woman's voice. From up the stairs—on ground level—a woman could be heard calling out.

"Who could that be?" he wondered aloud. Two-by-two, he sprinted up the stairs to see who was occupying this barren world with them.

Tavia. The vindictive vixen ignored Brady. She breezed past him, stomping towards the stairwell he'd just climbed.

The curls and bandanna atop Jenn's head came into view as she navigated the concrete stairs. Tavia didn't give Jenn an opening. As soon as she spotted her, the blond waitress left her feet.

Diving with little regard for her own well-being, she caught Jenn with a direct hit. The duo went flying down the stairs, landing with a loud thud that took Jenn's breath away. Tavia's fists rained down on her new enemy. "You know the old saying. 'If they won't join you... beat 'em!'"

☠☠☠

PRESENT DAY-ABOARD THE VILNAGROM-II
YEAR 0 + 286 DAYS (OCTOBER 12th)

Polo alerted as many of his fellow crew members as possible. Dorothea and Carver huddled around a monitor in their sleeping quarters. Armstrong and Monroe communicated from the theater, while Avis and Baron listened in from the Control Center.

The Cartographer reported, "The vital signs for Subject Silva have reached alarming levels!" he said with a great deal of urgency in his voice.

"Please be more specific," the ship's doctor insisted.

"Her blood pressure has risen to extreme levels. Heart rate has jumped significantly. Adrenaline is surging. Pulse-Ox is spiking up and down..."

Baron interrupted, "They are in virtual reality. What does it matter?"

Dorothea explained, "A specimen can be killed in VR. Subject Silva is experiencing her surroundings as if it is one hundred percent real. Even if she is not actually getting hit, her mind and her body are tricked into thinking she is. Stroke or heart attack is possible."

Polo offered to enter the life suspension tank to investigate. "If someone could assist me, I could link directly into the VR and report back..."

Being the youngest adult Nawerssian on the ship, Monroe almost always deferred to the senior members of the crew. *Not today. Not now.* She rose to her feet. "It is time for action!" she proclaimed. "We do not need to waste even a second investigating. Reports are unnecessary. There are no fools among us. We *know* what is happening. There is no reason to debate. I am going there immediately! Avis, connect this corridor with Corridor 16."

Without further explanation, she sprinted down the hallway and stood by the air lock.

A series of tones rang out from the control panel. Buzzing and humming sounds echoed through the hallway. Then came another tone. "Monroe. Electromagnetic Connection is complete. Enter the safety code when you are ready... And, please, be careful."

Armstrong was on her heels. "I will go with her."

Both Monroe and her adoptive father stepped through the door that took them from Corridor 2 to the air lock. Once the door was shut and securely sealed, they would have approximately two minutes before the door to Corridor 16 could be opened.

Armstrong disabled the communications link between the interior of the air lock and the Control Center. He used this pause in the action to speak frankly with his daughter. "You heard Hannibal and Oya?"

"Yes."

"You know the history? You are aware of how your mother and father were killed... the circumstances behind it?"

"Of course."

"Do you see the similarities?"

"Absolutely."

"The *Vilnagrom-III* will be entering this solar system in the very near future."

Monroe nodded. They would be clear to step into Corridor 16 at any moment.

She didn't choose the name Monroe. That designation was chosen by a mother who disappeared and a father who abandoned her before she ever had a chance to make a single memory with either of them.

In trying to connect with her biological parents in some sort of metaphysical way, she sought to look for an avenue into their collective mindset. She believed the best way to do so was by studying the icon who had been the inspiration of the name they had given her. As a youth, the Nawerssian watched every movie and read every article she could about Marilyn Monroe.

She discovered she was a beautiful woman who lived a tragic life. She possessed confidence and more wisdom than any of her contemporaries ever seemed to acknowledge. One of the celeb's most enlightened quotes seemed to fit the prevailing attitude of those on the *V-II:*

"Men are climbing to the moon, but they don't seem interested in the beating human heart."

The statement caught Armstrong off guard. "What?"

"The role we play in the lives of those we abduct... We are failing them. And in failing them, the entire purpose of Project *Vilnagrom* is corrupted. I want to change that."

Armstrong did not have time to respond. More humming, and additional tones sounded from the Control Panel. They would be free to open the door in seconds.

"Reactivating the communications link."

Avis spoke. Though there was so much he wanted to say, he kept it simple. "You are clear to enter Corridor 16. Good luck."

☠☠☠

IN THE VIRTUAL REALITY TANKS—ABOARD THE VILNAGROM-II YEAR 0 + 286 DAYS (OCTOBER 12th)

Upon entry into the virtual setting, the light was so intense that she couldn't see a thing. Her eyes adjusted quickly.

Monroe fought to get her bearings. Entering VR from a state of consciousness was difficult because the ears filled with life suspension fluid. It took longer for her hearing to normalize. She didn't have time to wait!

With the virtual world around sounding like she was underwater, Monroe spotted Tavia and Jenn as the co-ed stomped on the grappler again and again. The young woman was merciless in her attack.

Monroe raced towards the duo. Wanting to ensure it remained a fair fight, Cocoa tried to step in the way. The Nawerssian was at least three inches taller and twenty-five pounds heavier than the daughter of the wrestling legend. Her size advantage and the momentum she had built up while charging towards her allowed Monroe to plow over Cocoa like a fullback crossing into the endzone to score the winning touchdown.

Once she was within a few feet of the fighters, Monroe launched herself forward, driving her shoulder into Tavia's ribs. The blindside hit was effective in bringing an end to the attack and tricking Tavia's mind and body into responding as if she'd actually been tackled.

The surprising heroine continued her onslaught following the initial takedown. She pounded Tavia with several successive punches to the jaw, then rolled into a chokehold. "The fight ends now!"

VILNAGROM-I

CREW MEMBERS (AFTER 19 YEARS ORBITING EARTH)

ROLE	CODENAME
V-I 1/GENERAL	JAGGER (in the brig)
V-I 2/SKIPPER	MAGELLAN
V-I 3/EXPLORER	ARMSTRONG
V-I 7/PILOT	AVIS
V-I 14/UNASSIGNED	*MONROE* (child of Crockett & McCoy)

DECEASED:

V-I 4/CARTOGRAPHER	CROCKETT
V-I 6/PILOT	LINDY
V-I 9/BIOLOGICAL SCIENCE	*TEY-RIXIA*
V-I 10/DOCTOR	*McCOY*
V-I 11/UNASSIGNED	ADAM (child of Magellan & Tey-Rixia)

DEFECTED:

V-I 5/NAVIGATOR	*VALENTINA*
V-I 8/PHYSICAL SCIENCE	*MANTLE*
V-I 12/UNASSIGNED	MONTANA (child of Mantle & Lindy)
V-I 13/UNASSIGNED	*GRETA* (child of Crockett & McCoy)

VILNAGROM-II

CREW MEMBERS (AFTER 18 YEARS ORBITING EARTH)

ROLE	CODENAME
V-I 3/SENIOR EXPLORER	ARMSTRONG
V-I 7/PILOT	AVIS
V-I 16/UNASSIGNED	*MONROE*
V-II 1/GENERAL	HANNIBAL
V-II 2/SKIPPER	*OYA*
V-II 3/EXPLORER	ATLAS
V-II 4/CARTOGRAPHER	POLO
V-II 5/NAVIGATOR	BARON
V-II 6/PILOT	QUETZAL
V-II 7/PILOT	*HAZEL (presumed dead)*
V-II 8/PHYSICAL SCIENCE	MIDAS
V-II 9/BIOLOGICAL SCIENCE	*CARVER*
V-II 10/DOCTOR	*DOROTHEA*
V-II 11/UNASSIGNED	PTOLEMY (child of Carver & REDACTED)
V-II 12/UNASSIGNED	*CLEO* (child of Dorothea & REDACTED)

V-II 11/UNASSIGNED – PTOLEMY & V-II 12/UNASSIGNED - CLEO are children currently in the observation & learning period.

19: LOUD AND CLEAR

"Everyone in the building needs to shut their pie holes and listen up. I'm going to say this loud and clear, and I don't wanna hafta say it again... You ready? Here goes... No comment. Ha! I got nothing to say to you buffoons!"

-BUBBA BRUNOCELLI in-ring promo given prior to his Falls Count Anywhere Match against Hal Hitchcock as part of the AWWA's Third Annual Black & Blue Bonanza!

IN THE VIRTUAL REALITY TANKS
ABOARD THE VILNAGROM-II
YEAR 0 + 287 DAYS (OCTOBER 13th)

When she went to sleep, Jenn was in agony. Tavia had blindsided her, then dished out a brutal beatdown. Though she was living suspended in a virtual reality tank, the setting and the beating were convincing enough to fool her mind into feeling the lingering effect of every kick and every punch she received.

When she awakened, the only pain she felt was a kink in her neck. "Where are we now?" she said aloud as her eyes tried to adjust to the dimly lit surroundings.

The luchadora had gone to bed in one of the fanciest hotel suites that virtual St. Louis had to offer. But Jenn was no longer lying amongst an ocean of pillows in a comfy, king-size bed. She wasn't in a bed at all!

"What the hell?"

Her second exclamation woke Brady. "Are we back on the train?"

It was almost pitch black inside. The commuter car wasn't moving. But once Brady had identified where they were, the contour of the plastic seats became obvious. "What are we doing on a train?"

Brady replied, "Based on past experience, I don't think it's anything good." He reached for the back of a seat to pull himself into a standing position. "Ladies? You might want to wake up."

Tavia and Cocoa both grumbled about being prematurely awakened.

Monroe, however, was appreciative. She took a moment to assess her surroundings. "This is the train you were on when you were abducted?"

Cocoa answered, "Smells better, but from what I can tell, it looks the same."

"I think we should get off. Right now!"

The Nawerssian didn't have to say it twice to convince Jenn. She sprang to her feet. After taking Brady by the hand, she felt her way towards the front of the car. Once she located the emergency exit button, they were able to force the doors open and step off the train.

Jenn squinted to help her see in the dark underground station. "This is where we were when the train stopped and sat there for a really long time," she said.

Cocoa agreed. "The empty train went by in the opposite direction. Not a single rider, even though the thing should have been packed?"

"That's the one."

Tavia chimed in. "Whoop-de-doo! Are you guys gonna sing 'Kumbaya' or something to celebrate the happy homecoming? Or are we gonna get out of here?"

No one had time to take the bait.

A tremendous rumbling would have drowned out any retorts to Tavia's sarcasm. The entire Eighth & Pine Station shook. Tiles fell off the walls. Florescent light bulbs exploded, sending bits of glass raining onto the cement floor below. Towards the exits, sounds of explosions could be heard coming from the ground level above.

"Earthquake!" Brady yelled.

"Sounds like we're under attack!" guessed Jenn.

Large hunks of concrete began crumbling from the walls around them. Cocoa turned and moved to seek cover inside the train car.

Monroe instinctively grabbed the booker by her wrist. "No!" Pointing towards the dual escalators and the flight of steps leading out of the underground tunnel, she barked her instructions. "We need to get above ground!"

"You want to go towards the explosions?"

"If not, we could be buried alive!"

The group scrambled to the top of the stairwell. The climb was difficult. Cocoa held them up when she became frozen in fear once the blasts boomed one after another after another.

Everyone hesitated and desperately attempted to clutch something solid when the explosions were close. The aftershocks caused the steps beneath their feet to sway like a raft atop a raging ocean.

After making it to the surface, they looked up and saw the city being decimated by hundreds of alien ships. The fighters swooped through the air like hornets, indiscriminately firing laser cannons into every road, building, and vehicle in sight.

Tavia grabbed Monroe by the shoulder and swung her around. "Friends of yours? What the hell are they doing?"

"Those ships are not from my world. They are not Nawerssian. I have never seen anything like them."

Brady grabbed both Tavia and Monroe by their wrists. "We can't stand here and argue! We're sitting ducks out here! We need to take cover!"

The group raced through the streets. They searched for places to duck behind for protection. It was a search to find concrete barriers or hunks of displaced asphalt or other nooks and crannies that the alien attackers had already hit. *The raiders wouldn't hit those exact spots again, would they?*

The young man found shelter between a pile of rubble and what was left of a toppled brick wall. He prayed aloud, "Dear God, save us!"

☠☠☠

ONE DAY LATER
YEAR 0 + 288 DAYS (OCTOBER 14th)

Jenn sat on one of the few patches of green grass left in the counterfeit world that she had been forced to call home. It was a piece of St. Louis that her All-World Wrestling Association colleague Henri Arceneaux once called "under the shadow of the Arch."

She spat. It wasn't just her way of trying to rid her mouth of a bitter taste. She was trying to pry a fond memory out of her mind. Henri was always good for a laugh. The man was a talented wrestler with a tremendous upside. Like Jenn, he was committed to the idea kayfabe… so much so that he had managed to convince her, Cocoa, and the rest of the AWWA roster that he grew up in France (instead of America's Heartland).

"Shadow of the Arch? How ironic," she muttered as she focused on how much of the fallen landmark rested in the waters of the Mississippi River.

"Who are you talking to?"

The pirate nearly jumped out of her boots. Brady startled her with his question. She hadn't noticed that he and Monroe were approaching.

"Absolutely no one," she replied with an accompanying roll of the eyes.

"That didn't sound too inviting," said Brady. Though the luchadora had not indicated he was welcome to do so, the perpetually nice guy lowered himself to sit next to her on the ground.

Jenn shrugged. "I guess I'm in a pissed off mood and I'm not quite ready to be done being pissed off."

Looking for something positive to say, Brady offered, "It looks like your scrapes and bruises are all gone."

She responded by holding up her hands. Fresh blood covered her swollen knuckles. "All but these."

Monroe expressed surprise over the injuries. "Our avatars reset at the beginning of each 24-hour period. That is why wounds heal so quickly in VR. It also explains why you might go to sleep wearing pajamas but wake up wearing your default outfit of clothing."

"Then why are Jenn's hands bloody?"

Before Monroe could offer a hypothesis, Jenn gave the answer. "Because, just a few minutes ago, I punched a brick wall twenty or thirty times. Like I said, I'm not quite ready to be done being pissed off... Oh, by the way, I'm giving this version of Purple Goo Virtual Reality a 'zero-star review.' Post-Alien Attack St. Louis is literally Hell on Earth."

Brady motioned with his head for Monroe to give him and Jenn some privacy. Though she had never lived on Earth, the Nawerssian had studied its people and visited its surface enough to recognize the signal. She tiptoed away.

Once Monroe had made her exit, Brady told Jenn, "Believe it or not, what you see as 'Hell on Earth,' I find somewhat peaceful."

"Peaceful?"

"Absolutely," he said. His optimism greatly contrasted Jenn's frustration and cynicism. "It's peaceful... especially when compared to what we experienced a few weeks ago when we thought anyone and everyone we cared about had instantly vanished into thin air. They're all okay. Isn't that good news?"

"Unicorns and rainbows!" she said mockingly. She couldn't stomach his overly joyful spin. Not today. "Look around! This is *our* life now. And this place is a nightmare. Aliens have imprisoned

us in their little virtual reality fishbowls. If that wasn't bad enough,
now they've dumped us in a pile of garbage that looks and smells
like a post-nuclear war setting. That, my friend, is Hell on Earth."
Once she finished, she rose to her feet. She was ready to stomp off
in any other direction. It was time to get away from Brady and his
Pollyanna attitude.

He refused to give up. "I'm sorry if it's making you angry, but
no matter what you say, I find it peaceful."

Jenn couldn't help it. Frustration forced a smile to flash across
her face. Maybe a famous quote from *The Princess Bride* would
help her get her point across. "You keep using that word. I do not
think it means what you think it means."

"You don't? Inconceivable!" Brady returned the smile. (His
came much more voluntarily.) Then he patted the spot on the
ground that Jenn had vacated, inviting her to sit down again. Once
she did, he continued. "Think about it... Is 'peace' the absence of
violence and destruction? Or is it something else? When we first
got taken, confusion surrounded us everywhere we went. They
made it look like empty airplanes were crashing into bridges.
Thousands of people gone in an instant... Poof! We were
desperately searching for an explanation. We didn't get any sort of
answers. If we had, they would have been nothing but lies... Here,
we know we're in a phony world. It's a terrible setting, but there is
no genuine conflict. It's quiet, empty, and lonely. *Yes.* But it's also
a place where the only harm that can come to us comes from
within. We don't have to feel any confusion about what's
happening to us or why it's happening in the first place. We know
all that. Right?"

He continued, "I think about peace like this... When I was a
little boy, thunderstorms used to scare the crap out of me. My room
lit up every time there was a flash of lightning. I'd count, 'one

Mississippi, two Mississippi, three Mississippi.' I only stopped when I heard the thunder that followed. Then I knew how far away that deadly lightning bolt was from striking our house and killing me dead. If the count got under 'two Mississippi,' I'd go running to my mom and dad's bedroom. I'd snuggle in between my parents, and suddenly I felt one hundred percent safe... Not because the thunderstorm had gone away. But because, at least in *my* mind, my mom and my dad were bigger than any bolt of lightning that ever came out of the clouds. The violence and destruction? Those were still right outside my window. But my parents were a whole lot closer. So I felt *peace*."

Brady wasn't sure if his words of wisdom were helping. He wrapped things up by saying, "When you can focus your mind to look beyond the confusion, you can find peace no matter what your surroundings may look like. If you do that, it'll give you a leg up on whatever the bad guys are throwing at you."

☠☠☠

ABOARD THE VILNAGROM-II
YEAR 0 + 288 DAYS (OCTOBER 14th)

Pilots were assigned several duties aboard the *Vilnagrom-II*. Their primary role was to transport Explorers and Scouts to Earth for their reconnaissance and abduction missions. They also assisted the Skipper in maintaining the structural integrity of the spacecraft.

Most of their time, however, was spent manning the bridge and control center while the *V-II* was "docked." There was no piloting and no flying involved in the job. It was anything but exhilarating. It was nearly impossible to generate an adrenaline rush when they were relegated to long rotations of watching a bank of lights and monitors.

Avis stepped onto the deck to begin his regular shift. He was relieving his fellow shuttle jockey, Quetzal.

"Yet another quiet night on the flight deck. Nothing to report. It seems like all the recent excitement has been occurring on the ship. Personally, I would like to get in some flying time. It would be nice to get off this ship for a few hours."

Avis was uninterested in chit-chatting with the much younger pilot.

Quetzal (who insisted that his name be pronounced as if it rhymed with "pretzel") chose his name from the Aztec god of wind and air, Quetzalcoatl. He was a decorated pilot from a Nawerssian-Cyborg skirmish that occurred after Avis and the original *Vilnagrom-I* crew departed Na-Werss. Years after selecting his Earthly name, the arrogant flyboy still enjoyed reliving the stories of his wartime heroism. That joy was eclipsed only by explaining why naming himself after the wrathful feathered-serpent deity was the perfect choice for him.

Avis preferred to avoid the braggadocios proclamations. Instead, he hoped to complete the "handoff" by running through the checklist as quickly as possible. "What is that red light on the Communication Grid?"

"This is the first I have seen it," Quetzal admitted. Many on the crew would have felt great shame by missing a potentially important message. Not Quetzal. He was amazing behind the stick of a Nawerssian Fighter. His piloting skills were believed to be at a level far superior to those possessed by the aging Avis (or anyone else on the *V-II*, for that matter). But he made it no secret that he dreaded the tedium of working on the bridge.

Another factor contributed to Quetzal's apathy. The red light flashed somewhat regularly with warnings of incoming transmissions. Of all the times it lit up on his watch, he had never received an actual communication. Often, an intercepted satellite communication triggered the alarm. Other times, it was a magnetic pulse from a distant star or radio broadcast that bounced off the Earth's stratosphere.

Quetzal leaned forward and pressed the appropriate button to play the recording.

The message began with a long tone. A voice speaking in traditional Nawerssian followed. "Attention *Vilnagrom-II*... Greetings from Skipper Twee Zie'Naxx of the *Vilnagrom-III*. Our ship has successfully passed through and exited the wormhole. Please acknowledge receipt of this transmission."

The *V-III*'s greeting was followed by a timestamp. "Replay the message," Avis said, not caring that it sounded like he was giving a command instead of making a request.

"Our instructions are to contact the General and the Skipper immediately upon receipt of any Nawerssian communications."

"Replay the message!"

Avis listened carefully to the greeting, paying particular attention to the timestamp. "There must be a mistake. According to the digital markings, that message was sent weeks ago."

Quetzal was not nearly as alarmed. "I suspect their sensors were damaged during their passage through the wormhole... I'm going to inform the Skipper..."

"Please do that. In the meantime, I will acknowledge receipt of their communication as they requested."

After the hotshot yielded control of the Comm Grid to Avis, the veteran pilot broadcast the *V-II*'s reply: "Greetings, *Vilnagrom-III*. The *Vilnagrom-II* has received your transmission. Your timestamp settings may require calibration. Please check sensors against star charts."

Mission protocols required that the *V-III* send their transmission immediately after passage through the Eye of Jupiter Wormhole. Because Jupiter is approximately 450 million miles from Earth, communications between the two ships were expected to experience a four-hour lag in each direction.

Avis logged the time before he moved into the Captain's Chair. "Now we wait... We should receive a response from the *V-III* in approximately eight hours."

☠☠☠

FOUR HOURS LATER

News of the *V-III*'s transmission generated a lot of excitement among the crew of the *V-II*. Quetzal was joined by his good friend Baron. They shared a bottle of whiskey that he and Atlas had grabbed during a recent reconnaissance mission.

"Stop watching that board, Avis. You yourself said that we would not be receiving a reply to your most recent message for at least eight hours," the arrogant young pilot called across the distance that separated those who had gathered to celebrate and Avis, who was still trying to perform his assigned tasks. "Join us!"

Avis declined the offer. "Perhaps I will indulge after my shift is over."

Baron wrapped one arm around Quetzal's shoulder, while using the other to lift the bottle of booze to his thin lips. Beginning to feel the effects of the alcohol, he said, "If there is any left, you will be welcome to indulge."

Oya and the massive Hannibal also gathered on the bridge. They sipped on traditional Nawerssian Meezah along with Atlas and his brother, Midas.

Their presence served as a distraction to Avis, who was still trying to solve the mystery of the seemingly incorrect timestamp that accompanied the *V-III*'s communication. It wasn't the noise. It was the fact that the six of them made it no secret that they wanted to take an aggressive stance when dealing with the newest batch of specimens. The group believed that operating a ship clear of any significant problems would elevate their collective status in the annals of their people's storied history.

Were Avis, Armstrong, and Monroe seen as "problems," too? Did some of those on the bridge believe that eliminating the remnants of the initial Vilnagrom voyage might further elevate the prestige of the V-II crew?

It was a lot to think about.

Then the light on the Comm Grid flashed red again.

Avis took a deep breath, then called to the revelers across the deck. "Skipper... General... We have another red light on the Comm Grid. It could be a message from the *V-III*." The Pilot explained that the *V-III* was much too far away to have already received the reply he sent four hours earlier, responded, and have that response travel the incredible distance back to the *V-II*. "Their ship could have sustained serious damage in the passage through the wormhole. It could be a distress call."

Quetzal spoke for the group. "Or it could be a repeat of their first message. It could be a radio bounce from Earth. It is senseless to assume the worst when it may just be a score from the Green Bay Packers game."

Hannibal expressed the sentiment in fewer words. "Stop bickering. Play the message!"

"Greetings from Skipper Twee Zie'Naxx of the *Vilnagrom-III*. Rendezvous fast approaching. Modification G-0-1-7-7-1-N-1. Repeating: Modification G-0-1-7-7-1-N-1. End of transmission."

The code was unlike any Nawerssian message Avis had ever heard.

The communication generated more speculation and confusion on the flight desk. Had a recent advance in Nawerssian technology allowed the *V-III* to send its message instantaneously? Was the ship closer than expected? Or was Zie'Naxx somehow communicating with another ship?

"The timestamp?" Hannibal asked.

"Exactly two hours ago." Avis reported.

Quetzal offered an explanation, "This message was not responsive to the previous inquiry Avis made about their sensors. Perhaps the *V-III* is experiencing problems with their Communications Grid and this was nothing but a fragment they did not intend to broadcast."

"Play it again," Hannibal demanded.

Everyone in the room became silent.

After hearing it once more, Hannibal said, "That signal was loud and clear."

"How should I reply?"

Hannibal held up his hand. He flashed a Nawerssian gesture similar to an emphatic head shake. "The signal was clear. The message, however, did not follow our protocols. I am ordering that we go on High Alert Status... Immediately."

☠☠☠

THE NEXT MORNING
YEAR 0 + 289 DAYS (OCTOBER 15th)

With Monroe working inside the life suspension tanks, the remaining members of the crew shared her regular duties.

Dorothea was wrapping her silver robe around her as she greeted the day's instructor at her door. "Children... Explorer Armstrong is here for your daily lessons."

"Doctor, can I speak to you and Carver for a moment?" he asked. "It is a matter of utmost importance."

"Absolutely. But you will have to settle for only me. Carver is monitoring the food supply. Row after row of tanks, filled with all the synthetic organisms a crew can eat."

"I understand." Knowing that the children would soon be ready, Armstrong wasted little time. "Avis and I share concerns about the recent messages from the *Vilnagrom-III*. Specifically, he suspects—as do I— that these may not be the first transmissions that this ship has received from the *V-III*."

"What?" He was suggesting a possibility that Dorothea had never considered.

"Think back to our recent meeting, and how aggressively Hannibal and Oya wanted to exterminate the Earthly human test subjects... Now we get mysterious transmissions that indicate the *V-III* may be very close. Why would Hannibal and Oya keep that from us? Are they looking to modify the goals of the entire mission?"

"What do you mean?"

"What if those on the *V-III* have no intention of observing and reporting on the current occupants of Earth? What if they are looking to take a more aggressive approach to achieve the goal of 'return home?'"

Dorothea remained skeptical. "I acknowledge that Hannibal and Oya wanted to send Subjects Silva, Freeman, and Emerson out the launch tubes. But why do you think that means they want to attack the Earth?"

"Avis once referred to Project *Vilnagrom* as a 'suicide mission.' Perhaps there are some among us who do not like the idea of living remainder of their lives aboard a spacecraft. Perhaps they would like to accelerate the move to the surface of the Earth."

As the children approached, the Explorer expanded on his theory. "What if Quetzal had not missed the message indicator? Would we know that the *V-III* was in this solar system? Consider the possibility that Quetzal, Hannibal, and Oya have been secretly communicating with the *V-III* for weeks. Consider the ramifications if that mysterious code was signaling the details of a sinister plan against the people of Earth... or the people on this ship who might disapprove of taking any aggressive actions against the people of Earth... Avis and I have gone around and around. Unfortunately, we believe these concerns are not outrageous. We believe they may be a distinct possibility."

20: SHOW COLOR

*"Let me tell you one thing, Boris Sputnikov
thought he was pulling a fast one by busting that
Fabergé egg over my head. But that slimy
Russian found out that it takes a lot more than
that to stop Corporal Chambers. This American
BLEEDS red, white, and blue... U-S-A! U-S-A!
U-S-A!"*

*-CORPORAL CHAMBERS promo,
recorded during his feud with Boris Sputnikov at
the heart of the Cold War in the mid-1980s.*

SEVERAL MONTHS EARLIER
YEAR 0 + 2 DAYS (JANUARY 2nd)

Sounds of gunfire rattled the room. Images of World War II soldiers being gunned down blanketed across the TV screen. "Take that, you no good Nazi!"

Brady's roommate, Valērijs, was immersed in his first-person shooter video game.

Greg opened the door, inviting himself in like always.

"Die! Die, Nazi scum!" Val shouted again.

"Who me?" Greg laughed. This wasn't his first time witnessing the lanky Latvian being fully engrossed by war simulations.

Greg assessed the surroundings. A greasy pizza box and two empty Styrofoam cups of instant noodles rested on the coffee table in front of Val. "This explains why you didn't join us at The End Zone yesterday."

Without looking away from the TV, the gamer replied, "I was busy taking out bad guys in Northern Italy!"

Greg eyed the trash spread on and around the coffee table. Several drained energy drinks stood among the carnage. "When was the last time you slept?"

Brady walked into the room. "Oh hey, Greg. Come on in."

"Did you ask him?"

Still refusing to look away from the screen filled with digital depictions of German soldiers, Val pressed his roommate, "Who? Me? Ask me what?"

"Greg and Marshall and I are putting together a church league basketball team. We've got a couple other guys, but we need at least seven on the roster. Eight would be ideal."

Greg cut to the chase. "We thought you might like to play. Here's the kicker… It's a church league, so in order to remain eligible, you'd have to get off the couch and go with us to services at least once a week."

Brady didn't mind telling his roommate to get off the couch. However, he was a little uneasy pressuring Val on topics like church, God, religion, etc. He worried it might be crossing a line. "Do you ever go to church?"

"Oh, yes. As a child, I went often," he said as he put down his controller and shifted in his seat. The Latvian always seemed to exaggerate his Baltic accent when he told a story from his childhood. *Was this a tell? Was he about to launch into a tall tale?* "You see, my father worked as janitor at our church in Kuldīga. He always insisted on making the church spotless before services began. Early one Easter morning, he walked into building and saw that the baptismal pool had leaked. Water all over the sanctuary. He ran to the parsonage and told minister. He said, 'The baptismal pool is empty!' You must understand, in Latvian, the word is same for 'baptismal pool' and for 'tomb.' So when the minister heard, 'The tomb is empty!' he clapped his hands together and replied... 'Christ is risen indeed!'"

Brady fought the urge to laugh out loud. He caught himself and suppressed any audible sound. He and Valērijs had lived under the same roof for a year and a half, and he still had trouble reading him. *Was that a joke?*

Val allowed the awkward pause to linger for a moment before he picked up the controller. After unpausing the game and resuming the WWII bloodbath, he said, "I will play on your basketball team. I'm not exactly Kristaps Porziņģis, but I can put ball through hoop."

☠☠☠

THREE DAYS LATER
YEAR 0 + 5 DAYS (JANUARY 5th)

Sonlight Church. With two services on Saturday evening and three on Sunday morning, the non-denominational church held claim to the largest congregation in King City. The facilities were immaculate.

"Brady, Greg, Marshal... I see you've brought a friend with you." Pastor Winston never forgot a face. If someone was trying to remain anonymous among the masses who attended SC-KC, they were making a big mistake. The friendly minister always seemed to spot new visitors as soon as they stepped through the door.

"This is my housemate: Valērijs."

Pastor Winston made a good-faith effort to pronounce the Latvian's name correctly. "Val-jerris?"

"'Val' is fine," the visitor assured him.

"The College & Careers Class is going to put together a basketball team for the men's church league," Brady announced. "Val's going to start coming with us so he can play."

The pastor looked Val up and down. Even though the visitor was seated, he could tell that he stood over six feet tall. "Brought in a ringer. Smart... Val, it was very nice to meet you. Don't forget to fill out and sign the 'Who's Who in the Pew' form so we can send you a nice gift."

He stepped away to greet others who had entered the building.

A moment later, Marty Upshaw approached. The hometown celebrity was a former shooting guard and the all-time leading scorer for Central Illinois University. If he'd been a few inches taller, the master of the no-look pass would have made it to the

NBA. Unfortunately, he stood significantly below a height of six feet. That meant that his only offers came from teams in Europe.

His wife was a bit of a hometown celebrity, herself. Heather Tanner-Upshaw was a former contestant in the Miss Teen USA Pageant. Since she didn't want to move out of the Central Time Zone, Marty took a job selling pickup trucks at King Ford.

Now in his mid-thirties, Marty remained a formidable threat on the basketball court. He'd captained the church's "A Team" for the last eleven years. Everyone knew that his squad—who carried the well-earned nickname of "the Sonlight Devils"— were a lock to have their names engraved on the trophy for the twelfth straight year.

"I hear Sonlight's going to have a 'C-Team' in the men's division. That's great. Having three out of the ten teams in the league... I like the odds of SC-KC taking home the championship."

No one from "the Brady Bunch" replied with anything more than a head nod. Taking the hint, Marty meandered back to his beautiful bride. Before he did so, he offered, "Well, good luck, boys. See you at the gym."

☠ ☠ ☠

TWO MONTHS LATER
YEAR 0 + 69 DAYS (MARCH 10th)

"If you fall for the head fake, he'll drive right past you."

"I know. I know!"

Brady was understandably irritable. *"Nervous" may have been a better word.* Though the "C-Team" muddled through the regular season with three wins and six losses, they caught fire in the tournament and snuck into the Men's Church League Championship. Not surprisingly, they were matched up against the

Sonlight Devils. And Brady was the sacrificial lamb assigned to the task of guarding Marty "MVP" Upshaw.

The referee's whistle signaled it was time to break the huddle and meet at center court for the opening prayer that would kick off the contest.

"Stand your ground when you see that head fake," Greg leaned in and whispered (again) just before the jump ball.

The game began with a flurry of action. Valērijs won his first jump ball of the year. Despite being three inches shorter, he out jumped a school bus driver named Dallas. On the first possession, Greg fired up a wild shot, but Marshall snagged the rebound. He put it through the hoop for a 2-0 lead.

Upshaw made a remark about the C-Team using up all of their luck in the first minute of the game. Brady didn't acknowledge the comment, though. He was too busy hustling back down the court to take his defensive position.

After passing the ball around to his teammates, Upshaw looked to drive towards the basket. Brady did not flinch. The CIU legend plowed into his defensive counterpart. The legs of the hardwood combatants tangled, and they both dropped to the floor with a thud.

Upshaw was guilty of an offensive foul. The overzealous referee made sure that everyone gymnasium knew it. He blasted his whistle, and with a hand positioned against the back of his head, he yelled out, "Charging!"

Greg was the first one over. Trying to help his friend to his feet, he asked, "Are you okay? That sounded like it hurt?"

Brady nodded. "I'm fine."

A second later, he was on the receiving end of a push from Upshaw. "Get off of me!" complained the cocky car dealer.

The ref admonished them both to play a good, clean game. He also reminded them that the gymnasium they were playing in was an extension of "the Lord's House."

With his arms held outward, Brady protested, "What did *I* do?"

Following another bucket for the C-Team, the former Big Man on Campus locked eyes with Brady. *Upshaw's mad. He's going to try to run me over.*

A half-hearted head fake didn't fool Brady one bit. *He's going to try to run me over.*

Upshaw scowled and plowed forward. Attempting to draw a foul and send a stern message in one fell swoop, the hometown hero lowered his head while jumping forward.

His nose cracked against Brady's jaw. Bullseye! Blood sprayed everywhere. The ball squirted out of his hands and flew over the backboard.

The referee blew his whistle. "CHARGING!"

As representatives from each team helped Brady and Upshaw to their feet, the ref jumped in and told them that they had to get the blood cleaned up. He reminded both players, "You can't return to the court until the bleeding has completely stopped. And you can't have any blood on your clothing. League rules. Not a drop."

Once Brady realized that all the blood had come from his opponent's busted nose, he scrambled to the bench and swapped jerseys with another player.

Upshaw, on the other hand, had to tilt his head back and rush to the locker room for assistance. It was going to take some time to stop the crimson flow that he was experiencing.

Dallas the School Bus Driver tried to reassure his fellow A-Teamer. "We can beat these chumps without you. Get the fixed up and come back in."

Few people could have foreseen what happened next.

Valērijs caught fire.

The video game and energy drink aficionado hadn't scored more than four points in a single game. But lightning struck, struck twice, then struck again. Val hit six three-pointers in a row. By the time Heather Tanner-Upshaw was able to stop her husband's nosebleed and return him to the court, Brady's College & Careers Team led the Devils by the score of 24-2.

"What the heck got into you?" Greg asked his Latvian teammate during a timeout.

Brady had the answer. "I made him turn the video games off at midnight. It's amazing what the guy can accomplish if he gets eight hours of sleep!"

☠ ☠ ☠

IN THE VIRTUAL REALITY TANKS
ABOARD THE VILNAGROM-II
YEAR 0 + 291 DAYS (OCTOBER 17th)

Jenn turned towards Brady as he finished his story. She smiled. She couldn't help it. Over their extended period of time living together in virtual reality, she had come to learn that he was a young man who possessed a tremendous amount of wisdom... even if he did express it in strange ways and at odd times.

This one puzzled her, though. "Great story. But what does that possibly have to do with our current dilemma?"

He shrugged. "Maybe nothing. Or maybe it's just that telling that story reminds me of an old hymn we sang at church. You see, Sonlight went to contemporary music years ago. Still, there was a contingent of old timers that wanted to hear the classics... the old songs out of the dusty hymnals. To keep them happy, we always sang at least one 'oldie but goodie' at every service. You ever hear the song 'Power in the Blood?'"

Jenn shook her head "no."

"It was my dad's favorite." Brady rose to his feet. "Please excuse my miserable singing voice... If I remember correctly, the song goes like this:

'Would you be free from the burden of sin?/
There's power in the blood, power in the blood...
Would dah duh dah dah a victory win?/
There's wonderful power in the blood...
There is power, power, wonder-working power/
In the blood of the Lamb...
There is power, power, wonder-working power/
In the precious blood of the Lamb.'"

With his verse concluded, he sat back down. Almost apologetically, he said, "That's how the first part goes, anyway. Except for the 'dah duh dah dah' line. I forgot the words that go there."

Jenn placed her hand on Brady's knee. Detecting no resistance, she lowered her head onto his shoulder. "You don't have a miserable singing voice. It's actually quite nice." Then she laughed. "I do have one question, though... Other than perhaps giving us a spirit boost, how does that song help?"

Brady wiggled his shoulder. It was almost a subconscious move. He knew Jenn was married, and he didn't want to be tempted to make a move on another man's wife. "I don't know," he said. His words sounded like a confession. In reality, he was talking himself out of his plan before he ever articulated it. "Monroe thinks we've got a couple of allies on the ship. Allies that just might be willing to help us get back to Earth. Getting them to pull us out of the tank is the real challenge."

The luchadora picked up on his uncertainty. She looked him in the eyes. "If you've got an idea, I want you to tell me."

"I was thinking… What's the one time the aliens felt like they had to interrupt the simulation and jump into the tank? The one time something was happening in our virtual reality world that they didn't like, so they had to intervene?" Brady was gaining confidence in the plan. "When Tavia was kickin' the crap out of you!"

"Thanks for that reminder. She attacked me from behind, you know? It was a total blindside."

"I know, champ. That's not the point! You realize she never laid a finger on you. You and Tavia and the rest of us were in virtual reality. But the beating was so realistic and so intense that your mind convinced your body to react just like it would if she actually was beating you to within an inch of your life. It freaked these guys out so much that they sent Monroe into the tank with us to break it up!"

Jenn still wasn't completely following him. "Yeah?"

"When I drew those charges in the basketball game… When Marty Upshaw's wife had to take him into the locker room to stop his nose from bleeding… That's when we took control of the game."

"So whose nose are we supposed to bloody? Monroe's?"

"No. We bloody *my* nose… I want you to beat me and beat me and beat me some more. Kick my butt so bad that my brain tells my body it's the real deal. I can take it. Don't stop. Don't stop, no matter what… If they react like Monroe and I think they will, a bunch of blue men will come running and yank us out of the tank."

"Why would they take us out of the tank?"

"To put a stop to studying the four of us. Monroe says they're already close to deciding we're too much trouble... Basically, they'll pull us out of the tank so they can kill us," he explained.

"Wow! That sounds like a *great* idea!"

"We can't fight them as long as we're in the tank, can we? This is our only chance to get out. And it's our best chance to hit 'em when they're not expecting it."

Jenn smiled. The more she thought about it, the more she believed this was another one of Brady's surprising displays of wisdom. "That may be the greatest idea I've ever heard. Either that or maybe the stupidest."

"Why can't it be both?"

"I suppose it can."

Jenn leaned in. She lingered for a moment, a mere shallow whisper away from him. When he didn't pull away, she struck. She pressed her lips into his, then subtly parted them inviting Brady to explore.

The kiss was brief. But it was enough to send a chill up each of their spines. Both Jenn and Brady remained dangerously close to one another, their mouths hovering centimeters apart. Each fought the temptation to give into their urges any further. It would have been so easy to dive towards the other, beginning with another kiss and allowing the moment to take them wherever their desires chose to lead them.

But then Jenn pulled away. "Sorry about that... I shouldn't..."

Brady held up a hand. "Don't. I'm the one who should be apologizing. You're a married woman."

Jenn forced a smile in an effort to hide her disappointment. "Fair warning... If this crazy coup works, there's a good chance I'm going to want to kiss you again."

The feeling was mutual. Brady charted a plan of action. "That's
cool. One kiss. After that, we'll shake hands and I'll stay out of
your hair. I promise."

Jenn exhaled. She momentarily found herself at a loss for
words. "You're one amazing guy, Brady Emerson."

☠☠☠

THE NEXT MORNING
YEAR 0 + 292 DAYS (OCTOBER 18th)

She adjusted her leg brace while sitting on a massive hunk of
concrete. The slab had fallen from a toppled skyscraper in their
virtual post-apocalyptic setting. "Remember…" the luchadora told
herself as she sucked a massive amount of air into her lungs and
tried to get in the proper mindset for what needed to be done.
"You're Long Jenn Silva. Not 'Jennysys Quevedo.' Not just 'Jenn.'
And right now we need Long Jenn Silva to give Brady a massive
beatdown so these aliens will have no choice but to pull us from the
tanks. Remember this, Long Jenn Silva… you're the Queen of
Kayfabe. This ain't real. You need to sell it. This attack needs to
look and feel one hundred percent legit… You can do this."

The pirate marched across a vacant lot. Brady was still sleeping
on his own hunk of displaced concrete. Long Jenn Silva interrupted
his slumber when she drove her boot into the side of his head.

"HOW COULD YOU?" she screamed.

A split second later, she straddled her prone victim. Jenn
shelled him with a dizzying sequence of forearm smashes and
closed-fist punches. Though she had years of training and
experience inside the wrestling ring, there were no arm bars or
headlocks in this mauling. It was a primitive, but effective, ambush

comprised of kicks, stomps, slaps, punches, scratching, clawing, and choking, with a few blood-curdling screams thrown in for good measure.

Brady never got in a single lick. He'd suggested that she sneak up on him to make the attack feel more realistic to him and look more authentic to any observers.

Monroe ran over to "attempt" to intervene. She'd been given a "heads up" from Jenn, and agreed that the plan to force the Nawerssians to extract them from the tanks had potential. With no intention of actually bringing an end to the onslaught, the blue-skinned beauty sold a "ref bump" with precision.

"Jenn! What are you doing?" she yelled as she moved towards the fight. When she got too close to the action, she walked into the champ's elbow and sprawled backwards.

The bitter taste of adrenaline filled Jenn's mouth. She continued to pummel and strangle her friend. She was doing quite a number on Brady. The beating was enough to convince her that his distress was real.

She hoped her alien captors would step in soon.

21: DIVAS

"G'Day, Wrestling Fans. My name is Sydney, and I am the IWO's newest superstar. As you can tell from my accent, I come from Down Under. But I like being on top. That's where you'll find me very soon... on top of the IWO's Fighting Foxes!"

-SYDNEY's steamy in-ring promo filmed as she wore a string bikini in front of 15,000 screaming fans.

ABOARD THE VILNAGROM-II
YEAR 0 + 292 DAYS (OCTOBER 18th)

The alarms blared deafening tones. Dorothea and Carver raced down Corridor 16. Yet another emergency in the life suspension tanks! This time the sensors were indicating it was Subject Brady Emerson who was in distress.

Once in the compartment that housed Brady and the others, Dorothea entered a sequence of prompts into the panel on the wall. "I am extracting Subject Emerson first, then Monroe."

"Why was Monroe unable to prevent this?" Carver asked as she waited for a mechanical arm to remove Brady from the tank and lower him out for medical assistance.

The *V-II's* Doctor had kept their scheme a very closely held secret. She was confident her closest companion would side with her, Armstrong, Avis, and Monroe. But with every additional individual that knew of the plan came the greater the likelihood of discovery. They could not risk it. She would not share any information with anyone else until their group was poised to launch their mutiny.

Operating much like a Magic Claw Machine in an arcade, a mechanical device gripped Brady underneath each armpit, then pulled him out of the murky, purple liquid. It lowered him onto a slab for inspection by the medical personnel.

Brady lay motionless. He did not appear to be breathing.

"He has ingested a large amount of the LS Fluid!" Dorothea reported. *That was not part of the plan!* Everyone who went into virtual reality in the life suspension tanks swallowed some of the purple goo. Brady, however, had gulped down significantly more than usual. He risked drowning if it filled his lungs. He could be poisoned if he did not purge most of the toxic fluid from his system.

Carver acknowledged the report. "Understood." She couldn't assist Dorothea until Monroe had been extracted from the tank.

The Doctor pulled Brady into a seated position. With his back reclined against her, she wrapped her arms around him and pressed just below his ribcage. She let out a loud grunt as she squeezed with all her might.

Fluid splattered against the tank after it came blasting out of the young man's mouth. Brady coughed and gasped for air. The technology of Na-Werss was two thousand years ahead of that on Original Earth, but the Heimlich Maneuver (by whatever name it was known throughout the universe) remained the best way to save a choking humanoid.

Carver yelled at Monroe as the young Nawerssian was being lowered out of the tank. "Why were you unable to prevent this? You know that pulling someone in and out of VR drastically reduces the effectiveness of future experiments with that subject! Hannibal and Grace are going to want to expel him out the launch tubes!"

Brady continued to hack and cough and regurgitate more of the slime that had contaminated his lungs. Most of the disgusting substance had been swallowed while he was getting pulverized by Jenn.

"Is he alright?" Monroe asked.

Dorothea replied, "He will be fine."

Carver didn't necessarily agree. "He may well survive this episode. But, like I said, I expect that the Senior Officers will be united in their position. They are going to order that Emerson, Silva, and Freeman be euthanized... Monroe, how did this happen?"

"Perhaps you and Dorothea should talk while I extract the others from the tank."

Carver and Dorothea were stepping outside when Armstrong burst through the door. He brought a levitating box with him. "We do not have much time." He reached into the container and pulled out Brady's Pittsburgh Pirates jersey, followed by his shorts, shoes, and socks. Handing them to Monroe, he instructed her, "Help him get dressed."

"What about my hat?" he asked.

Armstrong chose not to answer. There was no time to waste talking about a baseball cap. Instead, he handed Jenn and Cocoa the clothing they had been wearing when they were abducted.

Once the clothing had been distributed, the veteran Nawerssian Explorer presented Jenn and Brady with sheathed daggers. They were the same daggers he had taken from Jagger after the *Vilnagrom-I* crew fractured.

"These weapons once were used for extremely evil purposes," Armstrong told them. "Today, it is my hope that, if you use these blades, justice will be the result."

Brady balanced the dagger in his palm. Then he asked, "Got any guns? My dad used to take me shooting all the time. I'm an excellent shot."

"Guns like you use on Earth? No way," Monroe answered. "One miss and the bullet would tear a hole through the wall. The corridor would depressurize and the entire arm might rip away from the ship. Only an idiot would fire a gun up here... That or someone with a death wish."

Brady required no more explanation. "Roger that."

Armstrong jumped in. He did not want his new allies to be caught off guard. "There are Stun Blasters on this ship. We have none to spare, and no time to teach you how to use them... Just remember, each blaster has the capacity to fire two stun shots or one kill shot. Then it must recharge."

Blasters! Did he say "Blasters?"

Jenn looked to her friend, hoping for some reassurance. "Are we really going to do this?"

Brady was ready. Looking down at his jersey, he declared, "We're pirates, right? Let's be pirates."

"What about the children?"

Armstrong jumped in. "They are with Avis in the Control Room... Monroe, protect them at all costs."

The youthful Nawerssian woman tapped Brady's shoulder with the back of her hand. "You're coming with me." Then the two of them ran out of the room and down the corridor.

Their quick exit frustrated Jenn. She'd spent the last three months with Brady. Over that time, they had grown very close. *Maybe a little too close.* The wrestling champ had been tasked with beating him to within an inch of his life. Though she shuddered to consider the possibility, one of them might die while taking part in this alien revolt. She didn't like the thought of their last moments together being spent with her kicking and pounding him so close to death.

Armstrong attempted to keep his team moving in the right direction. With the alarms continuing to put the rest of the crew on alert, they did not have much more time to get organized. "We need to keep moving!"

With Monroe and Brady on their way to protect the Nawerssian children, all eyes landed on Cocoa. She made no effort to scrub the purple film from her body. She stared at the life suspension tank. Her clothes remained neatly folded in her hands.

Armstrong gestured towards Cocoa. He asked Jenn, "Is she going to be a problem?"

The booker spoke for herself. "I'm right here. If you're talkin' 'bout me, I suggest you talk to me directly... To answer your question, I'm not gonna get in your way. But I'm not doing one thing to help you, either." She tapped the glass of the tank. "I'm gonna sit this silly little rebellion out. And whenever the dust settles, I'm gonna ask whoever wins to put me right back in there. I don't particularly care who wins in your battle of evil versus evil. I'll just let you put me back in the tank where I'm not in agonizing pain one hundred percent of the time."

☠☠☠

FOURTEEN MONTHS EARLIER
YEAR -1 + 238 DAYS (AUGUST 26th)

"You weren't kidding when you said there would be a lot of people here!"

Jenn and Cocoa walked into the packed convention center. Wrestling fans from all over the Midwest had traveled miles and miles of interstate highway to attend the Sixth Annual Heroes & Headlocks Convention. The center was filled with row after row of vendors hocking memorabilia, magazines, and T-shirts. Current and former wrestlers were present, raking in some extra cash in booths set up for photo ops and autographs.

"Just wait until tonight. Instead of a couple hundred people in the stands, we'll have at least five thousand in the audience," Cocoa promised. "This will be one of our biggest crowds of the year."

Before they could get ready for that night's matches, Jenn and Cocoa were told to put in a couple hours at the "Women of Wrestling" Autograph Station. "It's a good way to connect with some of our biggest fans," Cocoa told her friend as they approached their designated area. "As long as none of them get to cozy when they wrap their arms around you for a picture."

As their autograph table came into sight, they could see a gigantic flat screen television set up behind where they would be sitting. Clips of a scantily clad women's wrestler played on a loop. The blond bombshell could be seen riding in a convertible, being doused with water, riding on the back of a horse, running on the beach, riding a motorcycle, and occasionally tussling with other wrestle-babes... all of this was done while she wore just enough clothing to maintain a PG-13 rating.

Though she was considerably older than she was when the clips were filmed, the star of the video was shimmying into the middle of the three seats at their table.

Jenn stopped in her tracks. She held out her arms to impede Cocoa's progress. "Who is *that*?"

"Pops didn't tell you?" she said while rolling her eyes. "This afternoon we'll be sharing the spotlight with Sydney, a former Fighting Fox."

"Oh brother!" the pirate said while rolling her eyes.

The Fighting Foxes were women's wrestlers from an era in which they didn't do much actual wrestling. The top promotions recruited swimsuit models and pom pom girls to put on bikinis and parade around the ring between the matches. Occasionally they'd step through the ropes for a bout of their own. But those fights were usually gimmick-laden sideshows with not so clever names like "Naughty School Girl Match," "Bikini Car Wash Match," and "Take My T-Shirt Match."

After a quick replay of their conversation in her head, Cocoa held her hand out and stopped Jenn this time. "I'm also guessing Pops didn't tell you another important piece of information... You're scheduled to fight Sydney tonight."

"No. Tonight I'm fighting Kelly Ka-Pow in a match to determine the Number One Contender."

"I don't think so," the boss's daughter said while shaking her head. "Sydney got her start in the AWWA. Back then she was known as Outback Annie. She briefly wrestled with a crocodile hunter gimmick until she got lured away by Conrad Griffin. She begged her old friend Fireball to give her a match tonight, and you, New Girl, got stuck with the short straw... Sorry to tell you this, but it looks like he hasn't bothered to tell you that your big Number One Contenders match will have to wait for another day."

"That sucks!" Jenn said with a frown. Then the frown got even more extreme when she saw that Sydney's line for autographs was twice as long as Cocoa's... and that Jenn's line had only two people waiting to meet her.

☠☠☠

Cocoa was right. Jenn not only had to endure two hours of being gagged by the overwhelming aroma of Sydney's perfume, she was going to be subjected to some extra time in the ring with a woman who came from an era in which female combatants saw their value measured more by pin-ups than pinfalls.

Prior to the match, Fireball had given Jenn a list of moves she could not use against Sydney. No slams, no suplexes, no suicide dives. "Keep it simple. Kicks, slaps, and chops are fine. A six-minute match will be about perfect."

"Six minutes of getting my hair pulled before she pins me with a surprise roll up! I'm not sure 'perfect' is the word I'd use to describe it."

Cocoa was there to keep Jenn in check. "Careful, New Girl," she said, reminding the pirate that she was going to have to take one for the team.

The roof almost came off the convention center when Sydney paraded down to the ring. Jenn had plenty of experience playing the heel/*rudo*/bad guy. Still, she was none too happy to be doing so on this occasion.

Things didn't get any better when the opening bell rang and the fight began. Sydney came charging towards her with her claws out. The Aussie wasn't equipped for a contest with real holds or wrestling moves. She was limited to a line of attacks that included slapping, scratching, kicking, and yanking Jenn by the hair.

"Easy, Chica!" Jenn's opponent squealed when the pirate responded with a slap of her own.

Is this woman serious?

Thankfully, Fireball booked the match to end with Jenn's originally scheduled opponent— Kelly Ka-Pow (aka "The Chaotic Clown")— barging into the ring to attack both wrestlers. The referee had no choice but to end the match as a double-disqualification when the villain came running in with a mallet.

A DQ was a result the pirate could stomach. She may have never lived it down if she had been pinned by the bleach-blond bimbo.

☠ ☠ ☠

It was the end of the night. Jenn was packing up her gear when Sydney approached. Still a little perturbed about the last-minute change to her assignment, the luchadora offered an unenthusiastic "Hey."

The Aussie had enough exuberance for the both of them. "Long Jenn Silva! I'm glad I caught you before you left... I want to thank you for what you did and what you do!"

"Oh?"

"You women wrestlers these days... you're really something special. You do things in the ring that I could never dream about doing. Certainly not now. Not even fifteen, twenty years ago. When I worked for the IWO, they sometimes called it women's wrestling, but it was really a bunch of girls runnin' around in their knickers... Athletes like you have legitimized women's wrestling as a sport. I sincerely thank you for that."

Jenn didn't know what to say.

"I also wanted to thank you for agreeing to our match tonight. Fireball wasn't overly excited about having me face you. How'd he put it...? 'Syd, if my top prospect pitches a fit about it, I'm not gonna make her fight you.' From the bottom of my heart... Thanks for not pitching a fit."

Jenn shrugged and smiled. "It was no big deal."

"That's where you're wrong," Sydney continued. "Thanks to this match tonight, I'll have a whole new batch of fans who find their way onto my website. They'll watch my old matches on the internet. They'll order my 'Best of' DVD, my book, and... *other stuff*." (The "other stuff" she was referring to included a collection of semi-nude pictures and a lingerie calendar.) "Sure, there will be some creepy messages in the inboxes of my social media accounts. But it's mostly all good. Because of you, I probably just made enough money to pay for braces for my daughter."

She reached in and wrapped Jenn up in a massive hug.

Maybe her perfume doesn't smell that bad, after all.

☠☠☠

PRESENT DAY - ABOARD THE VILNAGROM-II
YEAR 0 + 292 DAYS (OCTOBER 18th)

Fear consumed Carver. The Nawerssian Biologist worried that she and Dorothea may have chosen the wrong side of the revolt. *If they failed, would Hannibal and Oya retaliate by euthanizing every human test subject aboard the spacecraft? What type of punishment would she and Dorothea face? What would happen to the children?*

She raced to Corridor 15 to extract Charlie Patton, as well as Mildred and Cornell Bledsoe, from the life suspension tanks. The elderly couple had been submerged for over twenty years. Explaining their predicament would not be easy.

The Bledsoes clung to one another after being removed from the tank. Carver covered them in silver robes. "I am sorry I do not have time to explain what is happening."

"I think we have a pretty good idea," Cornell said as he offered a sad smile. Though he could have been expected to be shocked or enamored by the sight of a blue-skinned native of an alien world, the old romantic refused to glance away from his wife for more than a few seconds. "Millie and I were abducted ten (maybe twenty) years ago. You and your people used advanced technology to simulate our surroundings from our home back on Earth... I suppose so you could study us in a setting close to our natural environment?"

Carver stood motionless. "How did you know?"

He chuckled. "Oh, I knew something was off the first time I took a drink of that slop that was supposed to pass for my home-distilled bourbon. Not long after that, I noticed Millie's cooking didn't taste nearly as good as it once did. We talked about it and we started looking for clues. I hadn't guessed your skin would be blue, but I'd say I got the rest of it pretty darn close."

The seventy-something lovebirds continued to nestle together while Carver extracted Charlie from the tank.

A metallic band covered his eyes, stretching from temple to temple. Though the young man was thrashing his body in an effort to get away, the Nawerssian scientist took great care to wipe the purple residue out of the grooves of his vision-aiding apparatus.

Unlike the Bledsoes, the sudden removal from the tank triggered a panicked response from Charlie. Cornell raised his voice to try to calm his friend. "Charlie...! Charlie...! Listen here. This woman is doing her best to help you. I know it's a scary situation. You're confused. Millie and I were too. But you need to calm down! It's important!"

"Charlie, can you see me?" Carver asked.

Violently shivering, he pulled his robe close to him for warmth. He managed to shake his head in response to her question. "I understand it is a lot to take in," she told Tavia's older brother over the incessant alarms that were being sounded, "But you need to come with us. We must move you. Your lives depend on it."

Cornell spoke up. "No, hon. You help Charlie. Take care of him. He's a kind soul." The old Kentuckian fought against the urge to cry.

Mildred took over for her husband. "If it's all the same, Cornell and I will stay behind. It'll be easier for you to help Charlie if we're not slowing you down."

Over Carver's protests, Cornell explained. "Sometimes Millie and I feel like we somehow cheated Death and lived an extra lifetime. It's been wonderful... spending so much time with the woman I adore more than anything. But we're tired. We're ready to go home. We've lived a good life. Two good lives, perhaps. But we're ready to see what awaits us on the other side... We'll do our best to hold off the bad guys from here."

Carver was speechless. As she stood there, she couldn't help but admire them. And she realized she may have learned more about the residents of Earth in the last five minutes than she had in her previous twenty years of observing the behavior of humans while aboard the *Vilnagrom-II*.

22: BATTLE ROYALE

*"You better be big, and you better be bad if
you're going to step through the ropes to fight
fifteen other people at once. You better be smart,
and you better be crafty if you want to survive in
a battle royale. Most of all, you better have
heart. There's no substitute for heart when your
neck is on the line."*

*-MANU "THE SAMOAN WARRIOR"
promo prior to fighting in a 12-man Battle
Royale as part of the AWWA's Third Annual
Black & Blue Bonanza.*

YEAR 0 + 291 DAYS (OCTOBER 18th)

The alarms had been blaring for several minutes. Avis and the children shared the bridge with Baron. Whether it was because the children were present or because Avis had twenty more years' worth of experience in space, the *V-II's* Navigator had been deferring to the old Pilot's judgment. But he was getting impatient.

"What exactly is happening?" Baron asked Avis in an accusatory tone. "You have told Hannibal and Oya that it is a false alarm, the result of a malfunction. But what I am seeing on these monitors tells a different story."

The crafty veteran offered a response designed to confuse his counterpart and distract him from watching the activities of his allies on the Control Center screens. "There is a simple explanation. I am assigned to instruct the children today. We are here because it is clear you had too much whiskey during the recent celebration, and I want to be certain we miss no more communications."

Despite the lingering effects the alcohol may have been having on him, Baron knew that something was amiss. He scanned the screens to observe the actions of his fellow crew members. Carver, Dorothea, and Armstrong were moving with great urgency. "Is that Monroe? When did she exit life suspension?"

A moment later, the monitor revealed Brady running along at Monroe's side.

Using his handheld communication link, Baron contacted the General. "Hannibal, this is Baron with an urgent report..."

After gesturing for Cleo and Ptolemy to move to the far end of the bridge, Avis closed the gap between him and Baron. The Pilot slipped his hand down to his hip. After sliding two fingers a few inches downward, he drew the Stun Blaster that had been concealed in the leg of his flight suit. Without hesitation, he fired. A blanket of electricity wrapped around Baron's body, temporarily paralyzing the Navigator and causing him to drop into a chair.

Though the stunned Nawerssian would remain unable to move a muscle for at least thirty minutes, Avis did not want to waste a moment. "Ptolemy, please go to the panel on the wall and enter code 7-7-1-3-Q. I need cords to constrain our prisoner."

Within moments, a pneumatic tube delivered the synthetic ropes that Avis would use to constrict Baron in his chair.

His next move was to step towards the Communications Grid. The mutineer lifted his blaster towards the grid and fired.

"We now have two advantages," Avis explained to the children in his charge. "That shot disabled all outside broadcasts to and from the *V-II*. It also disrupted person-to-person contact via communication links. Any radio messages between members of the crew must now go through the Control Center... Plus, we can assist our friends by helping them move from corridor to corridor through the air locks. Our enemies will have to travel through the hub along the bell of the ship."

One word confused Ptolemy and Cleo. "Enemies?"

☠☠☠

A frantic Oya appeared outside Quetzal's sleeping quarters. The pilot took a long time to open the door. When he did, he was undressed and clearly feeling the effects of the whiskey he'd downed the night before.

"Skipper? Why are you here?"

She was indignant. "Do you not hear the alarm tones?"

"Yes. We have been hearing those a lot lately."

"This time it is mutiny!" Oya placed a cube in Quetzal's hand. Approximately three times the size of a standard die, when plugged into a Nawerssian computer, the item could hold massive amounts of data. "Get dressed. Then get in a shuttle and fly away from here. Keep flying until you reach the *Vilnagrom-III*."

The news and the Skipper's order had a sobering effect on the war hero. "You are a pilot, too. Why send me?"

"Because you are the best we have. And my job requires I defend this ship... no matter what happens."

☠☠☠

Four feet long. Nearly four pounds. The musclebound Hannibal acquired his massive longsword during one of the *V-II's* first excursions to Earth. The General had been involved in the abduction of a college professor who fashioned himself a medieval war enthusiast. Even though such a practice was forbidden by those who drafted the protocols for Project *Vilnagrom*, he took the weapon as a trophy.

He dragged the blade behind him. As the edge dug into the floor, it created a metallic hiss that alerted his prey that they were being hunted. He did not fear the advanced warning would give his victims any advantage. He confidently boasted that it gave his opposition a slight chance at avoiding an otherwise imminent slaughter.

The blue giant looked in every compartment, checking the creases and crevices in each room. He was in the Corridor 15 library when he spotted Cornell and Millie Bledsoe. "This is not personal," Hannibal said as he raised his heavy sword.

Cornell kissed Millie on the forehead and held her tight. They truly were together "'til death do us part."

☠☠☠

Dorothea exited the Bell and raced down Corridor 2. She was searching for Polo, eager to sway the Cartographer to her side of the conflict.

Oya was searching for Polo, as well. Control of the bridge would be the key to crushing this revolt. She needed as many friends as possible to do that.

Dorothea did not break stride as she turned around a corner. The sudden movement and the appearance of a figure charging towards her triggered Oya's reflexes. She raised her Stun Blaster and fired a fully charged bolt.

The shot struck Dorothea in the stomach. The force knocked her off her feet, propelling her back into the wall behind her.

The Doctor looked downward. It didn't take long to assess that the wound was fatal. Then she looked up, her final gaze falling on the eyes of the woman who killed her.

Though they were on separate sides of the dispute, the two women had lived in close contact with one another for twenty years. They had been friends for much longer than they were foes. "Oh, Dorothea! I am so sorry!"

"Me too..." She replied. Then she whispered the sentiment once more. "Me too."

☠☠☠

Monroe and Brady arrived at the Control Center.

"Thank the Stars! You are here!" Avis assigned them the tasks of watching the bridge, guarding the prisoner, and protecting the children. The veteran pilot handed his Stun Blaster to Monroe. "Take this. I am going to pursue Quetzal. He left in a shuttle a few minutes ago. I presume he will attempt to rendezvous with the crew of the *V-III*... We cannot let that happen."

Brady argued that their primary objective should be to protect the children. However, he was met with resistance from young Ptolemy. "This is the most important spot on the ship. We can see everything that is happening. You can direct your friends where to go and tell them when enemies are approaching."

Monroe smiled. "The kid has a point. We would be foolish to leave. From here we can give a tremendous advantage to Armstrong, Jenn, Carver, and Dorothea."

"Not Dorothea." The softly spoken words came from Cleo. "My mother died a few minutes ago. She is dead."

☠☠☠

The low end of each corridor opened into the bell of the spacecraft. Once inside, one could take an elevator (or climb a ladder) up or down to other levels until reaching the appropriate passageway to additional corridors. One also could proceed deeper into the bell, advancing to the bridge, the landing bay, the launch tubes, the power generators, and the hydroponic farm that housed row after row of tanks in which the algae-like synthetic proteins were grown.

Armstrong and Jenn had advanced to this hub when they encountered Atlas and Midas.

Before being selected to be an Explorer on the *V-II*, Atlas was a sniper in the Nawerssian Military. Though a Stun Blaster wasn't as accurate or reliable as the long rifle he used on Na-Werss, he was excellent with a stun gun. His brother, Midas, was not. As they roamed the corridors of the *V-II*, Atlas was armed with two blasters, while Midas carried one.

Armstrong dropped to his knees the moment he was hit with a shot from his fellow Explorer. Thankfully, the weapon had been set to "stun." But now Jenn was outnumbered, two to one… They had blasters. She had a single dagger.

Midas raised his weapon and prepared to fire. His brief hesitation gave the luchadora an opportunity to duck and dodge his shot. As she did so, she somersaulted towards the Geologist. She reached up, grabbing the barrel of his blaster. The woman with the pirate persona instinctively tugged on the weapon. The momentum jerked Midas around and spun him into the path of the second shot from Atlas.

The Geologist fell atop Armstrong. Both were stunned, and would be rendered unable to fight for the duration of the struggle.

After pausing to check on his downed sibling, Atlas stared at Jenn. He held two blasters, both of which held enough charge for one stunning shot. She now held Midas's fully charged blaster.

Too bad I don't have a clue how to shoot this damn thing.

As they circled one another, the much larger Nawerssian said, "I understand fighting is your profession. I propose we drop these weapons and settle our differences one-on-one, hand-to-hand."

☠☠☠

Polo hesitated once he reached his destination. He had not expected to see Cocoa standing in front of the life suspension tank. *Was she a friend or a foe?*

"Lookin' for someone?"

The Cartographer spent countless hours studying Cocoa Freeman when she was immersed in a world of virtual reality. Observing her in a simulation had not given him enough information to measure where she stood at this moment.

"I am looking for assistance. I am looking for someone to help stop this madness."

The wrestler shook her head. "Like I told your friends—or maybe *not* your friends— Cocoa's sittin' this one out." Then she pointed to the single figure that remained hovering in purple liquid inside the tank. "Your girl Tavia might help... if you think you can trust her."

Polo moved to the panel on the wall and entered the sequence that would cause the mechanical arm to extract the angry co-ed from the purple goo. Minutes later, she was out of the tank, wearing black Nawerssian undergarments, and looking for clothing.

"I apologize. I did not think to bring anything for you to wear."

"Whatever," Tavia said, voicing her disgust. "I am so sick of everything about you people. I wouldn't put on one of your friggin' flight suits even if I was freezing to death."

Once she noticed the alarm tones, Tavia asked, "Where's my brother... How long was I in VR? Has Doc Dorothea finished with the surgeries yet?"

A jittery Polo did his best to fill her in on what was transpiring minute by minute. "Your brother is fine. Dorothea is dead."

"WHAT?" *If the doctor was dead, who was going to heal Charlie's blindness so the two of them could return to Earth?*

"The crew of the *Vilnagrom-III* will be here soon. They will have physicians aboard who can complete the surgeries. But we must quash this rebellion now. If we do not, the *V-III* will follow mission mandates. They will obliterate this ship upon arrival."

Tavia let Polo's words sink in. Then she asked, "Why should I believe you?"

"Who else are you going to believe? Armstrong? *He* is to blame for this fight. This happened once before, on the *Vilnagrom-I*... not long before this ship was scheduled to arrive. And now, when we get word that the *V-III* has entered the solar system, we have more bloodshed... It may not seem so, but trust me when I say he is a madman who seeks to create division and conflict in order to manipulate the new crew and the entire mission."

Much of the Nawerssian backstory was lost on Tavia. But Armstrong had left her in the life suspension tank. Alone. Alone after he extracted Monroe, Jenn, Brady, and even Cocoa. She looked at Polo and said, "All I care about is saving my brother. Tell me what you need me to do."

☠ ☠ ☠

Monroe stood behind Brady. She watched as her human friend demonstrated that he had understood her quick tutorial on operating the key functions on the control panel.

"Flip this to switch cameras. Press this and this into the communication board to speak directly through a monitor in a particular compartment... I think I've got it."

"And the blaster?"

Brady showed her that he knew how to hold the weapon, how a quick twist of his back wrist was needed to fire a shot, and how to switch the setting from the stun to kill. "I'm good with guns, remember?"

Monroe inhaled and exhaled a deep breath. "Yes, I remember," she said. Then she leaned in and kissed him. It was a long, deep, passionate kiss. *One like she had seen a hundred times before when watching the movies of Earth while studying the culture of the planet.*

When the kiss ended, Monroe could hear snickering Nawerssian children. She pulled away from Brady and admitted, "I never kissed anyone before."

The young man stood with his mouth agape. Though not unwanted, the kiss had caught him off guard. He didn't know what to say. (He'd later think of dozens of things he could have and should have said in this moment.)

Letting out another deep breath, Monroe nodded her head. "I am going to the launch tubes. I have to help Avis." She turned to Cleo and Ptolemy, "Stay with Brady. He is a good person. You can trust him..." She smiled before she finished her thought. "I do."

☠ ☠ ☠

Atlas dropped the blaster he had been holding in his left hand. His knees bent and he gradually lowered his body downward. "Shall we lay our weapons down at the count of three?"

Jenn nodded.

Her knees bent with his. She slowly sank into a squatting position. Never blinking, she knew that this could be a trick. She refused to take her eyes off her adversary.

"One... Two..."

There was a long pause after "Two." Though his blaster was nearly touching the floor, a sudden twist of his wrist would be all it took to fire a shot.

Jenn detected a twitch, a flinch. *The beginning of some sudden movement.* Instead of dropping her blaster, she sprang upwards. The reigning All-World Wrestling Association Women's Champion leapt over the head of Atlas. She narrowly missed being hit by the surge of electricity that went in the air when the *V-II's* Explorer fired his weapon.

Airborne, the professional grappler had Atlas where she wanted him. As the spacecraft's artificial gravity pulled her downward, she thrusted her right leg forward, planting the sole of her boot between the Nawerssian's red eyes.

She was uncertain how to shoot her blaster. But she knew how to use the thing as a club. Jenn hoped to deliver a knockout blow by pounding it against his oversized skull.

BAM!!!

Jenn hadn't tried to discharge her weapon. She wasn't sure she could do it again if she tried. But, as she was preparing to drive the 41st century ray gun into Atlas's cranium, she ended up blowing a hole through his skull. It was a messy victory, but a victory nonetheless.

She shrugged. "Serves him right for trying to take me out with a cheap shot."

☠☠☠

Quetzal had a significant head start on Avis. If the wily veteran was going to close the gap between his bullet shuttle and the one flown by the much younger ace, he would have to rely on his years of additional experience flying in space.

"When flying long distances through space, the fastest route most often is *not* a straight line," Avis had told Pilots Quetzal and Hazel (who was lost in a fiery crash five years ago) when the *Vilnagrom-II* first arrived. "The secret is to find an object with a high level of gravity. Then you slingshot around that object, utilizing its gravitational pull to increase your velocity beyond the capacity of the engine."

If Quetzal implemented that flying technique on his way to the *V-III*, his pursuer would never catch him. He could be caught, however, if he got careless or cocky.

Avis scanned the open space ahead of him. He kept an eye on Quetzal's shuttle far ahead of him, while hoping to discover an asteroid that might possess enough mass to allow him to narrow the distance that separated them.

Unfortunately, it was Avis who got sloppy.

A surge of electricity fried the dashboard and disabled his flight stick. The engine shut down. The blasters were useless. Oya had chased him down from behind. Worse than that, she'd nailed his shuttle with a stun shot.

Avis was adrift and he was in Oya's sights. His shuttle floated through the weightlessness of space. It would take less than a few minutes for the Skipper's blasters to fully recharge. Then she'd zoom in for a kill shot. There was nothing he could do to prevent it.

After forty years living in space, it comes down to this. Avis didn't feel any anger, certainly no rage. There was some regret. For the most part, his mind went to recalling the joyful times. *He remembered his first opportunity to fly the bullet shuttle through the skies of Na-Werss... He thought of the many happy memories he shared during a lifetime spent with Armstrong... And he was thankful for the opportunity to discover unexpected ways to show love when they adopted Monroe... It was all worth it.*

Oya's voice came over the radio. "I am sorry it has to end this way, my friend."

From his peripheral vision, Avis saw a bright flash of light. But the impact of that blast never hit him. The burst of light he had seen was Oya's shuttle exploding after being hit by a kill shot from Monroe!

Residual force from the magnitude of the nearby explosion did cause Avis's shuttle to go into a soft roll, but it was far better than the alternative.

Monroe greeted him over the radio. "I thought you could use some help. Turns out I was correct. Let me charge back up and I will come get you."

Avis tried to convince her to continue the chase. "Quetzal is too far ahead. I would never catch him," she said. She didn't bother mentioning that going after him would also seriously endanger the life of her adoptive father. His shuttle would not be operational for hours. In that amount of time, the odds were high that he would either freeze to death or run out of breathable oxygen in the cockpit. "Time to go back to the *V-II*. Let us hope that the good guys are winning the fight on the ship."

☠☠☠

Brady rested his hands against the control panel. His eyes constantly jumped from one screen to another as he tried to assess the action that was taking place aboard the *V-II*. Though communication with those outside the ship had been rendered impossible, he frequently attempted to contact Monroe.

Because he was distracted and overwhelmed by the massive bank of computers in front of him, the hopeful hero did not notice that Polo had stepped onto the bridge. He was startled when he heard the Cartographer announce his presence.

"Hello, Brady Emerson. Hello, children."

Brady swung around, brandishing the knife that Armstrong had given him an hour earlier.

Polo raised his hands. He did his best to assume a posture that an Earthly human would interpret as non-threatening. "Easy, Mr. Emerson. You have given me no reason to oppose you. And I would never harm these children."

"Whose side are you on?"

"I repeat... I would never harm the children, and you have given me no reason to think you and I oppose one another. Call me 'neutral.' And please allow me to do as you are. I would prefer to watch from here and wait for this skirmish to end."

The young man weighed his options. Driving the dagger deep into Polo's chest would be the safest route to take. But Brady was no murderer. He would only take this man's life as a last resort... *even if he was an alien who had played a major role in abducting Brady against his will.*

"Listen, my number one priority is to protect these children. I need to know whose side you are on."

"This again?" Polo's tone revealed he was getting frustrated. "I am on the side of Science. Am I on the side of my home planet of Na-Werss? Of course. Am I on the side of Project *Vilnagrom*? Does it matter? Your people are doomed. And that beautiful planet down there could be a safe and healthy alternative to where my friends and family currently live." He paused, then continued. "That does not mean I am unwilling to help you and the people of your planet. If we can help, we should... Doomsday on Earth could be a hundred years from now. Should we withhold assistance we can provide simply because your people will become extinct at some unknown point in the future? I do not believe so. In fact, I believe Earthly humans and Nawerssians could live on your planet together. I believe we should live together in harmony for as long as possible. That is the best answer I can give."

Brady nodded his head. He was satisfied. He continued to feel some hesitation, though. He used the dagger to gesture towards a row of seats on the far end of the bridge. "Sit over there. Stay out of my way. And leave the children alone."

☠☠☠

Hannibal dragged his sword into the hub along the edge of the ship's bell-shaped core. Upon spotting Long Jenn Silva, he declared, "You will suffer for those who died because of you. And then I will make each of the traitors you call 'friends' suffer too."

She wasn't going to back away from a fight. "Apparently trash talk is a universal language." Once he'd moved close enough for Jenn to see the fresh blood that had collected on his mighty blade, she knew she was in a battle of life and death. "Know this, ya blue bastard, you've gotta get through me first."

The General began the confrontation with an uncontrolled swing of his sword. It was as if he was swinging a sledgehammer like a baseball bat. It was a maneuver done solely for the purpose of trying to intimidate his opposition.

He stepped closer, swinging the gigantic blade with much more control. Jenn bent backwards as if she was in the finals of a limbo competition. It was an odd movement, but effective at dodging the attack.

The pirate responded to Hannibal's next swing of his sword by blocking it with her previously spent Stun Blaster. The blade dug several inches deep, causing the weapons to be fused together with the blade embedded deep into the casing of the firearm.

Discarding the sword, Hannibal moved in close. The musclebound giant nearly bear-hugged the life out of her during their initial tangle. It was obvious he intended to use his considerable size advantage to crush her this time around.

Jenn wasn't interested in a test of strength. He'd win that battle in an instant. As he advanced towards her, she nailed him with a boot to the shin. The Nawerssians were two thousand years of microevolution ahead of "Earthly humans," but the shins remained highly vulnerable.

Hannibal instinctively bent down and grabbed his injured leg. Jenn seized the opportunity and kicked her foe across his jaw. This forced him to stagger backwards, but he did not leave his feet.

The luchadora shifted into an offense posture, but not quickly enough. Hannibal lunged forward and drilled her with a football tackle. With both on the floor, it was obvious he was going to try to keep her on the ground so he could utilize his significant size advantage to squash her.

Remain calm!

Intergender competitions and mixed tag team matches were very popular in Mexico. Jenn often found herself in bouts where she was being slammed by men who outweighed her by 100 or even 150 pounds. It was a part of her Lucha Libre background that gave her an advantage over women wrestlers who never donned a mask south of the border.

Hannibal wrapped his right arm around Jenn's neck. It was perfectly positioned directly below her jaw. She was unable to suck in any oxygen. She'd be unconscious in no time if she wasn't able to get him to break the hold.

She first tried to dip her jaw downward to bite her opponent. That was a big no-no in the world of wrestling, but not when you were fighting for your life. Biting did not work, however. The material of the alien flight suit was too strong.

Next, she bashed her fist into her attacker's groin. However, the suit was reinforced in that area. That extra layer of advanced synthetic material was highly effective in absorbing such attacks. The attempted low blow had no effect.

Jenn felt herself fading fast. Though her mind was getting cloudy, she happened to remember a move a wrestler with mixed martial arts experience had executed a little too aggressively in an AWWA match. She reached for and located Hannibal's free hand. She grabbed his thumb with one hand and his fifth finger with the other.

Snap! She broke the long, blue digit... and the stranglehold!

Moving to her knees, Jenn tried to suck in as much air as quickly as possible. Hannibal would not allow her to catch her breath. While standing above her, he thumped her with a kick to the stomach.

Completely winded, Jenn fell into a seated position with her back against the wall. The angry General kicked her again. This time his boot caught her across the face and bloodied her nose.

The crimson fluid gushed into her mouth. It was a sensation that always led to her smiling in defiance. For some reason, the taste of blood across her lips always led to a surge of adrenaline... even when her system should have been depleted.

With Jenn looking like she was almost knocked out, Hannibal paused and scanned his surroundings for a means of finishing her off. He looked past the blasters scattered around. Instead, he opted for his treasured longsword.

He turned his back on Jenn only for an instant. It was all she needed. The pirate rolled towards him, clipping him behind the knee. She hopped up to a standing position, then caught him with a knee across the face.

Now the flesh across his face was bloody!

She attempted a running clothesline, but he was ready for it. The much larger foe grabbed her by the arm and used her momentum to sling her into the wall.

While still on his knees, the General shifted around the sword. He wasn't going to make the mistake of turning his back on Jenn

SCOTT QUINN

again. He yanked the blaster off his sword. Then he used his medieval weapon to slowly rise to a standing position.

With Hannibal bent at the waist, Jenn jumped up and charged towards him. She vaulted herself into the air, jumping over his head. The champion landed with her knees in the middle of his back and the tops of her feet resting against the bulging trapezius muscles atop his shoulders. While in midair, she slung her hands downward and wrapped them around his waist. Then she let gravity do the rest of the work.

Jenn hit the floor hard. She landed flat on her back, but left her knees cocked and pointing straight up in the air. Hannibal came crashing down over her, his momentum meeting a sudden stop and a violent end when her knees stabbed into the back of his lungs.

The General was stunned. All the air had been expelled from his lungs. Rapidly. Plus, the fibers of the flight suit weren't enough to absorb such an intense impact. He was breathless and in severe pain.

The fierce young woman rolled over. She picked up the longsword and plunged it into Hannibal's throat. She'd toppled the giant.

Then she dropped to the ground.

Long Jenn Silva had come out the victor in a big, bruising battle. She was exhausted and nearly unconscious.

As Jenn lay there, she heard a slow, deliberate clapping sound. She looked up and spotted Tavia standing about twenty feet away.

"Personally, I'm glad the big guy didn't finish you off. That pleasure should belong to me."

VILNAGROM-II

CREW MEMBERS (AFTER 20 YEARS ORBITING EARTH)

V-I 3/SENIOR EXPLORER	ARMSTRONG
V-I 7/PILOT	AVIS
V-I 16/UNASSIGNED	*MONROE*

V-II 4/CARTOGRAPHER	POLO
V-II 5/NAVIGATOR	BARON (in the brig)
V-II 6/PILOT	QUETZAL (bound for *V-III*)
V-II 8/PHYSICAL SCIENCE	MIDAS (in the brig)
V-II 9/BIOLOGICAL SCIENCE	*CARVER*

V-II 11/UNASSIGNED	PTOLEMY (child of Carver & REDACTED)
V-II 12/UNASSIGNED	*CLEO* (child of Dorothea & REDACTED)

DECEASED:

V-II 1/GENERAL	HANNIBAL
V-II 2/SKIPPER	*OYA*
V-II 3/EXPLORER	ATLAS
V-II 7/PILOT	*HAZEL (presumed dead)*
V-II 10/DOCTOR	*DOROTHEA*

23: THE MAIN EVENT

"I lifted weights until I was ready to pass out, then skipped dessert and cried myself to sleep. I spent holidays on the road away from loved ones. Broken nails, broken bones, and broken spirits. That's what comes with a career in wrestling. Never broken promises, though. I promised myself I'd become champion, and it's going to take everything you've got and more if you want to take this belt away from me."

-LONG JENN SILVA promo given prior to her first match defending the AWWA Women's Championship against Savannah Lyons.

ONE YEAR EARLIER
YEAR -1 + 182 DAYS (JULY 1st)

Seventeen-year-old Tavia had been looking forward to the trip to Memphis for weeks! Things had not gone as planned with Fireball Freeman and the All-World Wrestling Association tryout, but she still had big plans for the rest of the weekend. The enthusiastic young woman had mapped out "The Four Kings of Memphis" extravaganza. She and her brother would begin their epic vacation with a tour of Graceland, followed by a trip to the Civil Rights Museum. Then they'd give her new fake ID a test drive with a trip to two specific bars on Beale Street.

"Come on, Charlie! Wake up!" she pleaded.

The wrestling hopeful hadn't taken his rejection well. As soon as Tavia fell asleep, he slipped out of the room and purchased a cheap bottle of whiskey from a packaged liquor store. He downed half the bottle before dawn.

Tavia looked at the glowing red numbers on the hotel room's alarm clock. "Charlie... It's three o'clock. We've missed Graceland. We've missed the Civil Rights Museum. But we can still hit Beale Street!"

He could only muster a groan for an answer.

"Charlie, the front desk just called again. They said we were supposed to be out of the room two hours ago. We need to be out of here soon. Otherwise, they're either going to send security up here or charge us for another night!"

Knowing that he'd rather spend his hard-earned cash on alcohol than another night in the motel room, he rolled out of bed. On his way to the bathroom, he instructed his younger sister, "Call them back and tell them we'll be out of here in twenty minutes."

☠☠☠

FIVE HOURS LATER

"Beale Street was fun while it lasted," Tavia declared as she pulled the car door shut with exaggerated force.

"What? So you're mad now?" an indignant Charlie fired back. "That asshole was totally staring at your tits. I told him to move along, and he gave me lip. I should've followed through with my threat. I should've laid him out right there in the middle of the bar."

"First off, you might as well have knocked him silly because you still got us kicked out of the bar... We're lucky they didn't call the cops, because then they would've discovered I was in there on a fake ID. I could've gotten in big trouble!"

Charlie shook his head in disgust. "Woulda, coulda, shoulda... None of that happened. So why are you cryin' about it?"

Tavia ignored her brother's comment. "Second... Who cares if he was staring at my boobs? They're nice boobs. Sometimes guys are going to look, maybe even stare. Especially when there's alcohol involved."

"Ugggh!" Charlie screamed in frustration. "Why did I drive down here again? Oh, that's right… so Fireball Freeman could tell me I'm a loser with no shot of making it in the wrestling business. Making matters even more enjoyable, I get to hear my little sister go on and on about her anatomy!"

His sister whispered her response. "I wasn't going on and on."

After that, they drove in silence for quite a while.

Eventually Tavia signaled and pulled off the highway. "If I'm going to make this drive, I need to get some food in my stomach and some caffeine to keep me awake. Need anything?"

Charlie lifted his whiskey bottle. His escapades of the previous night meant it was already halfway empty. That didn't concern him, though. "I'm good."

Armed with a hot dog, a bag of corn chips, and a 44-ounce diet soda, Tavia was ready for four hours behind the wheel. Much to her dismay, Charlie was sitting in the driver's seat when she returned to the car. Brother and sister argued for several minutes before Tavia reluctantly plopped into the passenger seat.

☠ ☠ ☠

FOUR HOURS LATER

They were almost home. Tavia didn't feel home free, though, because Charlie continued to guzzle what was left from his bottle of whiskey. With every additional drop of alcohol in his system, he became more and more aggressive.

"You're tellin' me that Fireball Freeman liked me? That's great news! Right...? But yer also tellin' me that Cocoa Freeman and Captain Jenn... Long Jenn Silva... were the ones that talked him out of hiring me?"

"I knew I shouldn't have said anything. PLEASE! Keep your eyes on the road. Or better yet, pull over and let me drive!"

Much to Tavia's surprise, Charlie yanked the steering wheel and took the Gravois Road exit.

"Here we are. Historic Route 66," he said, sounding very much like their father announcing landmarks and points of interest on their family vacations.

Charlie pulled the car up to a pump at the filling station off the exit. "We're almost on 'E.' I'm gonna fill up. If you wanna slide over and drive the rest of the way, I won't fight you about it."

"Thank God!" the young woman said aloud.

After positioning herself behind the wheel, Tavia stared down at the nearly empty whiskey bottle. *Should she pitch it? Or could that set him off again? Maybe it would be best not to push the issue.*

She looked up. "Oh, what now?"

Charlie had crossed the street and was making his way up the fire escape of a three-story apartment building.

"CHARLIE!"

He wasn't listening. He was too busy giving an imaginary promo before a fictitious wrestling match. "Cocoa Freeman and Long Jenn Silva? Do they know what it's like to want something their entire lives... only to have it ripped away for no good reason?" He paused and considered his own rhetorical question. "I don't know. I don't know them that well. Maybe...? But one thing I know for sure... Cocoa Freeman and Long Jenn Silva wouldn't know a talented wrestler... if he bit them in the ass!"

"Charlie, get down from there! Please!"

He ignored her. Instead of climbing down from his moderately high perch above South St. Louis, he stepped into the role of ring announcer for his fantasy bout. "And now for the Main Event! Introducing first, the challenger... from Chesterfield, Missouri... weighing in at an even 200 pounds... Patton Charles!" Charlie stopped long enough to mimic the sounds of the crowd cheering for their hero. He chose to let those made up sounds drown out Tavia's desperate pleadings.

Charlie decided to give "his fans" a show. He pulled his shirt over his head and began flexing his muscles. He spun around, acting as if he was going to pose for the fans on the other side of his imaginary ring. While he was turning, however, he lost his balance.

Charlie Patton's fall was from approximately thirty feet above. His head smacked against the fire escape on the way down.

"CHARLIE!!!"

Tavia managed to call 9-1-1. She didn't remember doing so, and she didn't know how long it took her trembling hands to unlock the phone and dial the number. But she made the call. Even though she didn't know if her brother was alive or dead.

"Charlie! Please don't die! I need you! Charlie! I need you!"

"9-1-1... What is your emergency?"

☠☠☠

Tavia had not been on the line long when the first police car arrived. Captain Arnold Grayson stepped out of his vehicle but made no move towards Charlie and Tavia. Instead, the heavyset cop stood back. He studied the scene from afar. He did this while speaking into his radio.

Thirty seconds later, a second police vehicle pulled into the parking lot. As soon as the second officer exited her vehicle, both advanced towards Tavia and her injured brother.

"Good evening, young lady," Grayson said as he approached. "I'm Captain Grayson. I've been on the line with dispatch. Let me assure you, an ambulance will be here very shortly." He gestured towards an area away from Charlie's lifeless body. "Do you mind stepping over here? This is Officer Santiago. She has a few questions for you."

☠☠☠

ONE WEEK LATER
YEAR -1 + 189 DAYS (JULY 8th)

Mr. and Mrs. Patton went down to the hospital cafeteria. They recognized Tavia needed some time alone with her big brother.

Charlie smiled. His voice was weak. His forehead was bandaged like a mummy. "I thought they'd never leave."

"Yeah," his sister remarked while fighting back tears. "They've made it pretty clear that I'm grounded until the day I move into the dorms at CIU."

"What have I missed while I've been cooped up in this hospital room?"

"Fourth of July wasn't so great this year. It poured rain and there was even a tornado watch. They canceled the fireworks... Lots of people have called to see how you were doing. Boris, Lance, Parker, Liz..."

Charlie interrupted. "Liz, huh? She always did have the hots for me. She's already turned eighteen, right?"

Tavia simultaneously grinned and rolled her eyes. Under normal circumstances, she wouldn't tolerate her brother making perverted remarks about her best friend. Given the circumstances, she opted to let it slide. "Lots of people have called. Other than that, there's really nothing I can think to tell you. The last few days have been a big blur."

It was a poor choice of words. The doctors had told Tavia's parents that the fall may have permanently impacted Charlie's vision. "A big blur? For you and me both," he joked.

Would he be blind? Would his vision gradually return? The doctors refused to speculate about the magnitude of his brain injury. His blindness could linger for a few days or weeks. Then again, it could be permanent and irreversible. They would not dare venture a guess until after some of his swelling subsided and they were able to get a clear picture from the MRI.

Perhaps most obviously, the doctors would continue to remain in the dark until Charlie regained consciousness.

"They say that you might wake up any day now." Tavia squeezed her brother's hand. "I hate that I have to imagine our conversations. I hate that you climbed up onto the roof of that building... I'd do anything to turn the clock back. To make it like it was before. You and me... on top of the world. Just one step away from making it into the wrestling business... I would do anything... Anything."

☠☠☠

PRESENT DAY – ABOARD THE VILNAGROM-II
YEAR 0 + 292 DAYS (OCTOBER 18th)

Jenn was flat on her back. She looked up, desperately trying to focus on the lights above her. A sad smile briefly flashed across her face as she pictured herself as a young child lying down in the grass. She squinted her eyes, imagining the starlit sky, until she could only see the light from the very brightest of stars. The lesser beams blurred and blended into those of the brightest star. Her mind wandered. *Which one will win? Which star will outshine the other? If only she could squint to a point that her eyes were almost completely shut. Open only wide enough to see the brightest star.*

In the next instant, Jenn's body jerked at a painfully awkward angle. This movement jostled her out of her haze and away from her dream. She was being dragged by her feet, pulled to a section of the massive spacecraft that was completely foreign to her.

Thrashing her legs, Jenn pushed herself out of Tavia's grasp. The sudden movement sent her foe sprawling several steps away. The luchadora used this opening to pull herself up to a standing position. She collected herself and readied herself for the fight of her life. *(The second or third of the day!)*

The two fighters glared at each other in a manner that resembled a pair of dancers first eyeing their next partner from across the ballroom. They circled around one another, each desiring the perfect angle from which she could strike. It was a formal, gracefully flowing waltz from an age long before synthesizers and electric guitars. And Jenn and Tavia were the only dancers on the floor.

The two continued this masquerade as they circled one another. Each did her best to showcase her physique, hoping to intimidate their opponent and impress an imaginary audience.

Several quick spots followed. Tavia charged forward with a kick. Jenn somersaulted out of harm's way, then bounced back with a backhand chop of her own. They traded a number of these jabs. The maneuvers were useful in feeling out the opposition, with the hope that they might deliver a quick victory after catching the other by surprise.

The two stood face to face and joined hands. Locking up in this manner was a test of strength. It also served as a test of wills. Through gritted teeth, each boasted their strength was superior and claimed their cause as the righteous one. If one could overpower the other in this physical showdown, it could shatter the confidence of the weaker fighter.

With neither possessing a clear advantage in the test of strength, Tavia raced down a dark passageway. She sought to find a spot to hide long enough to surprise Jenn when she gave chase. An opening at the end of the corridor looked to be the perfect spot. The waitress-turned-warrior leapt inside and readied herself to ambush her enemy.

☠☠☠

Though both Brady and Polo made efforts to shield the eyes of the Nawerssian children, all four watched intently from the Control Center.

"She's going to blindside Jenn!" Brady observed. "We've got to do something! We need to warn her! How do I operate the comm system? And is there some way to cut the lights or maybe lock Tavia in that room?"

Young Ptolemy stepped forward. Polo raised his hand to signal the boy to stop. "No. This needs to be a fair fight. We must not interfere."

Brady looked at the glass of the monitor. Instead of focusing on the images being broadcast, he concentrated on the reflections that bounced off the screen and back at him. A number of questions short through his mind in an instant. Guessing the correct answer to each of those questions could be the difference between life and death.

Was Polo truly neutral?

Or was he secretly working with Tavia?

Did the children appear confident that they knew how to operate the control panel?

Was Polo close enough to be vulnerable to a sudden attack?

Without warning, Brady thrust his arm upwards and behind him. His elbow struck the taller Polo in the jaw. The alien's head whipped back, then fell forward. Remaining on the offensive, Brady pivoted, grasped the Cartographer's bulbous head, and pushed it downward until it crashed into his violently rising knee.

Polo was out cold.

"Kids, I need one of you to work on tying him up, while the other helps me with these controls."

The young boy stepped forward. Without a word, he pressed a sequence of buttons that hopefully would sway the battle in the favor of Long Jenn Silva.

☠ ☠ ☠

Tavia entered an enormous, domed opening. She had stepped into the room that housed tank after tank of the algae-like protein that served as the primary source of food for those aboard the ship.

The blond villain spotted a catwalk overhead. She scurried up a ladder and perched herself in a position high above. She let out a confident snarl and held out her arms in a superhero pose. She envisioned striking Jenn from above the moment she stepped through the door. And she reveled in the thought of destroying the post-apocalyptic pirate once and for all.

Jenn stepped through the doorway. Once Tavia caught a glimpse of the luchadora's outfit, she pushed off the railing and propelled herself over the edge of the catwalk. She was a few feet away from pummeling Jenn with a blindside attack from overhead.

But Tavia didn't drop like she expected. Instead, she floated above the rows and rows of protein tanks.

Jenn, too, found her body lifting upwards.

A voice came over a speaker. "This is Brady. I have disabled the artificial gravity. Now finish her, Jenn!"

Jenn "swam" through the weightlessness of space, waving her arms and pushing her body towards Tavia's. The fight/dance was going to continue with the waltzing warriors hovering twenty feet above the floor.

When the two grapplers met in the air, each instantly went for the other's throat. Jenn's hands wrapped around Tavia's neck, almost to the point that she could clasp her fingers together. If she succeeded, she would cut off all oxygen to the brain and it would be lights out for blondie in a matter of seconds.

But Tavia had a few tricks up her sleeve. While digging her fingernails from her left hand into the skin around Jenn's neck, she released the grip of her right hand. Before the veteran wrestler could react, Tavia jabbed her thumb into Jenn's eye!

The blast of pain forced Jenn to let go of her foe's neck. Momentarily blinded, Jenn knew that Tavia would likely be hitting her with a follow up attack. Trying to prevent receiving a knockout blow, Jenn thrust both legs forward hoping to strike Tavia and perhaps push her away.

Direct hit.

Both of Jenn's feet caught Tavia's midsection, launching her upwards towards the ceiling of the cavernous room.

The force also pushed Jenn back in the opposite direction. She now hovered considerably closer to the floor than her foe.

With Brady still manning the controls of the ship's artificial gravity, he turned the system on... hoping that the tremendous fall would be the end of Tavia Patton.

Tavia's body twisted and turned as she plunged toward the floor. She landed feet first in the narrow aisle between a pair of protein tanks.

"ARRRGGGGGHHHHHH!!!"

She let out a blood-curdling shriek the instant her left foot hit the ground. Her fibula split in two. The broken bone tore through the skin.

Though she did not fall from as great a distance, Jenn also suffered greatly upon impact. She landed directly atop one of the protein tanks. The glass shattered beneath her. She dropped to the bottom of the tank, fully submerged under two and a half feet of slimy liquid.

Algae-filled water rolled over her eyes as she looked upwards. Visions of her fight with Tavia flashed above her. Then she saw Lazz. She smiled as she remembered how the smell of his cologne complimented the musky smell of his sweaty body. It was an aroma she first noticed as they danced at their wedding. *("You should wear this cologne more often," she remembered telling him.)*

The vision changed again. This time, it was the night she first had her hand held high in victory as a luchadora in Mexico. Though Manny Vargas was an ugly bastard, his fatherly smile was one of the most beautiful things she'd ever seen.

She caught a glimpse of the night she won the AWWA Championship from Savannah Lyons. It was a surge of joy that came as the payoff to almost a decade of hard work in the wrestling business.

Then the in-ring images disappeared. Her dance continued. This time it was Brady who was in her arms. *Did she love him?* She didn't have time to wade through that quandary. But she knew she was fighting for LOVE. She didn't hate Tavia. Right now that didn't matter. If Tavia came out on top, Brady would be in grave danger. If Tavia won, Jenn would never return to Earth or see Lazz ever again.

The pirate sat up. Water blasted out of her mouth. Then she desperately gasped for air.

Dragging her left leg behind her, Tavia pushed against the rims of the glass tanks. With anguish written across her face, she maneuvered towards her rival.

By this point in their battle, the bodies of both women were completely worn down. Each was running on all heart, no strength.

Tavia leaned in, resting her forehead against Jenn's... just for a moment.

She had nearly drowned. Gasping for air, liquid droplets continued to spray out of her mouth as she tried to regulate her breathing.

Tavia refused to give in to her excruciating pain. Not long ago, she had been a college girl and a scantily clad waitress slinging burgers and cheap beer at a shameless sports bar. She told herself she was much more than that. Finishing Long Jenn Silva was the next step in her epic journey.

The co-ed wrapped her left arm around Jenn's neck, tucking the woman's head beneath her armpit. Next, she reached into the tank with her right arm, stopping when she reached the waist of Jenn's wrestling tights. With one final surge of strength, Tavia lifted her opponent into the air.

It was a perfect suplex. It was particularly beautiful considering she could only draw her power from one leg.

The classic wrestling move sent Jenn through the air, then through the glass of the protein tank in the next row over.

Once again submerged, this time Jenn had no chance to dream about her wrestling successes, her beloved husband, or her dear friend. Though she was screaming in agony, Tavia wrapped her hand around Jenn's neck and pushed her towards the bottom of the tank.

Jenn was drowning. No doubt about it. Though she thrashed her arms and kicked her legs, she didn't have the power to pull away from Tavia. The swashbuckler knew there was no getting up as long as she was being held down down.

Tavia continued to press downward with every ounce of strength within her. *Was this the end?*

Long Jenn Silva thought about Brady and what he had told her about inner peace. She thought about her previous boasts in the wrestling ring:

"You learn to expect attacks from all sides. And you learn to keep your cool no matter what the high seas throws at you..."

"There are only two things a pirate ever desires: gold and revenge."

"Let this serve as the only warning you'll get. I'm coming for you!"

"I'm Long Jenn Silva. And I'm a survivor!"

Jenn reached her hands up and wrapped them tightly around Tavia's throat. But the tightness quickly subsided. Soon, Jenn's grip loosened. Then her hands dropped, limply crashing into the water and falling to her side.

Tavia dropped to the ground. Now she was gasping for air and on the verge of passing out. She still managed a smile, however. She had toppled her mighty foe.

Then Jenn sat up in the tank. Straight up. She sucked in a massive gulp of air before pushing herself over the edge.

The champ dropped to the ground as soon as she hit the floor. Her appendages were cramping. It wasn't surprising due to her prolonged lack of oxygen. Nearly drowning hadn't killed her, but it had succeeded in turning her legs and arms into hundred pound bags of sand.

Tavia pulled herself into a standing position. The dance was long over. Her hands were balled into fists. She intended to smash those fists into that ridiculous pirate until she was long past dead. With a confident snarl, she pushed off with her right leg as she thrust herself towards Jenn.

Tavia never landed a punch.

As her momentum brought Tavia downward, Long Jenn Silva pulled Jagger's dagger out of its sheath. Raising the blade upwards, the luchadora caught her foe.

The dagger sank deep into Tavia's gut.

Wanting to eliminate the possibility of a recovery, Jenn extracted the blade. A second later, she had slashed it across Tavia's throat. The gash was a fatal one. It wouldn't take long for her to bleed out.

Jenn looked into the eyes of her adversary. "You were good. Really good. I wish we would have gotten the chance to fight in the ring instead of here on this damn spaceship."

She would never know if Tavia heard those sentiments. Tavia's eyes glazed over and seemed to look through Jenn. She seemed to be focusing on something else entirely. Though no sound came out, she struggled to mouth her last words.

"Get down, Charlie... I'll do anything!"

Tavia was lying on her back. The bright lights above the hydroponic tanks shined above her.

She was having difficulty keeping her eyes from rolling back in her head. She tapped into all her strength to open her eyes and raise one arm straight up in the air. But she could not say a word.

Then Tavia's arm dropped. A river of thick blood pushed away the puddles of spilled water that had collected on the floor.

24: DIRT SHEETS

"Clickbait. Fake News. I'm sick of it! One website says I'm about to sign with the IWO. Another says I'm leaving the AWWA to wrestle in Japan. I've even heard that I'm going to quit wrestling to play the bad guy in Hollywood's next big superhero movie! Don't believe any of it. Brick VanderWal is here to stay!"

-BRICK VANDERWAL promo given two weeks before he abruptly retired from wrestling to star as the villain in "The Snowflake Killer," an action-packed summer blockbuster.

SIX WEEKS LATER
YEAR 0 + 341 DAYS (DECEMBER 7th)

Whether the report aired on Fox News, CNN, Telemundo, the BBC, ESPN, or the Total Wrestling Network, the day's top news story began the same:

"Shocking news out of Orange Beach, Florida, this morning..." The news anchors always used this lead-in when beginning their report. It was as if the phrase "shocking news" was a pied piper's tune designed to bring additional viewers rushing in from the next room.

"Professional wrestler Jennysis Quevedo, known by fans of the sport as 'Long Jenn Silva', washed ashore at approximately 3:55 Central Standard Time this morning. She was rushed to a nearby medical facility due to fatigue, dehydration, and some superficial injuries.

"Recent college graduate, Brady Emerson of King City, Illinois, was with her. Silva and Emerson were two of the four people who mysteriously vanished from St. Louis commuter trains over four months ago. The whereabouts of the remaining two missing persons—professional wrestler Cocoa Freeman and St. Louis police officer Arnold Grayson— remain a mystery."

☠☠☠

5:15 AM EASTERN STANDARD TIME (4:15 CENTRAL)

Manuel Vargas was driven by his routine. Ten minutes after he rolled out of bed, he was in his car on the way to the gym. He'd spend the first few hours of each morning with eight prospects, training and teaching them everything he cared to share about the world of professional wrestling. A couple of his proteges had made it to the big time... none bigger than former All-World Wrestling Association Women's Champion Long Jenn Silva.

Once he was dressed, Manuel stopped only long enough to grab two bananas from the kitchen and his copy of the newspaper off the front step. Even with a brief detour in which he'd grab a large coffee and a breakfast burrito from a fast food joint, he'd pull into the gym by 5:30.

Spilling that large coffee all over The Orlando Sentinel was not part of the plan. "Give me a friggin' break!" the former wrestler muttered as he struggled to find the key to the door of the gym.

Several students would be arriving within minutes. In fact, his 26-year-old niece had already pulled into the parking lot. That meant he didn't have time to grab another paper. He'd have to stoop to relying on the television to catch him up with the latest things happening in the world.

He flipped through the channels until stopping on a local news broadcast.

"Is that Jenn on the TV?" asked his niece.

The video showed Jenn dressed in her trademark ring attire. The outfit had taken a beating. Her hair was wet. Her eyes looked a little sunk in as if she might be suffering from dehydration. But there was no mistaking what that were seeing.

With a smile from ear to ear, Manny forgot all about his spilled coffee and his soggy newspaper. "I'll be damned. Long Jenn Silva... resurrected from her watery grave!"

☠☠☠

6:15 AM EASTERN STANDARD TIME (7:15 CENTRAL)

Tentz 3000 created high end camping equipment at reasonable prices. Greg Puckett wore several hats working at his brother's

Atlanta-based start-up. One of his daily tasks was to generate buzz for the company's products over the Internet. As he once explained, "The first thing I do when I wake up is find out what's trending online. I've been on a half dozen social media platforms before I even brush my teeth."

He slid out of his bed and into the chair perched under a desk. With two taps onto the screen of his computer, he connected with the rest of the known universe. "Hashtag Long Jenn Silva?" he read aloud.

The women's wrestling champ had become quite famous over the last few months. Her name—along with that of Greg's buddy, Brady Emerson—flooded the news cycle for a few days following her mysterious disappearance. There were a lot of theories and a lot of questions. One minute she was seen riding a commuter train in St. Louis; the next minute, she had vanished into thin air.

Part of Greg wanted to resist the temptation. He told himself that following the links would serve no purpose. He guessed it would be more clickbait. More baseless gossip. Reading that garbage would drag him down and force him to mourn the loss of his pal all over again.

He couldn't avoid it. Everywhere he went, everywhere he logged in... they were teasing the same story.

CLICK.

He read the article as quickly as he could. When giving it a second look, he read it aloud to keep his lips from quivering.

"Brady is alive," he said after skimming through the article enough to be satisfied that he hadn't been lured in by "fake news" authored by someone with a sick sense of humor. Once he was convinced that the news was true, he leaned back in his chair and exhaled. It felt like he was letting out a breath that he'd been holding in for months.

Smiling, Greg grabbed his phone off its charger and spoke a command. "Send text message to my brother... Taking a personal day. Period. They found Brady. Period. I'm driving to Pensacola. Period... Send message."

☠ ☠ ☠

7:15 AM EASTERN STANDARD TIME (6:15 CENTRAL)

Fireball Freeman was in a deep slumber when he was awakened. Someone was pounding on his front door. Still in bed, the old wrestler maneuvered his body so he could read the number on his alarm clock. He squinted, because deciphering those large red numbers was difficult without his glasses.

6:15. *Who in tarnation would be at the door this early in the morning?*

As the annoyance continued, Fireball decided he needed to pull his aching body out of bed to find out. "Just a second!" he shouted while wrapping a plaid bathrobe around his frame.

That frame had grown rounder over the last few months. It was the result of stress eating. Recently he'd gobbled up plenty of pizza and fried foods. He made daily trips to the donut shop. He was choking down all those nasty foods that the doctor told him to avoid. It made no sense to avoid them ever since Cocoa disappeared.

More pounding.

"I'm coming!" he shouted again.

The pioneer of the wrestling industry looked to the cabinet where he stored his pistol. He decided retrieving it wasn't necessary only after he heard his son's voice.

"Pops! It's Kayzo!"

Once he unfastened the lock and two deadbolts, the old man looked at his son and demanded, "Why are you bangin' on my door at the ass crack o' dawn?"

KaPhonso scolded his father, "Because you didn't answer the phone the twenty times I tried calling you."

"I silence the ringer at night."

"Nevermind that... I'm guessing you haven't seen the news?"

Fireball gave his son a puzzled look. Of course he hadn't seen the news. He'd been asleep. He'd still be asleep... and would still be in bed for another couple of hours if Kayzo didn't come pounding on his door first thing in the morning. "What news?"

Pushing past his father, KaPhonso stepped into the house and moved towards the living room. "Just turn the TV on. You'll see."

As Kayzo predicted, file footage of one of Jenn's matches was being shown onscreen as soon as Fireball turned on his television.

The news anchor explained how local law enforcement officers and representatives from the Coast Guard had attempted to shield Jenn and Brady from countless photographers, cameramen, and journalists who arrived to report the story. Like the missing duo they were covering, these media members seemed to arrive out of thin air as soon as it was announced that Jenn and Brady had been located.

The returning heroes looked surprised and confused. They weren't being celebrated. No one on Earth knew where they had been or what they'd gone through for the last four months. The reporters wanted answers, and they shouted their questions in a deafening cacophony that did nothing but disorient the already weary duo.

"Miss Silva, where is Cocoa Freeman?" more than one reporter yelled.

Before she had an opportunity to respond, another person shouted, "Did you kill Officer Grayson?"

Others wanted to know, "Is this a wrestling hoax?"

The last question irritated Fireball. He shouted at the television. "'Wrestling hoax?' What kind of question is that? Shut up with that nonsense and let them answer the questions. Where is Cocoa?"

The Freemans would have to wait to get their answers.

The local sheriff jumped in. Through a thick southern accent, Sheriff Isaiah Landreaux announced, "Ms. Silva and Mr. Emerson have been through a tremendous ordeal. We're still in the process of ascertaining exactly what has happened. But at this point in time our first priority is to get them the medical attention they need."

The anchor declared her station's commitment to delivering the news in a timely fashion. "Action 5 News will break in with Special Reports when updates become available... In other news, officials are forecasting a record number of Christmas travelers..."

Fireball handed the remote control to his son. "Keep watchin'. I need to shave, shower, and get dressed. You know the drill. Then we're gonna get some answers. Even if we have to drive down to Florida to get them."

☠ ☠ ☠

10:15 AM EASTERN STANDARD TIME (9:15 CENTRAL)

Four months ago, four people stepped onto commuter trains in Downtown St. Louis. Then... POOF! They disappeared into thin air. Two of those missing persons washed onto a beach in Florida a little more than five hours earlier. Needless to say, the phone was ringing off the hook at the FBI's St. Louis Field Office.

Special Agent Oscar Ruffin was the lead investigator in the St. Louis Office. He'd personally studied every e-mail account and bank statement that belonged to Jennysis Quevedo (aka "Long Jenn Silva"), Brady Emerson, Cocoa Freeman, and Arnie Grayson. Not wanting to leave any stone unturned, he'd even poured through every page of each of their high school yearbooks! He was a man who was dedicated to finding out what why they vanished and where they went. Now there was a break in the case "a thousand friggin' miles away!" (That was a fact he was none too happy about.)

He snapped off instructions for his secretary. "Lexi, get me the number to this Sheriff Landreaux from 'Wherever's-ville, Florida! I wanna talk to that guy directly. And also Tabitha What's-her-name from the Pensacola office. She's a sharp one. I met her last year at that conference in Virginia."

"Sir, the messages are piling up," the secretary reported. "Media. Family members... Even that conspiracy theorist who constantly calls in claims it was UFOs that took our missing persons."

"Well, I certainly don't wanna talk to that nutjob. Hold all my calls until I've talked to Sheriff Landreaux or Tabitha..." Her name was on the tip of his tongue. He snapped his fingers a couple of times as he tried to remember it. "Tabitha *Stallings*. That's who I really wanna talk to."

While he was waiting for his secretary to track down Special Agent Stallings, Ruffin sat at his computer and re-watched the news report. He'd already viewed the footage a handful of times. But surely there was some detail to be gleaned.

Was Jenn Silva wearing a wedding ring?

There was something strange about the way Brady Emerson was holding his right hand. Was he holding something? Or could it possibly be broken?

He really wanted to know the connection between the commuter train disappearances and this other missing person... Tavia Patton. Emerson went to college with her. They were in a class together. And, he had been a customer in the restaurant where she was working the night she was last seen alive! He had enough experience to know that two missing persons with that many connections could not be a coincidence.

Lexi popped her head back into her boss's office. "I've got Tabitha Stallings on Line Four."

"Great. Thanks. Please shut the door."

☠☠☠

11:15 AM EASTERN STANDARD TIME (10:15 CENTRAL)

"You're listening to Satellite X-treme Sports Talk Radio with 'The Cobra' Carlos Larkin... Jeremy from Philly, thanks for calling. You're on the air. What's your question?"

"Thanks, Cobra. Long time listener, first time caller..."

As he always did to celebrate the initiation of sports talk rookies, the radio host interrupted with the piped-in effect of a blaring horn. It was a sound that was appropriate when the puck flew through the net of the home team during a professional hockey game. Broadcast over the airwaves of satellite radio, however, the noise had the potential to startle those who were listening in the car.

Laszlo Barba was at the wheel of his well-weathered Ford Explorer. He was doing his damnedest to make the seven-hour drive from Orlando to Pensacola in no more than six hours. That meant the accelerator was mashed into the floor.

The radio sound effect caught Lazz off guard. His attention had drifted away from sports talk. But he certainly heard the blast of a horn... and it just about scared the piss out of him.

He yelled out in a panic. In that split second, he almost jerked the steering wheel, which would have sent him barreling into the semi in the other lane. He thought to himself, *"Time to turn this joker off."*

But then he heard what the caller had to say.

"Keep in mind we're talking about a professional wrestler. Anything and everything they do is fake. Long Jenn Silva washing ashore could be an elaborate hoax designed to lure fans into watching her next match."

The host agreed. "I think you and I may be on the same page, Jeremy. In the wrestling biz, they call it 'a work.'"

"On the other hand, there's still the missing police officer. I'm not sure what his connection could possibly be to a hoax—or a work."

"A fair point."

The caller continued, "Plus, Long Jenn Silva washed ashore with this Brady guy. That has me thinking that we could be dealing with something entirely different. Like maybe they killed the other wrestler. The cop got in his way and they killed him too."

Now the host was skeptical. "I hear what you're saying. But, if there's one thing I've learned during my time in broadcasting, it's usually the simplest solution. Are they working a wrestling hoax? Or do we have a modern day Bonnie and Clyde? Dave from Knoxville, you've got a take on this situation?"

"Yes, I do. Great show, by the way..."

"Thanks, Dave. We've got about sixty seconds until the next commercial break."

"We need to be careful not to jump to any conclusions. In my opinion, suggesting they killed a couple people is ludicrous. We've got two men, two women... Maybe they just ran away together.

Long Jenn Silva's gorgeous. The guy that washed up on the beach with her was..."

The show's theme music began to play. The host jumped in. "He was a good-lookin' guy. I think everyone agrees on that... Thanks for the call, Dave. You were making a great point, but we've got to get to commercial... This is Satellite X-treme Sports Talk Radio with 'The Cobra' Carlos Larkin. We'll be back in a flash."

Lazz turned off the radio. He knew his wife's disappearance was no hoax. But it didn't take calls from "Jeremy from Philly" and "Dave from Knoxville" to spark his paranoia. *Who the hell was this Brady guy? Had Jenn run away with him? Were they a couple? How did Cocoa fall into the mix? Did Jenn snap after the booker had told her she'd be dropping the title to Ailani Diamond?* He didn't know what to think.

One crazy thought after another rumbled through his head. This continued for several minutes, until a customized ringtone broke the silence.

Lazz pressed a button on his dashboard to take the call on Hands Free Mode. "Hey... What's up?"

A woman's voice came over the speaker. She asked, "You hangin' in there?"

"I guess so. Traffic isn't bad. If it stays like this, I should be in Pensacola by one o'clock."

"Yeah, but where's your head at?"

When the weightlifter-turned-wrestler didn't respond, the woman on the other end spoke again. "I wish I could be there with you, honey."

"I'm going to see my wife at the hospital. My wife. My wife that I thought was dead." There was a long pause before he continued. "And now people are saying that she might have been having an affair. This whole thing doesn't make any sense."

Perhaps seeing an opportunity to drive a wedge between Lazz and his wife who had suddenly reemerged, "the other woman" looked to plant additional seeds of paranoia. "Lazz... How well did you really know Jenn? You two got married after only dating for a few months. You were on the road with one wrestling promotion, while she was on the road with another. You were apart far more often than you were together. I'm not saying she was cheating on you all along, but the possibility certainly exists."

"That thought definitely occurred to me, too."

25: ATTACKS FROM ALL SIDES

"Now that I've got this championship belt, I've got loads of people gunning for me. There's that no good Russian Boris Sputnikov, and his friends The Sultan & The Samarai... I'm ready for you! At the end of the match, Corporal Chambers will be waving the Stars 'n Stripes and chanting 'U-S-A! U-S-A! U-S-A!'"

-CORPORAL CHAMBERS promo, shortly after he won the IWO Heavyweight Championship at the heart of the Cold War in the mid-1980s.

YEAR 0 + 341 DAYS (DECEMBER 7th)

It was the middle of the night. Monroe flew one of the "bobsled shuttles" into the lower atmosphere and dropped her passengers into the Gulf of Mexico. They splashed into the water about a half mile offshore.

Tired. Wet. Confused. Hungry. Jenn and Brady were dressed in the same clothes they wore when they first disappeared four months ago.

They washed onto the white, sandy beach at about four in the morning. Dozens of news teams arrived at that same beach by 5:30.

"Miss Silva, where is Cocoa Freeman?" more than one reporter yelled.

"Did you kill Officer Grayson?" was another question that she heard again and again.

Others wanted to know, "Is this a wrestling hoax?"

Jenn and Brady were grateful that the local sheriff jumped in. Through a thick southern accent, Sheriff Isaiah Landreaux announced, "Ms. Silva and Mr. Emerson have been through a tremendous ordeal. We're still in the process of ascertaining exactly what has happened. But at this point in time, our number one priority is to get them the medical attention they need."

☠☠☠

Eight hours after Brady and Jenn washed ashore, Brady's lifelong friend Greg Puckett walked into his hospital room.

Completely disregarding the fact that his pal was being questioned by law enforcement officers from various agencies, Greg plowed through the group. "Brady! You're alive! I can't believe it! I made the drive down from Atlanta as soon as I heard the news. It should've taken me five hours, but I ran over a hubcap and blew out a tire near Montgomery. So that set me back..."

A woman clamped her hand on Greg's shoulder and spun him around. "Excuse me, sir! I don't know how you got past our man at the door, but you can't just march in here like a bull in a china shop. I am with the Federal Bureau of Investigation. You need to step back immediately, before you impede my investigation any further."

Greg sucked in a deep breath. He sheepishly responded, "There was no man at the door." While it was true that he had paid no attention to the others in the room, he hadn't intended his entrance or the excitement he showed to be disrespectful to anyone. And he certainly wasn't trying to disrupt an FBI investigation.

Then the woman's words hit him like a baseball bat across the face. *FBI investigation? Is Brady in some kind of trouble?*

Greg raised a single finger at the agent (whose hand continued to grip his shoulder). "One second..." He leaned towards Brady. He wanted to remind his blood brother that the other member of "the Brady Bunch" attended one of the finest law schools in the country. "I've been on the phone with Marshall. His parents have some airline points he can use if we need him to fly out here. I'm gonna call him and tell him to hop on the next flight out of LAX."

Special Agent Tabitha Stallings looked to Sheriff Isaiah Landreaux. "Sheriff, would you please escort this young man out of the room? I'd like to continue questioning Mr. Emerson."

"Don't bother."

These words came from one of two "suits" that were entering the room at that very second.

Each of the two men proudly held their identification in the air. The mouthpiece of the duo explained, "Preston Ivy and Dr. Yaron Harazi. We're from D.O.D. More specifically, the UAPTF..."

Sheriff Landreaux seemed confused. "U-A-P...?"

"UAPTF. Thank you for your time and trouble, but Dr. Harazi and I will take it from here."

Stallings and her colleagues from the FBI made no effort to hide their frustration. "We're talking about suspects in a potential kidnapping, possibly multiple murders. Jenn Silva and Brady Emerson fall under our jurisdiction."

"Sorry to burst your bubble, but this is a D.O.D. investigation. Who do you need to hear from? Homeland Security? The Secretary of Defense? The Attorney General? *The President?* Go ahead and make your calls. They're all going to tell you the same thing... This is OUR investigation."

While the suits from different government agencies clashed, Greg took the opportunity to look up "UAPTF" on his phone. The acronym stood for "Unidentified Aerial Phenomena (UAP) Task Force (UAPTF)." With talk of UFOs, kidnappings, murders, the Department of Defense, and even the President of the United States filling the room, Greg knew what he had to do. "I'm calling Marshall... Now."

☠☠☠

SIXTEEN DAYS LATER
YEAR 0 + 357 DAYS (DECEMBER 23rd)

As the days turned into weeks, things didn't get any easier for Brady. The media continued to buzz with one outrageous rumor after another. Nosy neighbors went through his garbage, looked through his windows, and even tried to steal his mail.

The strangest visit occurred on a December morning two days before Christmas.

Brady heard a soft knock at the door. *Who is it this time?* He peeked through the curtain and saw a familiar face.

Shawna Varsho occupied a dorm room down the hall from Brady during his Sophomore year at Central Illinois University. He took her out on a couple of dates, but there wasn't much of a spark.

Now Shawna had reemerged from out of the blue. She was knocking on his front door, while struggling to hold a toddler on her hip. *What could this be about?*

He opened the door. "Shawna Varsho?"

"I wasn't sure if you would recognize me with straight hair." Years earlier, she had sported tight curly auburn locks. Now her hair was styled longer, straighter, and back to a more natural appearing shade. "I also thought the baby might throw you off."

True. She didn't have that when she and Brady had dated.

"Come in, come in," he said, purposely downplaying the fact that she walked past him without accepting the friendly hug he was offering.

"This is Zoë. She just turned two."

Brady had very little experience with tiny tots. But he tried to make eye contact and smile as he spoke to the young child. "Nice to meet you, Zoë."

The kid ignored him. She was far more interested in the Christmas tree Brady had erected in his living room.

"Listen, I don't want to waste any more of your time—or my time, for that matter—than I have to... I need money."

Was this a plea for help or a demand?

Obviously well-practiced in doing so, Shawna gently pressed Zoë's right ear against her. As she did so, the mother wrapped her right arm over her daughter's left ear so she couldn't hear what she was about to say. "Zoë's father is a deadbeat. Hasn't paid me a dime of child support, and things are getting pretty tight."

Brady couldn't hold back his questions any longer. "I'm sorry to hear that. But why are you coming to me?"

She shrugged. She seemed to think the answer should be obvious. "You practically ruined my life. And now you're in the news. You've got reporters asking around about you. I've got some dirt on you and I don't mind sharing it. There's this guy from a big gossip site on the internet. (I'm not gonna tell you which one, but you've definitely heard of it.) He's offering me a thousand bucks for my story. You can keep me quiet for two thousand. That's my price. Two thousand dollars and you'll never have to hear from me again. The world will never know about the terrible thing you did to me."

Tilting his head to one side and squinting his eyes just a bit, Brady desperately tried to figure out what she could possibly be talking about.

Shawna read his expression as feigned confusion. "You can stop playing dumb." The young mother quickly covered her daughter's ears again. This time Zoë protested. Shawna talked over the shrill squeal of her child, "I know you remember taking pictures of me..." She mouthed the next words, "engaged in a graphic sexual act..." She returned to full volume while lowering her kid to the floor, "And then you sent those pictures to the sorority I was rushing. They kicked me out of the house, and I went into a major depression. A year later, I got pregnant. To make matters worse, I had to drop out of school and move back in with my parents."

She believes every word of what she just said. Brady spoke as kindly as he could. He didn't want to sound like he was arguing, but he needed to clear his name. He needed to make some sense of this confusion.

"Shawna, I never took any pictures. I never even *saw* any naughty pictures of you. And I would never send anything like that to your sorority or anyone else."

Brady's kind tone partially diffused Shawna's anger. The two settled onto the living room couch and pieced together the clues of this mystery.

After a few minutes of discussion, Brady believed he had solved the case. "I know the weekend you're talking about. Greg and Marshall road tripped up to Chicago for a concert, but I didn't go because I had to referee a couple of intramural games at the athletic center. Your roommate was hooking up with some guy from the football team..."

Shawna shook her head in agreement as the memory was beginning to be much less cloudy. "Not just some guy. It was Malcolm North, the star running back."

"Yep." Brady knew all about the CIU record setting rusher. "Drafted in the sixth round by the San Francisco 49ers. But he blew out his knee in the first preseason game."

After redirecting Zoë and stopping her from pulling ornaments off Brady's tree, Shawna and Brady discussed the events that led up to that horrible weekend in greater detail. Eventually, they got to the point when she came knocking on his dorm room door.

"You were pretty drunk. You looked like you'd been crying and you said you wanted to crash in my room... As soon as you got settled, I went out and slept on a chair in the TV lounge."

Shawna sat in silence. She replayed the scene in her head. She thought about the grudge she'd harbored for the last three years. She admitted, "You're right. It wasn't you that took the photos. You didn't have anything to do with it. It was those guys from down the hall. Those two guys from Minnesota."

"Theo Davis and... Nicolas Nixon? I think they were from Michigan, actually."

"Yeah, those guys. Theo and Nick. The ones that set the fire in the elevator during midterms. I should have..." Shawna stopped mid-apology. Zoë didn't have much of an attention span, and Brady's living room wasn't exactly built with toddlers in mind. "Zoë! Get that out of your mouth!"

Brady bounced up from his seat. "Here! I've got a couple of Kids' Meal toys. Would you like a rocket or a pink dinosaur?" He tore open the plastic packages and handed them to the child. "Actually, she can have both."

Shawna was grateful. "Thanks. That was quick thinking. But why do you have these?"

"When I go through a drive thru, two Kids' Meals are about the same price as one Value Meal. That's what I get so I can drink the milk instead of soda. I save the toys and give them out on Halloween instead of candy."

Shawna laughed. "I've got one question: Do dentists love you because you never have any cavities? Or do they hate you because you're bad for business?" After a short pause, she decided that she owed the young man an apology. "I should have known better. Brady, I'm so sorry. All these years, I've been going around thinking you're the creep who took pervy pictures of me then sent them to my sorority... basically ruining my life. In reality, you were buying Kids' Meals so you could drink the milk and give the toys to trick-or-treaters."

With the youngster now content to bang the toy rocket into the plastic dinosaur, the reconciled friends continued to talk for several minutes.

Shawna stood and patted her hands against her thighs to get her daughter's attention. "Okay, Zo-bot... Time to go." While brushing

a wisp of hair out of her eyes, Shawna smiled and looked at Brady.
"I know I just tried to blackmail you and all, but I only live about
thirty minutes from here. We could get together for a cup of coffee
sometime... If me having a kid doesn't scare you off."

"I'll keep that in mind." His tone revealed that he had no
intention of going on a date with her, and he knew it. "To be honest,
though, there's someone else I'm interested in. I'd like to see how
things play out with her."

Shawna flirtatiously gestured as if she was zipping her lips
shut. Then she nodded, indicating that she was accepting his
graceful rejection. "I hope things work out with you and her. And I
promise I won't say a word to the internet gossip guy." She leaned
in and kissed him on the cheek. "Merry Christmas, Brady
Emerson."

☠ ☠ ☠

Shawna had been gone for less than two minutes when Brady heard
more rapping at the front door. The knocks came so quickly behind
the young mother's departure that Brady suspected that Shawna had
left something behind.

Forgetting his newly forged habit of checking the peephole
before inviting anyone inside, Brady whipped open the door. He
was greeted by a badge-wielding FBI Agent.

Special Agent Oscar Ruffin barged in. As he did so, he
mentioned something about how he had put off his visit for long
enough. He used terms like "person of interest" and "awaiting
D.O.D. approval." It was a rapid-fire puzzle of legal jargon, and
Brady was having difficulty putting the pieces together.

Unlike the questions Special Agent Stallings had posed back in
the Pensacola hospital, this man's inquiries reached much deeper.

He wasn't there simply to harass someone he felt suspicious. And he wasn't just fishing around to see if he might stumble upon some answers about the whereabouts of Cocoa and Officer Grayson. Special Agent Ruffin was there with a set of specific objectives and expectations.

"I took the liberty of looking through your credit card bills while you were 'missing,'" he began, obnoxiously using air quotes to accompany his use of the word "missing."

Brady bowed his head and said a silent prayer. He knew he couldn't tell anyone what actually happened. People like Ruffin would want to throw him in jail. Others in the judicial system might want to lock him away in a mental institution. Perhaps worst of all, the U.S. Military would look to launch missiles into space until they brought Armstrong and his crew of blue-skinned, alien menaces crashing to Earth.

The young man thought about the advice Marshall had given him two weeks earlier. *"Don't say anything. If they think they have a single thread of evidence against you, they'll twist your words to sound like they've got enough evidence to file a rock-solid case. Then they'll arrest you for kidnapping, murder, or even something as simple as obstruction of justice."*

(Turns out Marshall was right. Ruffin threw out all of those possibilities in the first five minutes after he'd stepped through the front door.)

"You went to the End Zone on New Year's Day. Your waitress was a young lady named Tavia Patton." The detective opened a manila file and pulled out an 8x10 picture of the waitress/sorority girl that Brady knew as a vindictive turncoat. "You gave Miss Patton a nice tip... A big tip actually... Thirty percent... Funny thing is, the poor young lady went missing that very night. No one's

SCOTT QUINN

heard a single word from her ever since... Not one phone call. Not one e-mail. Not one post on social media."

"That doesn't sound the least bit funny."

"What?" Brady's cold response got Ruffin's dander up.

"*You* used the phrase 'funny thing is.' I don't think there's anything funny about it," Brady knew he was treading dangerous waters. He should be following the legal advice of his very good friend. But he didn't like Ruffin's attitude. And he didn't appreciate being on the wrong end of a baseless suggestion that he was somehow involved in Tavia's disappearance. "I know who Tavia Patton is. You don't have to show me a picture. My church prayed for her when she first went missing. I attended a vigil on campus for her... Eleven months ago. I'm sorry for whatever happened to her, but I had nothing to do with her going missing. Yes, I went to the End Zone on New Year's. So did half of King City. If you remember, CIU was playing in the Tumbleweed Bowl. Biggest game in the history of the university. Did you go pounding on the doors of all two hundred people who were in that restaurant that night?"

The Special Agent returned the verbal fire. "No... Because, out of all those names, yours is the only name on this important list: Brady Emerson, Jenn Silva, Cocoa Freeman, *Officer* Arnold Grayson..." He put extra emphasis on the word "Officer." Ruffin had an extra ax to grind because it appeared a brother in the field of law enforcement may have met an untimely demise. "Now let's add Tavia Patton to the list. That's *your* list."

Brady stood in silence.

"Where are they, Brady? I'm starting to think I may be looking at a cold-blooded serial killer. Prove me wrong. Tell me what you know. That's all you have to do. Then this all becomes a whole lot easier for everyone."

"Mr. Ruffin, I don't like where these questions are going. I've talked to an attorney, and he's instructed me not to say anything to the police without him being present. That being the case, I'm going to kindly ask you to leave. My lawyer's business card is on the fridge. I'll get it for you. Then, if you want to ask me any other questions about Tavia, Cocoa, Arnie or anything else, you'll need to call him first."

"You're gonna lawyer up, huh?" the agent asked, indignantly. His anger caused him to miss the fact that Brady had referred to Officer Arnold Grayson as "Arnie." Instead, he stood up, brushed imaginary dust away from his thighs for effect, and headed towards the door. "I gave you a chance to clear your name, to tell your story. But I guess I should've known that a cop killer doesn't typically have much to say... I'll promise you this... I'll be seein' you again, Emerson. When I arrest you... Then again when I testify against you at your trial... And also when the judge sentences you to life in prison. You're not gonna get away with this, smart guy!"

☠☠☠

Brady's heart was still pounding from his heated conversation with Agent Ruffin. He stood in the kitchen, staring into his fridge. *Was two o'clock in the afternoon way too early to crack open a beer? After all he'd endured, a couple of frosty ones sounded preferable to a tall glass of milk on this particular day.*

This internal debate was interrupted when a black SUV pulled into the driveway.

He looked through the window and saw a face he recognized. Though he couldn't remember the man's name, Brady knew he was the rank-pulling UFO chaser that had paid him a visit on his first day in the Pensacola hospital.

A second man exited from the passenger side of the vehicle. He, too, looked vaguely familiar. But it was the driver of the vehicle who had done all of the talking during their first exchange.

"Mr. Emerson," the agent said while acting out the cliché of deliberately removing his dark sunglasses. "I'm Preston Ivy with the UAPTF: Unidentified Aerial Phenomena Task Force. You and I met a little more than two weeks ago. This is my counterpart, Dr. Yaron Harazi. Would you mind if we came in to ask you a few questions?"

Brady nodded his head, saying nothing. He was becoming frustrated by the steady stream of uninvited visitors.

Agent Ivy wanted to carefully follow departmental protocols. "Is that a 'yes,' Mr. Emerson?"

Dr. Harazi barged in before Brady could answer. It was clear he was coming in with or without a formal invitation. Preston followed directly behind him, though he was somewhat uneasy entering without obtaining explicit approval from the subject of this investigation.

"Look, I already told the guy with the FBI..." Brady began to protest.

Harazi cut him off. "We don't care what you told the FBI, the local police, or anyone else, for that matter. That is to say, I don't believe that those working in traditional law enforcement would be interested in the same types of information that interest us."

Brady looked towards Ivy. He had done the talking during their initial interaction. He was deferring to the doctor this time around.

Ivy broke eye contact and looked towards the floor. He appeared uncomfortable with the situation. "Listen... Dr. Harazi has had too much coffee, and I haven't had enough. I'm going to step out and get some fresh air."

Seconds after the door shut behind him, Harazi made a statement intended to put Brady at ease. "Mr. Emerson, I don't care who you killed or who you didn't kill. Personally, I don't particularly think you killed anyone. I honestly do not care. The people I work with are far more concerned with where you were for four months. You vanished into thin air. We want to know... where did you go? What did you see? How were you treated? How did you get away? Perhaps most importantly, did you interact with them directly?"

These questions differed significantly from the others Brady had been asked over the last few days. Though over-caffeinated, the doctor seemed like a straight shooter. He wanted to trust him. But he had a long way to go before he earned that trust.

Dr. Harazi reached into a manila file that resembled the one Agent Ruffin had carried into the house just an hour earlier. The photograph Harazi presented, however, was drastically different.

Brady scanned another 8x10 photo. It was glossy black and white. Depicted was a naked being strapped to a metal table. The being looked like an adult, female Nawerssian. This one appeared much younger and far less wrinkled than Armstrong.

"Did you encounter any creatures that looked like this?" Harazi asked unapologetically.

Brady was a terrible liar and he knew it. If he tried to lie his way out of the situation, his miserable attempts to deceive would give him away in no time. "What? Is this some kind of joke?" he asked, while throwing in feigned laughter. "Aliens! You think I got abducted by aliens? You seriously think that's where I've been? You think I've was being studied by little green men? Do you need to check me for implants? Maybe search my house for some sort of advanced-tech radio transmitter?"

"Are you authorizing me and my associate to conduct such a search? We can get a warrant if we need to?"

"No! I was being sarcastic. Being studied by aliens! This is beginning to feel like a big, elaborate joke. Trust me, there's no implant. There's no radio transmitter."

"It's no joke, Mr. Emerson. I think you know that." Harazi's demeanor had changed in an instant. Now he was every bit as emotionless as the "aliens" about whom he was inquiring. "And I did not say anything about being studied. That was you who said that... More than once, I believe."

Pointing to the door, Brady insisted, "I want you to leave! I've spoken to an attorney. I have rights."

Harazi stood there, holding his ground in the kitchen. He didn't flinch. He didn't twitch. Instead, he peered at Brady for nearly half a minute before responding to the demands of the young man.

Finally, the alien expert nodded. Reeling in his level of aggression, he once again tried to reassure Brady. "Please do not feel threatened by me, Mr. Emerson. I'm on your side. I realize that it may not seem like it at the moment, but it's true. Since your return, I have taken measures to protect you and Ms. Quevedo... Long Jenn Silva. I want you to trust me. I do not want to bully you into achieving that trust. Mr. Ivy and I would like to speak with you again soon. Shortly after Christmas, if you'd like." Harazi pulled a business card out of his manilla file. "This is my card. My private cell phone number is on the back. Please call me any time."

Harazi left. Joining Ivy, the two returned to their black SUV.

Brady scrambled to get his phone. He texted: "Jenn! It's Brady! I'm freaking out right now! Please call me ASAP!"

26: DON'T CALL IT A COMEBACK

"Do I want to return to wrestling? Absolutely. Not right away, though. It takes a lot to become physically and mentally ready to step into the ring. I'll get there, but it's going to take some time."

-Excerpt from LONG JENN SILVA interview on an episode from "24/7 Sports News" given one week after her return.

YEAR 0 + 341 DAYS (DECEMBER 7th)

Exhausted, Jenn fell asleep at some point during the forty-minute ambulance ride to Pensacola. Despite protests from Special Agent Stallings and Sheriff Landreaux, the doctors gave Jenn enough medication to allow her to sleep comfortably for several hours.

When she awoke, everything appeared blurry. The combination of the fatigue, the drugs, and the brightness of the light coming through the window was nearly blinding to eyes that had grown accustomed to the dimness she'd experienced while living in space. Even so, she could make out the figure of her burly husband standing over her. "Lazz?" she asked, almost as if in disbelief.

After a momentary pause, she sat up in her bed, leaned forward and reached towards her gentle giant. He responded by backing up. His movement still permitted her to hold his hand. But she couldn't get close enough to embrace him. She couldn't give her husband the kiss she had dreamt of numerous times throughout her four month-long ordeal.

"Jenn, there are some people here who have a few questions…" he told her. The tone of his voice made it clear that he had no thoughts of stepping in to protect his wife. He wasn't going to do anything to prevent the interrogation. "Once they're done, I may have a few questions of my own."

☠☠☠

TWO DAYS LATER
YEAR 0 + 343 DAYS (DECEMBER 9th)

Jenn picked out a summery dress that she had purchased prior to being abducted. With a cowled neckline, an open back, and a seductive front slit that traveled far beyond her knee, she was confident that her outfit would get Lazz's attention.

She hoped to dazzle her husband with a one-two punch. She was not just dressed to kill. She filled the condominium with the aromas of Lazz's favorite dinner: Baked Ziti with Mushrooms and Spicy Italian Sausage. She added some fresh baked Garlic Bread and a Spinach Salad to gain even more points!

The door swung open. Her husband marched into the condo and moved straight towards the master bedroom. It wasn't entirely surprising. Jenn suspected that the former Olympic weightlifter was covered in sweat after he returned from his heavy-duty workout.

After pulling the garlic bread out of the oven, the pirate-turned-chef went to invite her hubby to the dinner table.

The shower was running in the en suite bathroom. Jenn tried the door. It was locked. *Strange. He never locked the bathroom door before.*

"*Querido...* Hurry up in there and come to dinner. I made baked ziti with mushrooms 'n sausage."

He didn't sound too enthused. "Eh... I got a fish sandwich and a milkshake on my way home."

"Maybe you could sit down and have a couple bites?"

Lazz made no effort to hurry. He eventually made his way to the table. Unlike Jenn, he didn't think of dressing up. He wore a pair of sweat shorts and a pit-stained white T-shirt.

Jenn scooped a forkful of salad into her mouth. Chewing on an oversized bite of baby spinach and fresh tomatoes was preferable to saying something she might regret.

"This is my first time wearing this dress. Do you like it?"

Her husband used his answer to imply that she had wronged him in some way. "I guess so. I knew you had it... I saw it hanging in the closet during those four months you were gone."

The meal continued to bounce back and forth between periods of awkward silence and vague remarks that sounded dangerously close to accusations. Finally, Jenn had enough. "Are you suggesting that I wanted to be gone all that time?"

Lazz spiked his napkin onto his plate. He stood up and began to walk away. Then he turned back around. "I don't know. I don't have a clue what I'm supposed to think. You haven't told me anything about why you disappeared, where you disappeared to, or who you were with! All I know is you were told you were gonna drop your title, then whammo! Gone. Vanished into thin air without a word. Months later, you and Handsome College Guy return without Cocoa Freeman. You've been back two full days, and you haven't offered one word of explanation... The food tastes great. Your dress is nice. Is that what you wanna hear? If I wasn't so angry and confused right now, I'd probably want to tear it off you and carry you into the bedroom. But, right now, what I really want from you is an honest discussion and a few answers."

She didn't tell him about the abduction. *She couldn't. It for his own good.* "I don't know what to say."

Lazz nodded his head as his shoulders sagged. "That's the problem, Jenn. That's the problem."

☠☠☠

TWELVE DAYS LATER
YEAR 0 + 355 DAYS (DECEMBER 21st)

Jenn had been back for two weeks. During that time, her name continued to be featured prominently in the mainstream media. It was trending nonstop throughout various social media platforms. One outrageous rumor followed another. Every thirty-six hour news cycle seemingly featured a new theory. Most were either total speculation or complete fiction. That didn't matter to headline hungry reporters. It didn't raise any concerns with the click-starved producers of Internet rubbish. And it certainly made no difference to the rabid consumers who gobbled up each and every spectacular story.

Jenn was on the business end of crazy looks at the grocery store, while she was out on her morning runs, and even when she tried to slip into the back row for a Sunday matinee. It was making her miserable.

"Half of the civilized world thinks I'm some kind of murderer," she told Manny when the two rendezvoused at a coffee shop not far from his gym. She went on to confide in her mentor. "Lazz says he can't even look me in the eye. Every time he sees my face, he has more and more questions he wants to ask... They're questions I can't answer. I would if I could. I can't."

"You know, your husband's not the only one with questions."

Jenn felt her heart shattering. "You too?"

"No, not me," her friend, mentor, and father figure chuckled as he attempted to assure her. "You could tell me that you'd spent the last four months playin' golf on Mars with Elvis, Andre the Giant, and Bigfoot. I'd believe you. You're like a daughter to me. And I know that you would tell me everything if you could. Knowing that is all I need..."

Where was he going with this? "But?"

"Fireball Freeman. You and his daughter disappeared together. You came back. She didn't... Word is 'you're dodging his calls.' You need to see him, Jenn. I can go with you if you like. But you need to see him."

She shook her head. "I know you're right. Maybe next week. Maybe after Christmas. I've got a lot on my plate right now. Mainly

trying to get things back to normal between me and my husband...
Although I have no idea where that's concerned."

☠ ☠ ☠

TWO DAYS LATER
YEAR 0 + 357 DAYS (DECEMBER 23rd)

Jenn sucked in a deep breath as she prepared to step into the
headquarters of wrestling's biggest promotion. She was no stranger
to this place. She had been there a couple years ago, when she was
rejected for being unwilling to ditch her pirate gimmick. Now she
was back again, desperate for work. *"Focus. You're here to get jobs
for you* and *Lazz,"* she thought to herself.

Surely a money grubber like Griffin Conrad would jump at the
chance to ink one of the biggest names out there. Even if it was just
for a couple shows. Jenn's name was all over the news. *"There's no
such thing as bad publicity, right?"* Putting her in the main event of
the next "Saturday Night Slamfest" would make some headlines
and bring in some big ratings. She could see the headlines: *"An
After Christmas Gift for Wrestling Fans Everywhere."*

She checked in with security. After that, she stepped towards
the elevator. It was there that she was joined by Santa Saws, the
monstrosity with a Kris Kringle/Chainsaw Massacre gimmick.

"Lookin' good, kid," he smiled as he stood over her.

Jenn pulled herself into him, nestling into his big beard as she
fought back the urge to cry. "It's so good to see a friendly face."

"'Friendly face.' That's one I don't hear too often."

The elevator dinged and the two wrestlers stepped in. "Going
up?" he asked, making his booming voice sound as friendly as
possible.

After the initial excitement of seeing her old friend began to wear off, Jenn flashed a puzzled squint in his direction. Though it seemed like ages ago, she knew that just a few months earlier the man was firmly entrenched as the All-World Wrestling Alliance's Hardcore Champion. It didn't make sense for him to be in another promotion's corporate offices. "What are you doing here?"

The elevator bell sounded again as they reached the top floor. Conrad's secretary immediately waived Jenn and Saws into the main office. Suddenly, Jenn realized she was about to be on the wrong end of an ambush.

"I thought this was going to be a one-on-one meeting," she said loudly enough to convey the message that she wasn't too happy about how this meeting was beginning to take shape.

"Jenn Silva!" Conrad jubilantly announced, again refusing to refer to the luchadora by her full pirate moniker. Though he was standing next to his desk, he motioned for her to take a seat. "Come in and sit down."

Saws stood behind her as she sank into the chair.

As soon as she was settled into her seat, the high-backed leather chair across the massive desk swiveled around. Fireball Freeman stared deep into Jenn's eyes, hoping to unnerve her.

"Mr. Freeman, it's good to see you," she said with a quiver in her voice. She was just a few weeks removed from battling quasi-aliens, but this surprise confrontation was enough to freak her out!

"You never called me 'Mr. Freeman' before. Call me 'Fireball.' Please." He sounded more like a cold-blooded gangster than a wrestling promoter... or a father concerned about the whereabouts of his daughter, for that matter.

She glanced around the room. "I didn't realize you and Mr. Conrad were friends." (She *knew* they *weren't* friends. They were bitter rivals.)

Conrad chimed in, "Some things transcend business."

"I'm just gonna cut to the chase here," Fireball said, leaning forward. "'Cause Griffin's not gonna hire you. Not for one match. And I'm not gonna hire you... What happened to Cocoa? Jenn... where's my daughter? What did you do to her?"

Saws put his hand on her shoulder. With that one simple action he conveyed two conflicting messages: He was her friend and he supported her, but he could and would crush her if the situation called for him to do so.

"Cocoa's not dead." Jenn wanted to get that out right away. "We were taken..."

Fireball cut her off. "Kidnapped?"

"More like abducted."

"*Who* exactly abducted you?"

"That I can't say."

"Can't? Or won't?"

Jenn shook her head in frustration. She knew she had to choose her words very, very carefully. "We were taken against our will. Me, Cocoa, Brady Emerson and the cop. All four of us. One minute we were passengers on a train. The next minute, we were gone. I can't explain how. We were in and out of consciousness for most of the time we were there. It's hard to say what was real and what wasn't. Brady and I escaped. As for Cocoa... she chose to stay."

"Why would she *choose* to stay?" he asked. There was much less bravado in his voice this time around. At least a small part of him recognized that what Jenn was saying might be true. That part of him recognized that, if she chose to stay wherever she was, he may have failed his daughter in some way.

Griffin Conrad couldn't resist the urge to jump in. He insisted on making her the heel. "I used to admire your commitment to kayfabe... now I see you for what you really are... a liar. Nothin' but a pathological liar. This man's daughter could be dead or dying somewhere, and you spew lie after lie after lie. You disgust me!"

Jenn ignored Conrad's rant. And she did her best to ignore the massive meat hook that rested on her shoulder. The pirate leaned in and looked straight into Fireball's eyes. "You can choose to believe me or leave here thinking I'm a liar, but that's the truth. One hundred percent. If I could've brought her back with me, I would have. But she was... she *is* a grown woman living in a lot of physical pain from taking a few too many bumps. She chose to stay, and I couldn't convince her otherwise in the short window of time I had. I'm sorry. I'm truly sorry she's not sitting right here with us right now."

Fireball dropped his head. He stared at the top of Conrad's desk for almost a minute. Finally, he managed to ask, "Why doesn't she call?"

That was a good question. Jenn quickly replayed the entire conversation in her head. She'd been forced to improvise. Thankfully, her career inside the squared circle had taught her to ad lib on the fly. She was fairly confident that she had framed her story to sound like they may have been snatched by some sort of cult.

"I'm not at all certain where we were or how we got there," she explained. "But calling you or anybody else? It's not possible."

The old wrestler was speechless. He nodded his head as a signal that he was satisfied with the answers he'd received.

Saws lifted his hand away from Jenn's shoulder. Then she left the room.

The meeting certainly hadn't gone as planned. It left Jenn shaken. With tears streaming down her face, she managed to text Lazz: "Can u pick me up? On a bench outside IWO HQ. No questions please."

☠☠☠

An SUV pulled up less than twenty minutes later.

Lazz reached across the passenger seat. He pulled on the handle, opening the door for his wife without having to get out of the car to do so.

"What are you doing here?" he asked as she was climbing into the vehicle.

"Please... no questions," Jenn insisted. "It's been a rough morning."

Throwing up his hands to show his frustration, he snapped back, "'No questions.' Where have I heard that before? Oh yeah... *you!* Every time I've tried asking you anything over the last couple of weeks! It's getting old, Jenn. It's getting old."

No one said a word for at least ten minutes. They were nearing the parking garage of the condominium when Jenn's phone vibrated.

It vibrated again.

Then it vibrated a third time.

"Sounds like someone's pretty desperate to reach you," her husband said, his voice sounding as if he believed the idea of rekindling their relationship might be hopeless. "Can I ask who? Better yet, why don't you read your messages out loud?"

Jenn looked down at her phone. She pursed her lips together as she read the texts. Even though she knew it was going to piss off her husband, she read the first one aloud. "Jenn. It's Brady. I'm freaking out right now. Please call me ASAP."

"What the hell does he want?" Lazz blurted out, making no effort to hide his disgust.

"Do you want me to text him back and find out?"

"That's the last thing I want you to do!"

"Fine. I won't call him back. But, honey... You don't need to feel threatened. I love you." Jenn reached for his hand and attempted to give him a reassuring squeeze.

"Would you please stop distracting me? Just let me keep my eyes on the road and my hands on the wheel."

☠☠☠

ONE DAY LATER
YEAR 0 + 358 DAYS (DECEMBER 24th)

Jenn started her morning with an hour on the treadmill. With headphones in her ears and a video on the display in front of her, it was almost enough to convince the luchadora that she was getting her morning exercise along the sandy beaches of Cancun. She would have preferred to take her seven-mile run through the neighborhoods of suburban Orlando. Unfortunately, the Florida weather didn't look like it was going to cooperate today. Plus, she had devised a plan to kickstart her relationship with her husband. Sticking around their condo would help her turn that idea into reality.

One she was done with her run, the wrestler-turned-pirate was eager to peel away her sweaty exercise clothes. "There's room in the shower for two if you're interested..." she called to her husband while en route to the bathroom.

There was no response.

"Lazz?"

He was nowhere to be seen.

"Laszlo?" she called out in a voice loud enough to be heard throughout the condo, but not so loud that it would have annoyed any neighbors who were sleeping in.

"Must've slipped out while I was on the treadmill," she guessed. Then she frowned. Her husband's rapid departure was another reminder of how rocky her marriage had been since she came back. "Oh well. His loss."

Jenn reached into the shower and turned on the hot water. Her heart nearly burst through her chest when she caught a glimpse of a figure in the mirror.

Armstrong.

He was standing just outside the doorway to the bathroom. He was completely unconcerned about invading Jenn's privacy. "I apologize for startling you."

"Armstrong! What do you think you're doing? Better yet, why are you here?"

"I am sorry if I have alarmed you. I will step out to allow you to wash and dress. But please do not be too long. We need to talk. And time is of the essence."

☠☠☠

She took one of the fastest showers in her life. She dressed quickly, throwing on a pair of leggings and a wrestling merch T-shirt that was at the top of a basket of clean laundry.

Armstrong was seated at the kitchen table. "There is no reason to be concerned about Mr. Barba. He is fine. However, I felt it advisable that you and I have this conversation without him being present."

"Am I in virtual reality right now?" she asked, more than a little perturbed.

"No. Your husband is."

Jenn knew enough about the process used in the life suspension tanks of the *Vilnagrom-II* to be confident that Lazz would never realize he was gone. Though it would take several hours to transport him from the Earth's surface to the ship floating above the planet, he'd be sedated the entire time. They could speed up or slow down the clock in VR. Once Polo hooked him up to the simulation in the tank of purple goo, he could manipulate the settings to make it seem like one day was a week or one year was a day. The Nawerssians would sedate him again for his return. Her husband would wake up in his bed in the morning completely unaware of the fact he'd missed a day or two of life on Earth.

Getting down to business, Armstrong told Jenn, "We have picked up new communications from the *Vilnagrom-III*. It will be here soon, orbiting the Earth. Avis and I have had some concerns that they may not be friendly towards my crew, especially since we believe Oya gave Quetzal a message for the *V-III* before he flew away."

"This is old news. Besides... what the hell do I care?"

"Cocoa Freeman, for one," he said, reminding Jenn that her friend had elected to remain on the *V-II*. "If our suspicions are correct, she could be in grave danger."

"I hate that. I really do. But, as her own father says, 'Cocoa's a grown ass woman.' She chose to live a life doped up in space."

Armstrong continued, "I also have some concerns that the crew of the *Vilnagrom-III* may be much more aggressive in their 'interactions' with the people of Earth."

"I don't understand. Are you talking alien invasion?"

Armstrong laughed at Jenn's use of the word "alien." Then he said, "That, too, is old news. But it is news that we chose not to share with you while you were on our ship."

"Why the hell not? Maybe I could've convinced Cocoa to come back home if she knew that the next batch of blue boys were all evil."

"We were unsure. We worried that the vague nature of their communications might be creating unnecessary paranoia among our people. But now we have additional reasons to believe that our initial fears were true."

Jenn rolled her eyes. "You're talkin' to me in riddles. Say what you're here to say."

"Our Navigator—Baron— previously sided with Hannibal and Oya. He has provided us with some new information. We now believe the crew of the *V-III* may possess intelligence that was not known or not made available to my original crew at the time we left Na-Werss almost forty Earth Years ago. Simply put, the doomsday of your planet is closer than was previously hypothesized."

Jenn spoke in a tone that made it clear that she wasn't interested in letting Armstrong and his crew (or any other Nawerssians) wreck her life any more than they already had. "If that's the case, so be it. Thanks for the warning, though. I hope you enjoyed scaring me half to death during your uninvited tour of my condo. Now get the hell out!"

Armstrong wasn't giving up on his effort to recruit her. "We need you. Everyone aboard the *V-II* needs you. Not just Cocoa. And not just me and Avis... You are smart..."

"That's me. Jenn the Genius," she interrupted. "If smart is what you're looking for, why don't you go a few miles up the road to Gainesville? The University of Florida is one of the top public schools in the country."

Ignoring Jenn's interruption (and her sarcasm), Armstrong continued his plea. "You are not just smart, you are quick on your feet, as well. And those are very different things. Those are attributes we likely will need in the fight that is to come. Fighters. Survivors. That perfectly describes 'Long Jenn Silva.' That is why I am here. And that is why, at this very moment, Monroe is having a similar conversation with Brady Emerson. We need both of you if we hope to prevent something terrible from occurring."

She remained unconvinced. "You're delusional! I just got off your damn spaceship. Now you want me to go back?"

"Did you exercise on your treadmill this morning because there was a twenty percent chance of rain in the forecast? Or did you run inside because you preferred to avoid what is on the other side of those walls?" Armstrong paused for effect. Once he detected that his point was hitting close to home, he continued. "Face facts, Jenn. Outside those walls is a world full of people who will not give you a job. A world of gossips saying you betrayed your closest friend. A world full of headhunters happy to accuse you of murder! They have made it clear *they* do not need you."

Jenn nodded her head and pressed her lips together. She desperately wanted to fight back any tears, but they were dangerously close to the surface. Armstrong was right. She knew it. This world would never be able to know her story. Sooner or later they'd act on their desires to crucify her.

Armstrong moved two fingers towards the neckline of his flight suit. Gliding those fingers downward, he "unzipped" the silver and blue outfit to the midpoint of his chest. He reached in and pulled out a tube. He removed a dagger. It was the one Jenn had used to defeat Tavia.

The Nawerssian held the dagger by the blade, offering the handle to the luchadora. "I am telling you that *WE* need you. Those of us on the *Vilnagrom-II*... and the people of Earth. This Earth. Your generation. Avis, Monroe, Carver, and I... even Polo and Baron... we believe there may be a way we can prevent this upcoming doomsday. But I cannot and will not try to do it on my own. Join me, Long Jenn Silva."

"When would we go?"

"Immediately."

That didn't phase her.

She moved on to her next question. "What about Lazz?"

"He can come with us or we can return him. You can take the next step of your journey with him at your side or you can leave him here. That is entirely up to you."

Jenn stood motionless. Her gaze landed above the collection of wrinkles on Armstrong's hairless head. She was weighing her options. Though things had been difficult since her return, she was no quitter. She wasn't ready to throw in the towel on her marriage.

Was she actually trying to convince herself that this wasn't completely ridiculous? Agreeing to voluntarily leave the comfort and familiarity of Earth? If she went with Armstrong, she'd likely become some sort of full-time space pirate.

Armstrong broke the silence. "I know you are deep in contemplation, but I need an answer soon."

Still buried in her thoughts, Jenn drifted towards the bedroom. "We're going to want to bring Lazz along with us. You want someone who is good in a fight? You can't ask for much better than Laszlo Barba."

She pulled her favorite piece of luggage out of the closet. It was a garment bag that folded over into a rolling suitcase. "I'm not wearing your traditional Nawerssian space suit all the time. And I'm sure not wearing those crazy silver robes," she explained.

Jenn pulled three wrestling outfits out of her closet, along with her favorite little black dress. *("Perfect for any occasion... on Earth or in space.")* She stuffed a pair of jeans, an extra pair of leggings, her three favorite bras, and a couple of her most treasured Lucha Libre T-shirts inside.

"Ready to go," she announced. "Let's hit the bricks before I lose my nerve and change my mind."

Armstrong smiled. "'Hit the bricks.' I do not recall hearing that particular figure of speech before. I like it... And I am pleased that you have decided to join us."

"Wait! ...One sec..." she said as she scurried back into her bedroom. A moment later she returned with the mask that she wore in Mexico, back when she was still known as "Lady Pirata." She thought back to the time professional wrestling's biggest corporate big shot insisted that she ditch the pirate gimmick, as well as the mask. They were some of the very things that defined the woman she had become. Long Jenn Silva had no intention of abandoning either one.

"You never know when a mask might come in handy."

27: THE DUSTY FINISH

"What's my secret? Whether we're talking about my wrestling career, my marriage, or life in general, I never stop learning. I know I can always improve. I can always be better. Once you decide you know all there is to know, you become unwilling to adapt. When that happens, you lose the match... your relationship falls apart... or you're dead. Those aren't options I'm willing to consider."

-LONG JENN SILVA interview on "Chatting with Champions" podcast.

TWENTY MONTHS EARLIER
YEAR -1 + 120 DAYS (APRIL 30th)

Jenn wore a pair of gray sweatpants and a well-worn black tank top. The shirt featured the image of a red, white, and green luchador mask printed on the front. Beneath the image were the words "Lucha Libre."

"Did you sleep in that?" Santa Saws asked as they stepped off the elevator together.

It was only 8:00 a.m. The post-apocalyptic pirate and the chainsaw-wielding St. Nick were among several AWWA stars who had fought at an event in Tokyo the previous night. They didn't make it back to their hotel until well after midnight.

"As a matter of fact, I did."

Jenn knocked on the door of Cocoa's 31st floor suite. As they waited for her to come to the door, she looked Saws up and down. He wore a plain white tank top, camouflage cargo shorts, and black combat boots.

"Did you sleep in that?"

"I sleep in the nude," he replied with a bit of a grunt.

The door swung open. Cocoa displayed a bit of surprise across her face. She, too, was wearing the clothes she had worn to bed. For her, it was a leopard print satin chemise that dropped just low enough to cover her backside.

"I... uh... didn't realize Saws was coming."

"I invited him to watch the pay-per-view with us," Jenn replied apologetically.

"What's the big deal?" the evil Santa deadpanned. "It's nothin' I haven't seen before. Remember, I see you when you're sleeping."

Jenn made a face. "Ew! Comments like that are why they make pepper spray."

Cocoa was feeling confident. She chose to not let the perverted remark ruin her mood. "Makes me no difference." She pivoted, giving Jenn and Saws a spectacular view of her ass as she walked away from the door. "Come on in. There's only one more match until the Main Event."

The indie wrestlers gathered in Cocoa's suite at 8:00 a.m. to watch the final match of the IWO's Montreal Madness pay-per-view event. With Tokyo being thirteen hours ahead of Quebec, 8:00 a.m. on Monday in Japan was 7:00 p.m. on Sunday in Montreal.

A fourth wrestler joined Jenn, Cocoa, and Saws. Japanese superstar Rokusaburo (pronounced "Rock-saw-boo-roo") stepped out of the bathroom. Droplets of water rolled down his chest. The only covering he wore was a bath towel wrapped around his waist.

"I'm starting to feel overdressed," Saws joked.

"Santa Saws! Good to see you again!" Rokusaburo proclaimed through a thick accent.

Rokusaburo had been victorious in a bruising match against The Great Kayzo, then apparently landed in Cocoa's bed by the end of the night. "Looks like you had quite the evening," Saws replied.

"That explains a lot," Jenn remarked, thinking specifically about the ravishing outfit Cocoa was wearing when she answered the door. She flashed a quick smile in Cocoa's direction. Her friend clearly had enjoyed her time in the Land of the Rising Sun. *Good for her.*

Cocoa told them, "I needed some help hooking up my laptop to the big screen so we could watch the match. All the instructions on the TV were in Japanese... Lucky for me, Rokusaburo came to help me out."

"Did your shower come with instructions in Japanese, too?" the luchadora joked.

Jenn's quip was met with a middle finger from Cocoa. Then the booker turned to Rokusaburo and said, "Put some pants on. The match is getting ready to start."

The foursome took their seats along the edges of the luxurious hotel room's two king-sized beds. They were just in time for the ring announcer to call out the particulars of both the challenger and reigning heavyweight title-holder.

"Introducing first, the challenger. Weighing in at 275 pounds, from Timisoara, Romania... Laszlo Barba!!!"

"Is he really from Romania?" Cocoa asked.

Jenn shook her head in the negative, but then added, "He grew up in Philly. But his grandparents were born in Romania. They came to the U.S. right around World War II."

Lazz finished his one-man parade into the ring. Some obligatory flexing of his muscles followed.

Cocoa elbowed Jenn and gave her a quick wink. "Damn, girl! Your man's got quite a physique."

"He's worked hard leading up to this match. He's been putting in even more hours at the gym than usual. And I don't think he's eaten a carb all month."

The music that was pumping through the arena's loudspeakers abruptly switched to the heel champion's theme. "His opponent, the International Wrestling Organization Heavyweight Champion... weighing in at 249 pounds, from Austin, Texas... Ace Cutler!!!"

"I fought Ace Cutler once. He is good," the Japanese main eventer informed everyone in the room. It was quite possible he was oblivious to the fact that everyone else was pulling for Jenn's musclebound fiancé.

Rokusaburo quickly figured out he was surrounded by Barba fans. Each time the "Romanian" landed a punch, kick or clothesline, the hotel room filled with cheers. There were plenty of opportunities for the indie wrestlers to hoot and holler for their friend. Lazz was having the match of his life. He found time to hit Ace with every move he had in his arsenal.

Jenn couldn't wipe the smile off her face. At one point late in the match, Lazz wrapped his hand around Ace's throat and lifted him high into the air. He chokeslammed the champion over the top rope. This move sent his opponent through a ringside table. Ace wailed and wiggled, dramatically playing up the amount of pain he sustained upon impact.

Saws threw in a bit of insider analysis. "Ace *is* good! He can sell a move like nobody else in the business! The way he's squirming around, you'd think that cowboy just got run over by an entire stampede of buffalo."

"I know Lazz is going to lose," Jenn admitted. "But I'm still excited. That's my man! And he's kicking ass and taking names in the biggest pay-per-view of the year!"

With wobbly legs barely able to hold him up, the champ forced himself to his feet and returned to the ring. He walked right into Lazz's finishing move— The Barba-Bomb Powerslam. The referee slid into position and brought his hand down three times: 1... 2... 3!

"Oh my God!!!" Cocoa shouted at the top of her lungs.

"AwwwwMawwwwGawwwwwd!!!" The shout from the mighty Saws echoed throughout the entire 31st floor of the hotel.

Jenn sat at the foot of the bed. She was speechless. With her hand covering her mouth, a tear rolled down her cheek.

Lazz's theme music blasted. The referee held the victor's arm in the air. The ring announcer declared to the fans across the globe, "Here is your winner... and NEW CHAMPION...!"

The announcement stopped abruptly. Griffin Conrad stomped down to the ring. The Chief Executive Officer of the world's most successful wrestling promotion came armed with his smart phone.

There was a lot of confusion in the crowd as Conrad put on his own scene-stealing performance.

"Why's he showing his phone to the referee?" Jenn asked. She was wrapped up in the excitement of what had just transpired. She momentarily forgot that she was watching sports entertainment... with an outcome that had been carefully scripted. *Even someone dedicated to the principle of kayfabe can be fooled when the wrestlers are on top of their game!*

"Oh, hell no!" Cocoa declared. "It's a damn Dusty Finish!"

Jenn's heart was racing. "Wait? What's a Dusty Finish?"

Jenn had been in the business for almost a decade. But much of that time was spent in Puerto Rico and Mexico. Every once in a while, someone threw out a bit of wrestling lingo that she'd never heard before. This was one of those times. And since the outcome of whether or not her boyfriend was going to be crowned champion hung in the balance, it annoyed her on this particular occasion.

"What's a Dusty Finish?" she asked much more emphatically.

"You've heard of Dusty Rhodes, right?"

"Of course," Jenn answered. The man was a ring legend.

Cocoa explained, "It's a wrestling trope where it appears that the babyface earned a victory. Then the rug gets yanked out from under him. Usually, the win gets overturned on a technicality... Dusty Rhodes used to pull that garbage all the time when he was booking matches."

An instant replay of the pinfall revealed that Ace managed to hang his foot on the bottom rope before the official had completed his three-count. After a lengthy discussion between Conrad, the official, and the two wrestlers, the timekeeper rang the bell. They were re-starting the match.

Lazz looked bewildered. He stepped towards the referee and continued to plead his case. Before he knew it, Ace came from behind and delivered his own finishing move— a lightning-fast neckbreaker he called "The Ace of Spades."

Lazz was down. The referee was right on top of the action. He performed one of the fastest 1-2-3's in wrestling history.

"That's a Dusty Finish, alright!" Saws bellowed, more than a little angered by the theater that had unfolded on the flat screen television. He jabbed his middle finger in the air as if someone on the other side of the world could see his display of anger. After that, he stomped towards the door. "Thanks for having us over to watch the match. I need a damn drink. I don't care if it *is* just 8:30 in the morning. It's prime drinkin' time back in the States."

With that dramatic exit behind them, Jenn turned to Rokusaburo and admitted, "I still don't understand why they call it a 'Dusty Finish.' Come to think of it, I'm not exactly sure I understand what just happened."

The Japanese star scrunched his face and shrugged. Jenn didn't know if her questions were lost in translation or if Rokusaburo was indicating that he shared similar confusion over the term.

Cocoa was ready to get some sleep. She stepped between Jenn and Rokusaburo to offer a bit of sisterly wisdom. "A couple of pieces of advice... When you call Lazz, make sure he knows that we all thought he did an amazing job. Even though the finish was scripted, you know ending the match of his life like that... it's gotta sting a little bit."

"What's the other piece of advice?"

"If you videochat with him, please don't wear that. You're dressed like you've been runnin' up the steps with Sylvester Stallone." Cocoa moved her hand up and down to model her lingerie. "Wear something sexy like this. The hotel's got a shop in the hotel lobby if you need something."

☠☠☠

PRESENT DAY
YEAR 0 + 358 DAYS (DECEMBER 24th)

Armstrong held his left hand against his ear. He was receiving a signal from his pilot. "Monroe will be here in a couple of minutes."

He opened the sliding glass doors and stepped onto the balcony of the condominium. Jenn followed.

Before she stepped onto the balcony, the luchadora turned back and scanned the condo one last time. Was there anything she might be forgetting? More importantly, was this the last time she'd ever set foot on Earth? She wasn't sure... but she was surprisingly excited about what the future held.

"May I ask what exactly it was that changed your mind? Why did you decide to come with us?"

"Coming back here," she shook her head from side to side as she searched for the words to articulate what she had been feeling. "It wasn't anything like I imagined it would be. I figured Lazz would be ecstatic to see me. Instead, the carpet gets pulled out from under me. Pretty much every minute we've spent together has been awkward. No matter what I try, it's not the outcome I expect. Being reunited with my husband was one of the things that motivated me to fight so hard up there. It's like I scored a big win, only to have someone or something come from out of nowhere to strip me of any real reason to celebrate... Not quite the happy ending I was expecting. Does that make any sense?"

"I am confused. Do you want us to keep your husband aboard the *V-II* or return him here?"

"I want him with me... up in outer space. He's been desperate for answers that I couldn't give him. If he's up there with me, I'll be able to tell him everything that happened."

A sound momentarily filled the air around them. It was as if someone had taken a wild swing with a tennis racket, striking nothing but air. Then the Nawerssian transport zipped through the sky until it hovered inches away from the balcony of Jenn's condo.

Monroe was piloting the shuttle. The seat directly behind her was empty. That was reserved for Armstrong. Brady occupied the third seat.

The sports enthusiast wore a new baseball jersey. Pittsburgh Pirates. It was not an inexpensive replica like the one he had worn when he and Jenn first met. This one was top dollar. Brady paid a couple hundred bucks to purchase a gray jersey with black and mustard yellow lettering. The word "Pirates" was sewn across the front, while the number "21" and the name "Clemente" arched across the back. "I just ordered it. A Christmas gift for myself. I got it because it reminded me of you," Brady explained. "You see, Roberto Clemente is probably Puerto Rico's most famous baseball player ever."

Jenn tossed her suitcase into the back, then climbed into the seat behind Brady. She offered the biggest smile that had appeared on her face in months. "I know who Roberto Clemente was. One of my first matches in Puerto Rico was in a school gym that was named after him."

A clear shield zoomed shut over their heads. This enclosed them in the transport. The roof above the passengers felt like metal to the touch, but from the inside it appeared as transparent as freshly cleaned glass.

"Traveling from Earth into space can be physically demanding. It could be particularly difficult on the two of you if you are not sedated like you were the first time," Monroe warned Jenn and Brady. "We could knock you out again if you prefer."

"Heck no! Not a chance!" Brady said, replying for the both of them. "This is a once in a lifetime experience. I wanna be one hundred percent awake and aware for this."

Those on the outside would have heard something that sounded like the cracking of a whip, followed by the tennis racket sound. Then nothing. Their ascent into space had no accompanying roar. They disappeared like a quickly forgotten breeze.

Inside the transport, the passengers shook violently as the silver bullet bounced against pockets of air and fought against the mighty tugs of gravity. Soon the sky around them was black instead of blue, and the turbulence was non-existent.

The sounds disappeared, too. It was silent. Observing the exaggerated quiet reminded Jenn of the eerie feeling she had experienced several months earlier, back when she was watching an airplane fall out of the sky. Back when she thought she might be one of just a few people left on Earth.

Brady turned around in his seat. He looked over his shoulder at the radiant sight of the Earth as it appeared smaller and smaller. Through his headset, he told Jenn, "You're missing it!" Hearing this jolted any melancholy thoughts out of her mind, and she joined Brady in gawking at the amazing sight.

The near silence was interrupted by a loud humming. "This next part might be difficult for a moment, but you will adjust," Monroe announced through her headset. The Nawerssian's voice had a metallic ring to it because of the rapid changes of pressure on the eardrums of the passengers. Now free of the Earth's atmosphere, the transport began to spiral as it propelled itself through space.

Neither Jenn nor Brady said a word. They were busy admiring the view... and desperately fighting the urge to vomit.

Monroe had made the trip dozens of times in her relatively young life. Her focus was on the spacecraft they were approaching. "What happened to our ship?" she asked.

Armstrong was silent.

Monroe's question caused Jenn and Brady to refocus their collective attention to the massive ship ahead of them. Both felt a nervous excitement about living aboard the *Vilnagrom*.

Monroe asked again, "What happened to our ship?" This time the young Nawerssian had much more urgency in her voice, because the massive vessel she was flying towards was covered with dings and scars. It looked as if it had spent the last decade flying through a belt of ice chunks and meteors.

Armstrong became gravely serious. "Abort the approach. Now! Abort the approach! That is not our ship."

"What do you mean 'not our ship?'"

"I have no explanation," the Explorer responded while Monroe mashed controls to allow the bobsled transport to drift. They were floating in the weightlessness of space.

A voice came over the radio. It was one that neither Jenn nor Brady had ever heard before. Armstrong, however, recognized it immediately.

"Armstrong? Is that me ol' buddy Armstrong who be approachin'?" The voice was far more gruff than that of any Nawerssian that Jenn had ever heard. It was almost as if he was imitating a swashbuckling character from *Pirates of the Caribbean* or *Treasure Island*.

Armstrong was frozen by rage. His enemy should have been executed two decades earlier. Someone must have betrayed him and the cause of the people of Na-werss.

He was also frozen by fear. They were in an extremely vulnerable position. The tiny transport had no armor. The vessel would provide virtually no protection if attacked. If the being on the other end of the transmission opened fire from the massive spacecraft, it would take no more than one direct hit for Armstrong and company to be absolutely obliterated. Making matters worse was the fact that they had no options. There was nowhere else they could go.

With Armstrong silent, Monroe felt the need to connect the dots for the passengers. "I believe that is the *Vilnagrom-I*."

"With Jagger at the helm," elaborated Armstrong. The Explorer sounded defeated.

"Avis and the *V-II* had ta make an unexpected departure. Good thing fer you, yer ol' mate Jagger drifted into the harbor at just the right time..."

Panic fell over Jenn. "If the V-II's gone, then where is Cocoa? Where is Lazz?"

Jagger continued taunting his rival. "I understand ye might have some pirates along wit' ye... Now why don't y'all come on aboard? We've got lotsa things to discuss... We'll call it a parley if that'll put ye at ease."

END OF BOOK ONE

COMING IN SPRING 2022:

PARTS UNKNOWN
LONG JENN SILVA SERIES: BOOK 2

PARTS UNKNOWN – CHAPTER 1: THE BLADE

YEAR 2 + 238 DAYS (AUGUST 26th)

"Welcome to The Middle of Nowhere. Our humble establishment has exactly what you seek."

These words rang out of a translator robot positioned at the door of the extraterrestrial tavern that served as both a watering hole and a brothel. Such "service bots" could perform few other functions. But with the recent influx of additional alien species that arrived on Oquezzi, the devices had become essential to transacting business at this crossroads for space travelers.

Peering through goggles, Ray Yandee appeared to be a typical Vattayan. He stood at a height of about four feet, six inches. Despite the outrageously hot temperatures on Oquezzi, the tiny alien wore a hooded coat lined with fur. A thick cloth covered his mouth and nose, leaving almost none of his ghostly grey skin exposed to the elements. He belched out a series of words in his native language. *The indecipherable syllables sounded like "Robba fobba bobba robba" to Jenn's untrained ear.*

After a brief pause, the bot provided the once highly popular women's wrestling champion with an interpretation. "Long Jenn Silva. Let me guess, are you here for a drink and a dance? Or are you finally going to take me up on my offer to come work for my crew?"

"Don't hold your breath, Yandee." Not waiting for the bot to spit out a translation, she stepped through the door and into The Middle of Nowhere.

Inside, Jenn immediately became engulfed by the sounds of thumping music. "Oquezzi Disco" featured a synthetic beat. The instruments sounded like a collection of electric guitars and steel drums. The vocals resembled the squawks of a teenage boy randomly attempting to rap words off the page of an algebra textbook. One of her fellow Earthlings once observed, "The music on this moon all sounds the same. It reminds me of the worst cover of 'We Didn't Start the Fire' you could possibly imagine."

The tavern was not well lit. That suited Jenn just fine. It obstructed her view of the shameless debauchery taking place all around her. Adventurers and mercenaries from at least a half dozen solar systems all came to The Middle of Nowhere. Though most were in search of inebriating substances, others came to sample the wares of the establishment's android entertainers. The soulless robots were extremely lifelike, and able to satisfy even the most extreme perversions.

Do they have to do it out in the open?

Patrons seated at the bar were downing shots of Villetra. The green liquor glowed florescent and was served warm. To Jenn, it tasted like someone had dumped grain alcohol into pea soup. But the potent beverage did the trick for those hoping to forget the past and drown their sorrows.

As far as she could tell, the luchadora somehow managed to make it to the back of the establishment without being spotted by any of Nixx-O-Fee's henchmen. Jenn eyed the door, sucking in a deep breath and saying a silent prayer before she stepped into the gangster's office.

He came from Hamurka, a planet whose natives regularly eclipsed seven feet in height. The males seldom donned any clothing above the waist. They preferred to show off their chiseled torsos and brick red skin. Hamurkan men customarily shaved their faces, but never cut their hair. Instead, their snowy white locks were woven into a single thick braid and often thrown over the front shoulder.

As expected, Nixx was not alone. He was enjoying the company of two beautiful cyborgs, female in form. Considerably different than the "pleasure bots" that had been entertaining various scoundrels within the brothel, these machines were born human. They were Nawerssian, cyborgs like the ones Jagger and Armstrong had battled decades earlier. Deadly levels of pollution in the southern hemisphere of the planet necessitated a series of surgeries in which the brains, hearts, and other key organs of healthy adults were transplanted into synthetic shells. The belief was that undergoing such a drastic transformation into bodies that were less susceptible to the toxins of their homeland was worth the cost if it meant doing so would add decades to their lives.

The first cyborg sat across the table from the Hamurkan. Her jacket was already on the floor. She slowly worked her way out of a gold, glittery dress. Before long she'd move on to seductively removing the unnecessary undergarments that covered her mechanical frame.

The second was positioned behind Nixx. This cyborg remained fully clothed. She had been assigned the task of massaging the muscles covering the vast landscape that was the gangster's upper back and shoulders.

Nixx spoke to Jenn in English. "I want to apologize for what transpired a few days ago... I understand you and he were extremely close."

Though he spoke the words, there wasn't a hint of an apology in his voice. The heartless bastard was rubbing it in. He was celebrating his triumph with no regard to who may have been impacted by his latest kill.

A bitter taste filled the pirate's mouth. She found herself wishing she had worn her wrestling mask. That might help obscure her facial expression. Instead, she was forced to rely on her days inside the squared circle. She did her best to utilize her talent of selling a particular angle. With a shrug, Jenn responded, "I'm not happy, but I get it. Business is business."

Nixx-O-Fee let out a low groan signifying his pleasure. Smiling, he glanced upwards towards the beauty that had been massaging his pronounced shoulder muscles. He brushed his thick braid to one side, then repositioned the cyborg's soft— but mechanical—hands so they rested at the base of his neck. "Right here, princess... That's it. Rub right there."

Jenn began to seethe. "Are we done?"

"Sadly, no," Nixx replied without making eye contact. He looked across the table, gesturing for the stripping cyborg to speed up her act. Only then did he make an effort to look towards the luchadora. "You said it yourself: 'Business is business.' From my perspective, you and your friends are loose ends. Unless we can figure something out, each one of you is going to meet the same fate as that chump you called a friend."

"That's why I'm standing here. I didn't come to get some phony apology. I came to tell you that the rest of my gang and I are going to join Ray Yandee. We'll be making some repairs to his ship. After that, we plan to stay aboard until time for The Slingshot. Oquezzi will be a distant memory. And we'll be outta your hair for good. That's not just a promise."

Nixx stroked the braided rope attached to his scalp. His smile grew even wider. "Good. That's what I like to hear... You should know, the Hamurka have a tradition. When a man and woman enter into an agreement, they seal the deal with a kiss."

Long Jenn Silva had no intention of kissing that slimeball. Not to memorialize an agreement. Not to maintain an illusion. Instead, she peeled away the glove that had been covering her left hand.

Nixx's eyes widened when his adversary quickly extracted the dagger she had sheathed along her hip. He settled back into his chair when Jenn said, "Back on Earth, pirates are known to seal a covenant in blood."

She glided the edge across the top of her exposed hand, causing crimson to flow to the surface. Revealing the murky liquid that ran along her brown skin, she instructed the gangster, "Now we blade *your* hand. We smear our blood together... Then our covenant cannot be broken."

Nixx gestured for the stripping cyborg to step aside to allow his uninvited guest to move closer. *Finally.* Then he planted his palm atop the table. Looking at Jenn, he said, "I like the way you conduct business."

The pirate's frown vanished. A smirk appeared a split second before she drove the dagger through the back of Nixx's meaty hand. The steel point lodged deep into the table, anchoring the Hamurkan's palm to the spot in which he had confidently planted it a moment earlier.

Turning to the nearly naked cyborg, Jenn spoke over the
scream of her foe. "Get dressed."

The screaming stopped. It was replaced by the sound of
crunching bones. The cyborg Nixx had called "Princess" now
clamped her soft, mechanical hands around his throat like a vice.
She would continue tightening her grip until she had squeezed the
life out of him.

The post-apocalyptic pirate pulled out a second dagger and
used it to saw off the monster's ponytail. "A trophy. A reminder to
everyone on Oquezzi... You don't cross Long Jenn Silva."

Now carrying the rope of Nixx-O-Fee's hair over her shoulder,
Jenn confidently led her cyborg accomplices across the tavern and
out the door. Once she had made her exit from The Middle of
Nowhere, she looked back and spoke to Ray Yandee. "Grab your
bot and come with us... if you still want to join *my crew*."

ABOUT THE AUTHOR

Scott Quinn may have waited until his mid-forties to publish his first book, but he's been writing since before he could read. What began as a kindergartener's fan fiction about his favorite cartoons and movies soon evolved into a hobby of creating unpublished short stories and screenplays. Following a detour through law school, he focused his efforts on authoring legal briefs and petitions. You can't stop a dreamer forever. This one ended up writing about pro wrestling champs and time-traveling aliens!

Made in the USA
Columbia, SC
13 October 2021